PRAISE FOR ROBERT BRYNDZA

'A rising star in British crime fiction.'

— *IRISH INDEPENDENT*

'Compelling at every turn, as we follow the brilliantly drawn Detective Erika Foster in her relentless hunt for one of the most horrific villains in modern crime fiction.'

— JEFFERY DEAVER, #1 INTERNATIONALLY BESTSELLING AUTHOR

'A spine-tingling thriller from the master of suspense.'

— MJ ARLIDGE, INTERNATIONAL BESTSELLING AUTHOR

'Sharply written and wonderfully wrought, this crime thriller sings with every twist and builds to a more-than-satisfying bang.'

— *PUBLISHERS WEEKLY*

'A riveting page-turner. An astonishingly good plot with perfectly drawn characters and sharp, detailed writing.'

— ROBERT DUGONI, #1 *WALL STREET JOURNAL* BESTSELLING AUTHOR

'Robert Bryndza's characters are so vividly drawn—even the slightest character—and fully human and uniquely imperfect. His plots are clever and original and cool, and his sense of timing is excruciatingly flawless.'

'An exciting, riveting read from a master storyteller who never disappoints.'

ALSO BY ROBERT BRYNDZA

A Very Coco Christmas

Coco Pinchard's Must-Have Toy Story

Miss Wrong and Mr Right

ROBERT BRYNDZA

A **DETECTIVE ERIKA FOSTER** NOVEL

LETHAL VENGEANCE

I dedicate this book to all my literary translators around the world.

Vengeance is in my heart, death in my hand, Blood and revenge are hammering in my head

— William Shakespeare, *Titus Andronicus*

1

Friday, January 13, 2023

Please, God, don't let this be a proposal, thought Detective Chief Inspector Erika Foster. She looked across the busy restaurant at Igor, who was talking to one of the white-jacketed waiters. A deal or arrangement was in the works. Was he asking for a ring to be buried in a chocolate soufflé?

Their dinner date was on a Friday evening in mid-January. It happened to be Friday the 13th, and everything had that bleached-out feel after the Christmas decorations had come down.

The restaurant was at the top of the OXO Tower, and they had a table by the window. Erika could see down to the Thames Embankment and the river rushing past like a slick of black ink, reflecting the London skyline lit up in the darkness. She was exhausted after a long day of paperwork and a court appearance to give evidence to the hostile barrister of a multiple rapist. This place was too posh. The waiters wore white gloves, and there were too many knives and forks on each side of her plate. And her smart dress was uncomfortable.

'Shit,' said Erika under her breath as Igor returned to the table. He'd scrubbed up nicely in his best black suit.

Then, louder, she asked, 'What was that?'

'Making sure the Champagne is cold,' replied Igor with a grin. The waiter appeared with a bottle of Champagne cradled in a white cloth and presented it to them like a newborn baby. Igor peered at it through his tortoiseshell glasses and nodded. The waiter strained a little with the effort and then pulled the cork free.

'That's a good pop,' said Igor.

'Yes, sir. We like to think so,' he replied, with just the right mix of deference and condescension. 'Would madam care to try?'

Madam would love you to leave the bottle and piss off, thought Erika, but she smiled and nodded.

He poured a little fizz into her glass and stepped back as she sipped. She didn't care much for Champagne and wished it were a cold can of dandelion and burdock to drink along with some chips, but she saw Igor waiting for her verdict and shook the thought away. She was being a bitch. How many single women would love to be taken out to a nice restaurant by the man they loved?

'It's very nice,' she said. The waiter leaned over and filled both their glasses. Looking down at them through flared nostrils.

'Is this a special occasion? A wedding anniversary?' he asked, fussing with a bucket on a stand and pushing the Champagne bottle into the ice.

'We're not married,' said Erika.

'Not yet,' said Igor with a wink. Erika's guts screamed a little, and she tensed her jaw.

Oh. My. God. He's going to get down on one knee amongst all of these people.

Even after four and a bit years, Erika didn't know what to call Igor. *Boyfriend?* No, they weren't teenagers. *Lover?* No. That

2

absolutely made her cringe. *Partner?* Yes, 'partner'. They weren't solicitors, but it was the best option.

'Would madam care for more artisan bread?'

'No.'

'Please enjoy our hand-curated olive oils. They pair beautifully with the bread.'

'Great,' said Erika, clenching her teeth into a smile.

'Do you have any questions about the menu?'

'No!' she snapped.

He clicked his heels together, gave them a little bow, and left. Igor regarded her across the table, then lifted his glass. They clinked. Erika took a flinching sip as he tipped his head back and downed most of the glass. The material of his jacket strained against his chest, and she noticed a bulge. Something was in his pocket. She felt a chill.

He's got a ring in a box, she thought.

Igor reached across the table, placed his hand on hers, and took a deep breath. 'Erika, I . . .'

Erika pulled her hand away and got up abruptly. 'I need to use the bathroom.'

'Okay,' he said, his brow furrowing. 'Everything all right?'

'Yeah. Fine.'

Erika crossed the busy dining room, almost colliding with two waiters carrying a giant birthday cake covered in burning candles.

I need air. The corridor outside the restaurant was narrow and bustling with waitstaff. She got into a crowded lift and hit the button to the ground floor. She could feel panic tightening in her chest. A feeling of not being able to catch her breath. The bodies pressed against her in the tiny lift didn't help, and when the doors opened, she pushed through them, ignoring their tutting and annoyed faces.

Only when she was outside, breathing in the crisp, freezing air next to the river, did she feel her heart slow. She gripped the railing along the Embankment wall, and the cold steel felt good against her skin.

Her phone was still on the table upstairs, but she had her purse and Met Police warrant card inside her glittery little going-out bag. She debated walking down to Waterloo station and hailing a cab home. It would put a stop to any proposal in the short term. Feeling around in the bag, she found a small packet of cigarettes. Old and slightly crumpled, but still smokable. A man was passing, and she asked him for a light. The lighter illuminated his thin, craggy face as she cupped her hands and lit the cigarette. She thanked him and inhaled gratefully.

'Not many of us left – smokers,' he said with a smile, and then he was gone.

Erika exhaled, feeling the powerful rush of the nicotine, and watched a tugboat go past, churning against the river's fast current. She'd started smoking again only recently. A cigarette here and there. Lately it had been more here than there. Was Igor really going to propose with no warning? They lived apart. Igor had his own place around the corner from her house in Blackheath, and he stayed over a few nights a week. If he proposed, then everything would change. He had a son, Tom, from his first marriage. She would be a wife and a stepmother.

No. She loved Igor and was very close to Tom, but she couldn't do it. Erika had been married before. Mark had worked with her in the police, and almost nine years ago, he'd been killed in a botched drug raid, along with four other colleagues. Erika had been heading up the raid. She'd been the senior officer that day and had taken the blame. She still held the responsibility and guilt. It was something that would never leave her.

She couldn't be a wife again. Mark had been her husband. And should still be her husband. The film *Sliding Doors* had affected her deeply: She wondered if there was another version of her life where the police van broke down on that fateful day. The raid never happened, and Erika and Mark lived happily ever after.

Far too fast, her cigarette was smoked. She took a last drag and flicked the butt into the water. She felt calmer here in the cold and quiet. She would just have to be honest. She loved Igor very much and their life together. Together, but with their own space, and that would have to do. He would have to accept this.

Erika realised she'd re-entered the building through a different door only when she was alone in the lift going up. She had just reached to press the button to take her back down to the ground floor when the lift stopped with a soft ding and the doors opened onto an empty corridor.

She heard a woman's echoing voice: 'Yeah, police, please . . . There's a body. A man is dead.'

Erika stepped out of the lift. Where was she? This seemed to be one of the building's residential floors. There were rows of white doors with gold numbers, and an older woman dressed in leggings and an old jumper stood beside a cleaner's cart next to an open door at the end of the corridor. She wore yellow rubber gloves and was wiping her eyes with her forearm. She had a messy nest of red hair and lots of orange make-up.

'It's in the OXO Tower building, the fourth floor on the Embankment. Yes, thank you.'

'Is everything okay?' Erika said.

The woman ended the call. 'This is a private floor,' she said with a gravelly voice. 'Residents only.'

'I'm a police officer.'

She looked Erika up and down, taking in her long, slightly ill-fitting evening dress. Erika was thankful she had her warrant card. She held it up, and the woman chewed her lip. *Oh,* her face seemed to say, and she looked relieved.

'There's a dead body in there,' she said, tilting her head to the open door. 'A man.'

Erika peered inside. She could see into a modern open-plan living room with windows overlooking the glowing London skyline.

'Is there anyone else inside?'

'No. He's in there on the bed.' Erika spied a pair of rubber gloves draped over the side of the cleaner's cart. 'It's usually empty when I clean. This is the first time I've seen him in . . . ages.'

Erika slipped on the rubber gloves.

'Stay here, please,' she said, and forgetting all about Igor waiting and her fears for their relationship, she stepped inside the apartment.

2

The wooden floorboards creaked, and an odd stillness held in the air, like the heavy feeling before a storm. The lights from the London skyline cast a sharp glare into a cavernous living room and kitchen, and a soft whirr punctuated the silence. A vast fish tank was built into the back wall behind a large pale, L-shaped sofa. A group of white-domed jellyfish flexed and moved across the tank in rhythm with the air pump, and two mournful flat grey fish hung, unblinking, amongst the bubbles.

Blue light from the fish tank reflected over the kitchen's expensive-looking steel cupboards and work surfaces. Devoid of appliances and clean and clear, it was the type of kitchen only used occasionally by hired caterers.

Erika crossed the floor, passing a veiny orange-and-brown slab of petrified rock, to a half-open door leading off the kitchen. She hesitated on the threshold when that oh-so-familiar fetid smell of death pricked her nostrils, then pushed the door open.

Thick curtains were drawn shut, leaving a six-inch gap in the middle. A strip of orange lit the pale body of a large white, naked man on the bed.

Erika couldn't find the light switch, so she yanked open the curtains, letting the light from outside fill the room. There was no other furniture apart from the king-sized bed with black sheets. The man lay on his front, hog-tied, his arms and legs bound behind his back and pulled up with a rope connecting the two. His head was arched up, so he faced the curtains, and there was masking tape over his mouth. His skin was pale and flabby, like raw pudding. Erika gingerly reached out and checked his pulse.

Yep. Dead all right.

A tan-coloured pair of trousers and a shirt and tie were heaped on the floor on the right side of the bed. Trying to disturb as little evidence as possible, Erika searched the trouser pockets and found a leather wallet and a small square white envelope. The wallet was empty, apart from a single ID card. It was a House of Commons pass for Neville Lomas, a Conservative member of Parliament for North East Surrey.

The envelope wasn't sealed, and inside were three Polaroid photographs. They showed Neville Lomas lying on the bed, clothed and seemingly alive, staring blankly at the camera. He was naked in the second Polaroid, lying on his back, and in the third, he was hog-tied. Barely holding the edges and taking care not to touch the photos, Erika turned them over. Each one had been signed with what looked like a black Sharpie pen in a looping, almost childlike signature:

ANNABELLE

'Are you all right?' said a voice.

Erika jumped, almost dropping the photos. The older woman with the gravelly voice and red hair stood in the doorway. Erika remembered that her phone was still up in the restaurant with Igor. She tucked the Polaroids back into the envelope. 'Can I use your phone, please?'

The woman's eyes moved to the man on the bed and back to Erika. 'Yeah,' she said.

Erika crossed to the woman and guided her out into the living room. She had to get a forensics team out here fast. She could feel the prickle of excitement. With a high-profile MP would come a high-profile murder case. The woman stopped at the sofa, putting a hand on the armrest.

'What's your name?' asked Erika.

'Ann-Marie Ross.' She let out a long breath. 'Can I sit down for a moment?'

Her craggy face was suddenly pale, and Erika could see her hands were shaking. 'I didn't see 'im in such . . . detail before.' She patted the pockets of her leggings, pulled out a crumpled pack of cigarettes, a small wooden effigy of the Virgin Mary, and then an old cracked smartphone. She went to place her cigarettes on the petrified rock coffee table, but Erika reached out and took them.

'No, this is a crime scene.'

Erika saw it wasn't an effigy of the Virgin Mary. It was a cigarette lighter.

'Sorry. It's made me woozy. I'll be all right in a sec . . . I got that in Lourdes,' she said, following Erika's gaze. 'I went with my sister. And my mum.'

'Are you religious?'

'No. And it didn't rub off on us. We all rowed the whole time.'

Ann-Marie handed Erika her phone, and she called the control room at Lewisham Row police station and asked for backup and forensics.

'What time did you arrive on this floor and open the door to this flat?'

'Just a couple of minutes before you.'

'Do you work here full time?'

'I work all over.'

'Are these residential flats?'

'Yeah, but they prefer you to call them "apartments". All this floor, and the one below and above. We go in and clean once a week.'

'We?'

'The agency I work for. Hoopers Limited.'

'Does the deceased man own the apartment?'

'I don't know. He's all trussed up.' Her voice cracked for the first time, and Erika could see she'd been putting on a brave face.

'Do you know any of the residents to talk to?'

'You think they talk to the likes of us? I see all sorts of people going in and out. Different every time. Sometimes we've had to clean up after a party . . .' She wrinkled her nose. 'You'd think that posh people are cleaner than the likes of us, but no. Filthy.'

There was a rumble as the lift moved past.

'Thank you for letting me use your phone,' said Erika, handing the phone, cigarettes, and lighter back to Ann-Marie. She helped her up, and they came back out into the corridor.

The lift doors opened with a ding, and two police officers in uniform emerged. A man and a woman, both white. Their young faces were flushed from the cold air outside, and raindrops spotted their high-visibility jackets.

'Fourth floor, apartment six; should be at the end of the corridor,' said a voice through the radio on the woman's lapel, repeating what Erika had said on the phone.

'Are you the cleaning staff? Can we ask you to vacate the area, please,' said the woman, seeing the open door to the apartment. She held out her arm to lead Erika and Ann-Marie away.

'I'm Detective Chief Inspector Erika Foster,' said Erika, a little bruised that this young woman thought she was the cleaner. The two officers looked her up and down, taking in the rubber gloves and black-sequinned evening dress.

'I'll be happy to be out of this,' said Ann-Marie, gripping the handle of her cleaning trolley and attempting to turn it in the small space.

'I'm Constable Dahlia Beck. This is my colleague Glenn Constance,' said the young officer. She was beautiful, with big brown eyes and a purse-lipped, pouty mouth. She made Erika think of a young actress who'd been cast as a police officer in a TV show, and her uniform was so new it looked almost like a costume. Her colleague, Glenn, was equally handsome. All strong jaw and matinee-idol looks, but he didn't seem to have Dahlia's confidence. Erika could see he kept swallowing, and his eyes belied a little fear.

'Evening, ma'am,' he said. Ann-Marie was now trying to manoeuvre her trolley past.

'Please can you leave that?' said Erika. 'I need you to stay and make a statement.'

Dahlia's radio beeped.

'This is control. Have you made contact?' said a voice.

Dahlia kept her eyes on Erika and gripped the radio. 'There's a lady here who says she's DCI Foster, but we haven't made a formal ID,' she said.

Irritation flared up in Erika. *A formal ID? I'm not the dead body.* At six feet, Erika was taller than Dahlia. She leaned over and grabbed the radio on her lapel. She was damned if she would flash her ID to this cocky little madam.

'This is Erika Foster. Is that you, Vicky? Over,' she said, recognising the same voice she'd spoken to on the call earlier.

'Yes, ma'am. Over.'

'Please confirm with PC Dahlia Beck here that we have backup and forensics on the way? Over.'

'They're about twelve minutes away. Over.'

Erika let go of the radio and could see Dahlia was equally annoyed.

'I'm just doing my job, ma'am.'

Erika turned to Glenn. 'Looks like the deceased is a Conservative MP, Neville Lomas. I don't have a formal ID, but please go to the front desk and see if you can find more info.'

'Yes, ma'am.'

'And I have a job for you,' said Erika to Dahlia. 'I need you to go to the restaurant on the top floor.'

3

Igor was wondering if Erika was ill. She'd been in the bathroom for a long time. The waiter had filled his Champagne glass twice, and now Igor felt light-headed.

'Is everything all right with madam, sir?' asked the maître d'.

'Not sure,' he said. He wiped his sweaty hands on his trousers. The collar of his shirt felt suddenly tight. Erika's phone sat on the table next to her plate.

'Chef informs me that your dishes are almost ready . . . Shall I push back?' Igor glanced at the door and ran a finger under his collar. 'Would that suit madam?'

'No. Bring it out. I'll go and check on her.'

Rain hammered against the window, and Igor felt the evening was backfiring. Erika hadn't been crazy about the idea of a posh dinner. He should have stuck with his first instinct: fish and chips. Igor put his napkin on the table and was about to get up when a good-looking young woman in a police uniform and high-visibility jacket entered the restaurant and made a beeline for his table. The dining room fell silent, and the plinky-plonky Muzak seemed louder.

'Are you Igor . . . Muck?' asked the woman, consulting a notepad.

'It's pronounced Mack, but yes, that's me. Is everything okay?'

The maître d' reappeared, all twinkly-eyed and slightly sweaty. 'Good evening, Officer. May I help you?'

She ignored him. 'I'm Constable Dahlia Beck,' she said to Igor with a bored air. 'I have a message for you from DCI Erika Foster.'

'What?'

'A message,' said Dahlia, speaking slowly. 'From Erika. You know her? She says she knows you.'

'Yes, what is it?'

'She asked me to inform you she's been called away to a crime scene—' Two steaming plates of food arrived at the table, and Dahlia stepped out of the way to let the waiters put them down. 'She's also asked me to retrieve her mobile phone.'

Igor checked his watch. Erika had been gone for twenty minutes.

'What crime scene?'

The waiters who delivered the food eyed Dahlia and returned to the kitchen, but the maître d' remained at the table. He gave a glib little laugh. 'Officer, could we discuss this matter elsewhere?'

'Where is this crime scene? In the building? In the toilets?' asked Igor.

'I can't comment on that,' said Dahlia.

'It must be in the building. We're supposed to be having dinner!'

Dahlia softened a little. *Downstairs,* she mouthed. 'Is this her phone?'

Igor nodded. 'Is Erika okay?'

'She's fine.' Dahlia leaned over, picked up the phone from the table, and left. An elderly gentleman, along with several other men in the restaurant, did a double take as she sashayed past.

Igor stared at the two plates of food. The maître d' gave Igor an oily smile.

'Bon appétit.'

Erika took a long statement from Ann-Marie, and then Isaac Strong, the forensic pathologist, called Erika back into the crime scene. The apartment was now busy with scenes-of-crime officers taking swab samples from the kitchen and bathroom floors. Dahlia and Glenn asked if they could view the crime scene with Erika. They were all given white forensics suits to wear, and a set of steel boxes, each spaced a foot apart, like a stepping stone bridge, had been set up through the apartment hallway and living room and into the bedroom so they could walk into the space without contaminating the scene.

The ropes on the man's body had been cut, but he still lay in the hog-tied position, with his arms and legs drawn up and back. His eyes were wide open. A gurney waited beside the bed, and a crime scene photographer was documenting every inch of the space.

'Good evening,' said Isaac. Only his brown eyes were visible, peering out over his face mask. He regarded Erika for a moment. 'You've had a change of plans this evening?' Erika and Isaac were close friends outside of work, and she'd been talking to him on the phone earlier about Igor's surprise invitation to take her to dinner.

'Yes . . . What can you tell us about all this?' asked Erika, looking down at the man's body and adding, 'Can you give me a time of death?'

'Nice try.'

'Could you give me a vague figure?'

Isaac sighed.

'His body is in the early stages of rigor mortis,' he said, indicating the man's arms and legs bent backward. 'Broadly speaking, I can estimate time of death in the last twenty-four hours.'

'So, from eight pm yesterday evening,' said Erika.

'At first examination, he has two, maybe three broken ribs in his chest, and his right arm has been dislocated from its socket, which could indicate a violent resistance to his bonds.'

Glenn was beside Erika, and he cleared his throat nervously.

'Do you think this was consensual sex?' he asked.

'Some guys like to be tied up,' said Dahlia.

'You'd know, would you?'

'Piss off, Glenn.'

'Hey! A little respect, please,' snapped Isaac, sharing Erika's irritation with the young officers. He moved closer to the man's head. 'Can I have more light,' he said to one of the SOCOs. They angled the nearest lamp closer. The dead man's wide-open eyes lit up with the reflection of the bright bulb. Isaac took a pair of flat-ended tweezers, gripped the edge of the masking tape, and gently peeled it away from the man's face. Underneath, his yellow teeth were bared in a rigor mortis grimace. Erika had seen his face before, on TV, during some parliamentary debate. He'd had the same grimace then, albeit more animated. Isaac stood back and deposited the piece of masking tape into a clear plastic evidence bag. He handed it to one of the SOCOs, who fixed a label on the side.

'We'll need a formal ID, but I'd say that's Neville Lomas, the same man in the House of Commons ID photo and the Polaroids,' said Isaac.

He handed Erika the three Polaroids, now in forensics bags. She flicked through them slowly, feeling the horror mount as the pictures seemed to progress and tell a story. The first showed Neville Lomas lying clothed on the bed, staring blankly at the camera. In the second photo, he was naked and trying to cover himself. In the third, he was hog-tied and his eyes were bloodshot.

'He looks out of it,' said Erika, flicking through the photos again. Isaac nodded.

'Who calls their kid Annabelle these days?' asked Dahlia, peering at the signature on each Polaroid.

'You could say the same for *Dahlia*,' said Glenn. She rolled her eyes.

'I'll try and get toxicology back to you asap,' said Isaac, giving the two younger officers the side-eye. There was fingerprint dust on each Polaroid.

'No prints on these photos – that's a pity,' said Erika. She looked around at the SOCOs dusting for prints on the bedpost. Fingerprint dust peppered more prints across the wall at the head of the bed and around the light switches. Erika moved out of the way to let the crime scene photographer access the pile of clothes still on the floor by the bed. 'There will be a lot of scrutiny on this one. Can I have prints processed as soon as possible?'

'Naturally,' said Isaac.

'That's a yes?'

'Yes.'

'What about cause of death?'

'Erika. I need to do my post-mortem.'

She looked back at the photos. 'Even if a Member of Parliament gets his kicks doing . . . this . . . whatever this was . . . do you really think he'd be happy to be photographed doing it?' She saw a look pass between Dahlia and Glenn. 'What? Spit it out.'

Dahlia pointed to one of the SOCOs, who stood in the bedroom doorway holding an umbrella stand filled with long leather riding crops.

'There's a cupboard in the hallway, filled with BDSM porn magazines and DVDs, and these,' said the SOCO.

'Any other horse-riding gear?' asked Erika.

'No. I don't think these were used for riding horses.'

'What about any illegal substances?'

She shook her head. 'Nothing. Yet.'

'Thank you. Bag it all up.' Erika looked at the evidence bags of Polaroids. 'This Annabelle could have been a prostitute he hired.'

'I think the preferred term is "sex worker",' said Dahlia.

Erika ignored her. 'There was no sign of a break-in. The cleaner unlocked the front door, came in, and found the body. This could have seen a sex game gone wrong, and whoever was involved panicked and fled. Or it's murder, made to look like a sex game.' Her words hung in the room for a while, and there was just the click and flash of the crime scene photographer's camera. 'Either way, we have a dead MP, and the clock is ticking until the media finds out.'

4

It was now ten pm. Erika removed her overalls and handed them over to be bagged by forensics. She checked her phone and saw a chain of messages from Igor asking what was going on.

Oh, crap. Igor.

Dahlia and Glenn handed in their overalls, and Erika asked them to start on a door-to-door of the apartments neighbouring number six and then went to speak to the doorman on the building's ground floor.

She saw that she'd come back from the river earlier through a separate residential entrance to the building, next to the restaurant's entrance. Erika found a small man sitting behind a desk in the lobby. He hadn't been there before. He had a suspicious ruddy little face with a protruding set of teeth that put Erika in mind of a middle-aged rabbit and regarded her with irritation when she flashed her ID.

'What's your name, please?' she asked.

'Oliver Grant,' he said, his teeth doing much of the work for the *aaa* sound in 'Grant'.

'Have you been here all day?'

'I came on at six. I understand that something has happened

up on the fourth floor? Are you here to furnish me with more information? I'm responsible for this building and don't like being in the dark.'

She could see a small bank of CCTV screens behind the desk showing different angles of the building.

'Do your CCTV feeds cover the internal corridors?' asked Erika, looking at the screen with the camera for the main entrance.

'They're not *my* video feeds. They belong to the building's cameras.'

'Of course,' said Erika, not taking the bait from this prickly, imperious little man.

'We take the privacy of our residents very seriously. We don't have anything covering the internal corridors.'

'What about inside the lifts?'

'The main two lifts which serve residential areas don't have CCTV inside,' he said.

'What does your CCTV cover?'

'The front entrance outside the Thames Path, the tradesmen's entrance, and the loading bay for the building and restaurant. The service lift for the restaurant, the entrance to the restaurant, and the brasserie bar. And the lobby here.'

'Do visitors have to sign in here?'

'Naturally.'

'Residents?'

'No.'

'How do you police that?'

'Er. We just know.'

'I entered here earlier, and you weren't at the desk.'

'I must have been in the back office.'

Erika saw the door to a small office further down the corridor. 'Were you working here yesterday evening?'

Before he could answer, the door opened behind them and a

brisk breeze came in from the river. A tall, dark man who looked to be in his late thirties with an acne-scarred face was flanked by another thin, balding man in a grey suit and long raincoat. He was pale and had a brown birthmark like a scab under his left eye.

'Mr Grant. Good evening,' said the younger man, ignoring Erika.

'Good evening, Superintendent Fisk,' said Oliver with a toothy smile.

'Superintendent?' asked Erika. She didn't recognise him or the other man.

'Yes.'

'I'm Detective Chief Inspector Erika Foster.' She noticed the two men looking her up and down in her evening dress.

'I'm Superintendent Dan Fisk, West End Central. Thank you for holding the fort,' he said with a smile. He didn't introduce the man with him, who had tiny black eyes which seemed to roam around the foyer and over Erika.

'Holding the fort? I was the first officer on the scene, sir,' said Erika.

The man in the suit pointed past the desk to a lift which had just opened. 'I'll head up,' he muttered. Dan nodded.

'Who is that?' asked Erika as he disappeared into the lift and the doors closed.

'Ah. That question is probably a bit out of your pay grade and mine,' said Dan. There was no hostility in his voice, but his jovial manner seemed forced. 'You are aware of, er, who our victim is?' he said, moving away from the desk and lowering his voice.

'We don't have a formal ID, but yes.'

'Good. Okay. I'll be taking over from here, Erika. Thank you for holding things down.'

'Hang on. Sir, who called you?'

He looked surprised at the question. 'Why is that relevant?'

'My rank is sufficient to ask.'

'Of course. This is no reflection on you. Another officer called me. Thought I would like to be aware of the sensitivity of this case.'

'Who?'

'Who called me?'

'Yes. Who called you?'

He seemed to have to ransack his mind for the person's name. 'One of my uniform officers, Dahlia Beck, responded to your call-out with another officer from West End Central.'

Erika stared at him for a beat. 'When did she call you?'

Dan laughed. Erika didn't like him. He was treating her like she was being unreasonable. 'About an hour ago.'

This was when Erika had been taking a statement from the cleaner, Ann-Marie.

'I'm just trying to understand why a uniformed officer, not long in uniform, would take it on herself to call you without telling me?'

'I understand you are based out of Lewisham Row station in South London?'

'Yes. But that's nothing to do with this. Sir, relaying information to senior staff is my job.'

He nodded and smiled maddeningly. He seemed impervious to what she was saying. His phone began to ring in his pocket.

'Sorry. I need to take this. Thank you, Erika. You are now free to go and enjoy the rest of your evening.' He answered his phone. 'Yes, Peter. I've just taken over.' A lift arrived, the doors opened, and he went inside.

Erika stared at him as the doors closed. He was deep in conversation. She turned back to Oliver. 'Were you working here last night?'

'No. I wasn't. And if you're leaving, you'll need to sign out,' he said with a triumphant, toothy smile.

Glenn Constance was taken off the door-to-door and assigned to take Erika home in his squad car.

She fumed silently as they drove out of central London and down the Old Kent Road. She'd made the mistake of sitting in the back seat, and could see Glenn eyeing her in the rearview mirror.

'I've never been to Blackheath,' he said, breaking the silence as they drove past New Cross station and the vast Sainsbury's superstore. 'I hear it's a nice area.'

'It is,' said Erika.

He nodded. 'I'm in Croydon.'

'That's a bit of a journey into central London.'

'Not really. I take the tram.'

'Is Superintendent Dan Fisk your guv'nor at West End Central?'

He smiled.

'What's funny?'

His face dropped. 'Sorry. You just don't hear that word often, "guv'nor".'

'Yeah. I'm old school. There was another guy with Superintendent Fisk who didn't introduce himself. Grey suit, bald. Birthmark under his eye.'

'He wanted to see the body.'

'Did he show any ID?'

'No. Superintendent Fisk signed in for him. He could have been civil service?' Erika nodded and looked out the window. She imagined they didn't want a story about an MP dying during a bizarre sex game splashed across the press to distract from policy and PR. Erika looked back. Glenn was still looking at her. 'It's good to meet you. I mean, work with you.'

'Is it? Why?'

He looked embarrassed.

'When I was training at Hendon, they used one of the cases you solved as part of training.'

'They do? Which case?'

'Elias Mills. The café owner who murdered nine women and served them up in curries. You suspected him, but he was able to hide everything . . . He was processing the meat into food, grinding up the bones and dumping the powder in the drains . . .'

This case stood out from her early years as a police officer in Manchester. Mark had worked with her on this one, too. 'You decided to concentrate on what he was doing with the hair. His girlfriend was a hairdresser at the local salon, and she was disposing of it.'

'And the scalps,' finished Erika, recalling the day they cracked the case and the smell of the rotting flesh.

'It was inspiring,' he said, and then he looked embarrassed by his enthusiasm.

'How old are you?'

'Twenty-five, ma'am.'

Jesus. Twenty-five. It was twenty-seven years since Erika passed out of Hendon Police College. An age ago. Back then she'd been living in the UK for only six years, and was engaged to Mark and full of hope about the future.

Looking at Glenn's reflection in the rearview mirror, she wanted to ask him if he was full of hope and what he dreamed of. But the question somehow seemed inappropriate. The moment passed, and they were silent for the rest of the journey. Erika couldn't shake off the evening's events. Superintendent Dan Fisk was also much younger than her, yet he had swooped in with his senior rank and taken over. Erika was proud of her rank of Detective Chief Inspector, but she'd always thought she would keep rising. She'd made enough enemies in the force to ensure her chances of promotion were scuppered. Until now, she'd been principled with how she'd navigated her career – often doing the right thing meant making an enemy – but lately, she felt frustrated. She was stuck.

She remembered her long day in court, watching a man she knew was guilty of rape get away with it, thanks to a good barrister. Would she ever be able to really make a difference? How long did she have left until she was sidelined and pressured to retire? Five years? Less?

When they reached Blackheath, Erika sent Igor a text:

I'm sorry. Are you awake?

A few minutes passed. He didn't answer. When they drew close to Erika's terraced house overlooking the heath, she could see the windows were dark.

When the car pulled up outside, Erika felt a sudden urge to impart some kind of wisdom or advice to Glenn, but she couldn't think of anything. So she just wished him goodnight.

5

Erika was greeted at the door by her cat, George. He stood on his hind legs and put his white-booted paws on her leg.

'Hello, fur ball,' said Erika, grateful for his unconditional love. She crouched down and gave him a cuddle. He rolled over and she scratched his shiny black fur. It was warm inside, and even though the new carpet had been laid a year ago, there was still a nice new-carpet smell whenever she came through the front door.

She went to the kitchen and opened the fridge. There was some leftover risotto, and she loaded up a plate and put it in the microwave. Erika had bought the house from an old lady who hadn't done anything to the property for years, and it was in a state when she moved in: bare floorboards and crumbling, water-stained plasterwork. The whole house had been slowly remodelled, thanks in part to Igor.

As the risotto spun in the microwave, Erika looked around at her cosy new kitchen, with its pale wooden countertops and sparkling silver appliances. She shouldn't have left Igor in the restaurant. She'd known that, but she still did it.

They'd been childhood sweethearts in Slovakia until Erika moved to Manchester when she was eighteen to be an au pair.

This was back in 1990. No internet, no mobile phones, and Erika looked after the two small children of a very austere forensic pathologist and his wife. They didn't mistreat her, but their hospitality didn't stretch to letting her use their landline to call home. After a bit of back-and-forth with letters, Erika and Igor's relationship fizzled out, and then a year later, Erika met Mark, and her life went in another direction.

When Erika bought the house in Blackheath four years ago, they met again when Igor delivered her new bed. He'd been divorced for a few years and working as an Argos delivery driver.

Erika noticed Igor's work ID was on top of the microwave. Three years ago, he'd had the opportunity to qualify as a London Tube train driver. Shortly afterwards, the pandemic hit, and they had both been classed as key workers. He had moved in with her so they could be in the same bubble. It had worked surprisingly well, and then he got back on his feet financially and bought a small flat around the corner.

It had all worked out perfectly. That was why Erika had freaked out at the thought of a marriage proposal crashing into her life like a wrecking ball.

The microwave pinged, and Erika took the food out. Igor had cooked the risotto the previous evening, and it tasted even better the next day. She found her phone and called him. It almost rang out when he picked it up.

'Your risotto beats any fancy restaurant,' she said. Igor was silent. 'You left your work ID here. I know you have a late shift tomorrow . . . You were planning to stay over until I abandoned you in the restaurant.'

'Did you solve the murder?'

Erika laughed awkwardly. 'No. I've already been chucked off the case, which is a record, even for me.'

'Oh. Sorry,' Igor said, sounding genuine, which made Erika feel even worse.

'No. I'm sorry. Sorry I left you.'

'Why?'

'I really did find a dead body. I went down to get some air and then came back through the wrong door.'

'Why didn't you just come and tell me? You sent some snotty rookie.'

Erika was secretly quite pleased he thought Dahlia was a snotty rookie.

'I went into the crime scene. There was a witness. Then forensics.'

'You were two floors down, and the guy was dead. You could have come up,' said Igor. His reasonable questioning made her feel worse.

'I'm sorry. It's like a disease, the way I get obsessed with murder cases.'

Igor was silent for a moment. 'Why have you been taken off the case?'

'I don't know. It's high profile, and I'm a loose cannon.'

'Hey, no one calls my girlfriend loose . . .'

Erika laughed. She pressed the fork into the steaming rice on her plate. 'You freaked me out with the posh meal. And . . . I thought . . . Were you going to propose to me?'

Igor made a choking noise, and she heard him spit beer back into the bottle.

'What? You thought I was going to propose? To you?'

'You don't have to protest that much!' said Erika, relieved. 'You had on your smart suit and that bloody waiter fussing with the Champagne. What was the surprise?'

Igor sighed.

'It wasn't a surprise, as such. It was something I wanted to ask you. Tell you what. I'll come over.'

Ten minutes later, Igor was building a fire in the grate in her front room, and Erika had opened a couple of beers. George was snoozing contentedly on the stool in front of the piano.

'There was something I wanted to ask you at dinner,' said Igor, turning to her.

'Okay,' Erika replied, feeling panic, even though he'd ruled out a marriage proposal.

'Don't look so scared.'

'I'm not scared.'

He went to the neatly piled wood and newspaper in the grate and lit a match. He put it on the paper, and with a whoomph, the fire started to burn.

Igor turned back to her. 'You're close to Tom?'

Tom was Igor's sixteen-year-old son from his marriage to Denise.

'Of course. I will never try to be a stepmother, but we get on well. Yes.'

'We'd like to have you listed as an emergency contact and have you added as a named person on the collection arrangement. If you ever take Tom to school. And when I say 'we', I mean myself and Denise. And Tom. He's excited that he might ride to school in a police car.'

'I drive an unmarked car,' said Erika with a smile.

'Yeah. But you've got a siren and blue lights.'

She looked at Igor. This was a significant step. An acknowledgement that their relationship was serious if she was being included in childcare arrangements.

'I'm flattered. I'd be happy to do all of that. I'll even take Tom to school sometimes, when I can. But why did you think you needed to take me out for some posh dinner to ask me?'

'Denise suggested it.'

'I'm very different from Denise,' said Erika, hoping she was making her point and being diplomatic.

'I'm really pleased. Thank you. It's kind of crazy if you think about it. The way things are done these days. We never had childcare arrangements back in Slovakia.'

'I know. I always walked across town to school by myself. And that was when I was eight. It's a different world now.'

He leaned down and kissed her. 'Good. That's settled, then. Now is there any more food left?'

'Did you eat at the restaurant?'

'I ate my food and yours, too, but the portions were tiny. I'm still hungry.'

Igor went off to the kitchen, and Erika sat by the fire. A niggling fear scratched at the back of her head. The fear of loving someone again after Mark, and relying on another person for her happiness.

She was happy with Igor, and it scared her.

6

Monday mornings in January were Erika's least favourite time of the year. Igor had stayed for the weekend, and his alarm went off at five thirty am. Erika lay in the darkness, staring at the ceiling as she heard him switch on the shower.

They'd spent the weekend at home, but the Neville Lomas case had been on her mind. She'd set a Google Alert to tell her when his murder hit the news, and her phone beeped. She sat up, bleary-eyed, groped around on the bedside table for her phone, and saw an article had just gone live on the BBC News:

Neville Lomas, MP for North East Surrey for 24 years, has died suddenly aged 66. Officers from the Met Police were called to his central London apartment at about 8.05 pm on Friday, where he was found unresponsive. At this time, his death is not thought to be suspicious. A kind family man, Neville was devoted to his local constituency and was the greatest champion of Surrey and the local area.

Erika spent some time researching Neville Lomas, and his CV read like the stereotypical sleazy MP's: He studied at Oxford, where he met his wife, Isabella. They had three children and a large house in their constituency. He'd been elected to the North East Surrey parliamentary safe seat in 1987. Throughout his career, he was involved in several scandals, none of which caused him to lose his seat. In fact, his majority had grown at each election. He was regularly accused of lobbying on behalf of various businesses that didn't have the interests of the British people at heart, and he had been implicated in three tabloid sex stings over the past thirty years. A journalist got hold of photos of him at a 'cocaine-fuelled orgy' in 1990 and at a 'bondage spanking orgy' with Russian prostitutes in 1993. Most recently, in 1999, a sex worker had sold her story to the press, saying that Neville Lomas paid her to humiliate him sexually. Apparently, he liked to be tied up, flogged, and urinated on.

His wife, Isabella, had stood by him through it all and, on two occasions, was pictured standing next to him on the lawn, tight-lipped in a twin set and padded hair-band as he apologised profusely to the same press for his actions.

The lurid details of Neville Lomas's sex life made Erika wonder whether his death was an accident or a sex game gone wrong. But something still bothered her about the Polaroids signed "Annabelle".

Igor appeared by the bed dressed in his Transport for London uniform.

'I made you a cup of tea,' he said, putting it on the bedside table. Erika sat up and showed him the article. 'So he wasn't murdered?'

'That's what they're reporting.'

'Do you think he was murdered?'

Erika took a sip of her tea and looked out the window at the tops of the bare trees against the orange street lights. She shrugged.

'It's a good thing. One less case to worry about. You said you have so many murder cases on the go. I'll see you tonight. Fish and chips?'

'On a Monday?'

'Yeah, let's go wild.'

Erika laughed. 'Okay.'

He gave her a kiss on the cheek and then left.

Lewisham Row police station was a twenty-minute drive from her house in Blackheath. The car park was half-empty when she pulled up at seven. The street lights illuminated a thick layer of frost on the tarmac. It was bitingly cold when she got out of the car, and she hurried inside, careful not to slip on the icy puddles dotted outside the main entrance.

It was changeover time from the night shift, and the corridor down to the offices was busy.

Erika met her colleague Detective Inspector Kate Moss at the door to the staff kitchen. When they went inside, Detective Inspector Peterson and Detective McGorry were huddled in front of the microwave, peering through the clear window at two bowls slowly turning.

'Morning, boss; morning, lads,' Moss said. She was a short, stocky woman with a bob of flame-red hair. Her face was covered with thousands of freckles, and her kind green eyes sparkled.

'Morning,' said Peterson and McGorry, turning blearily from the microwave.

'Good weekend?' asked Moss, unwinding her long scarf and removing her jacket.

Erika nodded, and Peterson and McGorry murmured yes without looking away from the microwave.

'Who needs Netflix?' said Moss, joining them. 'What are we watching? *True Crime Porridge*?'

'Ha ha,' said Peterson, turning to smile. 'This is – what is it?'

'Oat milk porridge with maple-flavoured Stevia syrup,' said McGorry.

Peterson was a tall, slender black man, slightly shorter than Erika at six feet, with an upright posture. He always made Erika think of a toy soldier. John McGorry was almost as tall as Erika. She'd first met him when he was a lean young lad, but now, more than six years later, he'd filled out quite a lot. The microwave pinged, and he opened the door, removing two steaming bowls of grey mush.

Moss took a paper bag from her coat pocket.

'I have a spare chocolate croissant if you fancy?' she said to Erika.

'Thanks. I'll take you up on that.'

Erika watched with amusement as Peterson and McGorry picked at their food and glanced over enviously as the women bit into the delicious buttery croissants.

'We're doing this new diet app and meal plan,' said Peterson.

Moss filled the kettle. 'Are you two drinking tea?'

'Black with lemon.'

'Oat milk for me,' said McGorry.

Moss looked at Erika.

'Milk and two sugars, please.'

'I read Friday night's duty log,' said Peterson. 'The death of that MP, Neville Lomas. You were there.'

'I was. But one of the superintendents from West End Central swooped in,' said Erika. 'We know stuff gets held back from the media, but whoever's been briefing the press has been quick to rule out murder.'

'You think it's suspicious?' asked McGorry. Erika quickly recapped what she'd seen.

'What did Isaac Strong think?' asked Moss.

'He wanted to withhold opinion until he'd done the post-mortem.'

'You should be happy it's not been added to our caseload,' said Moss. Erika thought of her caseload: eight active murder inquiries; two rape cases, including attempted murder; and two manslaughter charges. Moss was right; she didn't have the time or resources, but something about the Neville Lomas case was prickling her spider senses.

When Moss finished making the tea, Erika took her cup to her office. She opened the HOLMES database on her computer and logged in to see whether the death of Neville Lomas had been logged and a case file created. It had, but details were sparse. Superintendent Dan Fisk had created the file, and Erika reflected on the man who'd arrived with him. Who was he? Fisk hadn't introduced him as a police officer.

She closed HOLMES and looked up Superintendent Dan Fisk on the intranet. He had been working out of West End Central for the past few years, having been made a superintendent at age *thirty-five*. Erika sat back in her chair. Fisk was now thirty-nine, eleven years younger than Erika. He'd gone to Cambridge University and worked in finance until he decided to join the Met's fast-track recruitment scheme. Like Erika and many of her colleagues, he hadn't trodden the beat for years.

Erika was fifty years old. She would become eligible for early retirement in five years but could already feel she was being sidelined as one of the ancient dinosaurs. Just look at how those two young police officers had been around her, treating her like a relic of the past.

And maybe she was. Erika tapped her teeth with a pen and saw the pile of files on the table. So many cases were screaming for her attention. So much paperwork that she felt like a glorified admin. The feeling came to her again that she was drifting and rudderless. She looked around the tiny, cramped office with the crappy furniture and the view of a brick wall.

She picked up her phone and dialled Isaac's office at the morgue.

7

The morgue seemed to leach what little warmth Erika had left in her body as she hurried down the long, fluorescent-lit corridor to Isaac Strong's office.

The door was open, and she knocked on the frame. Isaac sat at his desk working. He wore a blue shirt open at the neck, black skinny jeans, and Crocs, and his dark hair was swept away from his high forehead. As usual, he projected an aura of calm and order compared to how frazzled Erika felt. The grey January light poured in through a window high on the wall. The room was lined with bookshelves, which Isaac had crammed with medical textbooks.

'Morning,' said Isaac softly. 'You got here fast.'

'I just bailed on my weekly team meeting and asked Moss to cover for me. She wasn't pleased . . . This isn't even my case.'

'I'm not judging you.'

'*I'm* judging me. I'm too old for this.'

'For what?'

'I don't know . . . Always going against authority.'

'Has anyone told you not to view the body?'

'No.'

'I have jurisdiction over the body of Neville Lomas. I invited you to view it. And less of this "too old" talk. We're the same age, Erika. Thank you,' he said with mock indignation.

'Yes, we're still young. Of course.'

Isaac smiled and got up from his desk. She followed him out and down the corridor to a tall steel door. He placed his pass-key on the sensor, and the door buzzed and popped open.

The chill air seemed to sink down and envelop them. The post-mortem room was a heady mix of steel and Victorian porcelain tile. Along one wall was a row of stainless-steel doors, and in the centre of the room were three post-mortem tables, also of stainless steel, surrounded by gutters. The body lay under a white sheet on the table closest to the door.

Isaac pulled on a pair of latex gloves and then gently folded the top portion of the sheet down. Neville Lomas seemed paler and more corpulent on the post-mortem table. His face was jowly in repose, and his chin rested atop a pile of three other chins. The only colour came from the thick purple thread of the stitches from the long Y-shaped incision across his chest, and they rose upwards with his mound of belly flesh.

'I read in the press that you ruled his death from natural causes?' said Erika.

'No. I actually ruled it as an open verdict,' said Isaac. 'But I also referred it to a colleague.' An open verdict meant exactly that: it acknowledged that a crime could have been committed, but didn't go as far as naming a criminal or the cause of death.

'Who put out the press release?'

'I don't know,' he said softly.

Erika glanced at his face. 'Let me guess – you had a visit from Dan Fisk and another man in a grey suit: short and balding, a brown birthmark under his left eye?'

Isaac nodded. 'He explained that Neville Lomas was known to engage in dangerous and sometimes violent sex acts. And they knew Neville Lomas to be in a terrible state, health-wise. I was also told discreetly, or not so discreetly, that two sex workers have previously sold stories to the tabloids about his taste for being beaten and flogged and how he liked to have suffocation simulated on him. And that the chief whip in the Houses of Parliament would be happy to furnish me with more details, off the record.'

Erika studied Neville Lomas's lifeless body lying on the post-mortem table, like a slab of spoiled meat. She recalled the crime scene where they'd found riding crops, sadomasochistic porn, and the look of fear in Neville's eyes in the Polaroid photos.

'What do you really think was the cause of death?'

'Suffocation, which led to heart failure. There were faint petechial haemorrhages and haemorrhages in the lungs. Of course, he could have asked to be suffocated, as part of a sex game.'

'Do you know how he was suffocated?'

Isaac nodded.

'He has faint bruising around his nostrils and chin. I thought it was a reaction to the masking tape. I think someone could have clamped their hand over his nose and pushed the jaw up to keep his mouth shut.' He leaned over to Erika and gently demonstrated on her face with his hands.

'That's horrible, even for a few seconds,' said Erika, pulling away.

'Notice I say, "could have". Neville Lomas also had a dislocated right shoulder and three broken ribs. He could have broken them trying to fight his restraints, but can you see, there are also two round bruises on his sternum.' He indicated two purple-hued circles on either side of the Y-shaped incision in Neville's chest. 'The costal cartilage was torn.'

'What's that?' said Erika.

'The ribcage is made up of twenty-four ribs, twelve on each

side,' said Isaac, indicating the sides of his chest. 'And then you have the sternum at the front, which is made up of a kind of diamond-shaped piece of bone,' he said, putting his hand on Neville's chest high up near the throat, 'and a longer piece underneath like a . . . like a long tongue shape. The sternum is connected to each rib with the costal cartilage, which is more flexible than bone.'

Erika nodded as she saw him splay his hands across the dead man's chest on each side.

Isaac went on: 'Neville's broken ribs were at the top of his chest, and the costal cartilage was also torn away from the sternum. This, coupled with the two bruises, makes me think that whoever suffocated him knelt on his chest while putting their hand over his mouth and nose. It's informally called the Burke and Hare technique. You've heard of Burke and Hare?'

'Of course; they're the two guys who killed people in the 1800s and sold their corpses for medical experiments. Burke and Hare would get their victims intoxicated, and then one would kneel on the victim's chest whilst the other put a hand or cloth over the victim's mouth. It stops them from drawing in any air and crushes the air out of the lungs.'

'Yes. But again, I'm being advised that Neville Lomas could have asked to have a sex worker kneel on his chest and suffocate him.'

'What about toxicology?' asked Erika.

'He was ten times over the legal alcohol limit and had flunitrazepam in his system.'

'Rohypnol? If it was consenting sex, why would he take Rohypnol?' finished Erika.

Isaac shook his head. 'He did have heart failure, potentially brought on by and coupled with suffocation. In fact, I'm surprised he was still alive in the first place. He had severe lung damage from smoking, furred-up arteries, osteoporosis, fatty liver, swollen lymph nodes, and a sizeable stomach tumour. He was morbidly obese and a type one diabetic, and there were two abscesses on his teeth – one burst during the post-mortem.'

Erika could see Isaac was stressed. He rarely showed stress. She put a hand on his arm. 'When Fisk and this grey-suited man came to the morgue, did they threaten you?'

'No. 'Course not. No. But you know what these people are like. They have this aura of dark power. I'm sure we would have recorded an open verdict even without their influence. I just would have liked the option of waiting to hear back from the colleague I referred it to. But now they've gone ahead and released the details to the press of Neville Lomas's death.'

They looked back at the body and were silent for a moment.

'When Superintendent Fisk came to the morgue, with our grey-suited friend. What did they ask you?'

'They didn't ask me anything. It was more like they wanted to press on me the information that Neville Lomas liked very rough sex. . . rough enough to cause a heart attack,' said Isaac.

'Nothing about the Annabelle Polaroids?'

'Nothing. What do you want to do?'

Erika hesitated and watched as Isaac carefully folded the sheet back over the body.

'I have eight active murder cases. Maybe I should concentrate on them and let the men in grey suits worry about this.'

TWO MONTHS LATER

8

Monday, March 6

It was early on a Monday morning in the first week of March, and Erika was driving Igor's son, Tom, to school for the first time. There had been a mix-up with Igor's and his ex-wife Denise's work schedules, so Igor had asked Erika if she could do the school run.

It was an overcast day, and the bright high-visibility jackets of the two parking stewards directing the traffic in the drop-off area outside the school drive hurt her eyes.

Erika really liked Tom. He was a funny, easy-going sixteen-year-old, but this was the first time she'd been alone with him, and she felt nervous.

'Is it like this every morning?' she asked as they joined the long line of cars. The main entrance had a sweeping set of steps leading up to it, and on each edge of the vast red-bricked building were small doors marked 'GIRLS' and 'BOYS'.

Tom nodded. He had a mop of rich chestnut, curly hair, his mother's heart-shaped face, and Igor's strong nose. He'd inherited the best of both of them, and was at that age where he wasn't quite boy or man.

'Is there a parking ticket machine?'

'It's not an airport,' he said with a grin. There were allotted times for dropping kids off, staggered between 8.00 am and 8.45 am. Igor told Erika that their time was 8.32 am, which also caused considerable stress. It was 8.28, and Erika was pleased she'd made it. She'd passed a small test. Competency to do the school run.

'What's that?' Tom asked, leaning between the seats and pointing at the magnetic light in its blue-domed plastic on the footwell in the passenger side.

'That's my blue light. I use it when I have to put on the siren.'

'Is that when you have to chase the bad guys?'

'Yes.'

'Do you ever use it when you want to get somewhere quicker?'

Erika smiled. 'Some officers do. Not me.'

Tom looked through the seats to where the line of cars had ground to a halt. The parent in the car at the front of the line was talking to the two stewards.

'Imagine if you put it on now. You could jump the queue. How do you switch the siren on?'

'This small button, here,' said Erika, indicating it on the dashboard.

'Does it sound loud inside the car?'

'It can do.'

The queue started to move forward again.

'Do you put criminals in the back here? Like when you arrest someone?'

'Not so much. I'm a plain clothes detective. I don't have the metal grilles for custody transfers.'

Tom looked around at the inside of the car and nodded. He looked completely absorbed. 'Have you *ever* had a criminal in the back?'

'Yes. Last week, there was an older woman who had killed her husband. She wasn't judged as a flight risk, so I took her in,' said Erika.

'Did this killer woman sit right here?'

Erika hesitated. 'Yeah.'

He bounced up and down in his seat a little, as if he could still feel the impression left by the murderer. 'How did she kill her husband?'

'She poisoned him.'

'Poison. Shi. . . I mean. Wow. How did she poison him? Can you tell me?'

'Anti-freeze. She put it in his food, a little at a time. Until . . .'

Tom was quiet. His eyes were wide. 'Until he, like, puked?'

'He was puking for a long time. He thought he was ill.'

They were almost at the drop-off point, and Erika thought she should steer the conversation to something more savoury for a teenager.

'How many times did he puke?'

'I don't know. A lot.'

'If he puked outside and it was icy weather, and he'd been eating anti-freeze, did it mean his puke wouldn't freeze?'

'You're clever. That's part of the way she was caught.'

'But he died, 'cos you said she was arrested for murder?'

'Yes.'

'When you put her in the car here, when you arrested her, did you do that thing where you put your hand on the top of her head when she got in?'

'Yes.'

'Dad joked that you would do that with me when you drove me today.'

Erika laughed. They were now at the main entrance.

There was a slight blonde-haired woman with a thin, pinched face and bright-blue eyes. She wore a high-visibility jacket over her smart houndstooth coat. She came to Tom's door and motioned for him to get out.

'Have a good day at school,' said Erika.

'Thanks for the lift. Are you coming back for the pick-up?'

'Your mum's going to pick you up tonight.'

'Oh. Okay.' He hesitated. 'Will you take me to school again sometime?'

'Yes, of course.'

He got out of the car and walked up the steps to where two of his mates were waiting. They were equally tall and handsome, with glossy brown hair. Tom said something, and they all turned. Erika gave him the thumbs up, thinking this might embarrass him less than if she waved. The woman in the high-visibility jacket motioned for her to wind down her window. Erika felt a cold breeze as the glass slid down.

'Morning, Denise. Oh, who are you?'

'I'm DC . . .' Erika hesitated. She was so used to introducing herself professionally. 'I'm Erika. Tom's father's, er. . .'

She didn't finish the sentence. Saying 'girlfriend' made her cringe.

'I'm Felicity Brogues-Houghton. We haven't been told that you would be dropping off Thomas.'

'I am on the contact list.'

Felicity flashed a chilly smile. 'Ah, yes. You're the *girlfriend*.'

It took Erika aback that this woman would choose to introduce herself in such a poisonous way.

'I'm also a police officer.'

Felicity raised an eyebrow. 'Oh. Right.'

'Yes. Right.'

Erika's phone began to ring. The number for the police control room flashed up on the dashboard.

'I better go. Good to meet you.' And before Felicity could say any more, she wound up the window, pulled the car forward, and answered the call.

'Morning, Erika. We've just had a call come in. The body of a twenty-three-year-old male has been found in the Greenwich One apartments.'

'That's next to Greenwich Park and the observatory,' said Erika, already keying the details into her satnav.

'The emergency call was made by the victim's mother—'

'Okay.'

'This hasn't been verified, but the victim is Jamie Teague.'

It took Erika a moment before she realised the significance of the name.

'He's a football player?'

'Yes. This one could generate a lot of press attention, so we're sending additional officers along with the forensics team.'

Erika's satnav calculated the journey, and the route appeared on the screen.

'I'm in Catford, only a couple of miles out, but it's rush hour. I'll be there asap.'

The line of cars in front wasn't moving. Erika saw in her wing mirror Felicity Brogues-Houghton marching over with a look of grim-set purpose on her face. She knocked on the window. Erika wound it down.

'I need you to fill in another form if you're going to drop off Thomas again,' she snapped, brandishing a piece of paper. 'And if you *are* a police officer, can I see some proof of ID?'

Erika reached down, picked up the magnetic blue light, leaned up, and slapped it on the car's roof.

'Sorry, Felicity. Duty calls.' The light and sirens blasted out, making Felicity jump. The line of cars parted, and she exited the school grounds, leaving Felicity open-mouthed, still holding the form.

9

The Greenwich One apartment block was a recently developed luxury high-rise overlooking Greenwich Park. Erika parked her car and walked through a landscaped plaza paved with butter-coloured stone. Greenwich One was twenty-four stories of blue-mirrored glass. It reflected the landscape of the park with a strange greyish hue, as if it were being shown in flashback. Where the glass windows were clear at the base of the building, there was a Starbucks coffee shop, though only a few people sat inside. The only clue that a murder investigation was unfolding was the black forensics van parked by the main entrance, next to a police car.

The entrance wasn't accessible to the public, and Erika had to press the intercom. When she cupped her hands and peered through the glass, she saw a familiar face across the lobby. It was the police officer from the Neville Lomas crime scene, Dahlia Beck. She hurried over to the door and opened it for Erika.

She was wearing a smart blue trouser suit and powder-blue Prada-branded trainers. Her long dark hair was tied back in a plait.

'Hello, Detective Chief Inspector Foster – *Erika?*'

'Why are you here?' asked Erika before she could stop herself.

'I'm on call, ma'am.'

'On call? You're not in uniform?'

'I've just been promoted to plain clothes. I'm really pleased to join your team this week on the murder squad at Lewisham Row.'

Erika stared at her, trying to take in all this new information. How old was Dahlia? Twelve? And she was now a plain clothes detective and due to join her team? Erika swallowed and composed herself. She didn't want this little . . . lady knowing she'd been blindsided.

'I'm pleased to hear that,' said Erika, trying to mean it. Dahlia beamed, and Erika wondered whether she was speaking to the same woman from two months ago. This version of Dahlia seemed polite. Maybe she only gave you the nice side of her face when she needed you? 'Have you been up to the crime scene?'

'No. I *literally* just got here and I've been talking to the doorman. He says that the forensics team are already in. And there's a couple of uniform officers upstairs. They answered the 999 call. The deceased is the footballer Jamie Teague.'

Dahlia led them across the marble floor to a large desk, where a slight man with thinning hair stood and hitched up his trousers. He pursed his lips and cocked his head inquisitively at Erika, who introduced herself and showed her warrant card.

'I'm Norbert Pope. The reception manager. Are you aware of the identity of the deceased young man?'

'We believe it's Jamie Teague,' said Erika.

Norbert shook his head sadly. 'He was a good defender. One of our best. I'm a Chelsea supporter. Always have been. He only just moved into the penthouse a couple of weeks ago.' Norbert spoke carefully and had a pronounced Kentish accent. He looked out of place in the vast marble reception area.

'Has the body been formally identified?' asked Erika.

He looked beadily between her and Dahlia. 'His mum found

his body, and she says it's 'im. I'd think his own mother would know. She's devastated. As you'd expect. One of your police officers is with 'er in the building manager's office.'

'Can we please go up to the penthouse?'

He nodded and handed Erika a white key card. 'Now. You use this card on the sensor and press *P* in the lift . . . Now, *P*, that's for "penthouse".'

'Thank you.'

He nodded sagely and sat down. 'What should I say if the press come?'

'Nothing. Don't let anyone in,' said Erika. They went to the bank of four lifts. The first in the line was open.

'I follow Jamie Teague on Instagram,' said Dahlia when they were inside and the doors closed. Erika pressed the button marked 'P'. 'He's got four million followers.'

Erika felt a queasy little lurch of her stomach as the lift sped up twenty-four floors. Dahlia was holding her phone. It looked too big to fit in the tight pockets of her trousers. She tapped the screen and then showed Erika Jamie Teague's Instagram profile. The top line of the grid showed photos of him dressed in white briefs at a modelling shoot on an exotic beach; another photo showed him dressed down in a baseball cap, visiting some deprived-looking children in an inner-city school; and in a third, he was dressed in a suit, standing in the middle of the grass of an empty sports stadium.

'This building is apparently the most secure in London, up there with The Shard,' said Dahlia. 'Loads of Arabs and tech people have invested in real estate here.'

Erika thought back to Norbert on the front desk, who looked like he could keel over at any minute, and made a mental note to ask about the security arrangements.

The lift opened into a large glass atrium with views over the Greenwich observatory, the palace, and the skyline of Canary

Wharf on the other side of the park. Erika had never seen such a panoramic view from this side of the capital. The trees were bare, and it was a grey day, and the tinted windows gave it an odd hue. Like they were watching it on a big video screen. The atrium led to a smaller lobby to the left, where a police officer had strung crime scene tape. It all seemed so eerily calm and disconnected from the real world. Farther along, a white sheet covered the carpet outside an open front door, where a scenes-of-crime officer was on his knees, taking a sample swab from the door-frame.

'Morning, ma'am,' said the police officer when Erika flashed her warrant card. Erika hated being called 'ma'am', but she had learned that no one ever listened when she protested, so she let it slide. Dahlia slid her warrant card from her trouser pocket and held it up, and he nodded, his eyes scanning her like a bar-code.

'How far along are forensics?' asked Erika.

'I've been told by the pathologist, Isaac Strong, that you can go in.' He lifted the police tape and they ducked underneath.

10

Erika and Dahlia suited up and crossed the threshold into Jamie Teague's apartment.

They walked right into a vast empty living space with wooden floors. A glass wall looked out over Greenwich Park and the London skyline, an enormous terrace with evergreen plants, and a Jacuzzi, where the steam escaped under the cover. Erika estimated the ceiling must have been four or five metres high. *Not the usual pad of a twenty-five-year-old,* she thought. The white walls and the space were bare, apart from a small blue sofa facing a flat-screen television. The apartment was crowded with scenes-of-crime officers in white overalls. Erika counted four in the main living area, swabbing, photographing, and lifting fingerprints, and another two in the kitchen, dusting an array of empty Champagne bottles and glasses on the dark marble countertops for prints. A long row of low metal boxes had been set up, allowing them to cross the living space. Isaac waited for them on the other side of this temporary bridge.

'Good morning,' he said, his voice slightly muffled by his face mask.

'Morning,' said Erika. 'Do you remember Detective Beck?'

'I do,' he replied. 'I hope you have a strong stomach, Detective Beck.'

'Yes, very strong,' said Dahlia. Erika could hear the nerves in her voice.

'We're in the master bedroom,' said Isaac.

They crossed over the boxes, which carried on down a long corridor to the main bedroom.

Isaac let Erika go inside first. The bedroom had the same high ceilings and floor-to-ceiling windows looking out over Greenwich Park. The walls were white, and the room was sparsely furnished, like the living area. The only piece of furniture was a four-poster bed in the middle of the room. It had a dark metal hue, and on closer inspection, Erika could see it was made of copper, just like the candelabra. Forensics had set up flood-lights, which glinted off the bed in brown-gold flashes and, in places, made Erika wince at the brightness.

Jamie Teague's body lay limply on its side, hog-tied, his arms and legs bound behind his back and pulled up with a rope connecting them. His head was arched up and back, so he faced the windows, and there was masking tape over his mouth.

He was lean and muscular, but his skin had a dull, yellow tinge. Erika felt a prickling of déjà vu about this crime scene.

'It's really him . . . ,' said Dahlia, putting a hand to her face.

'His clothes were piled next to the bed, and these were found in the left pocket in a small white envelope,' said Isaac. He handed Erika another plastic evidence bag. Inside were three Polaroid photos. Erika flicked through them with a heavy feeling in her chest. In the first, Jamie Teague was pictured from above, lying on the four-poster bed, wearing briefs. He stared at the camera with unfocused eyes and dilated pupils, but his eyes showed a glint of defiance. As if a small part of him were trying to resist. The second Polaroid was a close-up of his face, and he was flinching from something. *Was it the flash-bulb?* thought Erika. *Or something else.* In the third Polaroid, he was bound with the ropes, and a black-gloved hand reached into the shot, clamping his nose shut, with the fingers and palm pressed against his mouth. His eyes were open, and the muscles and tendons stood out on his body, as if he were fighting his bonds. The images had the same signature on the white strip at the bottom:

ANNABELLE

A look passed between Erika and Isaac.

'When his mother found the body. Did she see these photos?' Erika asked.

'I don't know. They were still in the pocket of his trousers when we arrived,' said Isaac. Erika looked around the room. 'He has three broken ribs,' he added, indicating Jamie Teague's chest, and where he lay on his side, Erika could see the broken bones in his ribcage underneath his taut, lean pectoral muscles. 'And two circular bruises on his chest.'

'Neville Lomas,' she said quietly.

'I know,' replied Isaac. Dahlia was silent, but her eyes darted between them.

'What about time of death?'

'Seventy-two hours or more. Rigor mortis has passed, and he was last seen alive in the early hours of Saturday morning. I'll know more when I open him up.'

Erika looked back at the Polaroids at Jamie Teague's huge dilated pupils. His eyes were like black holes, and it chilled her.

'And, of course, I'll follow up with toxicology as soon as possible,' added Isaac.

'The place is so empty. Where's all the furniture?'

'There's another bedroom next door, and it's filled with boxes.'

'He posted on Instagram last week that he was moving into a new apartment,' said Dahlia.

The crime scene photographer moved in and started to take close-up photos of Jamie Teague's body, and Isaac moved off to speak to one of the other SOCOs.

Erika felt uncharacteristically shaken by the crime scene and the body of Jamie Teague. They handed in their used overalls and then ducked back under the crime scene tape at the end of the corridor.

'Are you okay?' asked Dahlia.

'Of course. Are you?'

'I think so. My little brother has his poster on the wall. It seems harder when it's someone famous you admire.'

A slight man with thinning hair emerged from one of the lifts. He was dressed immaculately in a pin-striped three-piece suit, and his polka-dotted, blue handkerchief matched his tie.

'Good morning. Are you the police?' He spoke with a French accent, and he had very white teeth. Erika and Dahlia showed their warrant cards. 'My name is Jaques Durand. I'm the manager of Greenwich One. Janice Teague is waiting in my office. As you would understand, she's very distressed and becoming a little impatient.'

'I'd like to talk to her,' said Erika. 'Can you please arrange for all CCTV footage you have for the building for the past seventy-two hours to be sent here?' She added, handing him her business card, 'I take it your CCTV system is digital?'

'It is, and yes, of course.' He pocketed her card. 'Do you have a police media liaison I can contact with?'

'Dahlia, can you put Mr Durand in touch with Colleen Scanlan? She's the Met's media liaison. And can we get a statement from you?'

'Me? Why?' asked Jaque. He frowned.

'You are the building manager, and this unfortunate death has happened in your building.'

'I see,' he said coldly.

Erika turned to Dahlia. 'Perhaps if you sit down with Mr Durand for a few minutes, he can elaborate.'

'You have to appreciate I have high-profile clients who like to live discreetly, and I have signed non-disclosure agreements.'

Erika took a step closer to Jaque, and he seemed to notice for the first time that she was half a head taller than him.

'Mr Durand. This is a murder investigation,' she said quietly. 'And you should know as well as I do that non-disclosure agreements don't apply when answering questions concerning a police investigation. A murder investigation.'

'Murder?' he repeated, wide-eyed, and his accent sounded all the more pronounced.

'Yes. So, please. If you can make time now, it would be much appreciated. We can, of course, schedule a time for you to come into the station.'

'No, no, no. That won't be necessary, Detective.'

'Chief Inspector. Detective Chief Inspector. Good. Now. Please can you take me to Mrs Teague.'

11

Erika went into the office alone. Jamie Teague's mother sat on a sofa in the corner like a zombie, staring ahead with red, swollen eyes. She looked dishevelled with smudged mascara, her jet-black dyed hair contrasting her pale face.

Erika introduced herself, showing her warrant card. 'Mrs Teague. I'm very sorry I haven't been able to speak to you until now.'

She nodded and bit her lip. Pressing a balled-up piece of tissue to her nose. Erika looked around the stylish office. There were photos on the wall taken during the building's construction, bookended by two images: the then prime minister had been the one to break ground on the project, and then Prince Charles had unveiled a plaque to open the finished building.

'This is only the third time I've been here,' said Janice, following Erika's gaze over the photos. Her voice broke with emotion. 'Jamie only just moved in.'

Erika gave her a moment.

'Are you okay to answer some questions? It's just the sooner I speak to you, the fresher the details will be in your mind.'

'When else? Might as well be now,' she said.

Erika took out her notebook and pen. Janice had on an old pair of jeans with a sweater. A sensible waterproof jacket was draped over the arm of the sofa, and an expensive-looking Chanel-branded handbag looked out of place at her feet.

'Can I ask what time you arrived here today?'

Janice swallowed and held the tissue against her nose. 'It must have been about seven thirty. Today's the day I do his washing. I let myself in. I did that at his old place. I did the same here.'

'You have a key?'

'Yes, I just said I let myself in. He's my son.' There was a pause. Erika didn't correct her to the past tense, but Janice seemed to realise what she would now have to do. She looked up at the ceiling and, closing her eyes, took a deep breath. 'Yes, I have a key. He was meant to be at training today.'

'Do you live locally?'

'Deptford. Just down the road but a world away from this. It's where Jamie and his sister grew up.'

'Was the door open or locked when you arrived?'

'Locked.'

'Any sign of a break-in?'

'No.'

'Do you know what Jamie planned to do over the weekend?'

'He'd been at training all day and was getting ready to meet a couple of mates. One of them, Leon, just had a baby, and they were going out to wet the baby's head. That's when I . . . last spoke to him.'

Even though she'd lived in the UK for more than thirty years, Erika was still confused about where this saying came from, when the father and his mates go out and get drunk in the name of 'wetting the baby's head'. She knew that sometimes these nights out could get raucous.

'Do you know the names of his friends?'

'Of course I do,' she said tartly. 'Leon Bromfield and Finn

Horton. They were at the football academy with Jamie when they were younger. I know he was excited to see them.'

'I'll need their phone numbers.' Janice nodded and took out her phone, scrolling through. 'Do you know where they were going to go out?'

'Some fancy, expensive club in the West End. Jamie spends a fortune being a member of these posh nightclubs . . . He can't just go down the pub. He'd get mobbed. And . . .'

'And what?'

'Stalkers. He's had stalkers. His last flat in Highgate was broken into. The media hound him. Tabloid stories every bloody day, mostly lies. He can't have a real life.'

'Tell me about the break-in?'

'You lot were useless. Thank God he wasn't in when they broke in.'

'Was anything stolen?'

Janice sighed, exasperated. 'You should have this bloody information! He talked to you lot. I did too . . .' She watched Erika writing. 'How long is this going to take? Charles. My husband. He's away in Australia. He works for a plastics company. He doesn't know . . . I haven't been able to get hold of him yet. He's eleven hours ahead. He's going to be – Oh, God. I don't know how I'm going to tell him.'

Janice looked up with pleading, beseeching eyes, and Erika felt so much empathy for her.

'Are there any other family members we can call?'

'No. Our Karen, Jamie's sister. I've called her and left messages . . . Just knowing I know and neither of them knows.' Janice was suddenly very still. She looked up at Erika. 'I saw what was done to him. The . . . the ropes. I'm telling you here and now that he wasn't a pervert. No mother should have to see her son like . . . that.'

'Of course,' said Erika.

'What do you know? Have you got kids?'

Erika thought of Tom and how she would feel if she found his body tied up like that. It would be horrifying.

'No. I don't have children.'

'Have you had to see a person you loved die horribly?' she spat. Erika carried on writing. 'I'm asking you a question, Officer.'

Erika looked up. 'Yes. My husband was shot in front of me. He died in my arms.'

It came out a little too forcefully.

'When?'

'Eight years ago. It will be nine years in a few months.'

Janice's demeanour softened. 'I'm sorry.'

'Thank you.'

There was a long silence as Erika caught up with her notes.

'I feel this rage. Like it's going to consume me if I don't lash out. I want to punch you. But I'm not going to.'

'I felt like that for a long time, you know—'

Janice put her hand up. 'No. I don't want to hear about bloody psychologists. Do you hear me?'

'I'm just here to ask questions so we can find who did this.'

Erika had to get Janice to focus and give her as much information as possible whilst things were fresh in her mind. Before all the other mechanics and responsibilities of grief took over.

'What else do you want to know?'

'Was there anything else unusual inside the flat?' asked Erika, not wanting to lead Janice too much with regards to the Polaroid pictures.

'No. No. He'd just moved in. Everything is in boxes.'

'Does Jamie own a Polaroid camera?'

'What? No. I don't think so. He takes photos on his phone.'

'Was Jamie in a relationship with anyone?'

'*Girls*. He liked girls,' said Janice, eager to correct any assumptions.

'Did he have a girlfriend?'

'No.'

'Does the name Annabelle mean anything to you?'

Janice stared at her hands, thinking.

'No. He never mentioned that name. There hasn't been a girlfriend for a while. I know there were shenanigans. He's a young lad. And a football player. I suppose you're going to ask me about the allegations?'

Erika hesitated and racked her brain. Allegations? Yes. Jamie Teague, the footballer. Three years ago, he'd been tried for raping a young woman, and he'd been found not guilty.

'Yes. I know about the rape trial,' said Erika. The door opened as she was saying this, and a stocky woman wearing an expensive boxy black trouser suit entered with a balding middle-aged man. The woman looked anything between thirty and sixty. Her hair was ice-white blonde and scraped back in a ponytail, and her face had been pulled and plumped, and she had cat-like eyes.

'Oh my God! I've just heard. I'm so sorry, darlin',' said the woman, going to Janice. She also had a Scottish accent, but her voice was deep and gravelly. They embraced. The woman pulled back and fixed Janice with a stare. 'Sweetheart, what can I do?'

'Cheri. Get me the hell out of here. I can't get hold of Charles or Karen.'

'I'm Cheri Shelton, Jamie's football agent. This is his solicitor, Jack Grover,' said the woman, looking Erika up and down. The solicitor had his hands in his pockets, nodded awkwardly, and looked at the floor like he'd unknowingly walked into a women's changing room.

Erika showed them her warrant card. 'I was just asking some questions,' she said.

'I need to take Janice home,' said Cheri. She didn't seem too pleased that Erika was talking to Janice without her present.

'I'm almost done.'

'Is Janice under arrest?'

'No.'

'Good. Then she's free to go.'

'I have one more question. Did Jamie have any enemies, anyone he'd fallen out with recently?'

Janice got up, and Cheri held out her arm to lead her away, but she hesitated on the threshold, and her answer surprised Erika.

'He was so happy that his career was a success. The only problem was finding people who felt the same.'

Cheri indicated something impatiently to Jack.

'Ah, yes. Here is my card,' Jack said. 'If you need to speak to Janice, call me, and we can arrange a meeting when things have calmed down.'

They ushered Janice out of the room, and Erika was left looking at the card.

Marcus, Smoad, and Pilkington were an expensive law firm.

12

Later that afternoon, Erika joined her team for an emergency briefing in the incident room in the basement of Lewisham Row police station.

'Afternoon, everyone,' she said. The team assembled in front of her included Detective Inspector Moss, Detective Inspector James Peterson, Detective John McGorry, and Sergeant Crane, an officer with sand-coloured hair and a relaxed, easy-going vibe. There were also a group of civilian police admin workers and Dahlia, attending her first briefing as a team member. 'This morning, the body of the footballer Jamie Teague was found in his apartment in the new Greenwich One complex. We're still waiting for an official cause of death. There was no sign of forced entry into Jamie Teague's apartment. He was last seen on Friday night at the Red Velvet private members club in Soho with two friends.'

Superintendent Melanie Hudson entered the room and stood at the back. She was a tiny woman with silvery-blonde hair dressed informally in a black Adidas tracksuit. She was currently on annual leave, and if she'd broken off her holiday to attend this briefing, something was going on.

Erika switched off the lights, and the crime scene photos of

Jamie Teague appeared, projected on the enormous whiteboards covering the wall at the front of the room. There was silence as the images of his naked body hog-tied on his bed flashed up.

'Toxicology and post-mortem results are still pending, but we are treating his death as suspicious. There was also an envelope containing three Polaroid photos of the victim left at the scene, next to the bed, in the victim's trouser pocket,' said Erika. Scans of the Polaroids appeared on the wall. 'You can see these photos have all been signed with the name "Annabelle", using what looks like a black felt-tip or Sharpie-style pen . . . I don't know if you recall the murder of the Conservative MP for North East Surrey, Neville Lomas, two months ago in January? I was the first responder at the scene, and Neville Lomas's body was found tied up in the same way with masking tape across his mouth.'

The crime scene photos of Neville Lomas hog-tied and lying on his bed appeared on the screen. Even though he was a much larger, more corpulent man than Jamie Teague, the similarities in how they'd been tied up were startling.

'Three Polaroid photos were also found in a white envelope at the Neville Lomas crime scene, in the victim's trouser pockets, next to the bed. Also signed with the same signature: "Annabelle".' The Neville Lomas Polaroid photos flashed up on the whiteboards. Under the harsh glare of the camera flash, Neville Lomas's pale, sweaty skin looked all the more grotesque.

'If I remember correctly, Neville Lomas's death was ruled as an open verdict?' said Moss, perching on the edge of a desk with a cup of coffee. Erika had already tried calling Isaac to discuss this further, but his office had said he was busy.

'That's correct. But now we have two startlingly similar crime scenes with identical sets of signed Polaroids.' Erika hesitated. She thought back to the conversation she had with Isaac at the morgue in January. When he described his visit from the man in the grey suit. 'The Neville Lomas case was never ours.

Superintendent Dan Fisk from West End Central took over, and it's my understanding that Superintendent Fisk was encouraged not to dig too deeply into the background of Neville Lomas.'

'Erika, that's speculation,' said Melanie, speaking for the first time. A few officers who hadn't seen her in the room turned and looked surprised. *Aha; that's why you're here,* thought Erika. *Neville Lomas's death is a sensitive topic.*

'To be fair to Superintendent Fisk, if the evidence and circumstances of Neville Lomas's death had been presented in court at the time, and with Neville Lomas's sexual history and health problems, it would have been difficult to prove that his cause of death was murder and not a consensual sex game gone wrong. However, the link to Jamie Teague's death casts the circumstances of Neville Lomas's death in a whole new light. Which we will be investigating,' said Erika, directing the last sentence at Melanie.

'What about the person or sex worker who was with Neville Lomas when he died?' asked McGorry. 'They could be prosecuted for not reporting his death. Were they ever found?'

'I've just requested the case file,' said Erika. 'I should have it later this afternoon.'

'To clarify, again, Erika,' said Melanie, 'we're here today to start an investigation into the death of Jamie Teague. That is our priority. The Neville Lomas case will be reviewed in due course.'

Erika had a lot of time for Melanie. She was one of the few bosses who was respectful and had her back. Still, it was unusual for her to come down to the incident room and intervene like this.

'Okay,' said Erika. 'Our focus today is Jamie Teague. And the first thing we need to do is identify if anyone went back to his apartment on Friday night. I spoke to his mother this morning, and his previous home in Highgate was broken into recently. The mother also mentioned reporting a stalker to the police. We need to follow up on all this.'

The door to the incident room opened, and Commander Marsh entered. He was tall and craggily handsome with short-cropped blond hair. The room fell silent. It was rare to have a senior Met Police officer down on the floor of the police station.

'Good afternoon, everyone. Sorry to interrupt. Erika, Melanie, a word, please?' he asked. Erika turned to Moss, who gave the slightest raise of her eyebrow.

Erika returned the look. 'Could you carry on? Assign tasks, and get the case up and running in the system.'

'Of course,' said Moss.

Erika could see Marsh was sweating and looked very pale. She followed Melanie out into the corridor.

13

Erika, Melanie, and Commander Marsh were silent as they walked along the corridor. Whatever he wanted to say was going to be in private.

'How are you keeping, Erika?' asked Marsh when they got into the lift up to the top floor.

'Well, thank you, sir. How about you? All good?'

'Yes. It's been rather hectic for the past few months. I've moved offices again, which is always an upheaval.'

Melanie nodded along with him.

'I thought you all moved to the New Scotland Yard building a couple of years ago?' asked Erika.

'We did. I've moved up one floor.'

'Did you want a better view?'

'No, Erika. It was a productivity decision.'

'And has it made you more productive?'

'Yes. Commander Tate and myself now share a secretary.'

'You can both have her simultaneously,' said Erika. There was an awkward silence. Melanie was studying their interaction, much like someone watching one of those wildlife programmes narrated by David Attenborough. The cheetah chasing the gazelle. Erika liked to think she was the cheetah.

'I wouldn't put it like that,' he said haughtily. Erika wondered what Marsh's new office looked like. She remembered when he was superintendent here at Lewisham Row. His office had been a tip, a little like a teenage boy's bedroom, with papers everywhere, used coffee cups, and even sometimes old plates of food. Erika and Paul Marsh went back a long way. They'd trained together at Hendon, and Paul had been Mark's close friend. All that seemed like an age ago, especially now he was Commander Marsh in his shiny uniform. The row of silver buttons glittered under the lift's harsh lights. Untouched by the unwashed public. The only thing that Marsh came up against these days was the upholstery in a conference room. 'How is Igor?'

'He's well. How's Marcie?'

'Very good. She has an exhibition coming up. Boats . . . or is it fruit? I think she's going to invite you.'

'Lovely,' said Erika, forcing a smile on her face. Marsh's wife's paintings were awful.

The lift pinged, and Melanie looked relieved to get out. 'If you can come this way,' she said, allowing Marsh to leave first. He strode in front and took Melanie's chair in her office, forcing her to sit with Erika on the other side of the desk. This was a typical douchebag move, thought Erika. He pulled down his jacket, removed his cap, and placed it on the desk.

'Right. I've been asked to oversee this Jamie Keegan case.'

'It's Teague,' said Erika. 'Jamie Teague, sir. You might have been thinking of the footballer Kevin Keegan, who is still alive, and now in his seventies.'

'Yes, Jamie Teague,' he repeated, his neck flushing slightly with embarrassment. 'I've been brought in because this case has several intersectional elements.'

'Intersectional elements?' repeated Erika; she looked at Melanie, who seemed equally baffled.

'Yes. Jamie Teague was a Premiership footballer with a high profile. Famous, with a huge social media presence, the face of several big-name brands. As you also know, Neville Lomas, a senior Conservative MP, was murdered a few months ago with the same modus operandi.'

'Neville Lomas's death was ruled as an open verdict,' said Erika. 'And very quickly announced to the media as him dying of natural causes.'

Marsh hesitated, and then nodded. 'Yes. So you'll both agree we have the ingredients for a perfect storm. A potential serial killer who is targeting high-profile individuals.'

'Hang on, Paul,' said Erika. 'For once, I feel like we're on the wrong sides of the desk. I'm usually the one who jumps to conclusions. The murders may well be linked by the Polaroid photos left at the scene, but this is only the second murder. A serial killer is classed as at least three.'

'I know what a serial killer is, Erika! Our problem is that the Premier League season is still ongoing – Jamie Teague was due to be playing until May. We also have a contentious by-election coming up in two weeks, triggered by Neville Lomas's death. And this is all coming at a very delicate time in British politics. I have been briefed by several individuals at the Home Office, and there is a concern that these two murders could trigger social unrest.'

'Social unrest?' repeated Erika.

'I think the commander is saying it's a worst-case scenario—' Melanie started.

'Please. Don't put words in my mouth,' snapped Marsh. 'We have a perfect storm of inflation spiralling out of control. Britain is in the midst of the worst strikes since the 1970s, and the political conversation is more polarised than ever. Jamie Teague was a working-class hero. And the working class are—'

'Pretty pissed off?' finished Erika.

'I wouldn't put it like that.'

'I would.'

'There is a huge amount of hardship. And Jamie Teague's death, if not properly managed by the media and us as the police, could be seen as something that people could protest about.'

'Really?' asked Erika. 'I thought that people would protest about wages and living costs.'

'If it's seen that the cause of Neville Lomas's death was downplayed, even covered up, and a seriously disturbed individual went on to kill Jamie Teague, football fans could riot, triggering other protests.'

'*Was* Neville Lomas's death covered up?' asked Erika.

Marsh shifted uncomfortably in his chair. 'Neville Lomas was a polarizing figure in the Conservative Party. He was extremely right wing and from a privileged background. We will have to backtrack on the media coverage of his death being from natural causes.'

'An open verdict,' corrected Erika.

'Yes! This, linked with Jamie Teague's death, could fuel conspiracy theorists and negative media coverage for the Met.'

'I understand. But isn't this all rather speculative?' said Erika. 'Aren't you being alarmist?'

Melanie put her hand up. 'Okay. Thank you, Commander. I understand what you are telling us. What can we do for you?'

Marsh shifted on the chair and swallowed. His neck flushed again, and he rubbed at his temples.

'What?' said Erika. She could sense where this was going.

'You can't be on this case, Erika. I'm sorry,' said Marsh.

'Why not?'

'Top brass feel you are a loose cannon. And, come on – I'm sure you would admit this yourself, wouldn't you?'

'No. I refute that. And you are now top brass, sir. So are *you* telling me I'm a loose cannon?'

Marsh rolled his eyes, which always made him look like a petulant teenager. 'Superintendent Dan Fisk was the original officer who worked on the Neville Lomas case. He should take the lead.'

'No. Sir. *I* was the responding officer on the Neville Lomas case. And again, today, I was the responding officer!'

Erika could feel her anger mingled with a horrible, cold dread. She knew she was one of the best officers on the force; she always got results, but her mouth and direct manner had gotten her in trouble many times. The Met top brass wanted someone different, someone they could control, someone who would do what they were told and be part of the establishment.

Erika looked over at Melanie. 'I know the commander here can advise you, but he can't directly order me to be replaced.' Melanie was silent. Erika turned back to Marsh. 'Paul. You know how much experience I bring to these kinds of murder cases. Superintendent Dan Fisk is eleven years my junior. He's never trodden the beat. Even you trod the beat once. We trod the beat together, didn't we?'

Erika remembered their time as rookie police officers on the streets of Manchester. There was another awkward silence. Melanie leaned forward and placed her hand on the desk between Erika and Marsh.

'Commander. I respect this visit and your intervention in this case, but I don't have another officer with Erika's experience available to lead this investigation. Erika not only has the experience, but she also has the respect of a large team of talented, dedicated officers. She's able to take them with her . . . Could Dan Fisk be brought in as an adviser?'

Erika sat back and crossed her arms.

'No. Sorry, Melanie. If I'm in charge of a case, I need to be in charge and have the final say. If you want to promote me to superintendent, then go ahead. I've been waiting long enough . . .' Erika held out her hands. 'You could do it right now.'

Marsh slammed his hand down on the table, which made them both jump. 'Dammit, Erika! I feel like it's bloody Groundhog Day with you. We always seem to have these same conversations!'

'Okay, sir,' said Erika calmly. 'But I'll take that Groundhog Day analogy because you know the same thing happens every time.' She leaned forward and jabbed her finger on the desk. 'I always catch my killers.'

She stood up, feeling emboldened. 'And now, if that's everything, I have a murder case to go and work on.'

14

When Erika left the meeting, she was shaking. This was happening yet again. Why was she never good enough? Hadn't she always been straight as a die? She'd never been corrupt. Always did what was right, and here she was. Again.

She needed air and didn't want to run into Marsh as he left, so she took the lift down to the ground floor and came out the back door to the rear of the station. Two police officers stood under the plastic awning in the custody bay with a tall, elegant-looking man in his late fifties, wearing a suit. His right hand was cuffed to one of them, and he held a lit cigarette and a small packet of Marlboro Gold in his left. This was the entrance to the custody suite, where prisoners were processed after arrest.

It was raining, and the sky was grey. The sound of the raindrops hammered down on the awning. Erika was breathing heavily, and to her horror, she felt a tear in her eye. She quickly wiped it away with the back of her hand. The two officers glanced over at her. One returned to his phone while the other watched the elegant man.

'You look like you could do with a cigarette?' said the man.

'I've given up.'

He held out his hand and offered her the packet. 'Haven't we all.'

Screw it. Erika leaned over and took one from the packet.

'Thanks,' she said.

'Would you do the honours of a light, Officer?' he asked the police officer on his phone.

'Er. Yes. Here we are, ma'am,' he said, searching his pockets and handing her a pink cigarette lighter. Erika lit up and exhaled.

'Ma'am?' said the man with a raised eyebrow. 'Are you the queen?'

'I like to think so. Although not many people around here agree,' said Erika. The two police officers laughed nervously. 'What are you in for?'

'Some people think I defrauded them out of money.'

'Ah. And did you?'

'That's your time up,' said the officer he was cuffed to. The elegant man pulled a face as if their informal chat had been cut tragically short.

'Saved by the bell. Thanks for the cigarette,' said Erika.

'Maybe I'll see you again?'

'Maybe. Innocent until proven guilty.'

He smiled and nodded. The two police officers gave Erika a nod and led him back inside. She smoked alone for a moment, feeling the nicotine calm her. She closed her eyes and felt the rain on her face, and she saw the two bodies of Neville Lomas and Jamie Teague. Social unrest. Really? What a load of bollocks. It was smoke and mirrors. Someone hadn't wanted Neville Lomas's death to be looked into originally, and now they didn't have a choice. Why didn't they just fire her, instead of all this nonsense? It would be far easier.

Erika pulled out her phone and found the number for Dan

Fisk. He didn't answer, and his phone went straight to voicemail. Erika left a short message asking if he could call her.

Peterson came out of the back door, and Erika saw that he also had a packet of cigarettes.

'I didn't know you smoked?' she said, flicking the butt of her cigarette into a puddle.

'I just started again,' he said gruffly, lighting up. 'Moss finished the briefing,' he added, tipping his head back and blowing smoke up towards the grey sky.

'What do you think?'

'The two cases are linked, and this one could go further. The killer has established a modus operandi. They have a calling card with the Polaroids. Toxicology found flunitrazepam and alcohol in Neville Lomas's blood. Flunitrazepam is a date-rape drug, and it sheds new light on his so-called consent to rough sex.'

Erika nodded. 'Jamie Teague's mother mentioned his rape trial when I talked to her.'

'He was acquitted. But there was a hell of a storm on social media when they passed down the not-guilty verdict.'

'I bet.'

Erika had lost count of the rape trials she'd seen collapse, or where the defendant was found not guilty. It was depressing.

'Crane pulled the file on the rape case. It's on your desk.' Erika nodded. She thought back to Marsh's speech about social unrest. He hadn't mentioned the rape trial. Did he even know about it? Marsh wasn't a details man. 'Also, the new girl, Dahlia, spent eight months doing CCTV analysis. She's requested to be the one to study the CCTV footage when it comes in from Greenwich One.'

'Has she now.'

Peterson turned to Erika. 'You don't like her, do you? You haven't introduced her as a new team member.'

'I didn't have time.'

'I know you better than you think.'

Erika and Peterson had been in a relationship for several months, and they'd been serious for a time. He'd been Erika's first real relationship after Mark's death. And then Peterson was injured in the line of duty, and things cooled, cooling further when his ex-girlfriend showed up on his doorstep a few years back with a young lad and the news that he was a father. He was now married with another child on the way, and Erika was happy for him. Almost.

'Dahlia was at the scene the night Neville Lomas was murdered. She was a beat officer and happened to be in the area. I didn't like her attitude. She went above my head that night and called in Superintendent Fisk. He then took over the case. And now, she's been promoted and assigned to my team.'

'Who assigned her?'

'I don't know. I only found out a few hours ago, when she showed up at the Jamie Teague murder scene.'

Peterson considered this for a moment. 'What does Melanie say?'

'I haven't had the chance to ask. I just had a tense meeting with her and Marsh . . . He wants me off the case and Fisk on. Melanie backed me. For now.'

Peterson nodded. Erika went to say more but stopped herself. They were no longer in that place where she could moan to him about work. She was his boss.

'I think McGorry likes Dahlia. We're having to run behind him and clear up the drool.'

Erika rolled her eyes and laughed. 'What about you? What do you think of her?'

'I'm not wasting any drool on her.'

'Interesting answer.' Erika checked her watch. 'Okay. You're coming with me. I want to go and visit this nightclub in Soho where Jamie Teague went with his mates on Friday. And can you tell Crane I want him, and him alone, to review the CCTV from Greenwich One when it comes through. I'll meet you at my car in five minutes.'

Peterson nodded, flicked the butt of his cigarette into a puddle, and they headed back inside.

15

Erika was always struck by the size of London. She'd lived here for eight years, and there were still blink-and-you'll-miss-it areas she'd never seen before. The entrance to Red Velvet was accessed down a slender passageway on a road parallel to Old Compton Street. The walls seemed to close in, and the light was murky when they reached the dead end with a small door. Erika looked up at the strip of grey sky above.

'This is an exclusive members club?' muttered Peterson.

Erika glanced back down the alleyway. None of the people passing seemed to notice the club's entrance. *That may be the point.* She was pleased to see a small Perspex dome housing a CCTV camera mounted on the left-hand side of the wall looking down at the road. She turned back to the door. It was made of smooth steel and sunk flush into the brickwork. There was no door handle. A small square of red Perspex was affixed to the wall beside an intercom. Peterson pressed the button. Erika's phone buzzed in her pocket. She pulled it out and saw Melanie calling her for the third time.

'You should answer it,' said Peterson.

Erika ignored him and pocketed her phone. The door opened. An older lady with gnomic features peered up at them.

'Hello. Can we speak to the owner or manager?' asked Erika, holding up her warrant card. Peterson did the same.

'I'm the owner,' said the woman with a gravelly smoker's voice.

'What's your name, please?'

'Tulip Frost,' she said. She eyed them as they pocketed their warrant cards. 'Is this about Jamie Teague?'

'Why do you ask that?'

''Cos it's all over the news,' she said. 'How did he die?' Peterson glanced at Erika. She didn't like being blindsided, but she tried to keep her face neutral.

'I'm afraid we can't comment on that. Jamie Teague was here on Friday night?'

'Yeah.' She peered up the alleyway. 'You want to come in?'

'Please.'

She opened the door, and they followed her down a long passageway, almost like a tunnel lit by strip lighting. The walls were covered with thousands of LED light bulbs. Erika thought it must look dramatic when it was lit up. The amount of red velvet used in the décor of the bar was disarming – the floor, walls, and ceiling were all made of the same material. They crossed the dance floor in the centre, where a cleaning cart was parked. Over at the bar, a young lad, who looked only sixteen or seventeen, stacked glasses in a large dishwasher cage. He was almost painfully pale and wore a white, sleeveless T-shirt.

'This is Peter, my bar manager,' said Tulip. 'This is the police; they're here to ask about Jamie Teague.'

He nodded at them from under his cap but didn't seem fazed by this. 'You want coffee?'

'Yes, thank you,' said Peterson. Erika nodded. Tulip led them to one of the banquettes in the corner, and they sat down.

'Jamie Teague was a regular here,' said Tulip.

'How regular?' asked Erika.

'He'd come at least once a week, usually a Friday or Saturday night.'

'And members have to pay a fee?' asked Peterson.

'Of course. We have to remain exclusive.'

'Who does he normally come to the club with?' asked Erika.

'Sometimes a girl or two. Sometimes his teammates. He often brought his agent, Cheri Shelton. We insist on only Premiership footballers having membership and keep out the second- and third-division riffraff.'

'How well do you know his agent?' asked Peterson.

'Well enough to know they both have the same taste in women.'

'Was she here with him on Friday night?' asked Erika.

'No. He arrived with two other lads.'

'What time did they arrive?' asked Peterson. The barman, Peter, came to the table with two white mugs of what looked like milky instant coffee. They looked out of place when he put them down on the table's plush velvet surface.

'Pete, do you know what time? I think around nine, nine thirty.'

'Yeah. Think so. I can find the CCTV. He sat here,' said Peter, tucking the tray under his skinny arm and perching on the side of the banquette. 'He was with his mates and this bunch of girls. They all – Well, they all looked freakily the same. One of the security guards made a joke about there being a glitch in the matrix.'

'What do you mean?' asked Erika.

'You know, in the movie *The Matrix*. There's that scene where the identical guy in black shades appears over and over again. Those girls were like that. They weren't in suits with sunglasses on, but there were four or five of them, all dressed in identical black lace minidresses with identical black hair, and the same make-up. It was like they were impersonating someone, but no one well known.'

'Have you seen any of them here before?' asked Erika.

'No. What about you, Tue?' he said to Tulip.

She shook her head. 'I didn't really see 'em. Most of the slappers we get here tend to look like that.'

'They don't all look exactly like that. They're blonde or of different ethnicities,' said Peter.

'Were these women all white?' asked Erika.

'Fake tanned, but yeah, white.'

'Did they interact much with Jamie?' asked Peterson.

'Yeah. They were all in this banquette along with his mates. Jamie had bought a table with drinks.'

'How does that work?' asked Peterson.

'They get this banquette and the table for the night with three bottles of premium spirits, twelve beers, and mixers. They have to bring at least four guests, and they pay for other things on top of that.'

'What other things?'

'If they order wines or Champagne, it's extra.'

'This is an exclusive members club, so do you have details of every guest who comes through the door?' asked Peterson.

'Officially, our members can each bring two guests, but with our high-profile clients, it can be more,' said Tulip.

'Okay, you had these four or five women who all look alike. Do you know who they were guests of?' asked Erika.

Tulip sighed.

'I'll need to go over the sign-in data we have. It's going to take a while.'

'Was there anything else that stood out about Jamie Teague's visit? Was there any trouble? Anything out of the ordinary?'

Peter glanced over at Tulip. She sighed and shook her head.

'One of his mates was flagged by our security guard. He thought he saw him dealing drugs. Which we never tolerate. I'm telling you – if anyone is found with drugs, they're out, and we call the police. You hear me?' said Tulip, her eyes moving between Erika and Peterson.

'Of course,' said Erika. 'What happened?'

'Our security guard saw him and pulled him aside immediately to be searched. He didn't have anything on him.'

'What did the security guard think he was dealing with?' asked Erika.

'He thought he saw him with pills. Ecstasy or something like that,' said Peter. 'He was talking to one of these "glitch in the matrix" lookalike girls at the end of the bar.'

'The security guard thinks he sold this girl ecstasy?' asked Peterson.

'Yes. But he was searched and had nothing. We then had the problem of working out which girl it was.'

'And you didn't want to throw any of them out because they were with a very lucrative client?'

Peter put up his hands.

'It was the security guard who saw it. And then the guy agreed to be searched voluntarily. And there was nothing. He had nothing.'

'Do you know the name of the guy?' asked Erika.

'Jim or Finn. Finn. That was it,' he said.

Tulip had watched this whole exchange warily. 'Do you hear? There was nothing. No drugs. I've been cooperative with you both, and I'll continue to be, but I don't want any trouble or harassment from you lot.'

'I understand, and assure you there won't be,' said Erika. She took out her card. 'If you can send me the guest list information, plus all the CCTV footage you have from that night. All cameras. We would be very grateful.'

16

When Erika and Peterson returned to the street, she checked her watch. It was coming up to five pm. She'd missed lunch.

'You hungry?'

'Starving,' said Peterson.

Erika ordered four cheese croissants and two cappuccinos in a café on Old Compton Street. They sat in the window, looking out at the busy street. Erika felt ravenous and was about to bite into her croissant when her phone vibrated on the table. Melanie's name popped up on the screen.

'Answer it,' said Peterson, chewing.

She eyed her phone. This was the fifth call from the superintendent, and she wasn't doing herself favours by ignoring it.

'You're alive,' said Melanie.

'Me and Peterson were talking to the manager of the club where Jamie Teague was last seen.'

'Okay. And?'

Erika quickly outlined what had happened, and in the retelling, she had to admit it wasn't much.

'Am I still on the case?' she finished.

'Yes.'

'What about Marsh?'

'He wants me to keep him up to date with everything. Daily updates . . . and that means you have to answer your phone when I call.'

'Sorry.'

'Jamie Teague's family just released a statement through his sports agent, Cheri Shelton. They didn't give us a heads up.'

Erika could hear the exasperation in Melanie's voice.

'Released where?'

'Through his social media and the profiles of his sports agent. It's feeding through to the Associated Press.'

Peterson was chewing on his second croissant and held up his mobile phone.

'Okay. I've got it here,' said Erika, scanning the statement.

With deep sadness, we announce that Jamie Teague was found dead this morning at his home in London. We are working closely with the London Metropolitan Police and are not able to provide further information at this stage. We please ask that Jamie's family's privacy is respected in this difficult time of bereavement. The thoughts and prayers of everyone at Cheri Shelton Management and Chelsea Football Club are with his family, friends, and loved ones. A further statement will follow in due course.

'Marsh would like us to do a press conference tomorrow afternoon with the family.'

'I'm still waiting on post-mortem results, toxicology, CCTV. Witnesses. What are we going to say in a press conference?'

'You've requested CCTV?'

'Yes, from everywhere. I'm expecting it imminently.'

'Then you have twenty-four hours. We just need images of him out at that club and coming back to his flat, so we can appeal for eyewitnesses.'

'What about Neville Lomas, if the two cases are linked?'

'I don't know. I'll have to update you on that.'

'But the two cases are linked. I can't see what there is to update me on?'

'Erika,' said Melanie carefully. 'I'm on your side. I will update you shortly.'

'Can I ask you about Dahlia Beck? She's the detective who's recently been assigned to me. Who authorised that?' Melanie was quiet for a moment. 'Was it you?'

'No. Is there a problem with her?'

'I don't know. Back in January, she was on the beat the night of the call-out to the Neville Lomas crime scene. She then went over my head and called in Dan Fisk, and he turned up an hour later and took over the case . . . And today when I arrived at Greenwich One, Dahlia was already there waiting for me. She'd already been told she'd be joining my team.' Erika was going to mention the grey-suited man who had arrived at the Neville Lomas crime scene with Dan Fisk, but she suddenly felt uneasy about saying it on the phone. 'I think there's something else going on here. I'm not saying Dahlia is a bad police officer, but someone high up seems to be pushing her onto this case.'

There was a long silence.

'Erika. Sit tight. Refrain from jumping to conclusions. I'll look into it. Having her on your team could be useful if she worked on the Neville Lomas investigation in January. Listen, I have to go; I've got a meeting with Marsh and Colleen Scanlan about the press conference tomorrow.'

Melanie ended the call.

Erika eyed her two croissants on the table, picked up one, and bit into it.

'What did she say to piss you off?' asked Peterson.

'What are they scared of with Neville Lomas? I never told you: Isaac Strong had a visit from some grey-suited guy when he was doing the post-mortem. Encouraging him to report an open verdict on Lomas's death.'

'I thought Isaac was straight as a die? Well, you know what I mean. Work-wise.'

'He is. He said that he was going to rule an open verdict, and he referred the case to a colleague for a second opinion, but someone rushed out a press release saying Lomas died of natural causes.'

'Yeah, and wasn't there all that rubbish about him being a family man, blah, blah, blah.'

'It's hardly news these days, that politicians have sex lives. Even if they are into extreme stuff, like bondage.'

'Or it could be something darker,' said Peterson. Erika shuddered.

'And these Annabelle Polaroids are troubling. Jamie Teague and Neville Lomas have problematic pasts with women and sex. If there is a press conference, we should hold the details about the Polaroids back from the media. To help us sift through the nutcases and the time-wasters.'

'Erika. You can't say "nutcases".'

'Mentally deranged?'

'Not that either.'

'Then what do we call them?'

'Members of the public?' said Peterson, after a beat.

Erika laughed. 'Go on, say it. I'm being paranoid.'

He swallowed. 'I don't think you're paranoid. But I think the answer could be more banal. What if Dan Fisk is shagging Dahlia? I mean, I . . .' He stopped himself.

'You mean you'd shag her, too?'

'She's attractive, you have to admit.'

'So what if she's attractive? Is she a good police officer? Is she someone I can trust? At the moment, I'm coming back with no on both counts.'

'You do realise that apart from Moss, you don't have any other women on your team.'

'Half of my civilian support team are women.'

'But they're . . .'

'What are you going to say, James? Not hot?'

'No. I was going to say older. More mature ladies.'

This was true. The ladies on the civilian support teams were excellent at what they did, but they all had a matronly quality, and Erika wasn't threatened by them.

'Are you saying I should pay it forward? And think back to what it was like when I was a young female officer?'

'You don't have to go overboard. Just be civil to her and resist the urge to slap her.'

Erika grinned. It was good advice. He picked up her second croissant.

'Hey. Hands off my lunch, greedy guts.'

He put it back on the plate. 'Well, stop yapping and eat it. Do you want anything else? I'm going up.'

'I'd love a blueberry muffin for afters.'

Peterson got up and went back to the counter. Erika picked up her croissant and took a big bite, savouring the taste. She looked out at Old Compton Street. A red post office van was trundling along behind two young guys with bright-blue hair, walking up the middle of the road, deep in conversation. In Soho, the lines seemed to blur with pavement and road, and everyone treated it like a pedestrianised street. The van driver finally lost patience and beeped, and the two lads crossed. Opposite the coffee shop was a fetish store. Three silver, headless, muscular mannequins were adorned with leather studded jockstraps. Erika saw a small CCTV camera housed in a Perspex dome above the door. She left the coffee shop and crossed the street.

When she returned, Peterson was waiting with two blueberry muffins.

'Were you asking if they've got Igor's size?' asked Peterson, tilting his head towards the fetish shop.

Erika laughed.

'No. The owner has CCTV. I asked him to send us footage from last Friday, just on the off-chance Jamie Teague and his mates were on Old Compton Street before they went to Red Velvet.'

They sat down to eat the rest of what Erika was still calling lunch, though it was now five thirty, and the light was starting to fade.

17

Erika arrived home around eight thirty. The house was a little chilly, and George was waiting for her in the hall. He circled her legs, rubbing himself against her ankles, and she slipped off her coat, leaned down, and scratched behind his ears.

He followed her through to the kitchen and paced up and down impatiently as she put his food on a saucer, and whilst he lapped at it with his small pink tongue, she tried to work out whether she was hungry after eating lunch so late. She made some toast with Marmite and a cup of tea and brought them to the living room, followed by George.

Erika switched on the TV and knelt down to light a fire in the hearth. She kept an old wooden fruit box beside the grate with old newspapers and kindling, and George came and sat beside her as she built a pyramid of the small sticks of wood and stuffed it with crumpled-up pages from the local newspaper. She lit a match and held it to the paper. Within a few moments, the kindling was crackling, and a pleasant glow washed over the walls.

The late evening news came on, and Jamie Teague was the top story. The statement from his family had caused a massive amount of speculation, and they were reporting that his body had been found in 'suspicious circumstances'. The news report concentrated heavily on Jamie being a national sporting hero; there were clips of his best football matches, and of him posing in a suit with his MBE from Buckingham Palace. Janice was pictured with him, wearing a big hat and an even bigger smile. Erika thought back to the file she'd just read on his rape trial.

In late 2019 he'd been accused of drugging and assaulting a nineteen-year-old woman at his £3.8 million townhouse in Highgate. The woman had never been named for legal reasons, and Erika had put in a request for her name to be released to them for the purposes of their investigation. During the two-month trial at Southwark Crown Court, Teague had maintained that the woman had wanted to have sex with him and pursued him on the night in question. What he'd said on the stand had stuck in Erika's mind. He told the jury it was 'normal' for him to sleep with lots of different women, and being a famous footballer made it 'honestly, so easy' to pick up women at nightclubs and take them to his home.

Erika zoned out for a moment and stared into the licking flames. Her phone rang, and she saw it was Igor.

'Hello. You home?' he asked.

'Yes. You?'

'Yes. Tom's just gone to bed. I've been hearing all about the anti-freeze killer,' he said. It took Erika a moment to remember her conversation with Tom on the school run.

'Oh. Yes. Sorry. I kind of walked into that one. I didn't mean to go into details.'

Igor laughed. 'It's okay. Did you really catch the wife because her husband puked outside and it didn't freeze? Because he'd ingested anti-freeze?'

Erika smiled at his use of 'puke', like Tom.

'It was actually the doctor on call who spotted it. I made the link.'

'How?'

'Well, we had the husband's—'

'Puke?'

'His vomit tested after he died.'

'Tom was telling a teacher about it, and the teacher said that anti-freeze tastes very bitter.'

'Oh no. I've not been encouraging Tom and his mates to drink anti-freeze?'

Igor laughed again. 'No. It was a PE teacher. He said the wife couldn't have put anti-freeze in the husband's food and poisoned him because it tastes bitter and it's bright blue.'

'That's true with regular anti-freeze, the kind you buy at petrol stations – it's extremely bitter. Anti-freeze is made from the chemical ethylene glycol; in its pure form, it's odourless and slightly sweet. The wife was clever. She was having an affair with a man who worked in a big data centre in North London. Data centres have vast computer servers that must be kept cool. And they use pure ethylene glycol in their chilling and cooling systems.'

'Oh. So the lover got hold of some for her?'

'Yes. The pure version of ethylene glycol is a strictly regulated chemical, but this was a huge data centre and the guy was able to steal a small amount. The wife thought we wouldn't make the link between them. But I did.' Erika put her phone under her chin and added more wood to the fire.

'That's really interesting.'

'I'm saying it now, but it took a lot of time, energy, and dead ends to make the link.'

'Still. You must have been proud of yourself?' Erika sat back and had to think about this for a moment. She'd been doing the job for so long now and had started to lose sight of why she was doing it. Erika thought back to the day they arrested the wife. Had she stopped and reflected on her success? No. 'Tom also said you got caught by Felicity Brogues-Houghton . . . and he said you flicked on your lights and sirens and drove off!' He laughed.

'It wasn't quite like that. I was called to a murder scene.'

'Really?'

'Yes. And I was polite to her. I said I had to go. I didn't just bugger off.'

'Who was murdered?'

Erika hesitated. 'Felicity said they didn't have the paperwork to say I was a named person on the collection arrangement.'

'They do. I spoke to the school earlier. It was a mistake on her part.'

'Was it now.'

'Felicity likes to be difficult. Tom is asking if you could drop him off again this week?'

'I'd love to.' Erika felt warm and happy that Tom wanted her to do the school run again.

'Who was murdered? It wasn't Jamie Teague? Did you hear about that?'

Igor was probably joking, but Erika hesitated just a beat too long.

'No. I mean, yeah. I heard.'

'Bloody hell, Erika. It was him, wasn't it?'

'I can't talk about it.'

'Okay. But Jamie Teague was murdered? It said on the news that he was found dead in suspicious circumstances.'

'We're doing a press conference tomorrow. Igor, this can't get out.'

'You didn't tell me. I guessed. And, of course, I won't say anything. But *Jesus*. Who would murder him?'

'That's what I need to find out.'

'Is it going to be your case?'

'Yes.'

'Wow. That's cool.'

Erika laughed dryly. 'That's one way of putting it.'

'He was the most amazing footballer. Had his whole career ahead of him. When he was with Man U, he was like, our greatest asset. That penalty shoot-out . . . I was gutted when Chelsea bought him. It's interesting that on the mainstream news he's a hero. Have you seen social media?'

'No.'

'The coverage is *a lot* different. People talking about how he got away with raping that young woman. A lot of hate.' Erika poked at the fire again. She suddenly felt exhausted, and this was going to be a high-profile case. She was worried she didn't have the energy to solve it. 'You've gone quiet?'

'I'm listening, but you know I can't comment or tell you anything. It's been a long day.'

'Do you want to come over?'

'Sorry, no.'

'Do you want me to come over to you? I'm feeling horny . . . I'll be quick. You don't have to do anything. I won't be offended if you just want to lie there with a gormless look on your face.'

Erika laughed. 'As tempting as that sounds, no. I've still got work to do.'

'They don't pay you enough. Okay. I'll say goodnight. Love you.'

'Love you too. Night.'

'Oh. Find out if you have a morning free to drop off Tom this week.'

'I will.'

Erika ended the call, and she'd just started to eat her cold toast when her phone rang again. It was Sergeant Crane.

'Sorry to call you late,' he said. 'Have you got your laptop there? I've found something on the CCTV from Jamie Teague's apartment.'

18

Erika went through to the kitchen, opened her laptop, and switched it on.

'Are you still at the station?' she asked Crane as she sat down at the table.

'Yes. I've drunk too many coffees. And my wife is wondering if I exist anymore,' he said with a wry laugh. 'It's something I found on the CCTV from Greenwich One. I've just sent the files through to you, if you can open the first one.' His email came through with four video files attached. Erika opened the first. 'I've compiled pieces of the CCTV footage together. That first one is when Jamie Teague arrived back at Greenwich One early Saturday morning. There's no sound on the footage, as you would expect.'

Erika pressed play.

A view of the apartment building lobby appeared from a CCTV camera behind the desk facing the glass doors. The sky was dark outside, and the time stamp was 3.06 am. Jamie Teague entered the lobby with two other young men and a group of five women. The women were all dressed in identical lacy black minidresses and black gloves, and had long, dark hair and lots of make-up. They each carried a black clutch bag and wore matching silver high heels. The camera view cut to the group waiting at the lifts in the lobby.

'A glitch in the matrix,' said Erika.

'What?'

'It's how the barman at Red Velvet described the group of women with Jamie and his mates. How they all looked identical. There was five of them, and they all came back to Jamie Teague's apartment. All wearing black gloves.'

The camera view changed to inside the lift, where the eight of them were packed. The footage cut to them coming out of the lift on the penthouse floor, then moving across the lobby and down the corridor to Jamie Teague's apartment.

'If you click on the second video file,' said Crane.

'Got it.'

The second video was time-stamped at 5.16 am. Erika watched as Jamie's two friends appeared in the corridor again after leaving Jamie's flat. They stopped in the middle of the floor by the lifts. One was scrolling through his phone, and the other seemed to turn around to call out to someone. Two of the young women then joined them. The lift doors opened, and two more women hurried to join the group, just making it inside the lift as the doors closed. The video then cut to them moments later, emerging from the lift into the ground-floor lobby. They exited Greenwich One at 5.19 am.

'They all left apart from one of the women,' said Erika.

'Check the third video,' said Crane. Erika clicked on it. 'You can see the fifth woman leaves Jamie Teague's apartment at 11.14 am.'

'Almost six hours since the others left,' said Erika, unable to suppress a shudder.

'Watch how she walks out of his apartment to the lifts.'

It was daylight in the video of the lifts outside Jamie Teague's apartment. With slightly dishevelled hair, the young woman looked up at the camera the whole time she crossed to the lifts, carrying a small clutch.

'Hang on. She's leaving with a small bag. What did the women have for bags when they arrived?' said Erika. She found the first video and played it back.

'They all have little black bags,' said Crane.

'Identical little black clutch bags. I'm not a handbag kind of girl, but you can't keep very much in a clutch. What about the ropes used to tie him up? And she left Polaroids. A Polaroid camera is big and boxy. How did it all get inside his flat? If none of these women had room for it in their little bags?'

They were silent. Erika heard the click click of George's paws on the wooden floor, and he poked his head around the kitchen door to see what she was doing.

'Have a look at the first video again. In the lift up to Jamie's apartment,' said Crane. Erika clicked back to the part of the video taken from the camera mounted in the corner of the lift. All five women were looking up at the camera for the entirety of the journey in the lift.

'They're all staring up at the camera,' said Erika.

'Yeah. For the whole time. Like they meant to do it.'

Erika paused the video and zoomed in on the girls' faces one by one. 'Do you think their noses look weird?'

'Yeah. They've all had the same nose job or something?' said Crane.

'Or they have the same stick-on nose. I know that sounds silly, but their faces look like masks. Don't you think? The noses are too big for them all?'

'They all have the same odd eye colour. Their irises look black,' said Crane.

'They look like . . . They look like they're all in on it,' finished Erika for want of a better description. She pulled the video back and watched the section in the lift again as the women all stared up at the camera, faces neutral. Erika shuddered. It was like they were all looking directly at her. Like they could see into her kitchen. She jumped and let out a yell when she felt something on her leg.

'You okay?'

Erika looked down. George looked up at her and yowled.

'Sorry. It was the cat.'

'Erika. Do you think they *all* murdered Jamie Teague?'

'His two mates would have to be in on it, too. We still haven't had the exact time of death from Isaac. What if they wanted to make it hard for us to guess which one of the five women killed him? It looks like these young women agreed to look up at the camera simultaneously so the CCTV would get a good look at them.'

Erika watched as they exited the lift with Jamie and his mates. Each woman kept looking at the camera until they left.

'Do you have the CCTV from Red Velvet?'

'That's the fourth video you should have in your inbox,' said Crane.

'Got it,' said Erika. She pressed play.

'They arrived at 10.13 pm,' said Crane. 'There's no video cameras inside the club. This is the only camera they have – on the alleyway entrance. You'll see they all do it again. They look up at the camera.'

The short video showed the narrow alleyway leading up to the main entrance of Red Velvet. The five women entered the alleyway and walked in a tight group to the club door. They slowed as they passed and looked up at the camera.

'What time do they leave?'

'At 2.26 am. I've put in a request to Westminster City Council for CCTV from the road outside.'

'Did the guy from the fetish shop on Old Compton Street send over anything?'

'Not yet.'

They watched as the group of women left the club with Jamie Teague and his mates at 2.26 am and walked down the alleyway to the road at the end. The headlights from a passing car flared on the camera lens. The burst of white enveloped the group, and then they vanished from the shot.

19

Annabelle heard the sound of a key scraping along the pipe in the corridor outside the dormitory. The grinding of metal against metal, echoing off the stone walls, grew louder the closer he came.

They'd called him 'Pipes' in the children's home. And he was a carer. Hired to care. It was laughable to think this was his job title. The children always knew where Pipes was on his night-time rounds by the sound of that key on metal. If he was moving fast along the corridor, the pitch would be high, but if he slowed down, it would deepen, the tip of the key catching on the scrapes and indentations of the ancient heating pipe which snaked throughout the building.

The worst was if it slowed and stopped right outside your door.

The fear was still genuine after all these years. Pipes was long gone, but a scraping sound, any scraping sound when she was alone, induced a Pavlovian response in Annabelle – the pricking of cold sweat between her shoulder blades, nausea, and the kind of fear that blinds you to anything good.

In her years at the orphanage, Annabelle couldn't remember

many nights when the fear of hearing that sound wasn't present. Sometimes, the children would stay up late and visit between their dorms on the long corridor to play or eat sweets. And the meandering, menacing scrape of his key was a good warning system.

'Pipes is coming!' they would whisper, gripping each other, the fear mixed in with just a hint of excitement. And then the ones out of their dorms would scrabble around, trying to find slippers and toys or clear away the evidence of an illicit midnight feast, as the low grinding sound built and grew closer.

If you were caught outside your dorm after lights out, it wasn't just the case of getting a slap on the legs. If you were lucky and another carer caught you, that's all you'd get, but Pipes could be mean, and woe betide the poor child caught in the glare of his torch after hours.

But often you didn't have to do anything. The sound of the scraping key would stop in the corridor outside your dorm room, and then the door would slowly open. The arcing light of his torch would swing across the room, and even with your eyes closed, it was blinding.

Pipes never dragged Annabelle out of her bed, but it had happened to the girls around her. Silent and stealthy. Soft footsteps, a soft rustling, and a crackle of sparks as the nylon sheets were pulled back. Some girls would cry out, but if this wasn't the first time, they'd learned that it was better to keep quiet. Annabelle remembered hearing a soft 'No' or a whispered 'Please don't hurt me'.

On this cold March night in London, the sound of that key scraping on the pipe pervaded Annabelle's dreams. She woke, sweating and crying out in the dark. Even after she'd switched on the light by the bed, she could still hear that scrape. It took her a few minutes to remember she was now an adult. And she lived alone in her own flat in London, in a luxurious, secure complex high above the city. And it was silent.

Annabelle drank water from the glass next to her bed, slowly catching her breath as reality descended. The only thing she could hear was the sound of London. Ever present, like white noise. She kicked off the sheets and padded across the carpet to the window. The city spread out before her like a blanket of lights, pinpricks of colour against the smear of light pollution. A bright luminescence that you noticed only when it collided with the night sky in sweeps of orange, obliterating the stars. She was so high up that she could see past the light pollution to the faint stars above. Even aeroplanes didn't seem that far away when they moved across the sky.

As she gripped the windowsill, Annabelle came back fully to reality. It had been years since she had heard that scraping sound in her dreams. It was because she was close to finishing her work and getting closure on their past.

At two am, everything was still. The roads far below were empty, save for a few lone car headlights moving slowly. A red light progressed across the sky. And Annabelle wondered whether it was a private jet. Commercial planes didn't fly at night.

Very soon she would board a plane with a one-way ticket out of here. Far away from London, and England, and the memory of Pipes and his scraping key.

20

Across the city, Erika didn't sleep much, either, tossing and turning in the night. She kept seeing the image of the five 'glitch-in-the-matrix' girls, vanishing into the burst of light outside the Red Velvet nightclub. George spent the night lying on her legs, and every time he shifted, his warm, fidgety little body seemed to jolt her out of sleep, too.

At five am, the birds started chirping outside her window, so she got up and showered. Erika was about to throw on a dark pair of trousers and a pullover when she remembered that a press conference had been scheduled for the afternoon. Erika stood in front of her meagre wardrobe, hating that she needed to choose something smart to wear. And she could do with putting on some make-up. To quote a phrase Mark had used, she looked like boiled shite.

Erika settled on a smart black trouser suit, which was still in plastic since she'd had it dry-cleaned a year before, and a dark-blue blouse with slightly puffy sleeves and a pleated front, which she'd bought online last year for Moss's Christmas party. When dressed, she returned to the kitchen, made some coffee, and found the small black handbag where she kept her shoe polish, cloths, and brushes. George watched as she opened a round tin of Cherry Blossom, dipped in the bristles of the small stiff brush, and started to polish her black court shoes with the low heel.

The smell of the shoe polish and the old handbag reminded Erika of her days as a beat officer. In the early 1990s, female police officers were still called WPCs. In Manchester, she'd been issued a uniform which included a black skirt, black tights, and the small black leather handbag where she now kept her shoe polish. The handbag was scuffed and cracked, and the thin strap had long ago broken off. There had even been a small wooden 'ladies' truncheon made especially to fit inside the bag, but it was now lost somewhere. Her senior officers had been strict about appearance: clean uniforms and no ladders in your tights were a must, and above all, your shoes had to be shiny. One officer, in particular, had always stuck in her memory. A strict old-school WPC called Nanette Crosby – or Nanny Crosby, as she was known – insisted on wearing her skirt, even when the rules were changed, allowing female officers to wear trousers. Nanette always used to say, *'Ladies. I want your shoes so shiny that the bad guys can look at their reflection right before you kick them in the balls.'*

Erika smiled as she buffed her shoes to a shine. She had a feeling it would be the only task today which would have a clear outcome.

She fed George, gathered her things, and left the house just after six am.

The sky was a dark blue on the horizon, and a thin fog filled the crisp air as she drove to Lewisham. She found a message on her answerphone from Isaac, left in the early hours. And when she played it back through the hands-free speakers, his voice sounded tired and far away.

'Good evening, or should I say morning. Good Lord, it's almost three am . . . I just finished up on the post-mortem for Jamie Teague. I found flunitrazepam and alcohol in his system . . . The time of death was between six thirty and seven am, in the early hours of Saturday morning. He had five broken ribs, bruising on his chest, and petechial haemorrhaging in his lungs, indicating suffocation. And I would go as far as to ask if he suffocated in the same way as Neville Lomas. The Burke and Hare technique we talked about. My assistant will email over the files tomorrow morning. I just thought you'd want to know.'

Erika played the message again as the sky grew light, giving way to a bleak grey. Jamie's two friends and four of the girls had left his apartment at 5.16 am on Saturday morning. If the fifth girl, who stayed behind, killed him between 6.30 and 7.00 am, what was she doing until 11.14 am, when she left the flat? And Isaac thought she'd used the same Burke and Hare method to suffocate him as Neville Lomas and the Polaroids. Erika felt an uneasy prickle at the back of her neck and goose bumps on her skin. She had a feeling this one was only just getting going.

The station was empty when she arrived, and Erika went up to her office with a cup of the vile coffee from the machine outside the incident room. She spent an hour reviewing the CCTV videos from Red Velvet and Greenwich One and generated a series of still images that could be used for the press appeal.

Erika then printed out the post-mortem and toxicology reports from Isaac. Why was the only drug in his system flunitrazepam? Apart from being known as a date-rape drug, its original use was for treating severe insomnia or assisting with anaesthesia during medical procedures. Why would Jamie Teague take this on a night out with his friends, and mix it with alcohol? Had his drink been spiked? Erika made a note to ask Teague's friends about this.

Then she pulled up the post-mortem report for Neville Lomas and read it through again.

She hadn't noticed it before, but Isaac had even recorded the types of knots used on the ropes to bind Neville Lomas and Jamie Teague. They had both been tied up using a 'Munter hitch' knot and a 'Cow hitch' knot.

Erika moved the reports to one side, opened the HOLMES database, and ran a search on murder cases with male victims, who had flunitrazepam and alcohol in the blood, their bodies found tied, with tape on their mouths, with their ribs broken high on the chest, and a cause of death as suffocation.

Six results came up. When Erika refined the search and added that they were 'hog-tied' using the Munter hitch and Cow hitch knots, the results went down to one.

A third victim.

21

Erika went down to the incident room for the eight thirty briefing and examined the whiteboards as she waited for the team to arrive. They were now covered in photos and maps of the Embankment, Soho, and the area around Greenwich One, showing the timeline of the case so far. Photos from both crime scenes were displayed side by side to highlight the similarities. Erika saw the photo of Jamie Teague's kitchen, with the empty Champagne bottles and glasses strewn across the kitchen work surface. The kitchen in Neville Lomas's apartment had been clean and empty. There were no empty bottles or glasses; when had he ingested the alcohol and flunitrazepam?

'Morning,' said Moss, entering and looking a little flustered with windswept hair. 'I got you a cappuccino, but the barista wrote "Enrique" on your cup and "Moses" on mine. He's either hard of hearing or a very religious Enrique Iglesias fan.'

'Thank you,' said Erika, taking the cup. She took a sip. 'That's perfect. I was about to brave the coffee machine in the hall.'

Moss sat down and started sorting through the paperwork piled on her desk. Peterson arrived with Crane and McGorry, and her other team members drifted in. Dahlia was the last to arrive. She was on time, but Erika noted she arrived at the last possible moment. Erika started with a recap of the previous day's events. Then Crane went through the CCTV videos he'd sent Erika the night before highlighting the five identical young women who returned to Greenwich One with Jamie Teague and his friends. Melanie entered the incident room, but indicated for Erika to continue.

'We have a time of death for Jamie Teague which was after everyone left his flat at 5.16 am on Saturday morning, bar one of the young women. So we can discount the theory that more than one member of the group who accompanied him home killed him . . . I also have another update. I believe there could be a third victim.'

The room fell silent. Melanie looked shocked.

'I stress the words "could be" for a third victim. And if I'm correct, he would be the first victim chronologically. I have photos for the whiteboard.'

McGorry got up and switched off the lights. Erika tapped a button on her laptop, and an image of an elderly naked man hog-tied and lying on a grubby bed-sheet appeared on the wall.

'This is Terry DeVille, aged sixty-seven. His body was found in his house in Barnes, West London, on Monday, November 7, last year. The coroner's office recorded an open verdict on his death. As with Jamie Teague and Neville Lomas, his body was found hog-tied with masking tape on his mouth.

'He had alcohol and flunitrazepam in his blood, and his ribs were broken at the sternum. He also had two circular bruises on his chest, which indicate his chest could have been leaned on to suffocate him. Terry DeVille was also hog-tied using the Munter hitch and Cow hitch knots. The same knots were used to tie up Jamie Teague and Neville Lomas.'

'What about Polaroids?' asked Moss.

'No. No Polaroids were found at the scene, signed with the name Annabelle. The case file also says that a large volume of violent pornography was found in his home and materials, whips and restraints, that indicated he practised sadomasochistic sex. One of Terry's neighbours told the police that there were always male visitors to his house, often late at night, particularly in the weeks leading up to his death.'

'So, there are no Polaroids, and this victim was gay. Whereas Neville Lomas and Jamie Teague were heterosexual?' asked Melanie. Erika could feel the disappointment in the room that there were no Polaroids to clinch the deal.

'The fact that the house was filled with pornography depicting sadomasochistic sex could have meant that any Polaroids left at the scene depicting Terry DeVille tied up could have been overlooked. Especially if there were lots of similar-themed photos. Yes, I see the differences, but there are too many similarities for us not to look into this.'

'We have to prepare for a press appeal later today. What are we saying about this case? Are we going to mention that the murders of Jamie Teague and Neville Lomas are linked? And what about this guy, Terry DeVille?' asked McGorry.

'I have prepared some images from the lift and lobby CCTV at Jamie Teague's apartment, specifically focusing on these five women who went back with them on Friday night. We still have no CCTV from Neville Lomas's building on the night he was killed.'

Erika recalled that night in the lobby of Neville Lomas's building. When Dan Fisk arrived with the grey-suited man, she had been talking to the rude little doorman about CCTV.

'Dahlia, you worked on the case after Dan Fisk took over. Do you know what happened with the CCTV?'

'From what I remember, his death was ruled as an open

verdict very quickly, so no CCTV from his building was ever requested,' she said.

'Okay. And this gives us a problem if Neville Lomas's building only keeps CCTV for a certain time period before deleting it.'

'I put in a request yesterday afternoon,' said Crane. 'I'll follow it up again today.'

'Good. And can we review the statement I took from the cleaner who found Neville Lomas's body and anything gleaned from the door-to-door on the residential floors?'

'We didn't get anything from the door-to-door. No one was in,' said Dahlia.

'Then maybe you could revisit your enquiries? And we need to look into the death of Terry DeVille, find out everything we can about it. I'm just asking you, all of you, to dig deep with open minds.'

Everyone in the team nodded, apart from Dahlia, who looked rather sullen.

'As I always say, there are no stupid questions. Everything is up for grabs. I believe the CCTV video from Jamie Teague's flat shows us that his killer could have been female. But who's to say that one of these five identical women wasn't male?'

There was an awkward silence. The officers in the room looked uncomfortable.

'All I want you to do is keep asking questions. No one will ever do anything wrong asking questions when it comes to a brutal murder . . . Now, does anyone have any more to add?'

'So are we going to mention the other two murders at the press appeal?' repeated McGorry.

Erika looked to Melanie at the back of the room, waiting to speak to her. 'I will have an update on that shortly. Now, let's get to work.'

The team began to chatter noisily. Melanie came over to Erika.

'I'd prefer you to get your facts straight and in order before we start discussing a man in a dress. Let alone going on TV to talk about it,' she said in a low voice.

'I know.'

Erika followed Melanie out into the corridor. They could see the team through the glass windows, now going to work.

'We're scheduling the press conference for four pm upstairs in the main conference room. And Jamie Teague's family will be present.'

'What about Neville Lomas?'

Melanie pursed her lips and shook her head.

'Marsh wants to focus the press conference on Jamie Teague. As you said, we only have CCTV of the five women. Nothing for Neville Lomas. You know how these things work. If you do a public appeal, you must keep the messaging clear and concise.'

'But there could be a potential multiple murderer out there.'

'We'll be meeting before lunch to finalise everything. You'll have the chance to talk to Marsh then,' said Melanie, which Erika thought was a little slippery of her. 'We've got Jamie Teague's two friends, Leon Bromfield and Finn Horton, waiting for you upstairs in one of the offices.'

Erika was surprised. 'They're here now?'

'Yes.'

'They came voluntarily?'

'Yeah, with a solicitor. Also, Jamie Teague's manager, Cheri Shelton, wants to come in for a meeting at eleven. Can you make time to meet with her to talk about the press conference? Marsh will be there.'

'I thought that was the meeting before lunch?'

'No. They want another meeting before that.'

'So a meeting about having another meeting?'

Melanie sighed. 'Cheri Shelton is extremely well connected to the media, which will help our appeal. I'll get some nice sandwiches sent up to my office. It'll be very informal.'

'I hope she's paying, and it's not taxpayers' money?'

'Yes, she's paying.'

'In that case, I'll have the most expensive thing on the menu.'

Melanie laughed. 'See you at eleven. And let me know how it goes with Finn Horton and Leon Bromfield.'

22

Summer 2006

Annabelle didn't start out life in a children's home. She grew up with a mother and a stepfather in a flat on the top floor of a tall terraced house on a busy street in Greater London. It was just like thousands of other busy streets in the city's sprawling outskirts, where people hustled and worked and tried to play, living in flats and bed-sits cheek by jowl with cafés, hairdressers, Chinese and Indian takeaways, estate agents, fried chicken shops, and maybe, if they were lucky, a post office – and if they were very fortunate, a dentist.

Annabelle's earliest memories were of her mother in the next room screaming as Mac, her stepfather, beat her. And then, when the screaming stopped, Bren would come into Annabelle's room and crawl into her bed. Body warm, face wet with tears. Annabelle would watch her mother dab her wounds with antiseptic from the first aid kit if it was a bad beating.

And then, when Bren was calm, she would hold on to Annabelle and tell her that Mac wasn't a bad man. He looked after them. And he had a very stressful life. Annabelle remembered how she always smelt of peaches mixed in with the sharp scent of antiseptic.

Their house had a chicken shop on the ground floor. It always stank of frying chicken, and Mac was a constant presence in the background. He always seemed to be going up and down the stairs, moaning and smoking his horrible roll-up cigarettes or talking to other men who looked like him in the small concrete yard behind the house. The yard was closed with a high brick wall and a green gate with flaking paint. It led onto a narrow road behind, and the gate was always open in the day to take deliveries of oil and chicken and potatoes for the chicken shop, and then there were sometimes other things delivered late at night.

Even when she was so young, Annabelle wondered what her mother did that was so bad to make Mac so angry with her. Bren tried to hide the bruises on her arms and sometimes her neck, which she covered with long sleeves and high collars, even when it was baking hot behind the fryer in the chicken shop. Once, at the school nativity play, where Annabelle played the angel, Bren had a fat lip and a black eye, which she tried to cover with make-up. It didn't work.

When Annabelle was eight, Mac beat her mother badly, and then she fell down the stairs and died.

Annabelle recalled little of the memories and trauma of that time. Another woman called Tina arrived shortly after Bren died. Tina was cruel. She was the one who made Annabelle wear the scratchy tights and blue velvet dress to the church on the day Bren's coffin slid through the curtains and was burnt in the fire.

Annabelle's next clear memory was of a Saturday morning a few weeks after the funeral. She was in her bedroom watching cartoons on the small TV on the dresser when Mac opened the door. He was an ugly man with a round red face and crooked yellow teeth. Mac hardly ever came into her room, and if he did, he ignored her. He went to the curtains on the back windows looking over the yard and tore them open. They didn't quite meet in the middle, and Bren had pinned them together using bulldog clips to keep the light from the street out at night. The clips pinged off and clattered across the wooden floor.

Mac lifted the sash window and reached out, his backside sticking through the gap. On TV, Tom was chasing Jerry across a carpet, and with their effort to move quickly, the rug was bunching up under them. As the music played frantically, Annabelle saw the rug bunching up in the same way under Mac's feet as he reached out the window. His T-shirt had ridden up, showing acres of pale, hairy back and his big fuzzy arse crack. He placed one hand on the windowsill and leaned out farther. When Annabelle came to the window to see what he was doing, Mac was half hanging out of the window, with just one hand supporting him on the sill. With his other arm, he was trying to open a small metal chimney vent on the roof of the kitchen extension below. Once or twice she'd seen her mother do the same thing, like she was putting something there for safekeeping, but Bren's arms were longer than Mac's. She could reach.

On this sunny Saturday morning, as Mac hung out the window and the sun shone into the empty yard below, Annabelle saw a way to punish him. She couldn't remember having these exact thought processes; it was just an instinct. Mac's feet were off the ground, and his shabby Dr. Marten boots dangled just above her head. Annabelle was small, and it took little effort. Without thinking about the consequences if it went wrong, she stood between Mac's legs, put a hand under each of his boots, and lifted his ankles. It was as if he were as light as a feather, and his legs slithered past her and across the windowsill.

Mac yelled out, but only for a second, and then it was cut

short by a horrible crunching sound as he landed on his head in the concrete yard three stories below. Tina rushed into the bedroom a moment later and saw Annabelle standing at the open window. They both stared down at Mac's broken body.

'He fell,' said Annabelle.

23

Tuesday, March 7, 2023

Erika took Peterson with her up to the fourth floor, where Leon Bromfield and Finn Horton were waiting. They'd chosen a small conference room to conduct the interviews, as they were informal and voluntary. But the boys, having hired legal representation, sharpened Erika's senses nonetheless. They spoke to Finn Horton first. He was a big, broad, hairy bloke with a thick sandy-coloured beard and shoulder-length hair.

'Thank you for coming to talk to us,' said Erika as she and Peterson sat opposite him.

Finn wore jeans, big Timberland boots, and a red checked lumberjack shirt. He smelt a little of body odour. His solicitor was the type with an expensive suit and an oily smile. The type often hired by wealthy men who committed sexual assaults.

'There's nowt much to tell,' he said. He had a pronounced northern accent. His eyes slid from Erika to Peterson and back to Erika. 'You from up north?'

'No. I'm from Slovakia originally. My husband was from

Slaithwaite, and I learned English up there, so I caught the accent.'

'It's not a disease. Although lots of people down south seem to think so. You from down south, mate?' he added to Peterson.

'Yeah. London born and bred.'

Finn nodded. He looked at the solicitor. 'Am I supposed to start?'

'Well, this is an informal chat. You can leave at any time, so I'd rather hope that the officers have some questions for you?' said the solicitor, speaking with a clipped, almost farcically posh voice.

'Finn. Can we ask what you do for a living?' said Erika.

'I'm a builder.'

'Do you have your own firm?'

'Nope.'

'How did you know Jamie Teague?'

'We trained together at Chelsea Football Club Academy.'

'How old were you when you first met?' asked Peterson.

'Eleven. Yeah. Me mam and dad moved us down here the year before when Dad got work on Crossrail. You know, the rail tunnels. He worked on the construction teams.'

'How old are you now?' asked Erika.

'Twenty-four. A year younger than Jamie.'

'I take it you didn't become a professional football player?' said Peterson.

Finn's eyes narrowed, and he rolled them. 'That's correct, Mr Bergerac. What made you deduce that?'

'You said you work as a builder.'

Finn nodded and slumped lower in the chair, his arms crossed.

'I was gonna be. I was a better player than Jamie was. I had a bad knee injury when I was fifteen. Fucked it up. I couldn't play for a year and then was told I'd never be able to go professional. So here we are.'

Erika could see his arrogant bravado covering up embarrassment, and she felt a little pity for him.

'But you remained friends with Jamie?'

'Yeah, we kept in touch. Did you talk to Leon?'

'Not yet.'

'He's been the glue between us all, really. I'm good mates with Leon; he was also at the academy and kept us all in contact. We went out the other night to have a drink for Leon and his new baby.'

'That's what we need your help with,' said Erika. 'Whose plan was it to go to Red Velvet?'

'Jamie. I just wanted to go to a decent pub. There are a few in central London, tucked away. You know, horse brasses and horse-faced barmaids, that's my thing . . .' He gave a little smirk at his joke, but it went when he saw it wasn't reciprocated.

'Have you been to Red Velvet before?' asked Peterson.

'Bloody hell, no. Jamie pays something nuts to be a member there – twenty-five grand, he said, and then the drinks. I don't want to know what he paid, but we had this big table with a massive ice bucket filled with bottles of beer, Champagne, and spirits.'

'What about the group of girls you all spent the night with?' asked Erika. She opened a folder and took out images from the CCTV of the girls arriving at the alleyway to the club and then a couple of shots of them all in the lift up to Jamie's apartment.

'Jamie's mam thinks one of them did it,' he said, glaring at the photos.

'Who were they?'

'Girls,' he said, shrugging, as if this were all the answer needed.

'Do you know their names?'

'We drank a lot, and they all had really rhyming names; one was Anna, another was Joanna, and I think another was Savanna.

I think one even said she was called Rihanna, but we took it with a pinch of salt.'

'What about the name Annabelle?'

He sighed and then shook his head. 'Nope. That wasn't one of them. I told you, they all had rhyming names.'

'How did they join your group?' asked Peterson.

'One of them came over to me and asked about Jamie. She'd seen us all together and wanted to know if they could meet him.'

Erika hesitated. 'I know you're here voluntarily. But the manager of the club said that you were questioned by the bouncer about selling drugs.'

There was an icy silence, and the solicitor looked over at Finn and then sat up in his chair. 'My client is not here for you to go on a fishing trip. He's here to talk about events leading up to the murder of Jamie Teague.'

Finn gave his solicitor the side-eye and then seemed to slump farther in his chair. 'The girl asked me if I had any pills. I didn't. Then she got out some pills or something,' he said, waving his hand in the air vaguely.

'Prescription pills in a bottle? Or an illegal substance?' asked Erika.

He shrugged. 'I didn't see owt else, 'cos the bouncer was over to us like lightning. She showed him what they were. They had a doctor's label on them. The music was loud. She talked him down, and he left us alone. She said she'd done me a favour and I should introduce her and her mates to Jamie, so I did.'

Erika wanted to ask exactly how she'd done him a favour, but she wanted to stick to questions about the five young women.

'Did it strike you as odd that the women all looked so alike?' she asked.

'Yeah. That were weird. They told us they'd been to some model casting for a film or maybe a TV show about all these sisters, and they were all still in make-up. It was really loud in the club, and we were just dancing. And you would think that might be true, this being London and all that.'

'What happened when you all left?'

'Jamie invited everyone back to his new pad. We had to wait on the road for one of them big people cruiser taxis to take us all together.'

'Did you find out anything more about the girls?'

'Me and, er – actually me, I pulled one of them, and then three of the others were all over Jamie and . . .'

'Anything you say to us will remain confidential,' said Peterson.

'I don't think that's a promise you can make,' said the solicitor with a hollow laugh.

'I take it Leon may have been flirting or slept with one of the women?' Asked Peterson.

'I don't know.'

'But he's got a new baby?'

'You need to talk to Leon,' said Finn.

'Okay. Let's change tack. Was there anything odd about the women? Anything out of place which made you question who they were?'

Finn thought about it for a moment.

'Their noses were weird. Like the same. And they suited a couple of the girls, but the others looked like their noses were too big for their faces. And then . . . Well, I had sex with two of 'em, yeah? And they didn't want to kiss or let me touch their faces. I thought it was 'cos they were prostitutes, but it was as if they didn't want me to touch their noses . . . I was really drunk. Okay? But I did wonder if they had on fake noses, you know, really good ones.' He sighed and shook his head. 'I know it sounds weird, but I was drunk, and they kept saying that they'd been at this casting, so I didn't question it.'

'They each carried a small black bag. Do you know what they had inside?'

'No. I saw one of them get a lipstick out at one point. They were small bags. I don't know if any of them had much cash. They didn't pay, and I didn't see them on their phones, which was weird, especially with girls on a night out when they meet a famous footballer. They all want selfies, you know.'

'What did you all do back at Jamie's?' asked Peterson.

'Partied.'

'Can you be more specific?'

Finn fixed him with a hard stare.

'Jamie opened a load of Champagne bottles he had in the fridge. He tried to get the girls to go in the Jacuzzi on the terrace, but they weren't up for it. The girls just danced around to the MTV channel.'

'Did Jamie seem drunk, out of it? When you got back to his apartment?' asked Erika.

'A bit. We had sunk quite a few bevvies.'

'Do you think his drink was spiked with something?'

Finn thought about this for a moment. 'No. He was dancing like a madman, but I thought that was the drink.'

'Did Jamie or Leon sleep with any of the young women?'

'I can speak for myself. I went off with two of the girls into the guest bedroom. The other girls were with Jamie and Leon, but they could have been just drinking for all I know.'

'Which girls did you have sex with?' asked Peterson.

Finn sighed. 'I don't know.'

'The CCTV shows you arrived at Jamie's flat in Greenwich One at 3.06 am. Then you and Leon left with four of the women at 5.16 am on Saturday morning,' said Erika, taking the CCTV image from her folder and pushing it across the table.

'Well, yeah. If that's the time it says.'

'Do you know why the fifth young woman stayed at Jamie's flat?'

'We had an idea, but we didn't know she was gonna . . .' He went pale and seemed to look bereft for the first time during their conversation.

'Can you remember the name of the young woman who stayed?' asked Peterson.

'It could have been Anna, Savanna, Joanna, Rihanna . . . I think the fifth one said she was Hannah . . . I remember the other four were skivvying us along to leave, Leon and me. It was like they'd agreed that the fifth girl would stay with Jamie.'

'What happened after you left Greenwich One?'

'They all went off, said they had a cab. I never saw it, though. Me and Leon went into Greenwich and hung around until one of the caffs opened at six, and we had a fry-up; then we went home.'

'Did you hear anything from Jamie after you left?'

'No. Nothing. That was the last time we ever saw or spoke to Jamie.'

24

The same solicitor represented Leon Bromfield, but the contrast between Leon and Finn couldn't have been greater. Leon seemed to exude a calmness and confidence, which really impressed Erika. He was tall and lean and seemed to hold himself well. Whereas Finn shrank into himself and avoided eye contact, Leon did the opposite. He stood up and shook their hands when they entered the office as if he were welcoming them. The solicitor also seemed more relaxed in his presence.

'We know you trained at Chelsea Football Club Academy with Jamie and Finn, but now what do you do?' asked Erika.

'I'm a primary school teacher,' said Leon. 'Proud to be, too,' he added, seeming to direct this at Peterson.

'And you've just had a new baby.'

'Yeah. Danny. He's six weeks old. And he's sleeping through the night. Which accounts for the lack of bags under my eyes.'

Peterson smiled and nodded, and Erika could see he was trying not to get caught up in Leon's charisma.

'Thank you for talking to us. It's much appreciated. We just wanted you to take us through the night you spent with Jamie, in your own words,' said Erika.

Leon explained the reason for their night out and told a similar story to Finn. Taking them through the original plan to go to a regular pub, but Jamie was worried about being recognised, so they went to Red Velvet. Leon then described the group of girls as models and, without prompting, said that they all looked weirdly similar, with similar names like Anna, Savanna, Rihanna, and Hannah. He didn't think that any of them were called Annabelle, either.

'I think they'd all been out on some kind of casting for a new reality show. That's what one of them said. And they'd been asked to all dress the same,' finished Leon.

'One of the girls told you this?' asked Erika.

He nodded. 'I got the impression that she was glad of the fee.'

'What kind of fee? Do you mean that they got the job? The casting was a success?'

'She gave me the impression that they'd been paid for this job.'

Erika and Peterson exchanged a glance.

'They were sex workers?'

Leon put up his hands.

'Whoa. No, that's not what I'm saying. Finn got approached by one of the girls in the club to ask if they could come and join us in the VIP box or whatever it was. Jamie wasn't paying them anything.'

He'd lost his cool and suddenly looked agitated.

'Anything we talk about in here will remain confidential. If it's not related to the investigation, then it's not something we interfere in,' said Peterson.

Leon took a deep breath, and Erika could see he was shaking.

'Finn told you about me and one of the girls at Jamie's apartment?'

Peterson nodded, keeping eye contact with Leon. There was a long silence.

'I love my wife. Okay? And my son.'

'Like I said, we're here to investigate what happened to Jamie and who murdered him. We don't care about any affairs or infidelity.'

'Me and my wife have an understanding. An open relationship,' said Leon. Erika wondered if this agreement was still in force now that Leon and his wife had a baby. But she just nodded.

'Can we go back to the five women?' said Erika. She took out a CCTV photo of them all in the lift going up to Jamie's apartment. 'Is there anything you can tell us about them? Did you catch their surnames? Did you hear anything that could help us to find them? Anything, however small?'

Leon sat up and pulled the photo towards him. He studied it for a long time. Then he sat back and shook his head.

'It was noisy. We were all drinking.' He frowned.

'What? Anything you can remember would be helpful.'

'One of the girls I was talking to, she seemed a bit sad and depressed. She said she hadn't been allowed to take her phone with her.'

'To the nightclub?'

Leon shrugged. 'She was being vague. She said she had a kid at home and couldn't call her babysitter. It struck me as weird because I've just had a baby.'

'How many times did you phone your wife that evening?' asked Peterson pointedly. Erika shot him a look. This wasn't the time to antagonise Leon.

'I was texting her all evening,' said Leon, staring at Peterson.

'What was stopping this girl from having her phone with her?' asked Erika.

'I don't know. It was weird. She was bitching about one of the other girls, who seemed in charge.'

'Which girl seemed in charge?'

Leon pulled the photo closer again and peered at it. 'Jesus.

They all looked alike. Now I think about it, none of them had phones, apart from one.'

'Which one?'

He looked at the photo again and shook his head. 'None of them seemed to have any money. In fact, when this girl, the one I was talking to, opened her bag, it looked old and skanky.'

'It was vintage?'

'No, more like, grubby, and the make of the bag was something I'd never heard of: Folger. That stood out to me 'cos my wife is handbag crazy, and these young women seemed fashionable. Football skanks like them usually have designer bags, or knock-off designer bags.'

Erika made a note of this. It was the first tangible piece of information about the young women.

'Did you see what she had in her handbag?'

'Not really. I only saw the inside of the flap.'

'If you look at the photo, can you identify the young woman who stayed at Jamie's after the rest of you left his apartment?'

Leon peered at the photo again and then shook his head. 'I wish I could, but as the night wore on, it was a blur.'

'Do you think Jamie was on drugs? Or someone slipped something into his drink?'

Leon shook his head again. 'No, he just seemed drunk.'

'What can you tell us about the girl you had sex with at Jamie's apartment?'

Leon stared at the table. 'Nothing.'

'Did you think she was wearing a false nose?'

Leon looked up at them, and then across to his solicitor. 'Are you serious?'

'Yes.'

'No. I don't know; I don't think so. All I know is that it wasn't worth it. I love my wife.'

Afterwards, when they came out of the interview, Erika

thought about how broken he'd looked when he answered the final question.

When Erika and Peterson left the interview, Moss was outside in the corridor.

'Boss. A message from the superintendent. The press conference is now at one thirty pm, and it's been moved to the Marriott Hotel County Hall on the Embankment. Can you meet her down in reception?'

'Now?'

'Yes.'

Erika checked her watch. It was coming up to ten am.

'How did it go? With Finn and Leon?' asked Moss.

'They didn't expend much energy on getting to know these young women. It was a boozy night out. And we think the girls gave them fake names.'

'I've never heard of a group of women being involved in a murder like this,' said Moss.

'One of the girls let it slip they'd been hired for the night,' said Erika.

'Hired? As sex workers? By who?'

'We don't know.'

They started down the stairs back to the incident room.

'Does the fashion label "Folger" mean anything to you in terms of handbags?' asked Erika.

'Handbags?' repeated Moss with a chuckle. 'You're asking the wrong person. I'm all about the backpack. Isn't Folger an American brand of coffee?'

'Can you follow up on it? Leon Bromfield said he saw the brand "Folger" inside one of the girls' black handbags. If it's something obscure, and they all had identical bags, it might be something,' said Erika.

'Yes. Do you know if there will be a media appeal email or phone number issued during the press conference?' asked Moss. 'We're going to need manpower here if they want to use a live help-line.'

'As soon as I find out, I'll let you know.'

'I also came to tell you, the young woman Jamie was accused of raping is called Rebecca Reid. She was on the books of a modelling agency called Rush Models and was hired to accompany Jamie to a film premiere. After the trial, she signed an NDA and received a large payment from Cheri Shelton Management. She now lives on a farm in Devon.'

'Can you find out if she'll talk to us?'

'Of course.'

They reached the incident room, and Erika grabbed her coat and purse off her desk just as her phone rang. It was Igor.

'Can you talk?' he asked.

'Yes. Everything okay?'

'I know this is a long shot, but would you be free to pick Tom up from school at five pm today, after his football practice?'

'No. Sorry. I've got this press conference, and it's been moved to central London. I wish I could. Is there someone else?'

'I can move some things around, but Tom wanted me to ask you. I think he'd like to hear more about the anti-freeze killer.'

Erika looked at the incident room. It was buzzing with activity, and Dahlia was fixing enlarged photos of the faces of the 'glitch in the matrix girls' on the whiteboards at the back, and Crane and McGorry were sticking up the new photos from the Terry DeVille crime scene. She reminded herself again that she enjoyed her job. She got to do something she loved every day.

'I'll make some time one evening this week to tell him more gory stories. I could come over for dinner?'

'He'd love that. I would too,' said Igor with a chuckle. Erika heard a beep on her phone and saw that Melanie was calling her.

'Sorry. I've got to go. Look out for me on TV around one thirty pm.'

'I've set the sky box to record it,' said Igor.

25

Annabelle had a loose end to tie.

She'd debated long and hard if she needed to tie it or if leaving it loose would cause more confusion in a police investigation. No. It had to be tied off. Tight.

Door to door, it took only an hour to travel from her flat to Kensington High Street. Annabelle's journey had begun hours before, taking in a wide circuit of outer London to avoid CCTV cameras where possible. Her disguise was subtle, like all good disguises: a good-quality wig of blonde curls, red glasses, brown contact lenses, and make-up to subtly change her features – lips drawn smaller, and eyes more cat-like. She was dressed in jeans, trainers, and a black hoodie. A large holdall was her only luggage. Her burner phone was switched off, and she felt it against her hip in the bag alongside the brand-new metal monkey wrench.

It was bright and clear when Annabelle stepped off the train at Kensington High Street tube station. She stared up at every CCTV camera so they could get a good look at her disguise. Her appointment was at two pm, and she'd made good time.

Scarsdale Villas was a quiet suburban street of houses set back from Kensington High Street. Annabelle had done a couple of recce visits over the past couple of weeks. The small details mattered: Scarsdale Villas was a two-way street, so little traffic was being funnelled away from a main road along a one-way system. It was leafy with plenty of trees and filled with terraced houses converted into flats. It meant that there was a steady thrum of people coming and going.

Annabelle rang the bell at two pm on the dot, and a moment later, she heard Jessica Goldman through the crackly intercom.

'Hello?' She had a warm voice and made even a 'hello' sound like you wanted to know her.

'Hi, it's Casey,' said Annabelle. In real life, Annabelle's voice was South London, but when she was Casey, she spoke with a posher accent in a slightly higher, breathier register.

'Hey, Casey, come on in. I'm on the ground floor, end of the corridor.' There was a buzz, and the locking mechanism on the main entrance clicked. Annabelle took a deep breath and pushed the door open.

The floor in the communal hallway was made of scuffed herringbone parquet, and the walls mirrored the Art Deco style of the building outside. A cosy smell of floor polish was mixed in with dust and that funky smell of other people. There was a staircase to the left, and two doors painted pea green. Jessica lived at number two, on the right. Annabelle closed the front door behind her. The buzzing from the front door ceased, and the locking mechanism reactivated as she hurried down the hall.

Jessica opened the door and stared at Annabelle, annoyed. 'Why are you wearing the wig? And where are the garment bags I gave you?' she said, seeing the bulging holdall.

'I wanted to show you how good the wig looked,' said Annabelle. For a moment, she thought Jessica had guessed something weird was happening and wouldn't invite her in. 'And I was worried about squashing the wig on the Tube if I had it in a bag . . . ,' she added.

'You wore it on the Underground?' She leaned over and patted the curls. 'If it smells, I'm going to have to charge you for cleaning.'

'No worries,' she replied perkily. Casey was a bit ditzy and lovable, and Annabelle made sure to keep up her character.

Jessica rolled her eyes, smiled, and took a step back. 'Okay. Come on in. Let me have a look at it all.'

Annabelle stepped over the threshold and closed the door behind her with a click. She was in.

'Do you want tea?' asked Jessica, moving down the hallway. Annabelle followed. It was narrow, with the same wooden herringbone floor. There was a table on the left with a cordless landline phone and a stack of mail on top, and above it was a tall, thin mirror.

'Yes, please.'

'I hope you've got the wig-stand I gave you? They're not cheap . . . If not, I'll charge you for a new one.'

'It's in the bag,' said Annabelle, patting the holdall on her hip. She was suddenly nervous. A tiny bathroom was at the end of the hallway, and to the right was a bedroom. Annabelle followed Jessica through the door on the left.

It was a big kitchen/living area, light and airy with tall sash windows at the back. A long table filled the middle of the room and was covered with the paraphernalia of Jessica's job – pots of glue and all kinds of make-up. Three polystyrene heads stood in the middle, and stuck onto them were the fleshy components of a prosthetic face: noses, chins, and two fragments of angular latex to change the shape of the cheeks.

The room had no sofa, and the television was on the wall angled towards the kitchen table. On the back wall were scores of photos detailing the prosthetic make-up work she'd done on various film and TV projects.

Jessica headed for the sink, and Annabelle opened the holdall.

The monkey wrench was wrapped in a plastic freezer bag, sitting on top of the change of clothes. There were also two pairs of latex gloves in the inside pocket, and Annabelle had intended to slip them on, but she could now see there wasn't time.

Jessica was at the sink, filling up the kettle. The space on either side of the long table was too narrow for Annabelle and her bag. A sudden wave of nerves came over her. She'd killed the men for a purpose, but she liked Jessica. It wasn't her fault she was a loose end. Even as she stood there, Annabelle wondered if she could tie it off without killing her.

No.

'Milk and sugar?' asked Jessica, turning to her with the kettle in her hand.

'Both. Yes.'

Jessica stopped and stared at Annabelle. Holding the kettle in her hand. 'What did you say?'

Shit, thought Annabelle. She'd just used her own voice. Her South London, lower-register voice. She put her sweaty hand inside the bag, and took out the wrench and a length of thin rope.

'I'm really sorry,' said Annabelle. 'I liked you a lot.'

26

Erika met Melanie on the steps outside the station's main entrance.

'Change of plan—' said Melanie.

'Yes. Marriott Hotel County Hall by Westminster Bridge. What was wrong with the conference room here at the station?'

'Cheri Shelton thinks we'll reach a wider media pool if the press conference is held in central London. She requested it through Marsh.'

Erika rolled her eyes. '"Media pool". So, Cheri Shelton's running things?'

'It's not . . .' Her voice trailed off as Finn Horton and Leon Bromfield emerged from the main entrance with their solicitor. They were in a huddle. *A boys' huddle,* thought Erika. *All boys together, looking out for each other.* 'Thanks again, lads, for coming in to talk to us,' said Melanie, turning on the charm. They didn't reply and just gave her a nod as they walked over to the solicitor's black BMW and got in. 'The blond one looks like a bit of a bastard,' added Melanie. As the solicitor's BMW drove away, the boys were in the back seat and looked straight ahead with grim faces.

Erika quickly outlined what they'd talked about. 'We need to track down someone who can tell us more about this group of girls – young women. Sergeant Crane is waiting on CCTV from the area around the Red Velvet Club. We also need to find the cab driver who took them back to Jamie Teague's flat . . . I'm already worried about our manpower on this case, and now we're looking into the murder of Neville Lomas and Terry DeVille . . .'

A black stretch limousine turned off the main road and pulled up to the barrier to the car park.

'Is that Cheri Shelton?' asked Erika.

'She told me she'd send us her car service.' Melanie glanced back into the reception area of the station. 'This doesn't look good, us getting into a limo.'

The barrier opened, and the limo slid into the car park and drew beside them. It was so shiny, and as the light played over the paintwork, it looked like it was flowing. A tinted window slid down.

'Morning, ladies,' said Cheri.

A tall young man in a driver's uniform and hat got out and opened the door for Erika and Melanie.

'There's plenty of room,' said Cheri, shifting along and indicating the long leather seat. She wore a black trouser suit, and her blonde hair peeked out from under a black beret. Cheri had on lashings of pale foundation and smoky eye shadow with large black lashes, and her tiny mouth was overdrawn with red lipstick. Erika wondered whether she was attempting to look funereal, but she needed only a pair of white gloves, and she could busk as a mime artist. 'Can I get you a drink? Coffee? Something stronger?' A small bar in the corner had cans of soft drinks and bottles of water, wine, and beer.

'We're on duty,' said Erika.

'Just some water, thank you,' said Melanie.

'This is my office on wheels, and I can smoke. Unlike cabs,

trains, planes, and just about anywhere else.' She lit up a cigarette and offered the pack. Melanie and Erika both declined. 'Do you mind if I smoke?' she added, opening her window a crack and exhaling.

'Go ahead,' said Erika, and she saw Melanie was also nodding despite hating the smell of smoke. Erika's heart sank when she saw where the balance of power lay.

The limo pulled away. Cheri had a big personality, and Erika knew she and Melanie would need to assert their authority on the situation.

'So. How are things going?' asked Cheri. 'Any luck finding the bastard who did this?' She flicked her ash through the small gap in the window. She had long emerald-green fingernails and lots of rings on her fingers.

'We believe one of the five women who returned to Jamie's flat early Saturday morning killed him.'

'Jesus. Did any of them leave DNA?'

Erika thought of the black gloves they'd all worn, the empty Champagne glasses, and the beds in Jamie's apartment.

'We're still waiting on the DNA results,' she said.

Cheri's phone was in her lap, and it started to chime with alerts. When she picked it up, Erika saw the screen stacked with messages. Melanie took out her phone to check it.

'This must be an odd time for you. Balancing business with grieving?' said Erika.

Cheri didn't look up from her scrolling. 'It is. And I've got journalists circling. Waiting for the appropriate time to write their hit pieces.'

'Hit pieces?'

Cheri raised an eyebrow. 'Don't pretend, Detective. You know as well as I do what's doing the rounds on social media.'

'Did Jamie ever use the services of sex workers?'

Melanie looked up from her scrolling.

'He may have slept with a sex worker, and if he did, I doubt she charged him.'

'He was heterosexual?'

'He was. As far as I know, and I knew pretty much everything about him.'

'We're investigating Jamie's death in conjunction with the death of Neville Lomas—'

'That fat stinking pig dog of an MP?'

'Yes, he was an MP.' Erika explained the significance of a sex worker potentially being involved in his death. 'We are also at the early stages of identifying another victim.'

'No. Jamie never paid for sex workers. He had women throwing themselves at him.'

'What about Rebecca Reid?'

Cheri hesitated and bared her teeth in a smile. 'Rebecca Reid signed a non-disclosure agreement and was paid a substantial amount of cash. She now lives in blissful anonymity in a beautiful house on the coast in Devon. Quite a good payday for one night on her back.'

Erika was shocked at her venom.

'You don't believe that Jamie raped her?'

'No, I do not. Jamie wasn't a violent man, and he's not here to defend himself . . .' She struggled with her emotions for a moment and then composed herself. 'And what's crucial is that a judge and jury in a court of law ruled unanimously that he was innocent.' Erika could see she was getting worked up. 'Things got out of hand, yes, but she had a history of drug abuse and violence towards her ex-boyfriends. Jamie's defence team also had her phone turned over to them. Text messages between Rebecca and a friend showed she was planning to accuse Jamie of something in the hope of being offered a pay-off or a newspaper deal. Do you understand? Capisce?'

'I've never encountered a murder case before where the suspect could potentially be a female sex worker,' said Erika.

'And we're very much still using the word "potentially",' said Melanie, shooting Erika a look.

There was an icy silence. Cheri stared at them. Her phone chimed again, but she put it back in her lap and lit another cigarette.

'I'm a good friend of Commander Marsh. Paul,' she said. 'Me and Paul's wife, Marcie, were at Benenden together.' Benenden was one of the country's most prestigious girls' schools. Cheri was flexing her police connections. She didn't want to talk about Jamie Teague and sex workers. 'I've been assured by Commander Marsh that this press appeal will focus on finding Jamie's killer, not going on a fishing trip to besmirch his name.'

'This is my case, which is evolving rapidly, and—'

'Why don't we use this time to talk to you a little about your working relationship with Jamie and how he was in the days leading up to his murder?' said Melanie, shooting Erika another look. Cheri's eyes moved between them both.

'I was trying to get Jamie to agree to round-the-clock security. It was a big bone of contention between us. A few weeks ago, someone broke into his new place in Greenwich One and left a bottle of Champagne on the bed with a note.'

'What did the note say?' asked Erika.

'It was a love letter. It was written in rather explicit terms, but there was nothing violent. And it was a good bottle of Champagne, too. No rubbish.'

'Was the note signed with a name?'

'No. I don't think so. I have it at the office.'

'We'd like to see that letter,' said Melanie. Cheri nodded.

'Did you contact the police?' asked Erika.

'Yes, but I was told there wasn't much they – you – could do.'

'What about the CCTV cameras at Greenwich One? Did they record this intruder?' asked Melanie. Cheri sighed.

'The cameras weren't working. The building is completely new, and they were doing maintenance on the CCTV system or something. And lots of people were in and out of the flat: tradesmen, delivery people. Whoever got in managed it without anyone seeing them. I also didn't want Jamie to know. It was his new place. He would have then told his mother, and she worried terribly. Janice had a triple heart bypass last year, and if Jamie knew about the break-in, he would tell her. They were very close.'

'I thought you just said you wanted Jamie to have round-the-clock security?'

'Yes. But there were other reasons for Jamie to have security. He was very famous.'

Erika took out a photo of the CCTV showing the five young women grouped in the lift at Greenwich One with Jamie and passed it to her.

'These are the five women who returned from Red Velvet with Jamie and his friends early on Saturday morning. Do you recognise any of them?'

Cheri fumbled in her handbag by her feet, pulled out a pair of tortoiseshell glasses, and slipped them on. 'No. They look like the type, though,' she said as she studied the photo.

'What type?'

'The type of young women who hang around footballers,' she said with a snarl. 'Why are they all wearing black gloves?'

'We're not sure. Maybe they didn't want to leave fingerprints.'

'And you've never seen these women or anyone unusual hanging around Jamie. No repeat view of strangers around him, strange emails or threats in the past few weeks or months?' asked Erika.

Cheri looked back at the photo; her face was severe, the bravado gone.

'There are always lots of girls . . . He's always surrounded by women when he goes out, but none of these stand out to me.'

'We're going to make identifying them a key part of our press appeal,' said Erika.

'And we promise this will be an appeal which is respectful to Jamie's family and his memory,' added Melanie.

27

Cheri Shelton's limousine dropped them in front of the expansive Portland stone façade of the old County Hall building – now the Marriott Hotel. They walked down a vast arched tunnel approach, seven stories high, leading into an internal courtyard.

Cheri was concentrating on her phone, and the pings and chimes of new alerts echoed off the stone arches behind Erika and Melanie.

'Why were you making promises to her?' asked Erika.

'I've been ordered by Marsh to keep her happy.'

'Ordered?'

'Yes, Erika. I know you have a history with Marsh, but you need to remember that, as an officer, he holds the fifth highest rank in the Met.'

'You don't need to school me on this.'

'Maybe I do. Don't forget that I am your senior officer.' Melanie moved off towards the door at a quicker pace with a stony look on her face.

There was a fountain in the courtyard, splashing noisily, and Erika paused for a moment. The freezing spray was not unwelcome after the stuffy car journey. The steps at the main entrance led past a plaque on the wall. King George V and Queen Mary had opened the building in 1922. It had been used by the government and the General London Council before it was closed down, abandoned, and then sold to become a Marriott.

As she entered the lobby, Erika was struck by the building's palatial splendour. She found Melanie with Marsh and Colleen Scanlan, the Met Police media liaison officer, in the Library bar. He was in his dress uniform, sharp and immaculate as usual. Next to him, Colleen was somewhat dishevelled in a long skirt and checkerboard-pattern blouse. They had a table beside a window overlooking the grey Embankment and the London Eye. It was busy with people being blown by the wind coming off the Thames, which sloshed past, brown and sludgy.

'Ah, Erika. Where is Cherry?' said Marsh.

'She's just on her phone outside.'

'I hear you had a bit of a tense car journey?'

Erika looked over at Melanie and went to speak, but Cheri entered the restaurant.

'Paul, *darling*, how are you?' she said.

Marsh got up, and leaned down to kiss her on the cheek.

'Cherry. Lovely to see you. We're good. All good. They have lovely coffee here. Would you like one?' Erika noted that Marsh mispronounced her name, but she didn't correct him. He introduced Cheri to Colleen.

Erika saw Janice Teague enter the lobby with Fiona Watson, the police family liaison officer she vaguely recognised. With them were a short older man in a black suit and a tall young woman with long blonde hair, wearing a short dress and jacket. They must be Jamie's father and sister, thought Erika, and she noted how Janice and her daughter were a head taller than Jamie's father.

'Where do you want me to put them?' asked Fiona, indicating the family hovering in the lobby. Janice's eyes were red, and she was close to tears. The man looked uncomfortable and the young woman a bit bewildered and in awe of the hotel lobby.

'We have a space booked, I believe? For them to wait in,' asked Marsh. 'But we must say hello.'

'Janice. Darling!' said Cheri, beckoning them in. 'Charles! Karen! How are you all doing?' She embraced them all.

'Could be better,' said Charles, who also spoke with a thick Scottish accent.

'This is Commander Marsh from the Metropolitan Police and Superintendent Melanie Hudson. You've met Detective Chief Inspector Erika Foster, I think?'

'I have,' said Janice.

'Can I just say you have my deepest sympathy,' said Marsh, moving down the line to shake hands with the Teagues. 'And I want to assure you that we are doing everything possible to find the terrible person who did this. My best officers are working day and night. I can assure you.'

Janice and Karen gave him weak smiles.

'It's good to meet you officers,' said Charles with a brisk nod.

'I've brought some photos. I thought they might help with the appeal,' said Janice. She reached into her handbag and took out a plastic folder with some cute pictures of Jamie from when he was a young boy, including a school photo aged eight or nine, photos of him at the football academy in his teens, and another couple of family photos.

Marsh looked through the photos with a little too much enthusiasm. 'These are perfect. Perfect. Cherry? Don't you think we could use these during the appeal?'

'Yes, super photos, absolutely *super*,' she agreed. Behind them, a group of six men and women appeared in the lobby. They came to the doorway. Two men carried camera equipment, a long boom microphone, and a tripod camera.

'Hello, we're BBC News. I'm Alana Goldsmith, news

producer,' said one of the women. She introduced herself to everyone, giving the Teagues her sympathy.

'Yes. The press conference will be in here,' said Cheri, indicating the Library bar with a photo in her hand, of Jamie and Karen sitting on a donkey at Banham Zoo when they were small.

'I've brought some photos,' said Janice to Alana, fanning them out in her hands like a deck of playing cards.

'Brilliant. We can use these. Absolutely,' Alana said with detached enthusiasm, and then turned to Cheri. 'We've got the OB van outside. The doorman is being funny about us parking there.'

'Colleen, let's get the Teagues up to hospitality on the second floor,' said Marsh. 'They can have a coffee, and some refreshments whilst we let these good people set things up for the broadcast.' He smiled awkwardly at the Teagues and straightened his dress uniform.

Just as Colleen was trying to usher them out of the Library, another TV crew and a producer arrived, and two young men who worked on the hotel staff appeared carrying stacks of chairs.

Erika could feel the situation getting chaotic and asked to speak to Marsh and the producer.

'I'll need to be included in any conversation about the TV appeal,' said Cheri. Marsh waited until the Teagues had left with Fiona and then indicated to Erika, Melanie, and Cheri to move to a table in the corner of the bar.

'I would like to use the press conference to make a wider appeal, taking in two victims in addition to Jamie.'

'Hold on,' said Marsh, putting up his hand. 'Two additional victims?'

Erika quickly explained how she'd found Terry DeVille.

'This is something that just popped up a few hours ago? No,' said Marsh.

'Well, can we at least mention the death of Neville Lomas?

We've been able to link the two cases with the signed Polaroids. I would like to hold back that detail from the media at this stage, but it's enough for us to pursue a direct link.'

'I don't think Jamie's family know about the Polaroid photos,' said Cheri. 'And do you really want to upset them so close to the press appeal?'

'They're going to be upset,' said Erika. 'And I just said we don't want to mention the Polaroids at this stage.'

Melanie and Cheri both looked at Marsh. He started to speak, and then Alana returned with an iPad. Erika saw that she now had an earpiece.

'Sorry to interrupt. I have the visual materials for the broadcast.' Erika went to take them, but she handed them to Marsh instead. He scrolled through the still images of the five women, Jamie, and his friends from the CCTV in the lift at Greenwich One.

'These aren't the images I selected,' said Erika.

Alana looked between Erika and Marsh and then touched her earpiece. 'I'm needed in the OB van. Can I leave this with you to confirm the images asap?'

Erika nodded and took the iPad. 'I sent CCTV images to the press office and Colleen this morning. These are different.'

'Ah, yes. It looks like those are the CCTV screen grabs sent by my office,' said Marsh.

'And this isn't the statement I drafted,' said Erika, swiping through a document at the end.

'Yes. I was asked for my input on behalf of the family, isn't that right, Paul?' said Cheri.

'Erika, this is a simple case of accidental duplication,' said Marsh.

'I'm the lead officer on this case. Changing the statement isn't accidental duplication.'

'Erika, are these or are these not CCTV images from the night Jamie Teague was murdered?' asked Marsh.

'Well, yes.'

'And this statement gives the facts of Jamie Teague's life and last movements, yes? Cheri knew everything about him, so it would make sense for me to ask for her input. Yes?'

Erika handed back the iPad. She didn't like how Marsh tried to make her look unreasonable.

'I just don't think it's a good thing for continuity if we have two offices briefing on a case, sir. My team – my excellent team – is running this investigation out of Lewisham Row, so all communications should come through them via the press office.'

Alana came back to the table. 'Are we okay with everything?'

Marsh, Melanie, and Cheri looked at Erika, still holding the iPad, and she could see she was outnumbered.

28

An hour later, Erika emerged from the meeting and tried to find somewhere to have a cigarette. The only option was a small roped-off area in the corner of the courtyard. She lit up and watched as a third outside broadcast van arrived, churning up the neat gravel by the fountain opposite the hotel entrance. A considerable number of thick TV cables were now threading their way into the hotel, filling the revolving doors. Hotel patrons were being redirected through a smaller entrance next to it, much to the annoyance of the doorman in his coat and tails and top hat. It was strange how a television crew and a posh hotel elevated the whole death of Jamie Teague to a circus. The hotel had set up a line of metal crush barriers outside in the courtyard, and already people were lining the barrier, watching what was going on. *Where did they come from?* thought Erika. Did they even know what was going on? Had they been arranged by Cheri?

Erika smoked her cigarette and watched as one of the news crews began to film the people. She took out her phone and called Moss.

'How's it going there?' Moss asked.

'A farce,' said Erika. 'I've just come out of a meeting with

Marsh, Melanie, producers from BBC and ITN news, and Jamie Teague's manager. It seems this media appeal is turning into some kind of Jamie Teague memorial tribute. Marsh's office sent Cheri Shelton the materials I submitted through the press office. And they want to include all of these cutesy pictures of him from his childhood, and his mother has written a poem she wants to read. It's only short, but still.'

'What about the CCTV footage from the lift, of the "glitch in the matrix girls"?'

'Yes. They're including those images, and they just want to focus on that and issue a help-line number and email address, asking if anyone has any information.'

'Okay. And who's supposed to be manning these phone lines and email?' asked Moss.

'Melanie should be calling you.'

'It'll mean overtime. I'm not saying that's a problem, but no one is communicating with us . . . apart from you,' Moss added.

'Yes. I'm sorry.'

'It's not your fault.'

Erika took a drag of her cigarette and watched as a massive placard with the Met Police logo was pulled from the back of a van and carried in by two men.

'I've been told specifically by Marsh that we're not mentioning the murder of Neville Lomas, or Terry DeVille,' said Erika. 'I can understand about Terry DeVille, but Neville Lomas . . .'

'I've been in touch with the doorman at Neville Lomas's apartment. They only keep their CCTV footage for thirty days before it's deleted, so we don't have anything from the night he was murdered.'

'I thought that might be the case,' said Erika.

'There are CCTV cameras on the Embankment Path, and Crane has just spoken to one of his contacts at Southwark Council, whose cameras cover that area, and they manage the

CCTV, but we think it's going to be the same thing. They delete footage after thirty-one days, unless a crime has been committed in that particular location.'

'Fingers crossed for that then,' said Erika dryly.

'I just tracked down some info about Terry DeVille. There's an estate agent who's been trying to sell Terry's house in West London. He died intestate. He had no will, no dependents, and the house has damp and structural problems. Apparently, nothing has been touched in the house since forensics left last November.'

'Can you get someone over there to look around?'

'Not until tomorrow first thing.'

Erika sighed. 'Okay. That's good work.'

Moss was silent for a beat.

'Is the press conference going to be live on TV?' she asked.

'Yes.'

'Well. Anything can happen with live TV,' said Moss. Erika took a last drag of her cigarette and stubbed it under her shoe. The same thought had occurred to her.

'I better go,' she said. 'I'll make sure Melanie calls you about the help-line for the appeal.'

Annabelle walked slowly back to Kensington High Street. The road was busy with the usual Sloane types. There were a lot of mother-and-daughter combos walking along the road, all dressed like Kate Middleton, all sleek hair and shiny, rosy-cheeked faces. They stood out against the poor mortals who had to work for a living – the delivery drivers and shop workers.

Annabelle was surprised to feel hungry and bought herself a bagel and a coffee from the posh deli and walked to Kensington Palace. Her favourite bench was free, and she sat down. She took the bagel out of its paper bag. It was toasted poppy seed filled with peanut butter. She went to take a bite, and then she saw a tiny fleck of blood on her wrist, on the top of that small round jutty-out bone. It was dry blood, and she scrubbed at it with one of the napkins from the bagel bag. Suddenly she wasn't hungry anymore.

Her phone chimed with an alert. She put the bagel down, took it out, and saw with interest and trepidation that two of the Google Alerts she had set had gone off simultaneously. The Jamie Teague alert had been pinging regularly for the past few days, as she would expect. However, the Neville Lomas alert, which had remained silent for the past few months, was also pinging like crazy.

She clicked on the first and saw that it had been triggered by a police press appeal. With shaking hands, she clicked on the video link.

A thin, tired-looking woman with short blonde hair was speaking in front of a large Met Police banner. Written on a placard in front of her on the desk was DET. CHIEF INSPECTOR ERIKA FOSTER.

'We're also concerned that the murder of Jamie Teague may be connected to the recent death of the MP Neville Lomas—' she said.

'We should reiterate that this press appeal is for Jamie Teague,' a man's voice interrupted. The camera then pulled out to a police officer sitting beside her. COMMANDER MARSH was written on the sign on the desk in front of him. This wider shot showed Jamie Teague's mother, red-eyed, sitting next to him, and her husband was on the other side, with his arm around her shoulders.

'Yes. But we have evidence that links the murder of Neville Lomas with the murder of Jamie Teague,' said Detective Erika Foster. She spoke with passion. Insistently. 'We are also asking if anyone was in or around the OXO Tower, and the residential apartments on the Thames Embankment on Friday, January 13, this year, if they saw anything or anyone suspicious, they should call the hotline number on the screen.'

It was evident that Detective Erika was going off-script. There was an awkward silence, and the camera quickly cut between the officers and the family members sitting at the table. Then there was a wide view of the press attending – rows and rows of people with microphones and notebooks, and there were cameras set up in the four corners of the room.

'I just want to reiterate we're searching for anyone who has information about these women seen with Jamie Teague on the night he died,' said Commander Marsh, adjusting the microphone in front of him. Then a video was shown of CCTV from the lifts at Greenwich One. Annabelle's hands shook a little when she saw the five girls, all dressed in their lacy black dresses and long black wigs. And the make-up and prosthetics styled by Jessica.

Jesus. Jessica. *What if she'd seen this? And what if she'd then called the hotline number?* Annabelle had covered her tracks with pathological accuracy, but she could now see she'd made the right call to visit Jessica.

The video stopped, and a freeze-frame image flashed of the five women looking up at the CCTV in the lift. The camera slowly zoomed in on all their faces. 'We believe these women gave false names and they may have been wearing some kind of disguise to all look similar,' finished Commander Marsh. 'We're appealing to these women to come forward and help us with our investigations.'

The video clip ended. The appeal had only just gone out live. Annabelle's phone started to chime again with more alerts about Jamie Teague and Neville Lomas.

She looked up from her spot on the bench. The park was almost empty, and only a far-off woman was walking a small dog.

The police had joined the dots between Jamie Teague and Neville Lomas. It was happening. The chase was on.

Annabelle sat back and closed her eyes, feeling the weak sun on her face. Excitement and fear coursed through her veins in equal measure. It would be interesting to see if any of the four women made contact with the police. None of them had seen her without her disguise. Only Jessica had seen Annabelle before she was made up with the prosthetics, and now that loose end was tied up. And just in time. Another hour or two and she could have seen the appeal.

She returned to her phone, found the livestream of the press conference, and began to watch from the beginning. It wasn't often that you saw yourself on TV. Annabelle typed the phone number into her burner phone and made a call to the help-line.

29

Erika arrived home at six, exhausted. She ordered a takeaway and decided to light a fire.

George came and sat beside her as she built a pyramid of kindling and stuffed it with crumpled-up pages from the local newspaper.

She lit a match, and the paper was very dry, so it ignited with a whoomph. Within a few moments, the kindling was alight. Erika leaned past George to get more wood from the old fruit box by the hearth and saw only one huge gnarly log. It was far too big to dump on the fire this early. It would have to be fed with smaller pieces of wood. And that would mean a visit out to the shed.

Erika grabbed the box, unlocked the kitchen door, and stepped out into the garden. The security light above the back door flicked on, and she hurried across the dark lawn to the shed at the bottom of her small garden. George stayed inside the kitchen, watching her from the comfort of the mat. The cold immediately began to bite into her exposed hands, and she fumbled with the latch on the shed door.

Erika hated the shed and the garden at night. An alleyway ran along the wall at the bottom of her garden, and a few times, she'd heard the scuff of feet late at night. She hesitated, thinking she heard something again now, but the garden was silent.

The shed door gave a slight creak, and Erika shone her phone light over the woodpile. There was also something far worse in the shed. Spiders. She grabbed as many pieces of wood as she could carry in the old fruit box. Thankfully, there were no spiders, but the bright light from the phone lit up a wide, translucent web in the right-hand corner of the shed.

Ugh.

Gingerly reaching into the pile again, Erika gathered up more wood. When she turned around, a figure was standing outside the shed door. Erika shrieked and dropped the box and her phone, and the light dazzled her.

'I'm not going to hurt you,' said a man's voice. Erika grabbed her phone. The bald man with the grey suit and the birthmark under his eye winced and brought up a hand to block the bright light. 'I'm not going to hurt you,' he repeated. His voice was soft and very dry.

Erika was trapped in the shed's doorway. She went to step outside, and he moved to block her way. Erika kept the light shining in his face.

'Who are you?' she said, hearing the tremor in her voice.

'Please lower the light.'

Erika angled it away from his face. The silver pinstripes on his suit glittered in the harsh glare of the torch light.

'Who are you?'

'I can be a friend.'

'How did you get in?'

His big eyes swivelled around to the gate, which was ajar. The whites of his eyes made Erika think of veiny boiled eggs. He looked back at her, and his big black pupils contracted in the light.

'I always hope I only have to make myself clear once. You

don't want a second visit from me.' His voice was calm, with a sinister hypnotism.

'Can you move, please?' asked Erika. She wasn't afraid of the spiders now but wanted out of the cramped, dusty shed. He put up his hand and scratched his nose.

'I won't take up much of your evening.' He rested his other hand on the door-frame. He had stumpy, fat fingers and a gold ring with a green crest buried in the flesh of his index finger. Erika heard a little miaow, and George walked up to the man. He scooped George up and held him above his head, his legs dangling down. 'Who is this young fellow?'

'Put him down.'

'I think he likes me,' said the man. George miaowed again, more insistently. He lowered George and cradled him in his arms, running his stumpy fingers through George's black fur. George wiggled and tried to jump down.

'He doesn't like you.' The man gripped tighter, and George seemed to struggle and then submit, looking up at him like he'd been captured. 'You can make your point without hurting my cat.'

'Can I? You seem to be happy to defy orders . . . Shh, shh. There we are,' he added, stroking George, who was trying to get away. 'Neville Lomas is a murder victim, part of your investigation. You need to tread very carefully, Detective.'

'Please. Let him go and I'll talk to you.'

He brought George up to his face and kissed his neck. He then let go. George jumped down and darted off into the bushes.

'What did Neville Lomas do?'

'*Do?* He died, Detective. He was the victim of a brutal murder. Anything else you find out is immaterial.'

'Do you know who the killer is?'

He chuckled.

'That's a little below my pay grade, hunting down common or

garden murderers. We're happy to let you catch him or her, whoever they are.'

'I need the CCTV from Neville Lomas's apartment.'

'Detective. I'm not here to talk shop, and the nitty-gritty.'

'What do you want from me?'

'There are just some facts about Mr Lomas you don't need to know about, nor does anyone else. I could have broken your cat's neck with one twist, but no. I gained his trust. Trust me, and you'll be hunky-dory.'

'I don't like cover-ups,' said Erika weakly.

'Follow orders and you will have a long successful career.'

'And if not?' asked Erika, her bravado not reaching her voice. But he was gone, vanishing through the back gate into the shadows. Despite the cold, Erika was sweating and shaking. She leaned on the door-frame momentarily, took some deep breaths, then went to the back gate. She shone her phone torch up and down the narrow alleyway, but it was empty.

Erika thought of what Isaac had said about his visit from the grey-suited man. That they had an 'aura of dark power'. Erika had thought it an overdramatic phrase, but now she agreed. She closed the gate and hurried across the lawn and into the house, slamming the back door and locking it.

The fire had dwindled and gone out, so she started to rebuild it. Trying to keep calm. And trying not to feel so shaken.

Her doorbell rang, making her jump. And then her phone chimed. Her takeaway had arrived, but she was no longer hungry.

30

Erika didn't sleep much the night after her visit from the grey-suited man. George had returned through the cat flap in the early hours and settled down in the crook of her back for a cuddle. She was woken up by her phone ringing at six am, and was pleased to see it was McGorry calling.

'Morning,' she croaked. She cleared her throat and repeated it.

'Morning, boss. You okay?' asked McGorry.

'I will be after some coffee.'

There was a pause.

'For what it's worth, I think you did the right thing yesterday . . . The whole team does, even Dahlia.'

Erika was grateful for her team's support. It was even interesting to hear that Dahlia was on her side.

'Thank you, I appreciate that. Now, what can I do for you?'

'Moss gave me the details of Terry DeVille's estate agent, and I managed to get the keys last night for his house. Do you want to come with me to have a poke round? I figured you might want to avoid the station for a bit?'

For once Erika was pleased the call wasn't about Neville Lomas.

'Yes, that would be good.'

'Great. It's in Barnes. I'm just texting you the address now.'

When Erika hung up the phone, she saw she had angry messages from Melanie and Marsh, requesting that she come in for a meeting. George purred, rubbing his head against her leg.

'I wish I could teach you to make me coffee in the morning, when Igor's not here to do it,' said Erika, scratching him behind his ears. Last night she'd longed for Igor's presence in her bed, to make her feel safer. George purred and looked at her with his beautiful green eyes. 'Are you okay? I'm sorry I panicked. I should have hit him.'

George miaowed in agreement. Erika scooped him up in her arms and went downstairs in search of caffeine.

Erika left the house an hour later. She liked driving, and a long drive was a nice excuse to clear her head. Barnes was a small village sitting on the Thames and about as west as you could go before leaving Greater London.

Terry DeVille had lived in a large house at the end of a cul-de-sac parallel with the high street. McGorry was already there, waiting outside in his car. He had a coffee for her, which she appreciated. He didn't say anything more about the previous day's press conference.

'The estate agent said they've had trouble selling it since Terry DeVille's death. There are damp and structural issues; otherwise, it would be snapped up. It's through here,' said McGorry, guiding them down an alleyway between two crumbling terraced houses. They emerged into a small courtyard before an extended low cottage with sash windows. The front door had coloured glass in the frame.

Erika took the key from McGorry and unlocked the door. She

felt the resistance of unopened mail on the mat when she pushed the door. It was dimly lit inside and had a musty, damp smell.

'It's four months since he died,' said Erika.

'The solicitor said he's been in twice since then to check on things, but nothing's been touched since the police left the crime scene.'

'Do we know if they took anything away?'

'No.'

'Find out.'

They stepped into the gloom. Bunches of coats hung on the left-hand wall, which they had to squeeze past. A staircase was at the end of the hallway on the right-hand side. The hair on the back of Erika's neck prickled, and she felt alert to something. She glanced at McGorry, and he looked uneasy. Erika opened the door directly ahead. It was filled with furniture, and the curtains were closed. She skirted around the dark shapes and found a curtain pull. The curtains parted, flooding the room with light. A long row of windows looked out over a patio, a row of bushes, and on the other side, the river Thames, the water brown and sludgy.

'I didn't know he lived right on the Thames Path,' said McGorry.

'That wall of bushes is very low. It would be easy for someone to jump over.'

They turned to look at the living room. It was filled with dusty old sofas with tassels, and the walls were lined with creaking bookshelves. An ancient boxy Trinitron television was on wheels in one corner. Piled on top were newspapers and magazines, and above it was a long shelf filled with VHS tapes.

A deep fireplace with a thick brick surround sat between the bookshelves. A piano in the corner was covered with old cheese plants in earthenware pots, dried out with brown leaves. Dust swirled in the shards of sunlight.

On the bookshelf next to the television was a row of small

black binders stamped on the side with Polaroid branding. Erika grabbed the first one, slid it out, and opened it. She was hoping to find Polaroid photos signed by Annabelle, but inside the plastic pouches were scores of what looked like casting photos; in each one, a young man stared straight into the camera, holding up a piece of paper with his name written in black marker.

McGorry came to join Erika. As she flicked through, the photos became more informal, and some of the men were pictured shirtless. Tucked into a flap at the back was a stack of photos of young, naked men posing, lying on a grimy pink-and-green-striped sofa.

'That's this sofa,' said McGorry. Erika had one knee on the sofa, resting the album on her leg. She stepped back, replaced the Polaroids in the back flap, and took another album from the shelf.

She flicked through similar casting shots. Again there was a stack of Polaroids stuffed in the back, which were more explicit. One showed a young man kneeling in front of an unidentified man, giving him oral sex. McGorry grimaced at seeing a black-haired guy with a beard lying on the bed and spreading his legs for the camera.

'What kind of stuff did this guy do the casting for?' he asked.

'Lots of UK television shows, commercials, and some films.'

'And these guys would do anything for a lucky break?'

'I wonder when these were taken – there are no dates on them.' Erika scanned the shelf and the one above; there were more than twenty of these photo albums. 'We need to get these all bagged up and taken away. And then we have to search the bookshelves.'

'What if this Annabelle only started to leave Polaroids at the second crime scene?' asked McGorry.

Erika looked around the cluttered room. Then she wrinkled her nose. 'What's that smell? It's like meat.' Next to the fireplace was a box of firewood and another box with some empty tins, and beside it was an old tray with a loaf of bread and a packet of half-eaten Tesco Finest Brussels pâté. Erika touched the packet of pâté. 'It's chilled. If it's four months since Terry was killed, where did these come from?'

They heard a creak from upstairs, and footsteps moved across the ceiling.

'Please don't let that be his ghost,' whispered McGorry. Erika put her finger to her lips, and they left the room.

The hallway outside was now brighter since they'd opened the curtains. They tiptoed down the corridor towards another door. Erika opened it. The kitchen sink was piled high with dirty dishes, and the tap dripped slowly. A row of pale, stained blinds was pulled down over the windows, but they were thin enough to let the light in.

They carried on along the corridor towards the staircase. The sound of footsteps moved across the ceiling. They stood still for a moment in silence, and then Erika heard the stairs creak as someone seemed to be going back up slowly.

'Who's there?' she called out. 'We are police officers. My name is Erika Foster, and this is my colleague, John McGorry. You are trespassing.'

There was another beat of silence, and then a very tall, thin man wearing faded jeans and a black sweater came down the stairs with his hands above his head. His face was thin and angular, and he had a thick black beard.

He had something shoved in his back pocket, protruding from under his sweater.

'What's that in your pocket?'

He reached down and pulled out a half-full bottle of Robinsons blackcurrant squash.

'It's not neat squash,' he said, speaking in a broad Scouse accent. 'I've diluted the last of it.' Erika couldn't work out how old he was. He seemed to defy age and sit somewhere between twenty and forty.

'Who are you?'

'Me name's Russel Milligan.'

'Why are you here?'

'I'm 'omeless. Well, I was 'omeless. I knew Terry. We 'ad an acquaintance. He was me boyfriend, of sorts, until someone offed him. I found out his place was still empty. I lived here. I didn't break in,' he said.

'Are you one of the guys he photographed?' asked McGorry.

This flipped a switch in Russel.

'How do you know about that?' he said, advancing on them and raising his voice. He stopped when he reached the bottom of the stairs, and from close up, Erika could smell him. Unwashed and greasy.

She put up her hand. 'It's okay. You're not in any trouble.'

'I hope not. It's not illegal, you know, to take sex pictures in private, between two consenting adults.'

'How well did you know Terry?'

'I told you. We were a couple, on and off.'

'We're investigating Terry's murder.'

'I didn't do it. I wasn't 'ere when Terry died. I was away doing a tour. I only learned about 'im being offed when I returned to London.'

'Have you got time to talk to us?' asked Erika.

'I've got all the time in the world.'

31

Russel Milligan seemed to enjoy the sound of his own voice, because he sat on one end of a long sagging sofa and answered their questions without hesitation.

'I've been living 'ere, on and off, for the past four months. I 'ave a key,' he said, producing it from his jeans pocket. 'Which Terry gave me, I 'asten to add, and never asked for it back, so you can't do me for breaking and entering. And I'll 'ave you know, I paid the last leccy bill, and the water bill. Over two hundred quid it was, too. They were threatening to cut them off.'

'Did Terry give anyone else a key?' asked Erika.

'The cleaner 'ad one. The solicitor has one. 'E probably dished them out to other boyfriends in the past. And 'e 'ad a proper casting assistant for a time.'

'How do you mean, proper?' asked Erika.

'This young woman. It was the only time 'e 'ad an actual proper person to do the job, and not some boyfriend.'

'What was her name?'

'Eve . . . Eva, Evie? Something with an *E*, I forget which.'

'When was this?'

'Three or four years ago. She didn't last long. Terry fell out with 'er over something silly.'

'Do you have any contact details for this woman?'

'No, but 'er number could be 'ere, somewhere amongst all this,' he said, waving his hands over the mess.

'We've seen the Polaroid photos in these folders,' said McGorry, still standing by the shelf. He indicated the rows of photo albums on the bookshelves.

'Yes. Casting photos.'

'And the ones stuffed in the back?'

'Also casting photos. Into that, are you?'

'I'm straight.'

'That's what they all say, and a couple of bevvies later, their clothes are off and they're wearing their ankles as earrings.'

'A lot of these men look very *young*. And were you there, Russel, when these were taken? Holding the camera?' said McGorry.

Russel waggled his finger at the bookshelf. 'No, no, no. They were all consensual encounters. Check the photos. They've all got pubes. Terry was a stickler for that.'

Erika could see the distaste on McGorry's face, and she felt the same. 'Was Terry gay?' she asked.

'Is the pope a Catholic?' said Russel, flaring his nostrils and pursing his lips. He reached into the pocket of his jeans and took out a crumpled pack of cigarettes. He went to light one and dropped the lighter. Quick as a flash, Erika scooped it up off the floor.

'Now listen to me, Russel. You might think this is all hilarious and a performance, but we're dealing with a brutal murder. And you – well, shall we make a list? Sex with minors, creating explicit photos with minors.'

Erika was impressed that McGorry was making a big show of pulling on a pair of latex gloves. He shook out a substantial-sized clear plastic evidence bag from his pocket, went to the bookshelf, and slid the small Polaroid-branded albums into the bag. 'So I suggest you start taking our questions seriously.'

Russel blanched. He sat up straight. Erika handed him back the cigarette lighter. He lit up and was chaste for a moment. His hands were shaking, and his tone changed.

'Those men weren't underage. Terry always asked them for ID. They had to be over sixteen.'

'What kind of ID?' asked McGorry. He had filled the evidence bag with three of the albums and put them on the coffee table by the fire.

'Passport, driving licence,' he said insistently, his voice cracking.

'And if they didn't have that. What was it? You asked to see their last two utility bills?'

'Russel. Do you know the names of these men in the photos at the back?' asked Erika.

'Not all of them.'

'How did Terry find them?'

''E didn't find them. They found 'im. Terry was known in the business, and 'e was rich. I know this place doesn't look it. 'E would go out on the town a lot, to the London clubs, and flash the cash. There were always guys hanging around 'im. Terry also did that reality show a few years ago, where they were searching for the next soap star . . . I forget the name of it, but they were casting for a new family in that soap opera. It was like *The X Factor* for casting crappy TV.'

'What did these men get out of posing like this?' asked McGorry, holding up one of the photo albums with a young guy, naked, lying on his side on the sofa where Russel now sat.

'It was about the sex. The excitement,' said Russel, stubbing the butt of his cigarette out in an overflowing ashtray on the coffee table. He put his hand to his mouth, and his face creased. 'I know what this looks like. But it wasn't all . . . sordid. It's been tough, you know. Losing 'im.'

Erika sat on the end of the sofa, trying to push out the image of all the naked butts which had sat on there before. She decided to ask the next question outright.

'Have you seen any Polaroid photos in this house signed with the name Annabelle?'

'What? No. Terry never photographed girls. Women.'

Erika looked back at the windows overlooking the Thames Path and the river.

'This doesn't seem a very safe spot,' she said, pointing. 'Have you ever had trouble with burglaries?'

Russel followed her gaze, seeming to see the view for the first time.

'Not that I know of. The Thames Path on the other side is a good two meters lower than the 'eight of the garden there.'

'It says in the police report that a cleaner found Terry's body.'

'Yes.'

'Do you know the cleaner?'

He nodded. 'Yes. She was with Terry for years. Bev.'

'Did you talk to Bev after Terry died?'

'Yeah.'

'Did Bev know how Terry's killer broke in?'

'No. And there was no sign of a break-in. The police told 'er Terry must have let the person in.'

'Do you know where Bev is now?'

Russel took a deep breath and looked towards the window.

'She was sacked.'

'By who?'

'By the company, or should I say the solicitors, who've been tasked to try and work out what to do with Terry's estate. If no dependents are found, it will be auctioned off, and the money will go to the state . . . It's like *Downton Abbey*. They're trying to find some distant cousin or someone, but they haven't had any luck. I should have married 'im.'

'Can you give us Bev's phone number?'

'I can, but you won't get an answer. Bev died of a 'eart attack just after Christmas.'

'What about the other people in Terry's life?'

'You're looking at 'im. Terry had a work life, which was far more superficial. And then 'e had his private life. Me. Bev. 'Is mother, when she was alive.'

'What happened to Terry's phone?'

'The police took it.'

The room fell silent, and there was just the crackle of the plastic evidence bags as McGorry packed up the rest of the Polaroid albums.

'I'd like to have a look at the kitchen,' Erika said.

Russel sat hunched over with his packet of cigarettes, and he nodded. They left the living room and went down the corridor to the kitchen. Dirty plates were strewn across the surface. The windows were caked with grime, and weak grey light was attempting to shine through.

Like the living room, the kitchen was an Aladdin's cave, with three wooden Welsh dressers piled high with dying plants, cookbooks, and pots and pans.

'The police looked through everything,' said Russel. 'It was odd. It was the first time I'd seen a house look tidier after it was turned over by the authorities. Bev had a bit of a clean-up, too.'

McGorry went to the ancient, rusting fridge and opened it. The bottom two shelves were filled with jars of pickles and condiments, and the top shelf was stacked with boxes of Polaroid film. Erika peered inside and took one of the slim boxes out. It contained Polaroid Colour i-Type film, and each film was for eight photos. Several loose boxes were lined up on the shelf at the front, and then a big batch of the film was wrapped in cellophane.

'Terry got through quite a lot of Polaroid film?' asked McGorry.

'Yes. For castings,' said Russel. "E bought in bulk, as a business expense – it was all above board.'

McGorry closed the fridge door. Erika looked around. She stepped over a pile of dirty laundry and bed-sheets. There was something on the Welsh dresser next to the Aga. It was a small square girl's jewellery box. It was white with silver stars, and the silver paint had rubbed off in places.

'Do you know where this came from?' she asked.

'No. I thought it might be Terry's mother's, but she was a classy old bird. She wouldn't 'ave 'ad some teenage girl's jewellery box. I know the police dusted it for prints like they did everything. Bev filled a Hoover bag with that powder they use.'

Erika lifted it off the shelf and opened the lid. It was the type which had a tiny ballerina who turned if you wound it up. The inlay was some synthetic material to look like velvet, and it was scratched inside. Erika found the flat winding key with its smooth curved edges on the underside of the box and turned it once. The twinkling tone of "Dance of the Sugar Plum Fairy" from The Nutcracker sang out, and the tiny ballerina turned, the manic grin painted on her little plastic face. There was something about it that made Erika shudder. Why did young boys get tanks, trucks, and things that moved and built? And all girls got were dolls and stupid ballerinas who went round and round, looking pretty, doing nothing?

She went to put it back, but a strange thought went through her head – the memory of a thriller film. Erika never had one of these jewellery boxes when she was little, but she felt around the lining at the back of the lid, got her nail under the synthetic material, and pulled. It came away with a pop. Behind the false backing, there was a small white envelope.

'Shit, shit,' said McGorry, fumbling in his coat pocket for

another pair of latex gloves. He handed them to Erika, and in her excitement, they got stuck as she pulled them on. McGorry found a clean knife and handed it to her.

Taking care to hold the envelope at the edges, she used the tip of the knife to open the flap.

She put the knife down and pulled out a stack of three Polaroids.

They were photos of an older man tied up on a grubby mattress. In the first Polaroid, he was bound with rope in the same fashion as Neville Lomas. In the second, he was staring at the camera with a dazed look on his face, and in the third, he had a sex toy shoved down his throat, and his eyes were wide open.

The Polaroids were signed, using the same black marker pen:

ANNABELLE

32

They took two trips to carry the Polaroid albums in their evidence bags to the car. Erika felt a surge of adrenaline. They had another set of Polaroids. She could now link the three murders. They also had the jewellery box in an evidence bag.

'What do we do about this place and him?' asked McGorry. The wind had ceased outside the house, and Erika could hear the sound of the river on the other side of the building.

'I want forensics to come and have another look. The Polaroids were missed in the jewellery box.'

'Do you want to see if I can get him into emergency accommodation?' asked McGorry.

Russel appeared from the alleyway, wearing a long grubby houndstooth coat and huge sunglasses.

'Where are you going?' asked Erika.

'For a mooch; I'll knock on some friends' doors. I 'ave a few favours I can call in,' he said.

'Can you give me your phone number?'

Russel sighed and gave Erika his number, which she jotted down in her notebook.

'Can we give you a lift?' asked McGorry.

'No. I like to walk. I'm going to get a coffee and read the paper. Gather my thoughts.'

They watched as Russel went off down the road, seeming not to be in a hurry. Erika had a strange feeling. Not entirely of envy, but . . . She couldn't remember the last time she went for coffee without a plan or an idea of what she would do next. She shook the thought away.

The Polaroids. She had the Polaroids. She had a mandate to continue this investigation and hold her head high.

Erika reconvened her team that afternoon in the incident room. They had renewed energy, and she felt she had them on her side, but she was wary of how to approach the investigation into Neville Lomas, after her visit.

'We now have nine Polaroids,' said Erika, indicating them projected up on the whiteboard at the back of the incident room. 'I don't like to make assumptions, but this Annabelle looks to be playing the long game. She's spent the past four months watching and waiting for us to find the Polaroids hidden at the Terry DeVille crime scene. She didn't hide them at the Neville Lomas and Jamie Teague crime scenes, and she changed her modus operandi. At the last two crime scenes, she put them in a white envelope in the pockets of the victims' clothes . . . At Terry DeVille's house they were hidden. We've had these Polaroids tested, but like the others, there are no fingerprints.'

'Do we have anything from the media appeal yesterday? Did any of the five women get in contact with us?'

'Not yet,' said Moss, holding up a sheaf of papers. 'There are all the usual suspects – the conspiracy theorists and the time-wasters. The guy who always calls and says he was responsible for killing Princess Diana left his usual message. We're also dealing with a significant number of women and a couple of men who state that they were sexually assaulted by Jamie Teague.'

'I saw that the press conference generated a lot of heat around his previous acquittal for rape on social media,' Erika said.

'Yes. We've been advised that we need to refer all of these to another department in the CPS; we obviously need to take all of these seriously, but it will take us some time to work through everything.'

'Okay. Use all the staff you need to get through things quickly. What about CCTV?'

Crane put up his hand.

'That would be me, the one with square eyes,' he said. 'And Peterson.'

'Two sets of square eyes,' said Peterson.

'Yesterday afternoon, we had a huge data dump from Chelsea and Westminster's CCTV systems for the Soho area, and we've been working through it all.'

'Haven't actually been home,' added Peterson.

'I can see you're both quite chipper despite pulling an all-nighter?' asked Erika.

'Yes. We've started to trace these five young women's route before they met Jamie Teague and his mates,' said Crane. He tapped a couple of buttons on his laptop, and a view of central London appeared from Google Maps. 'Okay, so the young women travelled to the club in a taxi but didn't get dropped at Red Velvet. The taxi dropped them off on Old Compton Street opposite the Prince Edward Theatre . . .' Crane pressed a button, and a window with a CCTV clip from a lamp-post opposite appeared over the map. It was good quality. The road was bustling and brightly lit with coloured lights. The five 'glitch in the matrix girls' exited the taxi and stood on the pavement as the final girl to emerge leaned inside to pay the driver. Erika watched the other women as they waited. They were all wearing black gloves.

'They don't seem very excited to be on a night out,' said Erika. 'Look, they're all standing morosely on the pavement, not talking to each other.'

'They could have argued in the taxi,' said Dahlia, speaking for the first time. 'I've still got my group of girlfriends from school. We're close, but when we go out together and have a few drinks, there is always some kind of bickering.'

Erika tilted her head and watched the video as the five women moved along the pavement. The taxi pulled forward.

'And there. *Bam*,' said Crane, pausing the video. He zoomed in on the taxi.

'And we have a clear number-plate. Good work,' said Erika.

'It was a registered hackney carriage, so I've been able to trace the driver,' said Peterson. 'Samuel Rocanoe is the name of the driver. I left a message a couple of hours ago. Just waiting for a response. We've also requested the CCTV from inside the taxi, hoping it's one of the more modern taxis equipped with it.'

'Bloody hell, good work,' said Erika.

'We do have more,' said Crane. Another video window appeared over the map on the screen. 'Our group of young women walk past the theatre and G-A-Y nightclub. They go to G-A-Y, but before that, they all go into the international newsagent a couple of doors down.'

They watched the women move away from the first camera on the lamp-post and then walk into range of another camera opposite the newsagent. This video was more blurred than the first. Outside the newsagent, there were racks of magazines and piles of newspapers. The girls all filed into the newsagent.

'They stay inside for two minutes,' said Crane. The people streaming past on the road and pavements suddenly whizzed by as he forwarded the video. The women all filed out at normal speed.

'None of them have magazines or anything else you might suspect, like a drink or even cigarettes,' said Peterson.

'Unless they put whatever they bought in their bags,' said Erika.

'And then they go into G-A-Y nightclub,' said Crane.

'One of them is clutching her head,' said Erika as they watched the women double back and join the short queue waiting to go into the G-A-Y gay club.

'They could have gone inside that newsagent to buy painkillers,' said Dahlia.

'True,' said Erika.

'But if one of them bought painkillers, wouldn't they have to buy a drink to take the pills?' asked Peterson.

'Not necessarily. I get terrible cramps every month, and I'm so used to taking painkillers, I can swallow them dry,' said Dahlia.

Erika noticed Moss and another couple of women on the team nod in sympathy.

'It could have been cigarettes or painkillers they bought . . . or drugs,' said Erika. 'This international newsagent could be selling other stuff under the counter . . . What do they do next?'

'Okay, so they go into G-A-Y, where they stay for the next forty minutes,' said Crane. 'I've put the next clips of video together.' He minimised both video screens and then pulled up two more. 'There are two more cameras which caught their journey to Red Velvet. They left G-A-Y at 11.14 pm, walked up Old Compton Street, took a right onto Frith Street, and then were out of range as they took another left onto Romilly Street.'

Old Compton Street was now much busier than it had been an hour earlier, and it was difficult to make out much as the women moved through the throngs. They watched as the women passed the CCTV camera at the top of Frith Street.

'And then we have them arriving at Red Velvet, going down

the alleyway to the front entrance,' said Peterson as the clip of CCTV from Red Velvet's camera played.

'They still look bloody miserable,' said Erika. 'Like they're going to work . . . This is excellent work, guys.'

'Now we have this focal point of when they arrived, we're going to try and work backwards where they took the taxi from when we get in contact with the driver,' said Crane.

'There is no joy on the CCTV from Southwark Council on the night when Neville Lomas died. Everything from the cameras around his apartment on the Embankment is deleted every thirty-one days.'

'I thought that would be the case,' said Erika, and she hated that secretly she felt a little relieved. 'I don't know how much luck we'll have with CCTV close to where Terry DeVille lives, but see what you can do. Okay. How did we get on with the Folger name? Jamie Teague's friend Leon saw the name when one of the girls opened her handbag.'

'It's a costume hire warehouse,' said Dahlia.

'Where?' asked Erika.

'They have a big place in Acton in West London. They hire costumes for film and TV shoots. I've been contacting them, but no one is picking up.'

Erika looked around the room at the team and then back at the final image of the women frozen under the CCTV camera outside Red Velvet.

'That could be it. Costumes. They're wearing costumes.'

33

Erika decided to take Dahlia with her to visit Folger Costume Hire. She wanted to get to know her better, worrying she'd been too harsh to judge. She also wanted to loop back and pick her brains about the Neville Lomas case.

The drive out of Lewisham had been hectic through Camberwell and Peckham, and Dahlia had helped Erika navigate. It was only when they were driving along the river towards Battersea that the traffic was smooth, and an awkward silence fell over the car.

'How are you getting on? Are you settling in with the team?' asked Erika.

'Yeah. Everyone's been nice.'

She had this habit of running her fingers through her long hair and fluffing it up. Dahlia did that now and looked out the window.

'Can I talk to you about the Neville Lomas murder?' asked Erika. Dahlia smoothed her hair down and turned back to Erika.

'What about it?' There was caution in her voice.

'Did you feel like the murder investigation had any strange

elements?' There was a long silence. 'Did anything seem odd? Anything you say to me is confidential.'

'Is it?' asked Dahlia, looking over at her. Erika thought about how tired she looked. Tired but still very beautiful.

'Yes. You are on my team now, and I look after my officers.'

'I didn't think you liked me.'

'A lot of people think that. The night at the OXO Tower, I was the first officer on the scene when Neville Lomas's body was found. Then you arrived with the other officer . . .'

'Glenn.'

'Yes. I asked you to start door-to-door inquiries, but you took it upon yourself to call in Dan Fisk over my head—' Dahlia opened her mouth to protest. 'I'm not angry with you. I just want to know why you did that. Was it of your own accord?'

Dahlia turned to her. 'I thought you knew?'

'Knew what?'

'Knew that Dan had a special interest.'

Erika took a deep breath. 'What was Dan's special interest?'

'He told us when we were on the beat. We'd been told to keep a lookout around the OXO Tower apartments.'

'As a beat officer, you're supposed to keep a lookout.'

'No. A *specific* lookout. The month before, around Christmas, there was an incident where a young woman, covered in blood, bruised, was found wandering along the Embankment.'

Erika gripped the steering wheel. 'Were you on duty?'

'No. Another officer found her. He had her taken to the hospital, and she wanted to press charges against Neville Lomas. She said he beat her up. She was from an escort agency, and Neville Lomas said she had attacked *him*.'

Erika could feel the floor of the car sinking under her.

'And then what happened?'

'The woman discharged herself before we could take a statement, and she vanished.'

'What about the escort agency? She *was* from an agency?' asked Erika.

'The company says they provide secretarial services,' said Dahlia uncomfortably.

Erika snorted. Dahlia hesitated.

'They offer those services for a lot of high-profile people. Politicians. Some other famous people.'

'Were you asked to keep it quiet, what happened with Neville Lomas and this young woman, and cover this up?'

'No. Not to cover it up. We still don't know the young woman's real name. And she discharged herself before it could go any further.'

'I didn't see anything on record about this. Why didn't you mention this before or in the incident room?'

Erika could see Dahlia was getting stressed and defensive.

'I thought you knew. You're top brass. You're my senior officer.'

'Okay, so after this incident with the young woman, did Dan Fisk ask you to call him if anything else happened at Neville Lomas's flat?'

'Yes. It was an order. Dan Fisk was my senior—'

'Officer, yes. Now I am your senior officer, Dahlia . . . So what happened when Neville Lomas died? Did anyone go back to that same agency that provides secretarial services?'

'No.'

'Why not?'

'The incident room never got up and running. Neville Lomas's death was quickly ruled as misadventure. The case was over and done within a couple of days. They put the statement out in the press about him dying. That was it. So, you didn't know about all this?'

'No. I was taken off the case, or the case was never mine. Do you remember the name of the agency that provided secretarial services?'

'It was . . . Diamond Companions.'

'Which sounds both classy and seedy at the same time.'

Erika thought back to when she'd left a message with Dan Fisk. Monday. Why hadn't he called her back?

'Are you still in contact with Superintendent Fisk?'

'No.'

'Not even to text, or on social media?'

Dahlia turned to Erika and repeated, defiantly, 'No.'

They were interrupted by the satnav telling them that they had reached their destination.

They pulled up at a long corrugated warehouse building with a drop-down barrier and a tiny glass booth, where an elderly man sat reading the *Daily Sport*.

Erika stopped at the glass booth and wound down her window. He glanced up at her through rheumy eyes. He had the longest eyebrows Erika had seen, though his nose hair was giving them a run for their money.

'Folger Costume Hire?' she said, holding up her warrant card. The old man pressed a button, and the barrier popped up. 'Which building is it?'

'Go left,' was all he said. Erika drove through the barrier. The vast car park was empty, and weeds grew in the cracks at the edges.

'Acton. It used to be quite a big hub for TV production,' said Dahlia as Erika drove close to the main entrance and parked the car.

'Yeah?'

'My dad used to work for the BBC. There used to be a huge rehearsal room complex in Acton. They'd rehearse all the sitcoms and TV shows there. They demolished it a few years ago, and now it's flats.'

'What did your mum do?'

'She was a model before she had me and my brother. Catalogue stuff mainly, but she started doing Page Three – which I'm completely against.'

'When I first came to the UK, I was shocked by Page Three,' said Erika. 'We didn't have anything like it at home. Especially during communism.'

'As I said. I'm *completely* against it,' repeated Dahlia. She unbuckled her belt. The conversation was over. Erika watched Dahlia get out of the car. It troubled her that she hadn't thought to say anything about Neville Lomas. If Erika had been a young officer in her shoes, she'd have said something. She'd have questioned things and not just sat back and assumed that Erika knew. She would have to keep her eye on Dahlia. It was always the stupid people who were so sure of themselves. Erika hated having someone on her team that she couldn't trust completely, and couldn't rely on. Maybe she would have to find a way to fix that.

Erika unclipped her seat belt and joined Dahlia as she walked across the car park. They went to the main entrance, and the building looked empty. There was a list of companies next to a buzzer, and Erika found the button for Folger.

'Yes,' said a voice through the intercom. And Erika explained who they were and that they wanted to ask a few questions about some clothing hired. 'Go to the back,' said the voice. A moment later, the door clicked and popped open.

34

They walked through a long corridor with glass windows, looking into empty offices. Rows and rows of long communal office desks were bare and covered with dust and pieces of rubbish. At the end of the corridor was a small white door with FOLGER COSTUME HIRE LTD written on a sign.

A woman with long red, curly hair opened the door. She looked in her fifties and wore a long coat covered in a pattern of red roses with blue dungarees and a purple jumper. Her hair was tied up in a length of blue material.

'Are you really the police?' she asked. Erika and Dahlia showed her their warrant cards.

'What's your name, please?'

'Rah, spelled *R-A-haitch*. Rah Zahora. Come in . . . I'm not used to people coming around this way.'

'What other way is there?' asked Erika as they stepped inside.

'We have the loading bay on the main road,' she said, pointing over her shoulder with her thumb. 'This door never gets used.'

Rah led them down a short, brightly lit corridor to another door, which slid back, opening into a vast warehouse with a very high ceiling. It was freezing cold and smelt of dust and body odour. Racks and racks of costumes filled the space; in some places, they were two racks high. Erika turned to Dahlia, who raised an eyebrow.

'My office is through here,' said Rah, leading them through the racks. The aisles were so narrow that Erika felt her shoulder brush against some coarse material of what looked like caveman outfits.

'So, you're a fancy dress hire company?' asked Erika as the racks changed to rows and rows of shoes stacked on shelves.

'Wash your mouth out with soap and water,' she said with mock indignation. 'I supply costumes for film and TV . . . Some people sometimes come to borrow stuff for parties, but they tend to be in the industry. I'm not the kind of place for the acrylic-wig-and-naughty-nurse's-outfit crowd.'

They reached a wooden door, which was ajar. Inside was a small, cosy office. A messy desk was next to an oversized, squishy tartan-checked sofa, and under the desk was a gangly, doe-eyed greyhound lying under a knitted blanket. He gave a half-hearted growl.

'Wolsey, be nice. This is the police,' said Rah. Wolsey yawned and sat up. Erika looked around the room and saw one wall covered in a mishmash of actors' photos, some pinned on top of older ones curling up at the edges. Wolsey yawned again and lay back down, closing his eyes. A space heater was on, and it bathed the room in warmth and a red glow.

'It's always bloody freezing in here,' said Rah, seeing Erika looking at the heater. 'Would you like tea or coffee?'

Erika and Dahlia both asked for coffee. Rah indicated they should sit on the sofa.

'We're here to ask about some costumes you may have lent out,' said Erika.

'Okay. Well, that's what I do,' said Rah, checking a line of grubby-looking mugs and picking two. Erika took out her phone and found a close-up photo of one of the handbags the five girls were carrying in the CCTV video.

'It's a black handbag. Five bags, potentially,' said Erika, ready with her phone.

'Small black evening bags?' asked Rah, turning from loading a capsule into the little coffee machine next to the printer.

'Yes.'

Rah pressed a button, and the coffee machine began to whirr and fill the first cup. Wolsey growled and barked at the low humming sound the device made.

'Shush. Sorry, it's the new machine. He doesn't like the noise.'

Wolsey gave a little bark of agreement and lay back down.

Rah took Erika's phone and peered at the photo. 'Yeah. The black clutch bags were rented along with the black lace dresses and black gloves . . . What do they have to do with you guys?'

She returned Erika's phone and began loading up the second capsule.

'We think that one of these women was responsible for the murder of Jamie Teague.'

Rah froze with her hand holding another mug. 'Seriously?'

'Yes.'

She pressed the button on the coffee machine, and there was silence, broken only by the dog barking again. She handed them each a mug of coffee.

'I've just been looking at the story in the bloody newspaper,' she said, moving to her desk and picking up a copy of the *Sun*. She held it up to Erika and Dahlia. There was a lurid headline – even more lurid than Erika had expected: TEAGUE AND LOMAS MURDER LINK.

'I hadn't seen this,' said Erika, feeling slightly sick at the headline, and wondering what the man in the grey suit would think.

'I saw it this morning,' said Dahlia, shaking her head. Again,

Erika wondered why Dahlia hadn't mentioned this. And they'd been talking about the *Sun* newspaper in the car. Erika turned back to Rah.

'A group, this group, of young women were out with Jamie Teague and his friends, and one of them killed him when they returned to his apartment in Greenwich,' said Erika. She scanned the article and then turned to the second page. There was the CCTV photo of the 'glitch in the matrix girls' in the lift with Jamie Teague and his mates. And they had a montage of Neville Lomas photos; he was pictured speaking at the dispatch box in Parliament in a formal festive photo with his wife and two sons next to a Christmas tree. His two boys wore matching Christmas sweaters in this photo and shared his unfortunate piggish features. His wife was a tall, handsome woman with a strong jaw that didn't quite match her blonde feathered haircut, twin set, and pearls. The final photo showed him standing before a bookshelf in his office, beaming into the camera with tombstone-like teeth on display. Behind him on the shelf were desk diaries with dates going back thirty years.

Thank God they don't have the details of the Polaroids, thought Erika. 'Rah. What can you tell us about the person who hired the bags and the dresses?'

'She's a make-up artist,' said Rah. 'She was hiring them for a client.'

'What was her name?'

'Jessica Goldman.'

'How well do you know her?'

'Quite well, in work terms. She's been in the business for a long time. She mainly does prosthetics. Very talented. Oddly, she picked up the costumes for this gig, which isn't something she'd normally do. She said her client couldn't make it.'

'Did she tell you the client's name?'

'No. Why would she?'

'Okay. What kind of prosthetics?' asked Erika, her heart sinking at where this was headed.

'All kinds. Old-ageing make-up, injuries, sci-fi and fantasy stuff. You know, if someone is, for example, half-man, half-beast. She's always working. She's worked on make-up teams for some big films up at Leavesden and Pinewood Studios. That's where I've bumped into her before, when I've been transporting costumes.'

'What kind of make-up did this client want?' asked Erika.

Rah sighed and looked back at the newspaper, and she saw the CCTV photo of the five women. 'You've got to be . . . joking.'

'What?' asked Erika. Rah was quiet and held her hand to her mouth. Dahlia stared at her. 'What is it?'

'Jessica . . . She said the women on this gig were going to a casting for a reality show where they had to look like five sisters – sisters who all looked alike. She said it was a group of friends who were applying for this reality show.'

Rah picked up the newspaper and peered closely at the photos.

'And Jessica believed them?'

'Why wouldn't she? I think they hired her for half a day. And you're saying that one of these women killed Jamie Teague?' she said, tapping the paper with her finger.

'We think so. What kind of prosthetic make-up did Jessica say she did for these women?' asked Erika. Rah put down the newspaper, crouched down, and started to stroke the smooth grey fur on Wolsey's head. He looked balefully up at them.

'I'm sorry . . . It's just a lot to take in. It sounded like a fun, lucrative job for Jessica . . . She needed the extra money – her rent keeps going up. She lives in Kensington of all places . . . What was the question?'

'What kind of prosthetic make-up did Jessica do for these

women?' asked Erika, trying not to sound impatient. Rah patted Wolsey on the head and got up.

'The client wanted these girls to have prominent noses, like stereotypical South Europeans – can I say that? That's specifically what they asked her for. Does that make sense? And they all wanted the same hair. Long, dark, and curly. I provided the wigs and the dresses. And the contact lenses. I know Jessica didn't have any spare. We do all kinds of contact lenses. Oh, and they wanted teeth – prominent white teeth. Hollywood white teeth. I don't know where she got those from . . .' Rah stopped and turned to look at Erika. 'How did you know to come and ask me?'

'One of the women had your company's name in her handbag,' said Dahlia, speaking for the first time. 'It was spotted by one of Jamie Teague's mates.'

'Shit. Wow.'

'When did Jessica return the costumes?' asked Erika.

Rah perched on the edge of her desk, and she looked suddenly very scared.

'She didn't. They were due yesterday. It's very odd for her not to return something.'

'Can you give us her contact details?'

Rah looked between Erika and Dahlia. 'Do you think something has happened to her? Like I said, she was supposed to bring all the stuff back yesterday. It's not like I don't trust her. She could have been called away to do a last-minute job . . .'

Erika didn't like this, and despite the space heater next to her, she felt a sudden chill roll over her shoulders and she got goose bumps.

'If you can just give us all her details, it would be very helpful.'

35

'Jessica Goldman isn't answering her phone,' said Erika when she and Dahlia returned to the empty car park. It was now raining, and they hurried to get into the car.

Erika sat for a moment, listening to the rain hammer the roof. If Jessica had been hired to put prosthetic make-up on Annabelle and the other women in the group, it would mean Jessica saw Annabelle's real identity up close. And as a make-up artist, she would have studied her features for a long time. Erika called into control, asking them to send a squad car round to Jessica's Kensington flat. Then she tried Jessica's mobile again.

'She's a grown woman. She just might not be answering her phone?' said Dahlia.

Erika regarded her, sitting in the passenger seat and scrolling through Instagram on her phone. The lack of interest in this situation made Erika want to shake her. 'What would I do without your powers of detection?'

'Sorry, what was that?' Dahlia asked, looking up from her phone.

'Nothing. It's only four or five miles from here to Kensington. Let's go and meet the officers there.'

'Yeah. That's the best idea,' Dahlia said, and she did that thing with her hair again, running her fingers through it, which was rapidly becoming annoying.

Erika started the engine, and they pulled off into the rainstorm.

When they arrived at Scarsdale Villas twenty minutes later, the rain was hammering harder on the car roof, and there were roiling black clouds above the red-bricked terraced houses. The storm had darkened the sky so much that the street lights outside Jessica Goldman's building flickered on.

A lone police car sat outside, and as Erika pulled in behind, she could see the entrance to the building was propped open – never a good sign.

The smell of a decaying body hit them first in the communal hallway, and when they reached the open door to flat two, they saw a woman lying face-down just inside the door. The back of her head was a matted mess of congealing blood, and a monkey wrench lay on the floor beside her, wrapped in bloodied plastic. It was hot inside, and the air was alive with flies humming and crawling over the body and the blood spatter on the walls. A police officer appeared from one of the rooms.

He had the crook of his arm over his mouth and nose against the smell. Erika and Dahlia showed their warrant cards.

'Yes. Is this Jessica Goldman?' asked Erika, trying to breathe through her mouth.

'I don't know. I haven't made an ID,' he replied.

Erika knelt beside the body, pulled on a pair of latex gloves, and checked the woman's pockets. She found an iPhone in the right-hand pocket and held it up. The lock screen was activated with a long list of missed calls and alerts. Erika's number was listed twice.

'Do you have an evidence bag?' she asked Dahlia, who had her hand over her mouth.

'No.'

'I do,' said the officer, pulling a bag from a pouch on his utility belt. He held it out, and Erika dropped the phone inside. She then gently turned the body over. The woman's face was frozen in a grimace of pain and streaked with dried blood. There was a deep indentation in the centre of her forehead.

'We'll need a formal ID, but that's her mobile, and this is her flat,' said Erika, still supporting the body. Flies crawled over the woman's face, and Erika waved them away. Blood had soaked into the porous wooden floor, and Erika followed the arc of blood spatter up the walls to the mirror above the hall table.

Erika got up and moved carefully along the hallway. Directly opposite was a bathroom, which didn't have a window. A toilet and the edge of the bath and a shower curtain sat in the gloom. To her right was a bedroom, and to the left was a combined living room and kitchen. Both rooms looked like they'd been ransacked. Drawers had been turned out. Paperwork, folders, and books littered the floor in the living area. Clothes, cosmetics, and paperwork were also strewn across the bed and the bedroom floor. In the kitchen, the long table was covered with what looked like the paraphernalia of Jessica Goldman's work: pieces of prosthetic foam and latex in the shapes of noses, ears and bottles in all shapes and sizes, brushes, make-up, and several white Styrofoam heads. A desktop computer on a trolley in the corner had been turned over, and the screen lay on its side with the screensaver still glowing. Flies crawled up the bloodied walls, and one buzzed along the ceiling. Erika pulled out her phone and took quick shots of the living room, the bedroom, and the body in the hallway. 'Please, ma'am, we need to get out of here so we don't disturb anything for forensics,' said the police officer.

He was standing in the hallway outside the front door with Dahlia. Erika resisted the urge to look around the flat. She stepped carefully around the body and out into the corridor. 'Have you called forensics?'

'Yes. ETA one hour. Traffic, apparently.'

'Do you know who's on call?'

'No.'

'How did you get in?'

'I had to force the door open.'

'So, no sign of a break-in?'

'No.'

The rain was now roaring on the roof, and the cool air coming from the open door was welcome in the hallway. Erika's phone rang, and she saw it was Moss.

'What's that noise?' Moss asked.

Erika raised her voice. 'The rain.'

'Where are you? Did you say you were going to Acton?' asked Moss.

'I'm in Kensington, we've found—'

'Listen. I've just heard Marsh has a meeting at the Palace of Westminster with the chief whip about Neville Lomas. I just got a call from someone saying that your name is confirmed for security clearance, and that the meeting-room has been changed from 1a to 12b. The only problem is that the meeting is in thirty minutes.'

'What?' asked Erika, her blood running cold. 'I didn't know a meeting had been scheduled.' She checked her watch. It was three. A meeting with the chief whip in Parliament was a big deal. The chief whips were responsible for getting MPs to vote in line with party policy, and they knew everything about their MPs. Every bit of controversy and dirt. Erika thought back to the lurid newspaper headlines with Neville Lomas, and felt sick. What would happen if she was expected at this meeting and then didn't turn up? The tube journey from Kensington High Street to Westminster was just over twenty minutes. 'Can you text me all the details – I'm going to run and try and make that meeting,' said Erika. She ended the call. The police officer had now closed the front door to the crime scene, but the stench of death was still in the air, and some of the flies had escaped and now circled the ceiling light in the hallway. 'Dahlia, can you drive?' It was an odd question to have to ask a fellow police officer, but she wouldn't put it past Dahlia to be the only one on the force who couldn't.

'Yes.'

'Good, you need to drop me at High Street Kensington tube station, and then I need you to come back here to the crime scene and finish things up, and then take my car back to Lewisham Row. Okay?' Erika could hear a tremor in her voice, and her hands were shaking.

'Er. Okay. Yes.'

Erika took one of her business cards from her pocket and handed it to the young officer. 'Stay here and guard the door until forensics arrive. Please let me know about anything you find, and tell the forensics officers to contact me.'

'Use the side entrance when you get to High Street Ken,' said the officer. 'It's less busy.'

'Thank you,' said Erika, and then she and Dahlia hurried back out in the torrential rain.

36

Erika got drenched running the short distance across the road outside Kensington High Street tube station to catch the train. After vaulting the security barriers and showing her warrant card, she ran down the escalators to the platform. A District Line train was about to leave, and she slipped inside the carriage just as the doors closed.

She found a seat and slumped into it. Her leg muscles burned, and her heart was hammering. The seat opposite was empty, and when the train slid into the dark tunnel, she saw her face in the window. 'Haunted' was the word that best described her reflection. With hair plastered to her head, her gaunt face belied all her fear. Someone was messing with her. Why would they schedule a meeting, give her security clearance, and then not tell her? They, whoever they were, wanted her to feel afraid. Fear was the greatest weapon you could use to control someone.

Erika's phone vibrated. Moss had emailed her the details of the meeting. The Houses of Parliament and the Parliamentary Estate buildings were huge, and Moss had included a map attachment. The chief whip was a man called Richard Gaynor. He had a full head of dark hair cropped short and quite fashionably so. He was unlike the greasy male politicians she remembered seeing on TV in the early 1990s. The train seemed to crawl along, stopping at every station longer than necessary, even though very few people were getting on and off.

The train pulled into Westminster Tube station at 3.26 pm, with four minutes to go. After a blind dash up a never-ending escalator, Erika exited the station into the same lashing rainstorm on Westminster Bridge. The lights blazed yellow in the long, tall windows of the Houses of Parliament, and a strong wind roared up the river, causing the rain to beat her face. Squinting at the map again, Erika saw she had to go to the Cromwell Green entrance on the other side of the main Palace of Westminster building.

She finally arrived, out of breath, at the security checkpoint at 3.40 pm. Marsh was waiting farther down the line. Erika wiped her face and tried to do something with her hair, but she was soaking wet, as if she'd fallen into the Thames and been washed upstream from Kensington.

'Afternoon, sir,' said Erika, trying to compose herself and showing her warrant card to the man behind him.

Marsh turned and looked horrified to see her. He quickly recovered.

'Erika. You're here,' he said. He was as immaculate as ever and carrying a black umbrella.

'Your secretary let me know about the room change.'

'Did she?' His smile faltered. It was disturbing to think where she and Marsh had ended up. They'd started out as friends, even allies, when they were on the beat together in Manchester, and now she was an enemy. A problem. And yet, shouldn't they be on the same side and want the same thing?

'What is this meeting about? It's all been a bit sudden,' said Erika.

Marsh took a deep breath. 'Erm. There is some information

that the chief whip's office would like to share in strict confidence. And you were invited.'

'What information?'

'About . . . Neville Lomas,' he said quietly.

They reached the front of the security line and had to unload their belongings into plastic trays before going through the X-ray machine. They both showed their warrant cards, and a waiting secretary introduced herself on the other side. She looked curiously at Erika in her dripping-wet state.

'Here are your visitor passes. Please make sure they remain prominent about your person,' she said, handing them each a pass on the end of a lanyard.

They were taken down a long, gloomy corridor with strip lighting. A plain conference room had been booked, and when they arrived, Erika saw three other people waiting in the room, along with Richard Gaynor.

'Paul, it's good to see you again,' said Richard, getting up and pumping Marsh's hand enthusiastically.

Marsh is on first-name terms, thought Erika.

'And this is Detective Chief Inspector Erika Foster,' said Marsh, introducing them. He didn't pump her hand with quite the same enthusiasm but smiled briskly. Erika looked to the other three people, two rather grey and wan-looking older men in plain suits and a somewhat shiny-faced middle-aged woman with long, messy hair and an ill-fitting green dress. They didn't offer their names, and if they were surprised to see Erika, they didn't show it.

'I . . . We appreciate your time and that this is an extremely sensitive matter,' said Marsh, taking a seat at the head of the table. 'And I . . . We appreciate you meeting with us.' Erika took off her soaked coat, draped it over the chair next to Marsh, and sat. Marsh rubbed his chin, and his eyes darted about the room. *What's he nervous about?* thought Erika.

The men and woman studied them both as Richard touched his fingers to a folder on the desk in front of him.

'We understand you need to investigate the death of the right honourable Neville Lomas. We would like to offer, in confidence, some insight into a sensitive aspect of his life, which we believe will help inform the way you pursue those investigations.'

He spoke carefully, emphasising the weight of his words. Erika could feel the eyes of the two silent men and woman watching her. He paused and then continued.

'We don't believe that the information we wish to share with you has any connection to your investigations, but we believe you could benefit from our insight.'

Marsh was nodding along gravely.

'Of course. Thank you,' he said. Richard looked at Erika and seemed to want her to thank him as well. Much like a 'thank you' is expected from a small child offered sweets from a stranger.

'Yes, thank you,' murmured Erika. Richard nodded and then threw open the folder. He turned it and pushed it across the table towards them.

'This is Damsa Afridi,' he said, indicating an ID photo of a dark-haired young woman who looked to be in her early twenties. She was beautiful with very pale, flawless skin. She seemed to stare defiantly at the camera, as if looking into the room directly at them. 'Twenty-three years old. She is currently being held in an immigration detention centre awaiting deportation.' Richard leaned over and turned the page. There was a CCTV photo of Damsa, wearing tight jeans and a sleeveless T-shirt, in the foyer of Neville Lomas's apartment building next to the OXO Tower. He paged through more photos, which showed Neville Lomas walking along the Embankment with Damsa and then a picture of them getting into a car.

Erika looked at Marsh. She couldn't read his face. Did he know about this?

'How does this help my investigation?' asked Erika.

'We're not showing it to you to help your investigation. We're showing it to you because, at the time of Neville Lomas's death, he was being blackmailed by Damsa Afridi. She had been working as a prostitute whom Neville hired. And she became pregnant with his child.'

Erika heard Dahlia's voice saying, 'I think the preferred term is "sex worker".'

Richard turned the page to show a photo of Damsa walking along a London street with a swollen belly.

'When were these photos taken?' asked Erika. 'And are they all CCTV? There's no date stamp.'

Richard leaned over, slid the file back across the desk, and closed it. 'Damsa Afridi is an illegal immigrant in this country. She was working as a prostitute, who Neville Lomas hired and then made pregnant. This came to light just two days before Neville Lomas was murdered.'

'I'm working on the theory that Neville Lomas was potentially killed by a sex worker. And this potential sex worker's method of killing, links Neville Lomas's death to the death of Jamie Teague, and a third victim, Terry DeVille, who just came to light.'

Richard shook his head.

'No. We don't believe that Damsa Afridi had anything to do with the death of Neville Lomas. What we're concerned about is that she was blackmailing him. And she remains a risk. The media would have a field day if they knew, what with the party's stance on immigration and the current media narrative on immigration.'

'So, what are you asking?'

'We're not asking anything,' said Richard, glancing across at the woman and the two men who remained silent. 'We are sharing an insight with you and asking that you ensure the scope of your investigation doesn't deviate.'

'May I ask some questions?'

Wordlessly, the woman sitting at the end of the row opened a brown Manila file in front of her, removed a sheet of paper, and handed it to Richard. He held it out to Marsh, but Erika leaned over and took it. In small type at the top of the page was the name of an escort agency, Diamond Companions; underneath it were a mobile phone number and the name Marie.

'The person listed here can help with all your inquiries concerning your investigation.'

'Who is she? There's no surname.'

'Erika. Do you really believe anyone working in one of these agencies will give you their real name? You have my word that this contact is genuine.'

'And she knows what we discussed and has been briefed to talk to me?'

'She knows that a police officer will call to make specific inquiries about one of their employees on the night of January 13. That's all she will discuss.'

'What do you know about the night of January 13?' asked Erika. 'You seem to know everything. Is Damsa Afridi the same sex worker who Neville Lomas assaulted, and left with a bloody nose? Who was found walking along the Embankment late at night?'

'That was a separate incident, Erika, and the young woman vanished before the police were able to take a statement so she could press charges.'

'The incident hasn't been logged in the HOLMES system.'

For the first time Richard seemed to lose his cool. 'The young woman vanished before the police were able to take a . . .'

'Erika Foster is your married name; before that, you were Erika Bole-diš-ova,' said the woman, speaking for the first time. 'You were born in Nitra, Slovakia. Your father, Branislav, was a Communist Party member. He worked in the Plastika factory until he died in an accident in the factory in 1980, when you were eight. Your mother had relationships with three men between 1980 and 2005, none of whom you or your sister, Lenka, approved of. She worked in the same factory and died of alcoholism in 2005.' Erika stared, unable to hide her shock. 'We make a point of knowing everything, Erika. We know everything about Neville Lomas. And we know everything about you . . . We have invited you today as a courtesy. You need to understand that we are dealing with things well above your pay grade. You should be grateful for our help, and I advise you to refrain from pursuing any inquiries outside of what we've discussed.'

Erika thought back to what Dahlia had told her about the night the sex worker escaped from Neville Lomas's apartment, bloody and bruised. Were these people involved in covering that up? Or did this young woman really manage to evade the police before they could get more details?

'I didn't catch your name?' said Erika to the woman. 'I make a point of knowing the names of the people threatening me.'

'Jesus, Erika!' snapped Marsh.

The woman regarded her coldly for a beat and then pushed her chair out and stood. The two men followed.

'Good afternoon,' she said, and they all left the room. Richard seemed to relax a little when the door closed behind them.

Marsh blew out his cheeks and sat back. 'We really appreciate this, Richard. This is very helpful.'

Richard opened another folder on the desk in front of him. 'I'll need you both to sign to say you won't share any of the information we've just discussed.'

Erika could see that they would be signing a form regarding the Official Secrets Act governing Crime and Special Investigation powers. Marsh seized the pen and signed without reading. He held it out to Erika, and she took it, feeling sick. Why had she brought up the details of the second woman? As Erika signed, Richard stood up and clasped Marsh's hands when they shook.

'I hope this helps you to stop that bitch,' he said. For a split second, Erika wondered if he was talking about her or the serial killer.

37

The rainstorm had intensified when they emerged from the Cromwell Green entrance. Erika wasn't any drier than when she'd arrived, but her body had warmed the soaked material of her clothes. A strange long-ago recollection of wetting the bed came back to her – age five or six, waking up and her pyjamas being wet and warm. She shook the horrible memory away.

Erika and Marsh huddled under the awning, peering hopefully at the dark sky and the rain pouring down. She felt the cold air on her collar, and shivered.

Erika could see Marsh was weighing up whether to offer her shelter under his umbrella and a lift, or leave her to the elements. She turned to him.

'Don't start,' he snapped.

'Can we talk about that meeting?'

'No, we can't. We just signed that we bloody well can't.'

'I would have appreciated a heads up on a meeting I was invited to attend.'

'Okay. *Yes.* I didn't want you to come. Do you know why?'

'Why?'

'I didn't want to burden you with sensitive information.'

'That's not the first visit I've had with those secret service types.'

'It isn't?' asked Marsh, who seemed surprised.

'I've already been warned. And I was worried if I didn't show today, there would be repercussions.'

Marsh frowned. 'I'm sorry. I genuinely didn't know.' He peered up at the water cascading down the ancient gutter pipes with a frothy gurgle. 'Where are you headed?'

'The station – or actually, looking at the time, home.'

'I'm going that way. Do you want a lift?'

'Yes. Thank you.'

He had a posh umbrella that opened with a whoomph at the touch of a button. He offered up his arm, and Erika took it as they hurried the short distance across the car park.

When they were inside his car, the windows immediately began to steam up. Marsh switched on the cold air and started the engine.

'Who were those three people in there?' asked Erika.

Marsh gave her the side-eye as he steered the car to the main entrance barrier. 'You think I know? They could have been senior civil service, or MI5.'

'You say that a little blasé. You're fifth in command of the Met Police.'

'It's the reality of the situation. I know of two other occasions when you've had to sign the Official Secrets Act. I've lost count of the times I have.'

Marsh waited for a gap in the traffic and then pulled out onto the main road. The rain was easing and leaving behind vast puddles and flooded patches of road.

Erika's phone rang. She didn't recognise the number but answered.

'Ma'am. This is PC Mortimer from the Scarsdale Villas crime

scene. You gave me your card.'

'Thanks for calling. What's happening?'

'Forensics are still here. It looks like it will take a long time to dust the place for prints. There is so much stuff here and fingerprints on everything. We think Jessica worked from home.'

'Have relatives been informed? What about a formal ID?'

'We're having trouble getting in contact with anyone. There are no siblings. Her mother is in a home up north. Father is deceased. We don't know if there was a partner; she was registered as living here alone.'

Erika made a mental note to call Rah at Folger Costume Hire and ask if Jessica had a partner.

'What about her computers and phone?'

'Bagged up and winging their way to cybercrime. I'm texting you the reference number. The lady's body has just gone off to the morgue. Listen, one of the reasons I'm calling is that we found a desk diary. Lots of handwritten stuff, appointments, phone numbers, and details of her movements since January.'

'Where did you find it?'

'It was on top of the toilet cistern with a pile of magazines. Reading material for, well, you know what I mean.'

Erika thought back to how the flat had been ransacked. The bathroom was the last place the ransacker would have expected to find a diary. Erika wondered if Jessica Goldman had been looking at the diary when she was on the pot and left it there by mistake.

'Has the diary been dusted for prints?'

'Yes, ma'am.'

Marsh was taking her home, but the traffic was slow. And she needed to get out of her wet clothes. The last thing she needed was to get ill during such a high-profile investigation.

'Can you have the diary biked over to my home address? I can text it to you.'

'Yes, ma'am. I'm going to stay here until things are wound down. And your colleague, Dahlia, is here, overseeing things.'

'Can you put her on?'

'No, ma'am. She's in the crime scene with forensics, and I'm not wearing protective gear. I can get her to call you?'

'It's okay. I'll text her. And thank you; good work, Officer.'

Erika ended the call and sent Dahlia a text, asking if she could drive her car back to her house in Blackheath and bring the diary. She then stared ahead at another set of traffic lights. The reflection of the red lights was streaking in the rain on the windshield, and she couldn't tell whether it was starting to get dark or clouds were darkening the sky again. She filled in Marsh about Folger Costume Hire and the link to Jessica Goldman. They drew up at yet another set of lights. Rush hour was now in full swing.

Marsh looked across at her, and his face softened. 'That's good work.' Erika nodded. 'You know, you are my oldest friend.'

'I'm not that old.'

He did that eye-roll again. 'Don't be silly. You know what I mean. It's difficult to balance being your friend, your boss, and looking out for you. I promised Mark I'd look out for you.'

Erika looked over at him. He hadn't mentioned Mark's name for a long time.

Marsh put his hand on her leg. 'You're soaked.'

Erika lifted his hand using the sleeve of his jacket and placed it on his own leg. 'That's what happens when you get caught in the rain.'

'I should have given you a towel to sit on,' he said, the petulance back in his voice.

Erika and Marsh had dated briefly years ago, when they were at police training college, before Mark came along, and then there had been a lapse of judgement a few years back, but Marsh was still giving her mixed signals, like mentioning Mark in the same breath as touching her leg. Erika shifted her leg across and unfolded the piece of paper with the contact name at Diamond Companions.

'I take it there are a lot of high-profile individuals who use this escort agency?'

'I don't!' he said. 'I'm – I'm happily married to Marcie.'

'I wasn't talking about you, but I take it from your indignant response that senior Met Police officers use this escort agency?'

'I didn't respond indignantly!' Erika recalled a time a few years ago when she called Marsh late at night and Marcie answered, letting slip that they were sleeping in different rooms. Marsh sighed. 'I've heard rumours. I'm not telling you who.'

'Superintendent Dan Fisk? He seemed to be the one who was there to clear up Neville Lomas's mess, with the sex worker. The sex worker that somehow managed to evade the police when she was half-naked and beaten up.' Marsh didn't answer. They had now crossed the river at Blackfriars Bridge, and the traffic cleared. 'At what point do you stop being a policeman, and it becomes all about damage limitation?' asked Erika. 'It's a genuine question.'

Marsh hesitated. 'I don't know. Maybe it's the point where you saddle yourself with a colossal mortgage and two daughters at expensive private schools . . . Then your wife's father has to go into a home. And, of course, he has to go somewhere nice . . . I know I pressure you a great deal, Erika, but if I'm pressuring you about stuff, think how much pressure I get. It's a whole other level. But to be clear. I'm a genuine policeman, Erika. Okay?'

Erika thought about that for a moment. On the one hand, she felt sorry for Marsh, but on the other . . . Was he confessing that he'd sold his soul to the devil?

'Okay,' she said. 'How do I approach this?' She held up the piece of paper.

Marsh eyed it. 'Don't go digging up unnecessary dirt. Or

anything you can't now talk about. And if you find anything outside your investigation's scope, I have to be the first to know.'

There was something pleading and pathetic about the way he asked.

Erika nodded. 'I promise.'

She hoped it was a promise she could keep.

38

When Marsh dropped Erika home, she got the impression that he wanted to come in, but when he saw there was a light on in the front window, he said he had to get back home.

'Thanks for the lift,' said Erika.

Marsh turned to her. 'Please don't do anything stupid,' he asked, insistently.

'Goodnight,' said Erika. She got out of the car and watched him drive away. She heard the faint sounds of the piano coming up the path, and she remembered that she had agreed for Tom to come over and practise.

When she let herself in the front door, she heard a complicated arrangement of the *Star Wars* theme tune being played with thumping bass and twiddly high notes. George was waiting for her in the hall, and she leaned down, scratched him behind his ears. He rubbed his sleek little body against her and purred.

Erika went to the living room door, listening to the music and watching with awe as Tom sat on the piano stool, his hands splayed and working furiously across the keyboard. Igor was perched on the sofa by the fire, and when he saw her, he grinned, mouthing, *Hi.*

Tom finished playing and then sat back, out of breath. He turned and saw Erika.

'Ahoj,' he said.

'Wow, that was amazing! You're getting really good,' said Erika.

'He found a YouTube video of this woman playing the *Star Wars* theme on the piano and learnt it by ear. She was playing a piano in the shape of the *Millennium Falcon*,' said Igor.

'Calm down, Dad,' said Tom with a smile at Igor's enthusiasm.

'Why are you telling me to calm down. You have talent. I'd kill to have some kind of talent. You could be in a band. I sung in a band, remember?' said Igor.

Erika looked between Tom and Igor and shook her head.

'There were a lot of good bands in Nitra when we were growing up,' she said. 'I don't remember yours.'

'Can you even sing, Dad?'

'I can sing. I always sing along to stuff on the radio.'

Tom rolled his eyes and laughed. Igor got up and went to Erika. He leaned in and gave her a kiss. Then felt her clothes. 'You're soaking wet.'

'I got caught in the rain.'

'I'll run you a bath. Did you eat?'

'Did I eat? I don't think I did.'

'There's chilli con carne on the stove,' said Igor. Erika got herself some food whilst Igor ran her a bath. When she returned to the living room, Tom was practising something different on the piano using a metronome, which made a crisp clicking sound.

Erika didn't realise how starving she was until she started to eat. Igor's chilli was delicious and hot, and she added a dollop of sour cream to the steaming pile of meat and rice. She scarfed her food and watched Tom playing a slowed-down version of something she vaguely recognised. He got to a part he was stuck on. And stopped. The metronome carried on in the silence: click, click, click.

'Sorry. Do you want to watch TV?' Tom asked, seeing her on the sofa.

'No. I like to listen. What were you playing?'

He stopped the metronome. 'Half of the *Hungarian Rhapsody No. 2* for duelling pianos.'

'Why do I know it?'

'They used it in the movie *Who Framed Roger Rabbit?* When Donald Duck and Daffy Duck are both playing the pianos in the club.'

Erika laughed.

'Yes. That's it.' She scraped her bowl and ate the last rice and meat off the spoon, and got up to go to the kitchen.

'Got any good murder investigations on the go?' he asked hopefully, following her into the kitchen; whilst she talked, he poured them glasses of Coke from the bottle in the fridge.

'Yes.'

'What did this murderer do?'

Erika wondered how much she should say. She could tell him if she spoke with general terms.

'Killed three men and a woman. I think they killed a woman. We found another body today.'

'Where was her body?'

Like when she was in the car, Erika didn't know if she should give him this much detail, but he was sixteen, and she wanted to talk to him like an adult. He handed her a glass of fizzing Coke filled up to the brim. She could see he was enthralled.

'Lying in the hallway. And there was a monkey wrench on the floor beside her body.'

'Did the killer use the monkey wrench?'

Erika nodded. 'Hit her on the . . .' She gripped her glass. She suddenly saw the crime scene from the killer's point of view, standing behind Jessica Goldman and hitting her over the head once and twice. There was plenty of blood. It was a frenzied attack. It had been such a fraught and busy day that Erika hadn't stopped to think about the configuration of the crime scene. The location of the blood spatter. And where the monkey wrench was dropped on the hall floor.

'What is it?' asked Tom. Erika realised she'd gone very quiet, like she was in a trance.

'Sorry, Tom; something just occurred to me.'

'Like a clue?'

'Yeah. Maybe.' Erika went to her coat hanging on the banister in the hallway and took out her phone. Dahlia answered after the first ring.

'Are you still at the crime scene?' Erika said without preamble.

'No. I'm just pulling into your road in your car. I've got the diary with me.'

'Okay. I'll meet you outside in a sec.'

———

Igor came down the stairs just as the front door slammed shut.

'Where's Erika?' he said, wiping soap suds off his hands with a towel.

'She thinks she's discovered a clue, and she's gone outside to meet someone who has her car,' said Tom.

'Who has her car? I've just run her a bath.' Igor noticed Erika's coat was still hanging on the post at the bottom of the stairs. 'And she's gone outside in her wet clothes. It's bloody freezing.'

39

The cold air hit Erika when she exited the front door. The street light opposite was broken, and her house sat in a pool of shadow. There was a free space outside the front door, and Dahlia parked by the kerb. Erika indicated she should unlock the passenger door, and she got inside.

'Hi. Everything okay?' asked Dahlia, reaching behind the seat to get her bag. 'I've got an Uber coming.'

'Now?'

'A few minutes.'

'Okay. This will be quick.'

Dahlia stared at Erika's hand, and Erika realised she was still holding the glass of Coke from Tom.

'This is the diary,' said Dahlia, opening her bag. She handed Erika an A4 desk diary in bright yellow, enclosed in a police evidence bag. There was a silvery smattering of fingerprint powder on the cover and the spine. She switched off the headlights and engine, and they were plunged into darkness. 'Did you make it to the meeting at Parliament?'

'I did. I've just had a thought. Was the murder weapon on the left or the right of Jessica Goldman's body?'

'We think it's Jessica Goldman. We don't have an official ID on the body.'

'Forget that for a moment. Can you remember which side the murder weapon was on?'

Dahlia hesitated. 'It was on the left-hand side of her body.'

'Yes. And the blood spatter was more pronounced on the left-hand side of the wall in the hallway?'

'There was blood everywhere, but yes,' said Dahlia. 'Are you thinking if the killer was left- or right-handed?'

'Yes. The killer must have been left-handed. It would indicate that they, she, brought the monkey wrench down from above using her left hand, and followed through with it on the left-hand side of Jessica Goldman's body each time she struck her on the back of the head,' said Erika, demonstrating the movement with her left hand. It felt odd for her to use that hand because she was right-handed.

'Can we be sure it's the same person who killed Terry DeVille, Neville Lomas, and Jamie Teague?'

'There is a very strong probability,' said Erika, not wanting to think about it if she was wrong. There was a knock on the window beside Dahlia. She jumped, and Erika saw it was Igor.

'It's okay. That's my . . . boyfriend,' said Erika.

Dahlia switched on the ignition and rolled down her window. 'Hi. She's on the other side.'

'I've got Erika's coat here,' he said, holding it up. 'She's soaked through from travelling today, and I didn't want her to get cold.'

Dahlia passed the coat across the seat.

'Thanks,' said Erika, juggling it with the diary in the evidence bag, and the full glass of Coke.

'Hi. I'm Detective Dahlia Beck.'

'We met before, at the restaurant? Back in January, at the OXO Tower? The night that the politician died . . . ,' said Igor.

'Oh, yes. Hi,' said Dahlia. Erika could tell she didn't remember Igor.

He put his hand through the window, and they shook. 'Erika. Your bath's ready.'

'I'll be in in a minute.'

'Don't get cold.'

'Sorry about that,' said Erika when he'd gone.

'No. He's sweet.'

Erika didn't like that way she said 'sweet' but ignored it.

'Anyway. I was saying about the killer being left-handed. It's made me realise something. If we know she's left-handed, we might be able to narrow down the five "glitch in the matrix women" in the CCTV videos and see which of them are right-handed and which of them are left.'

'You don't think any of the "glitch in the matrix girls" will respond to the media appeal?'

Erika thought how funny it was that the phrase 'glitch in the matrix girls' had become the shorthand for these women so quickly.

'They could be scared to come forward. I really hope we can make the link between Jessica Goldman doing the prosthetics for them.'

'The woman at Folger confirmed that she'd rented the costumes.'

'Yes, but that's all we have. We need to know where Jessica did their make-up. Who paid her? Was one of them in on it, or were they all in?'

'You mean, was it a paid hit job?' asked Dahlia.

'When you put it like that, I don't think so. We don't know what the motive could be . . . Did Jamie Teague have life insurance? If so, would his death have benefited anyone?'

Erika looked out at the empty, dark road. Farther along, the street light was working, and a black cat darted across the pool of light. Erika wondered if it was George. She always worried about him when he was out at night crossing roads.

'Erika?'

'McGorry flagged the team to find out if Jamie Teague had an insurance policy. Have you had the chance to look at this?' asked Erika, looking down at the diary in the bag.

'No. As soon as forensics arrived, everyone in the building seemed to be coming home from work. Getting forensic evidence from the communal hallway was a bit of a nightmare.'

'What about the neighbours?'

'There's an older lady who lives on the ground floor next to Jessica Goldman's flat, but she's very deaf and old, and she didn't see or hear anything . . . What happened with your meeting?'

Erika hesitated. She had to be able to trust Dahlia. She was on her team and party to everything.

'I've been given a contact, first name only, of a person working at Diamond Companions.'

'Have you called this person?'

'I was about to before you arrived. Do you remember the name of the girl – the one you said was found on the Embankment with a bloody nose after Neville Lomas was alleged to beat her up?'

'Sorry, no . . .' A headlight appeared behind them, and her phone beeped. 'That's my Uber. Don't forget your bath.'

Erika waited until Dahlia was safely in her Uber and it had driven away.

Something was still bothering Erika about Dahlia and her link to Dan Fisk. She put the glass, the diary, and her coat on the wall outside and made a call to the control room at Lewisham Row.

'Is that Vicky? It's Erika Foster. Can you tell me if Superintendent Dan Fisk is on duty, or when he'll next be on?'

There was a short silence on the end of the phone, and then a burst of talking from the other officers in the background.

'He's gone on holiday,' said Vicky, one of the control room

operators. 'It specifically says he's out of the country for the next three weeks.'

'Oh. Do you know when he went on leave?'

'Hang on.' Erika heard keys tapping. 'Yesterday. Do you want me to send a message to his inbox?'

'No. Thank you.'

Erika hung up. She'd called Dan Fisk on Monday. His voicemail had mentioned nothing about going away the next day for three weeks, as was customary. It was odd. Erika shivered. There was a thin wisp of fog drifting above the street lights. She picked up her things and hurried back inside. Closing the front door quietly, she crept past the door to the living room and went upstairs to have her bath.

Before she got into the steaming water, Erika tried the number on the piece of paper Richard Gaynor had given her at the Houses of Parliament. It rang out and then went to a generic answerphone service. Erika tried it again. On the third try, she left a short message saying who she was, with her number, asking to be called back on a discreet matter.

The bath was deliciously hot, but Erika couldn't relax or stop thinking. She lay staring up at the ceiling at the sound of the piano playing downstairs. The story she'd been told by Richard Gaynor about Damsa Afridi, the sex worker who was an illegal immigrant. It seemed too . . . convenient. Yes, it would have been explosive and highly damaging if the news got out. But why would it still be damaging after Neville Lomas's death? The chief whip was in charge of whipping MPs to vote in line with party policy. They kept dirt on their MPs so they could control them. Now Neville was dead, and his vote didn't matter. He was no longer an MP. And it was much easier to spin a bad story about a dead man. There was something else, too. The CCTV photos of Damsa Afridi clutching her swollen belly and being pictured with Neville Lomas. Why had the time stamp been cut off the top of the images? Were they even real? Had they just fed Erika and Marsh a load of bullshit dressed up as a secret that needed to be kept, so they could interfere and stop the real story from being uncovered? After a few minutes, she washed her hair and got out.

She pulled on a robe and went to the tiny spare room she used as a small home office. The diary was still in its plastic bag on the desk, but she had another idea. Over her long career, Erika had been in contact with many narks. Low-level criminals kept an eye out for things and passed information to the police for a small fee, using a ten- or twenty-pound note. Erika hadn't seen much of her regular narks since before the pandemic, but she'd thought of one while in the bath. Curly Sue. She'd been a 'high-class' call girl for a few years, and then she'd moved over to the administration side of things, helping to run one of the biggest escort agencies in West London. Erika was rummaging in the drawers, looking for one of her older address books, when Igor appeared at the door.

'Did you finish in the bath?' he asked, seeing her crouching in her dressing gown with wet hair.

'No, I'm still lying there with shampoo in my hair,' she snapped. Then she saw Tom was with him. She took a deep breath. 'Sorry.'

Erika still wasn't used to having her house full of people when she was working on a case. She got up and fastened her dressing gown tighter.

'We're going to head off,' said Igor.

'Sorry, Tom. I was talking to you, and then I got called away.'

'Dad said you can pick me up from school sometime this week?' asked Tom.

Erika looked at Igor. 'Yes. Let me think. Today's Wednesday. How about tomorrow?'

'Cool!'

'You can definitely do tomorrow?' asked Igor.

'Of course.'

Igor leaned in and gave her a kiss. 'Okay. I'll give you a call.'

'High five,' said Tom, holding up his hand. They high-fived, and by the time they were halfway down the stairs, Erika was lost in her address book and the desk diary from Jessica Goldman's flat.

40

Erika was back at the station by seven, working in her office. She'd managed only a few hours' fitful sleep. The meeting with Marsh played heavily on her mind, and it had made her at turns fearful about pursuing the investigation and angry that her hands were now tied when it came to investigating Neville Lomas. She'd woken at five, unable to get back to sleep, with a sore throat, which she was trying to ignore and blot out with painkillers.

Jessica Goldman's diary was on the desk in front of her, and she went through it again. She wrote private entries in blue ink and used red ink for business. She'd been busy throughout the year, with around fifteen to twenty days of work per month. Erika noted that she wrote down the names of the production companies, and she had entries for BBC Studios and then some independent production companies: Fountain Films and EBA Entertainment. She'd written 'FOLGER, 2 pm' in blue ink on March 2.

Erika sat back in her chair. She knew that self-employed people often kept a diary with work commitments, which they could show the taxman if investigated. And this worked for when they had work they wanted to keep off the books, like the job for Annabelle.

It was coming up to eight am. Erika picked up the phone and called Rah Zahora.

'This is Detective Chief Inspector Erika Foster. We spoke yesterday . . .'

Erika heard the dog, Wolsey, barking in the background. She told Rah about Jessica Goldman.

'Oh my word,' she said. 'I didn't know.'

'Yes. It hasn't been made public yet. We're treating Jessica's death as suspicious.'

Rah sounded frightened. 'Do you think it has something to do with that job we discussed yesterday?'

'I do. Are you okay to answer some questions?'

'On the phone – now?'

'Yes. This has to stay confidential.'

Erika heard the springs creak in a chair as Rah sat down.

'Naturally. You're frightening me.'

'You have no reason to be frightened. I've got Jessica's diary here in front of me.'

'Is my name in her diary?'

Erika glanced down at the word 'FOLGER' written in neat blue writing.

'No. Your name isn't in here.'

'Oh. That's good to hear,' Rah said, sounding relieved. 'I had a sleepless night thinking about what you told me yesterday. I was worried they might come after me. I'm all alone on this industrial estate most of the day . . . and Wolsey is not much of a guard dog.'

'No. You're not linked. And the prosthetics make-up job we think Jessica did for the five women isn't listed in her diary.'

'She probably did it cash in hand, then,' said Rah after a beat.

'Did she pay cash to hire the costumes?' asked Erika. Rah sighed, and her voice was still shaky.

'Am I going to get in trouble with the taxman if I say yes?'

'No. I'm not interested in any of that. I just care about this murder investigation.'

'Yes. And just this once, I hired out the costumes to her for cash. That's why Jessica came to pick them up herself. So there's no link to her credit card and my business, either.'

Again, Rah sounded relieved. Erika didn't want to remind her that the name of Folger Costume Hire was in all the handbags the 'glitch in the matrix girls' were carrying.

'Do you know what Jessica would charge for a day's work doing these prosthetics?'

'She was one of the best I knew. I think her rate was around five hundred pounds per day, plus materials. Well, that was if she did a twelve-hour day on set. I don't know if she would have charged a bit more or less with a private client,' said Rah.

'And do you know where she would buy her materials from? Is there a place where you buy prosthetic features? I don't even know what they're called.'

'It's more complicated. You can buy generic pieces, but when you get to Jessica's level, you can use special modelling latex materials to create moulds. Sometimes the artists might use a plaster cast of the head if the job involves completely transforming the features.'

Erika had a sinking feeling.

'You told us that the five women wanted false noses, black wigs, and contact lenses.'

'Yes.'

'It looks like Jessica worked from home. Did she have a separate office or workspace?'

'No. Jessica couldn't afford to. Her big regret was that she couldn't expand her business. She had dreams of doing big special-effects projects.'

'Is there anything else she said about this job? Anything.'

Rah sighed.

'She did say something about the job being at a hotel in Marylebone. I don't know if the casting was there. Or they'd hired a room.'

'Okay. Thank you. Please keep in touch if you hear anything else from your colleagues.'

'I thought you asked me not to give away any details?'

'I meant don't talk to the newspapers.'

'Don't worry. I don't need any bad press.'

She hung up the phone, and just as Erika was making notes, her phone rang again. It was Curly Sue, the nark she'd contacted the night before, and she took the call.

Half an hour later, Erika went down to the incident room and briefed the team on the previous day's events – leaving out the details of her meeting in Parliament. Dahlia had already updated the display of photos on the whiteboard wall, including the crime scene photos of Jessica Goldman.

'I've just spoken to Rah Zahora at Folger Costume Hire, and she said Jessica mentioned that the "casting" for this reality show with the five identical women was being held at a hotel in Marylebone. Can you find out if Jessica Goldman booked a hotel room in Marylebone on Friday, the 3rd of March? She didn't specify which hotel. Also, it's a very long shot, but find out if any of the hotels had a casting booked in their conference rooms for some kind of TV show.'

'I thought the TV show thing was made up?' asked McGorry.

'I think it was, but what if this Annabelle booked a conference room under the pretence that there was some kind of casting to cover her tracks?'

Erika went over to the whiteboards and pointed to the crime

scene photos of Jessica Goldman's body lying in the hallway, next to the monkey wrench.

'I think this Annabelle had to go back and kill Jessica Goldman, because she may be the only link we'd have to finding her. We don't have an official time of death, but I imagine that she was killed before the press appeal went out. I've been through the log of people who called and emailed the appeal, and Jessica Goldman isn't on the list. If we find out the details of this prosthetics job she did, then that could lead us to Annabelle.'

'What if she's going to go after the other four women who went to Jamie Teague's flat?' asked McGorry.

'If I was smart enough to hire someone to do prosthetics on me, to make me look different to commit a murder, I'd make sure the only person who saw me out of make-up was the make-up artist who did the prosthetics. I could be wrong, but the other four women might not have realised what they were getting into. They might have thought this reality show was real. So they could have been made up later on that day. Hence the need for a hotel room or conference room to make it all look legit. That also reminds me – see if there were any reality show castings advertised in the trade presses in the past few weeks.'

Moss held up a piece of paper.

'I've got the text for another media appeal we want to make through our social media channels – Facebook, Twitter, TikTok – for the "glitch in the matrix women",' she said. Erika took the piece of paper and read through the text.

'Hang on. The Met Police have a TikTok account?' she said, looking up at her officers.

'Yeah. It's got almost a hundred thousand followers,' said McGorry. He took out his phone and held it up. Erika went over to him and saw that the videos on the @Metpolice TikTok had more than a million likes in addition to all the followers. She scrolled down and saw McGorry's face in a video from a few weeks previous. 'What's this?'

'I did a video for the TikTok account. I was asked to show a day in the life of a Met Police plain clothes detective,' he said sheepishly.

'You have to watch. It's hilarious,' said Peterson.

'It got the most likes for that account.'

'Until they did the video about the police sniffer dog with the cute furry face.'

The officers in the incident room laughed. Erika handed McGorry back his phone. She made a mental note to watch the video later on.

'Okay, okay. Can we concentrate? This appeal text is fine. It can be posted.' Erika wondered in all seriousness if there was a TikTok office, and saw a sudden image of Marsh doing a choreographed dance in his office with Commander Tate and their shared secretary. She pushed it out of her head.

'There have been several successful appeals posted on the TikTok account,' said McGorry. His pride still looked like it was hurt. 'My video helped us gain followers.'

'And that's why it's important that we put out this appeal for the five women on social media. It's good that we've included in this text that the women don't have to worry about being arrested,' she added to Moss.

'And we're going to stick to that?' asked Moss with a wry smile.

'That's what we're putting in the post. We'll have to see what happens,' said Erika. She checked her watch.

'Okay. If you can all follow up on what we've discussed. I have an appointment to go and meet one of my narks who used to work as an escort to try and shed some light on Diamond Companions. We'll reconvene tomorrow morning.'

41

'I can't comment on the rest of those poor men, but Neville Lomas . . . I'm not political, but maybe he deserved to die painfully,' said Curly Sue. Erika was sitting opposite her in the Brasserie of Light bar on the first floor of the Selfridges department store. She had just given Sue a brief outline of the murder case, withholding the information about the Polaroids found at the murder scenes.

Curly Sue's real name was Susan Forrester. She was a similar age to Erika and had started as a call girl in the late 1980s. She still had the long black, curly hair that had given her the nickname, even if it was now obvious it was dyed. Sue was reassuringly old school with her big hair and oversized shoulder pads, and she wore enough make-up to give Joan Collins a run for her money. Like Joan Collins, she liked the finer things in life. Erika would never usually meet a witness, let alone a nark, in such a luxurious bar, but Sue knew everything about the escort trade in London and wider afield.

'Why do you think he deserved to die painfully?'

'Nasty bastard.'

'Did you ever?'

'Have him as a punter?' She bit her lip, having to think about it. 'I never had sex with him. I might have walked over his back once wearing a pair of stilettos . . .' Her voice trailed off when the waiter arrived with their drinks. A Negroni cocktail for Sue and a black coffee for Erika. When the waiter had gone, she picked up her glass. 'Lovely, shall we say cheers?'

'Cheers,' said Erika, clinking her china cup. Sue took a long pull on the drink. Her mouth creased, and Erika could see where the lipstick bled into the deep smoker's wrinkles around her lips.

'As you know, the trade has changed since my day. It's more evil. Albanian mafia trafficking young girls against their will. And Russian and Eastern European girls who'll do all sorts for much less. There's still a market for the girl-next-door types, and a few still out there who treat it like a business, and if you strike while the iron's hot, there's a lot of money to be made.'

'Are you still working for Savannah Secretarial Services?' asked Erika.

'No. I packed it all in back in March 2020. I'd just turned fifty and put my priorities straight. I've got a few rental properties. I stopped when I hit forty – my tits were no longer roadworthy, so I started doing admin for Savannah. Isn't it awful how your tits go south? You're lucky to have small ones . . .' She barely paused to take another deep pull on her Negroni. 'And I had a good long run. Forty isn't old by any means, but in whoring terms, you've got to be careful and know when to pack it in. One day you can be flown to exotic locations and showered with cash, and the next, you're doling out hand-jobs on the Old Kent Road for fifteen quid a pop.'

Erika smiled. 'Back to Neville Lomas?'

'Sorry, love. Yeah. I remember a few occasions when Neville got rough with our Savannah ladies.'

'When was this?'

'Years ago. The early 2000s, maybe.'

'Did he ever beat up a woman badly?'

Sue's face clouded over. 'He broke a poor girl's nose once.'

'Did the girl press charges?'

Sue shook her head. 'He paid her off. The agency took a cut,' she added, raising a thin eyebrow.

'How much did he pay her off?'

'I don't remember, Erika, but it was enough for her to take two weeks off and go on a nice holiday.'

Erika thought back to the photos she'd seen of the sex worker, Damsa Afridi, who had allegedly been pregnant with Neville Lomas's baby and blackmailing him.

'Were there ever any rumours or stories of sex workers blackmailing their clients? In particular, Neville Lomas?'

'Blackmail? No. Most of the Savannah girls were earning an absolute fortune. I do know of those kiss-and-tell stories in the tabloids about Lomas. The sex workers involved were paid a lot of money, but that was back in the late eighties, nineties.'

'Did you ever have illegal immigrants on the books?'

Sue pulled a face. 'What do you think? How many choices do desperate women have to make money? 'Course we did.'

'What do you know about the agency Diamond Companions?'

'Quite a big outfit. Based online. Savannah went fully online in 2007.'

'And the difference with online as opposed to a working brothel?' asked Erika.

Sue raised an eyebrow. 'Are you fishing? You know the answer to that. Most brothels – not all, but most in London now – traffic young women from abroad. It's slavery and not the kind of business I'd ever be involved with. Online agencies are more legit and introduction-only portals. Then, whatever happens, it's between the girls and their clients. The clients pay upfront and online, and the girls pay the website a cut.'

'And they visit the clients? As opposed to there being a place the clients go to?'

'Yeah. Hotels, at home, and sometimes at an office. Some of them use their homes, or they rent places. That can be tricky with neighbours seeing a stream of men coming and going, so using different hotels is the safest. What's happening with Neville Lomas?'

Erika hesitated and bit her lip. She had to be careful. 'I was given a contact at Diamond Companions about Neville Lomas.'

Sue took another pull on her cocktail. 'By who?'

'I can't say.'

'Can you tell me the name of the contact?'

'Marie.'

'No surname?'

'No surname.'

Sue shifted in her chair. 'What made you call me? And not go to their offices, if this is a murder investigation?'

'If I go blundering into one of these agencies with my badge and truncheon, then everyone clams up, and by the time I get a warrant approved, if I get one approved, then everything has been shredded, and they've moved offices.'

Sue drained the last of her cocktail and indicated to the waiter behind the bar he should bring another. Negroni cocktails were twenty quid a pop, so Erika hoped she would get something from her before she ordered a third.

'Can you tell me anything else about Neville Lomas?'

Sue hesitated. 'You might know this. We were told in the office that if Neville Lomas hired one of the girls on our books at Savannah and something happened to her . . . if he . . . got rough, we should call a police officer.'

'Was it Superintendent Dan Fisk?'

Sue hesitated and flinched a little at the name. 'Erika. I don't work for them anymore.'

'Did he threaten you?'

'No, but we were told we had to be discreet. And then, of course, there was *the dossier*.'

Erika made a split-second decision to pretend she knew what Sue was talking about.

'Yes. The dossier.'

'Which I've never seen, I hasten to add,' she said, putting up both her hands. 'I've just heard the rumour that it exists. And it's another reason they, you lot, keep tabs on the agency.'

'What do you think is in the dossier? Exactly,' asked Erika, her mind whirring with questions.

Sue shifted uncomfortably.

'Them pictures, obviously. Those stupid old fools get blind drunk or high on drugs, and then, she, whoever it is, takes pictures of them.' Erika's heart was racing. She took a sip of her coffee and tried to remain looking nonchalant. 'For blackmail,' Sue said, nodding.

'And as you might know, a lot of high-profile men use Savannah and Diamond Companions. Ministers, celebrities, High Court judges.'

Bloody hell, thought Erika. *Is that what Richard Gaynor and his stooges in Westminster are trying to keep quiet?*

'How long have you known about the dossier?' asked Erika, trying to keep her voice even.

Sue had to think for a moment.

'A few years. No one knows who the girl is taking the photos. I know at Savannah, your colleague put us under pressure to find out, but it's such a secretive business. We're an introduction portal, as I say.'

'What about Diamond Companions? Were they put under pressure to investigate?'

Sue looked at Erika. 'You tell me.' Erika was grateful that the waiter appeared at the table with Sue's second Negroni cocktail. 'That was fast, thank you,' Sue said, taking it from him. She took a big gulp. Erika waited until the waiter had gone back to the bar. 'What were you saying?'

'Why do you think she takes pictures of all these rich and powerful men?' asked Erika, keeping her tone light, a little more gossipy.

'It's more secure. You can't hack something if it exists as a single hard-copy image.'

'We, the police, don't know who the girl is taking these photos of wealthy, influential men. Presumably, the photos are—'

'Explicit and damaging,' finished Sue, swallowing another quarter of the ruby-red fluid. Erika could see Sue's movements were slower, and she was slurring her words.

'How do you think the information got out if no one knows the source? Who this woman is? Is there a name?'

Sue put down her drink, picked up her handbag from the floor, and took out her phone. 'My husband's a car mechanic, does MOT repairs. He's always got a lad on one of those apprentice schemes. If the lad is tall and well built, I'll put some work his way as a walker. They earn bugger-all when they're training.'

'A walker is a man who accompanies sex workers when they arrive at hotels for a client?' clarified Erika.

Sue nodded, took out a diary, and found a piece of paper.

'This lad, Daniel. He's been doing walking jobs for the last few years for Savannah. And I think he does a bit for Diamond, too. He's about to qualify as a mechanic, so he won't be doing it much longer.' She wrote down a number. 'First name only. I can't promise he'll want to meet you. He's always got his nose to the ground. He's working with a lot of the women. He might know something. If he doesn't, then leave him alone. Yes?'

'Thank you,' said Erika.

42

Today Annabelle was visiting one of her regulars, Alan. He wasn't an evil man or even a particularly interesting one. A banker close to retirement whose wife had lost interest in him. He paid her £1,000 in cash weekly for two hours in a hotel.

'God, you're so beautiful,' he hissed a moment before he ejaculated. He collapsed on top of her, pressing his substantial, sweaty body against her. His grey hair was coarse, and unusually for a man his age, he had a full head of it.

Annabelle wrapped her legs around his back as best she could and listened to his heart beating, thrum thrum, against her chest. She clung to him tight. He was one of her most lucrative regulars, one of five who paid cash weekly. Four months ago, Annabelle had quit the two agencies who had displayed her photo in their directories. She'd retained fourteen regulars. And then, slowly, that had dwindled to five. No matter. It wasn't long now. She would soon fly away, never to return.

'Eve. You're so beautiful,' repeated Alan. He pulled out of her and rolled to one side, taking up most of the king-sized bed. He smoothed down his huge thatch of grey hair.

'Would you like a glass of water?' she asked.

'Yes, please, darling girl.'

Annabelle slid to the bed's edge and smoothed down her long hair. Alan liked her to wear red stockings, suspenders, and high heels. She got up slowly, running her hands over her breasts and down to her waist, where she adjusted the red suspender belt. There was a glass on the bedside table. It wasn't low, but she bent over, exposing herself. She could feel his eyes on her, and she looked back.

'Naughty boy.' She smiled. She crossed the carpet to the bathroom, feeling the high heels accentuating her bottom and legs.

'Let the tap run for a moment,' he added, dropping the dirty talk and falling back into Alan, the perfectionist.

Alan was worth a lot of money but always insisted on drinking tap-water. In his mind, bottled water was one of the biggest rip-offs.

Annabelle turned on the tap and let the water run. She saw herself in the mirror. She was beautiful and sexy, but the shine was dulling on her youth. Her body had lost that brief 'honey glow', as another girl once termed it. The insatiable youthfulness men seemed to love in women aged eighteen to twenty-three. She was now twenty-five. And didn't turn on the light in the hotel bathroom anymore.

When she returned with Alan's glass of water, he was sitting up, with his huge belly and ball sack on display. He'd put his glasses on and was now fiddling with the TV remote.

Annabelle forced a smile on her face. All she had to do was lie with him for the next forty-five minutes whilst he drank his tap-water and watched Bloomberg, and then she could go.

Alan always left the hotel room first. She took a shower, removed all her make-up, and then changed into clean workout gear: thin tracksuit bottoms, a cosy hoodie, and trainers. The rest of her stuff was shoved into a holdall. It was easy to blend in wearing workout gear and no make-up. People thought she was a yummy mummy or a student, and it was easier to come and go in London hotels if you weren't dressed up to the nines. Annabelle returned home to her building half an hour later.

Annabelle liked the hush and quiet of her small apartment. She locked the front door and went straight to the bedroom, sliding the wardrobe door open to reveal a small metal floor safe. Annabelle punched the four-digit code into the keypad, and the lid popped open to reveal a small cavity in the wardrobe floor. Sitting on top was a green cardboard folder. She took it out and placed it carefully to one side on the floor, then heaved out a wide metal cash box, set it down, and opened it with a little silver key.

It was filled with £30,000 in neatly stacked bundles of fifty-pound notes. Annabelle added the £1,000 cash from Alan, closed and locked the cash box, and then lowered it back into the floor safe. £31,000 was a little over three weeks' wages. It was becoming harder to deposit the money, and Annabelle used various credit cards and bank accounts to deposit the cash in small amounts without raising alarms. She also held money in stocks, bonds, and cryptocurrency. Back in the days of being a fully-fledged escort with a web profile, one of her clients had been a cryptocurrency geek, and he'd taught her a great deal about investing as wisely as possible.

Annabelle then turned her attention to the green folder. She opened it and turned to the first page of the Polaroid photos she'd been steadily collecting for the past few years. The man's face in the first photos was well known. He was a serious, powerful man, a "family man", but in the pictures, he was naked, high on drugs, his legs were spread, and he had a giant sex toy protruding from his anus. She carried on flicking through the images of depravity. This was her dossier of rich and powerful men, filled with photos like this of them. Embarrassing and explicit images. Images that could end a marriage . . . and lose a career, or even an election. It was her insurance policy.

Annabelle put the green folder back in the safe, then closed and keyed in the code to lock it. On her way out of the bedroom she stopped and looked at the frame on the wall. It was a cel from the original animated Disney film *The Ugly Duckling.* The duckling sat on a log, looking mournfully at the reflection in the water. It had cost Annabelle £8,000 at auction. But this wasn't just an investment. It was a reminder to her that she'd survived and that she would survive.

Annabelle had been an ugly duckling herself. She'd been a small, thin, ratty-looking child until just before her sixteenth birthday, when she suddenly blossomed into a beautiful young woman. It had been her saving grace at the children's home. The other young girls who looked pretty had suffered from unwanted attention, and in the case of one of them, the attention had been all-consuming and terrifying.

By the time Annabelle blossomed into a beauty, she had only a few weeks left until she was sixteen and classed as legally responsible for herself. She was free to leave the children's home.

She'd spent almost eight years living at Drexel Hill, and some of the things she saw there would be forever etched on her brain. But there was always a maturity to Annabelle. She never permitted herself to be lost in the present. Something in the back of her mind always told her nothing was forever. She was going to leave this place and go on to greater things.

She'd lifted Mac's legs on that sunny day just after her mother died, and he'd fallen out the window. It taught her that she had the power to change things.

And she had one more thing to change before she moved on for good.

43

When Erika arrived back at Lewisham Row, the incident room was half-empty. Moss and Crane were working at their desks.

'Where's everyone?' she asked, taking off her coat and draping it over her chair.

'Canteen or gone to grab a sandwich,' said Moss.

'What about your lunch?'

'My lovely wife packed me up a portion of homemade shepherd's pie,' said Moss, holding up an empty container.

'I wish my wife could cook,' said Crane. 'I bought her a lovely little Le Creuset Dutch oven. Perfect for two, but she uses it as a fruit bowl.'

Erika went over to Crane's desk and saw he was searching through CCTV of Oxford Street on the night of Friday, March 3. She noted the time stamp was 9.47 pm.

'What's this?' she asked.

Crane gave a dry laugh and rubbed his eyes. 'Do you remember I got the license plate number for the cab driver who dropped the "glitch in the matrix girls" off in Old Compton Street?'

'Yes. You'd left two messages for him, the last you told me.'

Crane picked up his notebook and flicked through the pages.

'He did pick up earlier today. Just as I traced the cab journey back through CCTV to Camden. Which was a bloody nightmare, but thankfully I had time codes and a friend who works in the TFL central CCTV building. Anyway, just as I traced them back to Camden, their cab driver called me back. He remembers the girls. He picked them up from outside Camden Market.'

'Where in Camden Market?'

Crane searched through the windows on his computer and found a CCTV video clip.

'This is Jamestown Road, close to the iron bridge at Camden Lock. They were all waiting outside the Wagamama.'

In the video, the road was very busy with people, but they could see the five girls waiting on the pavement outside what looked like an office block. The Wagamama sign was above the door on the ground floor. The girls all stood awkwardly with their arms crossed, and then the black cab drew up and they got inside.

'Did they eat at the restaurant?'

'No. Well, they didn't come from there. They stand outside for six minutes, not talking to each other, waiting for the cab . . .' Crane ran the video back. Pedestrians zipped past, but the five 'glitch in the matrix girls' with their little black dresses, black gloves, and long dark hair stayed still, unsmiling and seeming to talk to each other only occasionally. 'Here, look, they came from across the road.' The five girls walked in reverse across the road. 'Out of the covered market.'

'Shit. Jessica Goldman told the woman at the costume hire that the make-up and prosthetics job she did for them was in Marylebone.'

'They could have been in Marylebone earlier in the day, but I'm going to have to now try and track their movements back through the covered market, find where they went inside. And when. It was easier to trace the black cab because I had a time code and location.'

'I know. Good work,' said Erika, patting him on the shoulder. 'Did you have lunch?'

'I had some cheesy Wotsits.'

Erika rummaged in her bag and took out a twenty-pound note and the cheap cheese sandwich she'd bought. 'Go get some fresh air and something proper to eat.'

He smiled and shook his head. 'Boss, you don't need to do that.'

Erika shook her head and pushed the note into his hand.

'You've been working round the clock on this CCTV. It hasn't gone unnoticed. Now go and get a hot meal. Take an hour or longer if you need. That's an order.'

'I'll be an hour tops, and then I'll get cracking on the CCTV,' he said.

Crane picked up his coat and left smiling.

'You should practise what you preach,' said Moss, eyeing the value cheese sandwich in Erika's hand. 'You look a bit peaky.'

Erika's throat was feeling worse, and she'd just taken more painkillers. She found the number for Daniel that Curly Sue had given her. Every time they had a new piece of information or what felt like a breakthrough, it arrived with a caveat. The CCTV footage of the girls' journey was followed, but they ended up at a dead end. Erika had been to Camden Market several times, and once, she chased a couple of drug dealers through the market, but it was such a warren of long corridors and small buildings that it was easy for anyone to get lost. Erika looked at Moss, working so hard and so loyal. It felt wrong that she had to withhold the information she'd gleaned at the meeting yesterday with Marsh at the chief whip's office, and what about this dossier of explicit photos this sex worker was rumoured to have compiled?

She thought back to what the woman said at the meeting in

Westminster: *'You need to understand that we are dealing with things well above your pay grade. You should be grateful for our help, and I advise you to refrain from pursuing any inquiries outside of what we've discussed.'*

With the revelations about this dossier, she was all the more convinced that their story about Neville Lomas and the pregnant illegal immigrant Damsa Afridi was a cover – had she stumbled into something dangerous?

'Are you sure you're okay, boss?' asked Moss.

Erika was staring transfixed into the middle distance with half her sandwich held in mid-air. 'Yes. Thank you, just a bit tired.'

With a heavy heart, Erika turned back to her desk, and swallowed the last of her sandwich with a wince. She picked up her phone and dialled Daniel's number.

'Yeah,' said a deep voice without saying 'hello' or announcing a name. Erika was caught unawares. She explained who she was and who had given her his number.

'Dunno what you're talking about,' he mumbled and hung up. When Erika tried the number again, it was cancelled after two rings and went to his answering machine. She didn't leave a message. What could she expect? Why hadn't Curly Sue given him a heads up?

Erika was suddenly very thirsty and got up. People were starting to come back to the incident room after their lunch. Erika was searching her desk drawer to see if she had any spare change for the vending machine in the corridor when she heard Moss give a whistle.

'What is it?'

'We've just had a message come into the appeal line from someone who says she's one of the "glitch in the matrix girls",' said Moss.

44

Erika went to Moss's desk. It had been sent through the Met Police portal, which was linked to the social media accounts. The message looked like it had been written in haste by someone stressed.

DEAR MET POLICE,

HI, IVE JUST SEEN YOUR APPEAL ON SOCIAL MEDIA/TIKTOK. I'M AN ACTOR. I WAS HIRED FOR A CASTING FOR A SHOW ON TLC NETWORK CALLED 'GIRLS NIGHTS OUTS' I WAS PAID, BUT I WAS ALSO ASKED TO SIGN AN NDA AND A RELEASE FORM. I SAW THE NEWS ABOUT JAMIE TEAGUE BEING KILLED. I'VE BEEN SCARED TO CONTACT YOU IN CASE YOU THINK THAT I HAD ANYTHING TO DO WITH HIM DYING. I DIDN'T. WE WERE ASKED NOT TO TALK TO EACH OTHER, BUT ME AND ANOTHER

OF THE GIRLS SWAPPED NUMBERS AFTER THE
'NIGHT OUT', AND THAT'S WHEN WE STARTED
TALKING ABOUT THE WIERDNESS OF IT ALL. WE
ARE WILLING TO COME AND TALK TO YOU AND
GIVE U A STATEMENT, WE JUST NEED TO KNOW
THAT WE WON'T BE CHARGED WITH ANY CRIME,
'CAUSE WE DIDN'T COMMIT ANY CRIME. I DON'T
KNOW ABOUT THE OTHER TWO GIRLS. THERE WAS
ONE WHO WAS IN CHARGE, BUT I DON'T HAVE ANY
NAMES.
I LIVE IN ORPINGTON. I'M 22 YEARS OLD AND LIVE
WITH MY PARENTS. THEY DON'T KNOW ABOUT
THIS, SO PLEASE CAN I COME IN & SPEAK TO YOU
AND NOT THE OTHER WAY ROUND.

FROM KIRSTY VARDY.

There was silence, and Erika saw Dahlia, Peterson, and a few
other team members were now behind her, reading Moss's
computer screen.

'What do you want me to reply?' asked Moss.

'Get her in. Offer to send a car, an unmarked car. Orpington's,
what, half an hour away? Stress that this is voluntary, of course,
but put a little pressure on her to talk.'

Moss scrolled down the screen. 'She's left a mobile number. I'll
text her now.'

Erika returned to the whiteboards with the crime scene photos
of their four victims. In chronological order, they were Terry
DeVille, the casting director, in November last year; Neville
Lomas, the politician, in January; Jamie Teague, the footballer, on
March 3; and most recently, Jessica Goldman, the make-up artist.

How were they all connected? Erika had thought the connection was with sex workers who came into contact with Neville and Jamie. Still, they had the response from Kirsty, who wrote that she had attended what she thought was a casting for a reality TV show, and the casting needed make-up and prosthetics done by Jessica Goldman. Could this somehow be connected with Terry DeVille? And if so, how? He had been a casting director, but his interest was in male actors and models.

There was a massive map of London on the wall, and red arrows had been placed at each crime scene: Barnes, the Embankment, Greenwich, and then Kensington. Terry DeVille and Jessica Goldman worked in the entertainment industry, albeit in very different fields. However, they both lived in West London.

'What's our progress on Terry DeVille?' she asked. She felt like he had been sidelined in her mind during the investigation.

McGorry was just taking off his coat. 'I had all the Polaroids we took from his house, including the Annabelle ones, dusted for prints. I got them back from forensics early this morning. I'm going to have them all scanned.'

'What do forensics say?'

'They won't have any results on the fingerprints and DNA for a couple of days. I'll have to work through them and see if I can identify any of the guys in the explicit, naked photos.'

'What about Terry's work? Do we have any details of the casting projects he worked on? And the people he knew? Friends, colleagues in the entertainment business?'

McGorry went to his desk and picked up his notebook.

'He was a member of the CDG, which is the Casting Directors Guild. I emailed them to ask if any members could give me more information, but I haven't heard anything back.'

This always seemed to be the catchphrase in policing: 'I haven't heard anything back.'

'What about the guy who was squatting in his house?'

'Russel Milligan,' said McGorry, flicking through his notebook.

'Yes. Where is Russel now?'

'He's been staying in a hostel in Neasden.'

'What if we asked him to come in and talk. And in return, we'll turn a blind eye to him going back to the house in Barnes. He has a key, and they're not going sell it anytime soon, by the looks of it.'

'Okay. I'll call Russel. When?'

'As soon as possible. Time is ticking.'

'I also had an email back earlier about Jamie Teague's life insurance policy,' said McGorry. 'His mother and his sister were the beneficiaries.'

'How much will they get?'

'Half a mil.'

'What about his will? He wasn't married. Wouldn't the family inherit?'

'There's no will; he died intestate, so the family should inherit.'

Erika looked back at the whiteboards and the crime scene photos of Jamie Teague tied up. His bloodshot eyes staring at the camera. She'd been looking at these pictures daily, and it was difficult not to get used to them and stop seeing them for what they were.

Dahlia came over to McGorry's desk.

'Boss, this is a weird one. Jamie Teague's sister, Karen . . . It's just popped up in the news that she's started an OnlyFans page.'

'What?'

'I saw this in the paper while having lunch across the road in the Starbucks.' It showed a full spread of Karen Teague. There were three pictures, one of her on a beach in Spain, leaning back against a rocky cliff. She wore nothing but a pair of sunglasses, and her long dark hair was slicked back. The newspaper had superimposed three gold stars over her nipples and crotch. In the other two photos, she lay back on a bed wearing stockings, suspenders, and little red devil horns; again, three yellow stars had been superimposed on her body.

Erika read the article underneath:

Karen Teague, the sister of Jamie Teague, shared a TikTok video announcing that she's joined OnlyFans. The model, the younger sister of the recently deceased Premiership footballer, turned 21 in February and told fans: 'People think I'm being disrespectful, launching my OnlyFans profile, but I'd been talking to Jamie about doing this for months. He supported me 1000 percent and would have wanted me to do it. He was proud of me, and I can still feel his presence. He's with me every hour of every day, and I miss him so much.'

OnlyFans is an internet content subscription service mainly focusing on sex workers who produce pornography for a subscription fee. It also hosts the work of other content creators, such as personal trainers and musicians.

What do you think? Is it too soon for Karen Teague to join OnlyFans? Do you have a story about Karen? *Email us!*

'What's she doing?' said McGorry. 'Does she really need nineteen ninety-nine a month from a few thousand guys? If she's going to inherit her brother's millions?'

'Is that how much it costs a month?' asked Dahlia. Both she and Erika looked at McGorry.

'I've heard that's how much it costs,' he replied, blushing.

Erika looked back at the article. 'Can you get on to Cheri

Shelton and see if this is true? Again, we've got another aspect of sex work coming into our investigations.'

'Boss,' said Moss, calling over from her desk. 'Kirsty Vardy just replied to my text. She can come in later this afternoon and talk to us.'

45

August 2006

The woman nodded briskly. She had short dyed-brown hair, crooked teeth, and thick, round glasses.

'My name's Sal. I'm here to take you to your new home,' she said, stiffly. Coldly. The night Mac had died, Annabelle had been taken into foster care with a nice older lady called Margaret, who had a warm, cosy house, where Annabelle had her own room looking out over the garden. But her time with Margaret had been short-lived. Three days later, Annabelle had been given a place at Drexel Hill Children's Home.

'Goodbye, love,' said Margaret. Kneeling down to hug her, she pressed something into Annabelle's small sweaty hand.

Sal picked up Annabelle's suitcase, and they went to a waiting minibus, where a man sat in the driver's seat.

Margaret waved from her front door as Annabelle climbed into the back seat. The sliding door of the minibus slammed shut, and the woman got in next to her.

'Put your seat belt on,' she said. Her eyes were huge, and her pale skin was like crepe. She turned to look through the rear window, and Annabelle saw the top of a pale-blue spider-web tattoo poking above her collar. 'You're good to go, Gav.'

Annabelle saw only the back of Gav's head and his meaty, red neck as they set off through the busy streets.

'What have you got in your hand?' asked Sal. The top point of the spider's web settled in the flesh folds at her collar, and she smelt horrible – cigarettes and stale garlic. And she was sweating under her grubby blue pullover. Her hair was wet where it met her shirt collar. Annabelle opened her hand. There was a note folded four times, and when she opened it out, she saw it was a fifty-pound note.

'It's a pinkie,' said Annabelle. That's what she'd heard Mac call them. Sal's eyes widened behind her glasses, and she looked up to see if Gav was watching. There were yellow deposits of dried sleep in the corners of her eyes. Eye bogies.

'Children aren't allowed cash outside their weekly pocket money,' she murmured, grabbing the note and stuffing it into her pocket. 'Do you get carsick?'

'No.'

'Good. 'Cos if you're sick, you clear it up.'

'Where are we going?'

'Your new home,' said Sal. She scooted along the seat, and Annabelle saw that she left a trail of moisture on the scuffed plastic.

It took two hours to drive to the children's home. The journey seemed to stretch in Annabelle's memory, and she remembered how dark it was when she first saw Drexel Hill. It was a large country house set back from the main road in a leafy, hilly part of Kent. When they passed between two tall granite gateposts, the landscape changed. It was August, but the trees lining each side of the gravel driveway were dead. The sun dappled through their bare branches, and the ground surrounding the mottled trunks had a reddish tinge. Annabelle found out later that the trees had all been infected with a fungus, but back then, on that never-ending drive, Annabelle thought she'd travelled through time and somehow they'd driven to a place where it was now winter.

Drexel Hill was a cold place. The staff were mean, and the food was terrible. But Annabelle was blessed, she realised, because she was ugly. She was rat-faced, and her hair was short. The embodiment of an ugly duckling. She also had confidence in herself, and this, coupled with her unattractiveness, kept the predators, of which there were many, at bay.

Annabelle quickly learned that abuse came in many forms. There were the sadistic orderlies, like Sal, who never struck you, but took pleasure in discomfort. Sal was older. And a couple of other older women weren't kind and warm but were fair. And deep down, you could tell they cared, but Sal was their boss.

There were a couple of young orderlies who were barely into their adulthood themselves – a handsome boy called Fred and another beautiful young woman named Tamsin. They would often have their favourite children, and they could be overfamiliar with how they touched the kids and the attention they gave their favourites. So subtle that it was hard to think it was anything other than accidental.

And then there was Pipes . . . Annabelle didn't learn his real name until a few weeks into her first year. Lewis. Lewis Crowe. But the children called him Pipes.

Pipes should have been good-looking. He was tall and muscular. He had a bald head, a swarthy face, a chiselled chin, and a broad nose. He would arrive every day clean-shaven, but by the afternoon, he always had a five o'clock shadow three hours early. His eyes were large and brown, and the whites of his eyes were so white as to be alarming when he was happy and downright terrifying when he was angry.

Sal was in charge, but so was Pipes. They were a unit. They seemed to have a bond with each other. He would work a week of day shifts and then switch to nights, but even on his day shifts, he could crop up at night, running the key along the pipes as he made his progress through the dark corridors.

Drexel Hill Children's Home had been a stately home before the First World War. The family who owned it had fallen on hard times. It was empty for years and then commandeered by the army during the Second World War. During this time, the government had partitioned off walls and added a vast vented heating system fed by a giant furnace in the basement.

The heating system no longer worked. But the long network of pipes ran throughout the hallways and dorms, and where heat was once channelled into the rooms during the Second World War, all that was channelled through now was the sound of Pipes and his key.

One night, a year after Annabelle came to live at Drexel Hill, she woke in the night needing to use the toilet. She shared a dorm with seven other girls, and it had a large draughty communal bathroom. The windows were kept open, even at night, and the stone floor was freezing cold when Annabelle hurried to the loos. She went to the fourth cubicle on the end, which was the only one which didn't have a creaky door. She'd just finished peeing when she heard the heavy footsteps of an orderly.

Annabelle leaned forward and peered through the crack in the edge of the toilet door. Sal was standing opposite the next toilet stall and shining a torch into the dark tangle of old heating pipes running along the corner of the ceiling. Her iguana-like eyes magnified by her glasses. There was a soft rustle and a faint scrape of metal as she put something there. Annabelle was holding her breath, and the plastic toilet seat creaked as she moved. Sal turned. Annabelle lifted her legs off the floor, balancing on the seat as she shrank back into the shadows.

Sal shone her torch underneath the stalls, the arc of light

moving left and right. And then she turned and walked towards the door.

No! thought Annabelle. *If she sees that I'm out of bed, she'll know I was in here and saw something!*

Sal left the bathroom, a moment passed, and then she heard the door to the dormitory open and close.

A pretty blonde-haired girl who was a couple of years older than Annabelle entered the bathroom. She was dressed in an older girl's clothes, a long red dress with strappy sleeves. And she had a small bag on her arm. Annabelle watched her through the gap as she stared in the mirror. It was quite dark in the bathroom, with just a little moonlight filtering through the frosted glass, and the girl stared at her reflection for a long time with an odd look on her face, a mixture of fear and revulsion.

Annabelle watched as she pumped some of the pink soap out of the horrible plastic dispenser, scrubbing at the inside of her mouth and tongue, reaching her fingers back into her throat to scrub. She rinsed, did this twice more, and left the bathroom.

This girl stayed in their dorm, but she was often missing. Annabelle thought that she was frequently ill, but she was arriving late at night from somewhere.

After a couple of minutes, Annabelle got up from the toilet. She couldn't feel her feet anymore. They were so numb. Slowly she crept over to the sink where Sal had been standing with the torch, and she looked up. She couldn't see anything between the two large brown pipes.

Annabelle wasn't afraid of the dark, and she was curious. The sinks were made of heavy porcelain and stood on porcelain pedestals. Annabelle hitched up her nightdress and climbed up onto one of the sinks in the row. She stood inside and reached into the darkness between the pipes.

Feeling around in the spider-webs and the dust, she found a small place on top of the pipe, which was flat, with a little door. It lifted easily and soundlessly, and Annabelle could smell oil. It had been freshly oiled. She felt around inside the pipe, and her hands closed over something, like a small book.

Gently she lifted it out and then crouched down in the sink. It was a burgundy colour, and where it caught the moonlight, the image of a lion glittered.

It was a passport. Annabelle opened the front cover and saw it belonged to the girl in the red dress. In her photo, she stared at the camera defiantly.

A movement by the door caught Annabelle's eye, and she looked up. The young girl had now changed out of her red dress and was standing in the doorway staring at Annabelle.

'Put it back. They'll kill us both if you don't,' she whispered.

46

Thursday, March 9, 2023

Kirsty Vardy arrived at Lewisham Row with another young woman called Ella Berry. Erika and Moss met them down in the station reception. They were both dressed in expensive-looking designer tracksuits, wore a lot of make-up and long manicured nails, and carried designer handbags. They had an attitude about them – a confidence that Erika admired.

'I asked Ella to come with me,' said Kirsty. 'We've been texting.'

Ella had huge cornflower-blue eyes painted with the boldest and most beautiful eye make-up Erika had ever seen. Kirsty had a small doll-like face, brown eyes, and equally beautiful smoky eye make-up.

'Thank you for coming so fast. And to reiterate, you are both here of your own accord and free to go at any time,' said Erika.

Ella's dark hair was scraped back into a long ponytail, shining like a flat piece of polished mahogany. She looked around the dank, smelly reception area, taking in the row of green plastic chairs screwed to the floor and the noticeboard heaving with posters for missing persons. She looked frightened and disgusted in equal measure.

'We've got a nice, cosy office waiting for you upstairs. We can order Starbucks,' said Moss, giving the girls her best smile. 'It'll just be an informal chat. You can really help us with what you know.'

They led the girls through the staff entrance and along the corridor to the office of one of the civilian support workers. She had a blue sofa with multicoloured cushions and pictures of her dogs on the desk. It was still an office but felt far from a police station.

Moss let the girls choose from the Starbucks menu on her delivery app. They each chose a Cotton Candy Frappuccino with cream, which horrified Erika; she'd never met anyone who'd ordered one before.

Whilst they waited for the drinks, Erika asked them to sit down.

'Just to repeat, you are not in any trouble. You can leave at any time, but you are the only two people we've met who have seen the killer.'

The girls put their bags on the floor and sat on the sofa. They looked at each other, trying to work out who would speak first.

'Did she kill Jamie Teague?' asked Ella.

'Yes. After you all left Jamie's flat.'

'She said she was a producer. I believed her.'

'I did, too,' said Kirsty.

Moss pulled out two chairs and gave one to Erika. They sat down opposite the girls.

'Could we start from the beginning? How did the casting or the meeting come about?' asked Erika.

'I saw it advertised on a website called Casting Call. They post modelling jobs and some TV stuff,' said Kirsty.

'I saw it there, too,' said Ella.

'When was it posted?'

'Two weeks ago,' said Kirsty. She'd been holding her mobile phone in her hand the whole time, and she looked down and started to scroll and swipe, her long nails clicking against the screen. Ella looked over at what she was doing. 'Here,' said Kirsty, holding out her phone. Erika took it. The job ad was fairly basic.

ONLINE SCRIPTED SHOW PILOT

POSTED: FEBRUARY 23, 2023, LONDON

SCRIPTED SHOW, GBP 350 DAILY

DESCRIPTION: SEEKING TALENT FOR AN ONLINE SHOW ABOUT FEMALE FRIENDSHIP.

DATES & LOCATIONS: SHOOTS MARCH 3. IN LONDON.

Erika passed the phone back to Kirsty. 'How did you respond to the ad? Was there a phone number or email address?'

'On Casting Call, you reply to a job ad through the online portal. So you don't have to give away any personal details at the beginning,' said Kirsty.

'We've both got profiles on Casting Call. So you reply and send a message with your profile,' said Ella.

'What does your profile show?' asked Moss.

'We've got photos on there, our measurements. Height, hair and eye colour, past work, if you can dance or play an instrument. Things like that.'

'I got contacted a day later,' said Kirsty.

'What day was that?' asked Erika.

'February 24.'

'Same as me,' said Ella.

'And who contacted you?'

'The production company. A woman called Michelle,' said Kirsty. She tapped at her phone again and handed it over.

Hi, this is Michelle from Bandit Productions, we really like your look, and we'd like to invite you to a casting on March 3rd in central London. This will be a half day, starting at 1 pm and carrying on into the evening, and we're offering the day rate of £350 plus travel expenses and a meal. Costume and make-up will be provided, and you will be required to sign an NDA. Please respond if you are interested. 07093467792.

Erika handed the mobile phone back to Kirsty.

'Can we have copies of these messages?'

'Yes.'

'You both got this message and were asked to call back on the mobile phone number?'

'That's normal with these kinds of castings. It was unusual that it was a paid casting and good money for a half day's work,' said Kirsty.

'Can you remember the person you spoke to?'

'It was this woman, Michelle. She sounded English and didn't have an accent. Maybe a bit older than us; she was nice. She explained a bit about the whole casting. She said that it was for a show about friends who spy on their family members when they go out,' said Ella.

Erika and Moss exchanged a glance.

'How?' asked Moss.

'She said the idea was that, for example, they get someone's dad or brother or uncle or some male friend to go on a night out with mates,' said Kirsty. 'And then they get a group of girls, and one of the group is the man's wife or sister or mother. They're in disguise, and they play pranks on the guy.'

'Do you mean like a hidden-camera show?' asked Erika.

'Yeah, something like that. Michelle, the woman on the phone, said that the format was still being developed, but we would be hired to try out make-up and filming effects. We would go on a night out, and they would do some covert filming to see how it all worked.'

Shit, that's sneaky and clever, thought Erika.

'And it was three hundred and fifty pounds in cash in hand, plus expenses and a meal,' said Ella. 'I have to pay my mum a hundred and fifty pounds housekeeping a month, so it was good money, for me.'

'Me too,' said Kirsty.

'Did you do any research into this company? Bandit Productions?' asked Moss. The girls looked at her blankly.

'We never normally do. Casting Call is a good site. They don't normally have anything dodgy on there,' replied Kirsty, after a beat.

'Have you ladies had much experience of going to castings?'

'I haven't, really,' said Ella. 'I only joined Casting Call a few months ago. This was the first actual job I got.'

'I've done a couple of corporate videos. A stock photo shoot,' said Kirsty.

'Have either of you ever heard of a casting director called Terry DeVille?' asked Erika. The girls shook their heads.

'What does he do casting for?' asked Kirsty.

'He did TV and film; he was based in West London in Barnes.'

Kirsty shook her head.

'I've only ever met women doing castings,' said Ella.

There was a long silence. *That would have been too easy,* thought Erika. *If they'd known Terry.*

'Okay. So you were offered the job with this Bandit

Productions. What happened next?' asked Moss. A look passed between the girls.

'What?' asked Erika.

Kirsty opened her bag and took a crumple of folded papers out. 'We've both signed these NDAs – non-disclosure agreements,' she said.

Erika took them and read. The gist was that the girls had signed an NDA saying that if they talked about anything to do with the job or the TV show format, they could be sued for £250,000 plus damages and expenses.

'This isn't a proper legal NDA,' said Erika, passing it to Moss. Ella and Kirsty both looked scared.

'How do you know?' asked Kirsty.

'Because a legal NDA, one governed by UK law, will always have a clause that reads something like "Nothing in this Agreement will prevent the Recipient from making any disclosure of the Confidential Information required by law or by any competent authority." So even if this were a real NDA, which it isn't, talking to the police would exempt you from being sued.'

Kirsty breathed in and out again. Ella stared straight ahead.

'Can we make a copy of these?'

The girls nodded.

'Good. Let's go back to what happened after you got the job. You both had a text message with the details of the work?'

'Yes. The message said we had to meet Samantha, the show's producer, in the lobby of the Landmark hotel in Marylebone Friday afternoon, at four pm,' said Kirsty. Ella nodded.

Rah Zahora at Folger said that Jessica Goldman had been booked at a hotel in Marylebone, thought Erika. She could feel her heart thumping. Was she close to finding out who this Annabelle was?

Kirsty went on. 'I was there first, and you came just afterwards.'

'Yeah, and the other two girls arrived shortly after,' said Ella. 'We'd all been asked to wait in the lobby, which is this huge, posh marble place. And then Samantha came over to us.'

'What did she look like?' asked Erika.

'She looked kind of weird. But she told us right away that she was wearing the make-up we were due to wear,' said Kirsty.

'What make-up?'

'A long black wig. Little lace dress, silver pumps, and she said that we would all be made up to look like a group of sisters. We were all the same age and the same height. All thin. She said we would have prosthetic noses and maybe some other subtle stuff put on us.'

'That's when she made us sign the NDA agreements,' said Ella.

'Can you remember her voice? What it sounded like?'

'Sort of posh, quite high-pitched and excited. Sam was nice and said how excited she was for us to do this work on the pilot.'

'She had a room booked on the fourth floor. It wasn't huge, but it was a junior suite, she said, 'cos there was a big bedroom, two bathrooms, and a sort of living room area, and when we got up there, there was this make-up woman, Jessica, who seemed totally legit.'

'She was a real make-up artist. And she thought the same thing as you guys did, that the job was legitimate,' said Moss.

'Did you talk to her?' asked Ella.

Erika leaned forward. 'No. We found Jessica Goldman's body yesterday. She was murdered in her flat in South Kensington.'

47

There was a knock at the door, which made them all jump. Erika saw through the glass that it was McGorry with their order from Starbucks. Moss got up and fetched the coffees.

'Jessica's dead?' asked Kirsty.

Erika nodded. 'Yes.'

Moss returned with the cardboard tray and their giant pink drinks, topped with cream and cherries. They somehow seemed deeply inappropriate at this point in the conversation.

There was silence as the girls unwrapped paper straws.

'Who do you think killed her?' asked Ella, her cornflower-blue eyes wide.

'We think it was Samantha. The woman who was in charge,' said Erika. 'Can I pick up where you went up to the hotel room? What happened then?'

'Sam – Samantha – told us that we'd be doing covert filming to see what the make-up looked like against real people.'

'Jessica was a bit funny about that,' said Kirsty. 'She said her make-up and prosthetics were good for HD broadcast TV. And when she asked Sam where the camera crew was, Sam told her that we would only be recording on an iPhone, and she'd also arranged for the production company to have CCTV from the places we were due to visit.'

'Didn't you think this was odd?' asked Moss.

'It seemed so legit – the posh hotel. We went through the casting portal. Jessica, in her make-up box, had a couple of old visitor passes from Leavesden Studios, where they filmed Harry Potter, and from BBC Studios. And the release forms. And she paid us the cash before the job. Three hundred and fifty pounds each, and she said the job would be no longer than eight hours,' said Ella. She rummaged around for tissue and blotted her eyes.

'What kind of make-up did Jessica do on you?' asked Moss.

'Sam asked her to make us look like her. So I had a false nose put on; Jessica also changed the shape of my chin and my cheeks because my face is quite narrow,' said Kirsty.

'I just had a different nose put on and some stuff on my cheeks. Like two little squares of silicone,' said Ella. 'I didn't see the other two girls or what they had done. When Jessica finished on us, then Sam took us off to try on the dresses and give us our bags, details of our characters, and the other props.'

'Props?' asked Erika.

'Yeah. One of the things Sam said that the producers wanted us to do in the show was when they revealed the prank, the guy who's pranked gets lassoed by us all.'

'Lassoed?' asked Moss.

'Yeah. We each had a long piece of rope in our handbags.'

A look passed between Erika and Moss. *The rope.*

'What?' asked Kirsty. Erika shook her head; she didn't want to tell them what Sam, or Annabelle, had used the rope for. She could see from their faces that the girls didn't know.

'Nothing. Please, go on.'

'While we waited for the other girls to do their make-up, Sam let us order whatever we wanted on room service . . . And there were free drinks and Netflix in the room,' said Ella.

'Was there anything about Sam that you can remember? Anything that sticks out to you about the way she walked or spoke. Anything.'

Ella and Kirsty were quiet for a moment.

'She was nice,' said Kirsty. 'Until one of the girls didn't want to wear the gloves.'

'The black gloves you all wore?'

'Yeah. Holly said she looked stupid in them, like a croupier. Sam said she had to wear them. Sam had been wearing them since we arrived, and she never took them off.'

'So she didn't leave any fingerprints. No one knew what she looked like, apart from Jessica,' said Moss to Erika.

'When you were ready, in your make-up, what happened?' asked Erika.

'We got a cab from outside the hotel,' said Kirsty.

'No. Before that something happened that I was pissed – sorry, annoyed – about,' said Ella. 'When we got down to the hotel's foyer, we had to give in our mobiles!'

'Where?'

'A safety deposit box behind the hotel desk. And we were told we'd have to return to the hotel and get them. My life is on my mobile. But then, she'd put in the NDA that we had to give over our mobiles, and we were all scared, so we did.'

'What time did you leave the hotel?'

'Around eight thirty pm.'

'Yeah. After that, we all got in a cab and went all over London. It seemed like that. And then we ended up at Covent Garden and went to a pub under the Arches. And we messed about. She took a video of us. And kept buying us drinks.'

'Lots of drinks. It began to feel like a night out,' said Ella. 'We went to a few pubs, and Sam kept going up to the bar-staff and speaking to them. She told us that she was arranging for the TV company to get the CCTV footage of us in the bar.'

'Did you believe her?' asked Erika. There was a long silence. Ella and Kirsty shifted uncomfortably in their seats.

'I feel like an idiot,' said Kirsty. 'But at the time, it all seemed too real: the hotel, Jessica, the NDAs, and being paid in cash. We finished in Camden, and Sam said she'd organised a special treat for us. And would we like to meet a celebrity?'

'And that's when we got a cab over to Soho . . . Hang on!' said Ella. 'Sam's nose, her fake nose was coming loose, and when we got to Soho, we stopped at a newsagent, and she bought some glue.'

'What kind of glue?' asked Erika, thinking back to the CCTV Crane had found of them.

'Copydex, the one that smells like fish. One of the other girls helped her with the nose in the toilets at G-A-Y bar, where we went after.'

'Do you know the name of the girl?'

'Jenny, I think,' said Kirsty.

'We had more drinks at G-A-Y, and then Sam said she'd arranged for us to go to Red Velvet, this club. And that's where we saw Jamie Teague. We were very drunk, but Sam said the production company had arranged for us to meet Jamie Teague, and then there he was. There was no reason to think she was lying.'

'What happened at the club?' asked Erika.

'We drank more. It was so loud.'

'Didn't Jamie Teague and his friends question you having fake noses and prosthetics on?' asked Moss.

'No,' said Kirsty. 'Jessica was excellent, and the lads were more invested in touching us in other places than our faces.'

'Did anyone do any drugs?'

The two girls exchanged a look.

'It's okay. You're not going to be in trouble,' said Erika.

'One of Jamie Teague's friends had drugs on him. I think it was speed. His name was Jim or Finn. It was Finn.'

'Did this Sam know the friend had drugs?'

'She bought some of the pills from him. A couple of the other girls took it, and we didn't, did we?'

Ella shook her head.

'The night went so fast. Jamie was so nice to us. He was nicer than his friends, and he was so sexy. He invited us back to his flat. So we went,' she said.

'What happened at his flat?' asked Moss.

'When we got there, Sam took us all off to the bathroom, and she said she wanted us to give her the rope we all had in our bags.'

'Did either of you have sex with Jamie Teague?' asked Erika.

'No. The other girls went off with his friends, but we talked on his balcony and smoked cigarettes. Sam was with us the whole time. She'd been trying to get Jamie to take speed all night, but he didn't want to because of his training.' Ella put her long acrylic nails to her forehead.

'What is it?' asked Erika.

'Sam told us around five am that we should all go 'cos she'd only paid the hotel for the safety deposit box until seven am . . . Our phones were in it. So we left with Jamie's mates. But Sam wanted to stay, so she did.' Ella was crying now. 'God. I feel like an idiot.'

Kirsty nodded.

'What did you do afterwards?'

'There was a car waiting for us, an Uber, and it took us back to the hotel. They gave us our phones. The other two girls got their stuff and left. I think they lived in London. We stayed in the room. She hadn't told us how to get the make-up off. We used soap and hot water, literally ripping it off our faces. Then we got coffee and left.'

'My mum was so angry that I hadn't called her,' said Kirsty.

'My parents were crazy worried, too.'

There was a long silence. The two girls had finished their drinks and stared at the empty cups.

'Did she tie him up?' asked Kirsty.

'Yes,' said Erika.

'How did she kill him?'

'She knelt on his chest, put her hand over his mouth, and suffocated him. Would you two look at the CCTV video of the night from Red Velvet and Jamie's flat? It would help us if you could point yourself out on the video and which one was Sam.'

Or Annabelle, thought Erika.

48

McGorry and Crane came up to the office with a laptop so Crane could show Ella and Kirsty the CCTV footage from their night out on March 3. Erika checked her phone for the first time since lunch and saw eight missed calls from Igor. And two more from an unknown number.

Oh no. No, no, no. Erika checked her watch. It was quarter past six. Tom. She'd forgotten to pick up Tom from school at three thirty.

She excused herself and left the office; the corridor was busy, and she found one of the small break rooms. She closed the door and dialled Igor.

'Erika, are you okay?' he asked, his voice filled with concern, making Erika feel even worse.

'Yes. I'm fine.'

'What happened? You were supposed to collect Tom from school.'

It was on the tip of her tongue to lie; she could just lie and make an excuse, but she couldn't. Telling the truth was a bad habit she'd picked up.

'Igor. I'm so sorry. This case I've been working on distracted me.'

'You forgot?'

'Yes. I'm so sorry.'

There was a long pause.

'Are you still there?' Erika asked.

'You know what really pisses me off? I don't care so much if you stand me up. This was my son. You left him waiting outside the school.'

'Is he okay?'

'Yes, he's okay. That's not the point. Felicity Brogues-Houghton was on duty, and she gave him a lift home.'

'That's good.'

'No, it's not good. Felicity has taken great delight in pointing out that me and Denise forgot to pick him up!' Igor lowered his voice, and she heard him move to another room and close the door.

'But, he's sixteen,' said Erika.

'That's not the point.'

Erika bit her lip. She had been about to say that Tom could have taken a bus, but the school was in a rough area. 'You've said that twice now. I'm really sorry. What is the point?'

'Denise just told me she's pregnant.'

'Really? Who's the father?'

'Frank. Her partner.'

'Yes, of course. Sorry.'

'Not only that, but Denise and Frank are suddenly talking about moving to Spain! He wants to start a business there. He has enough to get a golden visa and work there . . .'

'When do they want to move?'

'As soon as they can, this summer. End of June maybe. And Denise doesn't want to leave Tom behind.'

Erika could hear how broken he sounded on the other end of the phone.

'Okay. But he's sixteen?' she said, repeating herself. 'He can choose.'

'Erika. Since the divorce, we have a child arrangements order, and right now, we have a legal arrangement in place until the end of the year, until Tom turns seventeen. He lives with Denise and spends two nights a week with me. I told you the divorce was messy.'

'A court will consider where a child wants to live after age sixteen.'

'I don't want to have to go to court!' he snapped.

Erika gripped the phone. She'd had no idea this was going on with Igor and Denise.

'No, of course not. Where are you?'

'I'm at my flat with Tom, and Denise is here. They're in the other room.'

'I can come over right now. Blame me for it all. I can be the bad guy. I am the bad guy, but if you want to yell and scream at me, that's fine. I had no idea about all of this.'

'Why didn't you just bloody pick him up, Erika? Why can't I rely on you?'

Erika felt awful. Like she was the lowest of the low.

'You can rely on me.' The door to the break room opened, and a young woman who worked in the custody suite went to the fridge.

'I'm coming now to yours,' said Erika, and she hung up. She ran into Moss in the corridor.

'There you are, boss. Kirsty and Ella have identified themselves on the CCTV video, and the other two young women, so we know which of the "glitch in the matrix girls" is this Annabelle.'

'Can you make sure the girls get home safely? And also, have someone on the team follow up on Bandit Productions, this Casting Call website, and if you can get screenshots of the messages between them and this "Sam" producer alias we think Annabelle was using.'

'Yes, and we're going to find out who booked the hotel room in the Landmark hotel and arranged for the safety deposit box to keep the girls' phones in . . . Everything all right?'

Erika grimaced and rubbed at the headache forming behind her eyes. 'I forgot to pick up Tom, Igor's son, from school.'

'Shit. He's sixteen, though, isn't he?'

'Yes, but it's caused a huge issue, which I need to deal with.'

'If it's any consolation, me and Celia have forgotten to pick up Jake from school. Twice.'

'Yes, but you're both his mothers. And I made a promise. I'm the wicked other woman, though,' said Erika.

Moss pulled a face. 'Sorry. I hope you can sort it out.'

'Thanks, I'll see you tomorrow.'

It was dark when Erika left the station. She drove back to Blackheath, feeling more and more guilty. She would just have to take her lashings and grovel. How could she have forgotten? She loved Tom. How was she going to move on and have a life if she kept fucking things up?

Igor's flat was two streets back from hers, and as she parked outside, she saw Tom coming out the front door with his backpack. Erika got out of the car.

'Tom. I'm so sorry about today,' she said, hurrying over to him.

He looked up and gave her a smile. 'It's okay.'

'That's nice of you, but it's not okay. The investigation I'm working on – it's complicated and not going well, and I managed to get two witnesses in today for an interview, and the day just escaped me. I should have put a reminder on my phone. I'm sorry.'

'Is that the case of the woman who murdered four people?'

'Yes.'

'And you're trying to find the woman?'

'Yeah. We think she's using a disguise.'

'Really?'

'I'll tell you all about it when I solve it.'

'Will you show me crime scene photos?'

Erika laughed. 'I don't know if your mum would like that, or your dad. And I'm probably not very popular with them right now.'

'I've seen crime scene photos before, online.'

'Where are your mum and dad?' asked Erika, changing the subject.

'Upstairs,' he said, indicating the second-floor flat with a tilt of his head. 'Screaming at each other.'

'Oh. I'm really sorry. I fucked up.' Tom looked at the ground and kicked his heels on some loose gravel and smiled. 'What?'

'You just said the F-word.'

'Oh. I did, didn't I? Is that the first time you've heard it?'

He laughed. 'No. It's just that most adults in my life have a go at me for swearing.'

'You didn't swear. I did.' Erika put her hand on his shoulder and pulled him in for a hug. 'Sorry. Really.' Erika let go of him. 'Are we okay?'

He smoothed down his curly hair. 'Will you show me the case files of the murders, when you've solved them?'

Erika hesitated. 'I'll think about it.'

The front door of the flats slammed, and Denise came stomping out, pulling on her purple puffer jacket. She saw Erika and stopped, hooking her handbag over her shoulder.

'Evening,' she said; her lips had thinned to nothing. When

Denise was happy, she was beautiful, with her delicate features, but when she was annoyed, she looked quite hard-faced. Erika wondered how far along in her pregnancy she was, and if Tom knew. Erika hadn't seen her for a couple of months, but she didn't look like she was showing.

'Hi, Denise. I'm sorry about the mix-up with the school pickup. I've just apologised to Tom.'

'You should have told us if you couldn't do it. Bishop's isn't in the nicest area, and this one doesn't look tough enough to walk the streets around there by himself,' said Denise.

'What's that supposed to mean?' said Tom.

'I'm complimenting you.'

'I'm just a pretty boy, am I?'

Denise gave an exasperated tut and looked to Erika for support. 'Did I say that?'

'I'd say he's handsome,' said Erika. She didn't want to undermine Denise, but boosting Tom's confidence seemed more important.

Denise took a box of gum from her bag and tipped a piece into her mouth. 'He's up there. Sulking. He's all yours . . . Come on, Tom. You've got homework.'

'Sorry again,' said Erika.

Denise waved it away. 'I doubt we'll have to ask you again.'

'Bye,' said Tom, giving Erika a smile. They went off to Denise's car. Erika went to the front door and rang the intercom. It took a moment for Igor to answer.

'Hi. It's me.'

'Erika. I'm not in the mood right now for seeing you.'

Erika crossed her arms against the cold. 'I've just apologised to Tom and Denise.'

'What about me?'

'I apologised to you on the phone, but I'll do it again, if you let me up?'

There was silence. Erika glanced over her shoulder and saw Denise drive slowly past, watching her talking through the intercom. Erika waved, but she drove away without reciprocating.

'Come on, this is silly. Let's talk about it.'

'I just need a bit of space,' he said. This troubled Erika. She knew that this was about more than just her. Denise moving on with a new family and potentially taking Tom with her. If Tom went to Spain, would he want to come back?

'Okay. Call me, if you want me to come back. Night.'

There was a click as he put down the intercom. Erika turned and started to walk back home.

49

Summer 2008

During her time at Drexel Hill Children's Home, Annabelle made two friends. Two other kids whom she could trust.

The girl with the passport was called Casey. She was two years older than Annabelle.

The other friend was a boy; he was the same age as Casey, and called Zach. Annabelle liked the sound of her friends' names – Zach and Casey, Casey and Zach – and over the next couple of years, they hung around together and looked out for each other.

Annabelle realised, years later, that their friendship with her was a form of escape. Zach and Casey had a beauty about them. Even Annabelle could see that. And they attracted attention from the wrong people: adults.

Annabelle never pushed them to talk about the things that happened to them, but from bits and pieces that she heard, Sal and Pipes were the agents of this disgusting cruelty. A few years later, Annabelle discovered from Zach that the abuse from Pipes always happened with him outside, on the grounds of the children's home. For Casey, it was different. Nothing terrible ever happened to her at Drexel Hill. It all happened far, far away in another country, and it was Sal.

Sal had applied for her passport. All the children at Drexel Hill were 'cared for', and there was a legal care order for the orderlies at the home to look after them until they were aged sixteen. So Sal had been able to apply for a passport in Casey's name, and there were regular trips to a house in France. There were other men, and sometimes women, in this house, as well as other children.

Annabelle made sure that when they were all together – she, Zach, and Casey – they had fun, or as much fun as they could.

One of their favourite games was to mess with Sal. Since she'd come to pick up Annabelle from her home to bring her to Drexel Hill, Annabelle had hated Sal. She was mean for sport and was known to send kids to bed early without supper for the slightest infraction. She also liked to supervise when the girls took showers, and she'd removed the lock from the communal bathroom door. And her involvement with Pipes meant her actions took on a darker dimension as she became his enabler.

One summer day, the children were taken out on a day trip to nearby Hepworth House, a stately home with extensive gardens. They'd had a picnic on the grounds, and there had been pony rides and games. In the afternoon, they took a walk through the gardens, where there was a vast greenhouse filled with exotic plants.

Zach always had his head in a book from the library and knew quite a lot about plants. Annabelle didn't think much of the greenhouse. It was too hot, and they were being made to look at boring trees and shrubs with funny, long names in Latin. She remembered Zach stopping beside a small plant with pretty yellow flowers and what looked like pea pods hanging off. He checked no one was looking and gathered up a pile of the pea pods which lay on the soil below.

'Don't say anything,' he hissed as he stuffed them into the pockets of his jeans.

Annabelle didn't think much of it until a couple of days later, when Zach told them to come to the bathroom in the boys' dorm.

Zach went to a cubicle at the end, stood on the toilet seat, and reached up to the tank high on the ceiling. All the bathrooms in Drexel Hill had old toilets, where you pulled a long chain when you were done, and gravity did the rest of the work, pulling the water down from the massive tank through a pipe to the bowl below to make it flush.

'This stuff is explosive,' he said, pulling a tall glass jar from the tank and showing it to Annabelle and Casey. It was filled with dark-brown water and pods, and he shook it, stirring up the sediment inside.

'What is it?' Annabelle asked.

'Senna pods. A couple of teaspoons of this, and you'll be shitting like a volcano.'

Annabelle remembered how wide Casey's eyes went when she saw it.

'What are you going to do with it?' she asked.

Zach smiled. 'If I tell you, you might get into trouble,' he said.

'You're not going to give it to us?' asked Annabelle.

'Don't be daft. We're family. I wouldn't do that to you,' said Zach.

'What does it taste of?' asked Casey.

'I read it's bitter,' said Zach. Very carefully, he opened the lid of the jar and let them have a sniff. It had a strange bittersweet smell. 'The pods from the plant can be used as a laxative. You wouldn't want to drink even a tiny thimbleful of this. Who should we give it to?'

'Sal,' they all said in unison.

Annabelle didn't know how he did it but clearly remembered what happened the next night.

It was a hot evening, and Sal was on duty. She'd forbidden the girls from opening the windows in their dorm, even though it was a sweltering night, because she said the mosquitoes would get in.

The heat was unbearable on that August night, and one of the girls, a big girl who sweated terribly during the heat, had opened the window a little bit above her bed.

Annabelle didn't know what time it was, but the door to their dormitory was suddenly thrown open, and Sal stood in the doorway.

'Who opened a window!' she shouted, flicking on the light. 'I've been bitten!' The window opener had chosen a bad time to fall asleep, and Sal saw it open a crack. She strode over, prepared to drag the girl out of bed, and then stopped with her hand hovering above the girl's chestnut-brown hair. Sal gave a terrible groan and doubled over. Her stomach made a wretched gurgling sound, and she ran for the toilets.

Over the next few hours, the girls sat up in bed with the windows open, listening to Sal on the toilet as she groaned, swore, and cried out in pain. Annabelle didn't know how Zach had done it. Afterwards, years later, Zach told the story of how he'd managed to pour a few teaspoons into Sal's Thermos full of tea that she always carried with her when she was on duty.

It was a horrible story, really, Annabelle reflected years later. So many children have happier memories of things that made them laugh.

But that hot summer night, listening to Sal shit her guts out made every child who'd suffered her cruelty feel like there was justice in the world.

Annabelle had never told anyone about Zach and the senna pods. And she'd kept Casey's secrets, too.

Even now that both Zach and Casey were dead.

50

Thursday, March 9, 2023

Erika started to walk home through the dark streets. Igor had sounded very depressed. It wasn't good for him to be on his own. Erika decided to buy fish and chips and take them back to his flat, where they could talk things through. As she turned the corner and saw the steamed-up windows of Wetherby's, the heavenly smell of fresh fried fish and chips hit her nose. It was busy, and the queue of people waiting reached the door. Erika lined up behind a man with a little boy, who she often saw getting chips.

'It's a cold one, isn't it?' he said, rubbing his hands together.

'Yes. I'm hoping spring is just around the corner,' replied Erika. He was young – well, young to Erika. He was in his late thirties, and he had on a flat cap. The little boy was rugged up with a thick woolly hat, coat, and mittens, and his cheeks were flushed with the cold. The queue moved forward, and Erika could shut the door behind her. The warm fug inside enveloped her. Erika thought of Igor and his fears of losing Tom, and she ransacked her mind for any contacts she might have who could help with their custody situation. The family courts were notoriously secretive, but surely, at his age, it wouldn't come to that? Erika wondered who Tom would live with if he had to make the choice.

It was an old-fashioned British chippy with a long green Formica counter next to a big silver fryer with a glass-fronted shelf where the battered fish was placed to drain.

The queue moved quickly, and when the man in front ordered, he lifted the little boy up to see the fish.

'Is that a sea-worm?' asked the little boy, pointing behind the glass.

'No, that's a battered sausage. Sausages come from pigs.'

'Little Peppa Pig?' he asked, swivelling his head around to look up at his dad.

'All our fish and pigs die of old age after very long, happy lives,' said the older man behind the counter, dipping fresh fish fillets into a raw batter container. The little boy looked back at his dad, who nodded in agreement.

'How old is Peppa Pig?'

'Four or five. Peppa's got plenty of good years left in her,' said the dad, glancing over at Erika. She nodded and smiled.

When Erika reached the counter, she ordered two portions of cod and chips with mushy peas and two cans of dandelion and burdock. As she paid and collected the clear plastic bag filled with the paper-wrapped food, she got a text from Igor.

I've just been called in for a last-minute night shift.

Speak tomorrow.

When Erika stepped out of the chip shop, the cold air hit her. Even though she knew this situation with Tom wasn't about her,

Erika still felt like the bad guy. She felt rotten for forgetting to pick up Tom from school, but it had been an honest mistake, and she hadn't lied about forgetting. Tom seemed to have forgiven her more than Igor. No, this wasn't really about her. Igor was upset, and taking it out on her was easier than the other people in his life.

And on top of this, the events of the day's case still hung on her. She thought back to the interview with Kirsty and Ella. What if no one knew what Annabelle looked like? What if even the hotel CCTV showed a woman arriving in disguise? What if Joanna was the only one who'd seen Annabelle? Every piece of CCTV with her dressed in disguise was useless. Everything that Kirsty and Ella had told them helped them form a timeline of the case, but it was also useless. And then there was Neville Lomas – what a mess. And Terry DeVille seemed to have faded into the background, but he was just as much part of her investigation.

Erika slowed and realised she was passing Isaac's house. He lived on a quiet mews street, set back from the heath. Isaac's house was the only one with a light shining. Risking the element of surprise, Erika rang his bell.

Isaac opened the door, wearing a dark tracksuit and bare feet, and his long black hair was messy and tucked behind his ears.

'You busy? I have cod and chips,' said Erika, holding up the bag.

'Wow. What a treat. I was just contemplating a tin of baked beans, so your timing is perfect,' Isaac said. He stood to one side to let Erika come in.

'You've been quiet the past couple of days.'

Isaac closed the front door and regarded her for a moment. 'Fancy a drink?' he said.

'Yes, very much.'

'Come through.'

He led her into the kitchen. It was elegant and very white:

hand-painted white cabinets, work surfaces of pale wood, and a heavy butler sink in white ceramic. Even the American-style fridge was white. Erika always wondered whether, as a forensic pathologist, Isaac made sure he steered clear of stainless-steel surfaces.

'Wine okay?' he asked, taking out plates and cutlery. He laid two place settings next to each other on the kitchen island, facing the TV fixed to the opposite wall.

'White, please,' said Erika. She unwrapped the fish and chips and put them, still in the paper, on the two plates. Isaac returned with a thin-stemmed glass of white wine with condensation. They clinked glasses, and Erika took a sip.

'Thank you, that's lovely,' she said.

They sat down to eat, and unusually for Isaac, he switched on the TV to the news. As they ate, he watched intently, and he seemed tense when there was a small piece at the end of the programme about Jamie Teague. The news anchor said there had been strong responses to the appeal, and police were working on several leads.

'*Several leads.* What does she know?' said Erika. The anchor went on to say that the body of Jamie Teague would be released to his family shortly so they could plan his funeral, which was expected to be in three weeks. 'Is that true, his body is due to be released? First I've heard.'

Isaac was staring intently at the screen and absent-mindedly dipping his last chip in the remnants of mushy peas.

Erika wiped her hands and pushed her empty plate away. 'What's going on? I thought you would have called me to tell me about Jamie Teague's body.'

Isaac wiped his mouth and took the plates to the sink. 'I've been replaced as the forensic pathologist on this case. A colleague of mine, Maurice Calderwood, has taken over.'

'Replaced? By who?'

'It's more accurate to say I've taken a step back.' Isaac put the plates down on the counter and turned away from her. 'Neville Lomas's body will be exhumed tomorrow, and Maurice will conduct another post-mortem.'

'Why don't I know about any of this?' She watched Isaac's back as he stacked the plates in the dishwasher and closed the door. He came back over to Erika. She could see Isaac looked frightened, and then he did something that shocked her. He broke down. He sat back on the chair beside her and put his head in his hands.

Erika put her hand on his shoulder. 'What is it? You're scaring me.'

He wiped his eyes and sat up.

'Sorry. I didn't mean to do that.' He cleared his throat and tried to compose himself. 'Sorry.'

'Isaac. Tell me . . . You can tell me.'

'I really can't. I don't want to put you in a situation.'

'Did they make you sign the Official Secrets Act? Because I've had to.' Isaac turned to her and raised a perfectly shaped eyebrow. Erika nodded. 'At a meeting with the chief whip's office in the palace of Westminster.'

Isaac shook his head in sympathy.

'A couple of nights ago, I was sitting here in the kitchen, minding my own business with a glass of wine, when there was a knock here at the back door. It was the man in the grey suit with the birthmark below his left eye,' said Isaac, sipping his wine. Erika could see his hand was shaking. 'No one ever knocks on the back door. He did it deliberately to scare me.'

'He appeared in my garden late the other night, when I was getting firewood from the shed.'

'What a brave man.'

'What did he want from you?'

'He told me I have to take the blame for incorrectly certifying the death of Neville Lomas as natural causes.'

'Hang on. Didn't the same people put you under pressure to rule that Neville Lomas did die of natural causes?'

Isaac gave a rueful smile. 'Yes. I told him that; that's when he got quite nasty . . . They know everything about me, Erika. About Stephen and things before. Like when I was arrested as a medical student for cruising in a public toilet in London. I was let off without charge. I also got caught with a small amount of cocaine when I was a student in halls. It was the caretaker who caught me, Erika. Not the police. And still, this guy knew about it.'

Erika thought back to Stephen Linley. He'd been Isaac's boyfriend during the Night Stalker case she'd worked on seven years previously. Stephen had been the killer's second victim, and Isaac had briefly been a suspect.

'He left me in no doubt they have their special file on me. And they won't be afraid to use it if I don't do what they ask.'

It wasn't that any of this stuff shocked Erika; everyone had a past. She just felt terrible for Isaac. How deep did all this go?

'What do you have to do?'

'When they exhume Neville Lomas, I have to come forward and say that my findings were incorrect.'

Erika stared at him.

'It happens. . . mistakes are made in forensic science,' she said.

'And I have to ask to take a short sabbatical.'

'You can't be serious?'

'You think I'm making this up!'

'No. Not at all. I'm thinking out loud.'

'He told me that the damage would be limited. I can return to work after things have died down. But I have to fall on my sword.'

Erika took a sip of her wine. 'Are you okay? Apart from that?'

'No. This is about ethics. My ethics. And they want to use me to cover something up. I was put under pressure to say Neville

Lomas died of natural causes in the first place, and now that his death has been undeniably linked to a multiple murder case, they're leaning on me to help them clear up their mistakes. I will be a distraction from what they've been trying to do.'

'And what if you say no?'

'Have you been listening to me?'

Erika put up her hands. 'Okay.'

'I'm telling you because I trust you.'

'Of course.'

'I need another glass of wine. What about you?'

Erika nodded. He went to the fridge, retrieved the bottle, and filled their glasses. The news report finished, and there was an advert for one of the soap operas. He switched off the TV. Erika took a sip of wine, and considered things for a moment. How much were they going to lean on the police, and would there come a point where they tried to shut down the murder investigation altogether? No, thought Erika. She wasn't going to let that happen.

'There's something connected to the case and Neville Lomas that they don't want to be made public,' she said. 'I can't tell you.'

'Let me guess, something embarrassing for the Establishment?'

Erika thought about it for a moment. She'd been warned off talking about Damsa Afridi, and she'd been asked to sign the Official Secrets Act specifically for this. She'd signed nothing to say she wouldn't talk about a dossier of damaging photos. But no, she didn't want to burden Isaac with this information if it could be dangerous for him.

'Yes,' she said after a long pause. 'And now I'm having to tiptoe around my own team, and work out what I can and can't investigate.'

'What would you do if you couldn't be a police officer anymore?' asked Isaac.

'I don't know. I can't see myself slipping away quietly. I could be a private detective. Although it would drive me insane not to have any resources. What about you?'

'If I had to stop being a forensic pathologist right now? I don't know. I love my job, but this has shaken my faith in the world. I always thought I could swim against the tide of bad things and do some good. But what if the system is rotten to the core, and there's nothing we can do to stop bad things happening?'

'You can't let bad win over good,' said Erika. 'What are you going to do?'

'I'm going to do what they tell me. And you're going to forget we ever had this conversation.'

51

It was past midnight when Erika and Isaac stepped out into the street. He insisted on walking her home, even though it was two streets away.

'What will you do with your time off?' asked Erika.

'I'm going to go abroad, I think. Travel for a couple of months.'

'When?'

'I have to write to the director of Forensic Services tomorrow. I don't doubt that the new post-mortem conclusions on Neville Lomas will be released soon.'

'You know everything is going to be okay,' said Erika. She wasn't sure she believed it. 'What about Neville Lomas's family?' she asked as they turned the corner into her street.

'I don't know if his wife has been leaned on or if they got to the grown-up children, too,' said Isaac.

'I need to talk to the wife. She's been ignoring our calls. I don't know how much she knows.' They reached Erika's front door. 'You know, Isaac . . . this might all just blow over. These people have plenty of other fires to put out.' Even as Erika said it, she knew it sounded stupid. She opened the front door, and George was waiting. Isaac leaned down in the hallway and stroked behind the cat's ears.

'I think what's been eye-opening and slightly scary about all this is how things have been decided by an unknown quantity. They released the news of Neville's death being natural causes even before I'd officially written my verdict. Someone must have been watching my computer . . . And I'm supposed to be the forensic pathologist. The only one who can make the legal decision.'

'Do you want to come in for a last drink?'

'No. Thank you. I'm knackered.'

'You'll keep in touch?' asked Erika.

'Yes.'

He gave her a hug, and then he was gone. Erika closed the front door and stood in the dark house with her back pressed against the door for a moment. She was exhausted and had to go to a meeting early the following day with Marsh and Melanie to brief them on what was happening, but she wondered whether it shouldn't be the other way around. Surely Marsh knew more about the case than she did.

Erika picked up George and went upstairs. She was getting ready for bed and took out her mobile phone to set the alarm for six when she saw a missed call and a voicemail from an unknown number.

When she listened, it was a message from a young man with a mumbling voice. 'Hello, this is Daniel. Sue gave me your number. She said you wanted to talk to me about walking. Said you're kosher . . . Listen, I don't do it much now, and I only did it for a bit, but I was walking for a couple of girls for Diamonds. I can meet you. Sue says you pay a bit of money. I'm behind on my mobile phone bill. You can pay that, and we can talk.'

It took Erika a moment in her tired state to realise who this was. It was the number Curly Sue had given her for the guy who worked as a walker for sex workers.

Erika texted him, asking if he could meet the following morning. After a moment, despite the late hour, he wrote back to say he could meet, adding,

CAN U PAY CASH? MY PHONE BILL IS £40.

Erika usually gave narks a twenty for their time – Curly Sue cost her more, and now there was this lad. But beggars couldn't be choosers. She replied yes to the text message, then flopped onto the bed, fully dressed. She stared at the ceiling, too exhausted to process the day's events.

Erika was worried about Isaac, and the conflict she felt being his colleague and also his friend. She'd just promised to keep his confidence. What if she had to break her word?

It was too early in the morning, and Erika was too tired to grope her way through a moral maze. She fell into a shallow, restless sleep.

***

'The body of Neville Lomas is due to be exhumed today,' said Marsh. It was the following morning, and they were sitting in Melanie's office.

'Who did you hear this from?' asked Erika. She looked across at Melanie; it seemed like news to her, too.

'The director of Forensic Services at the Metropolitan Police Service was asked to look again at the Neville Lomas post-mortem results. Some irregularities have been flagged to the director regarding Isaac Strong's work . . . I know he is a close colleague of yours,' said Marsh.

Erika put her hand up. 'He's always very professional,' she said.

Marsh eyed her for a moment. 'Yes, but Isaac could have been rather careless this time.'

'How did the director of Forensic Services come to that conclusion?' asked Erika. 'If Neville Lomas's body hasn't yet been exhumed?'

'He told me he found irregularities in Isaac's report.'

'I thought irregularities had been flagged?'

'Yes.'

'He flagged them to . . . himself?'

Marsh closed his eyes and sighed, as if she were a small child who wasn't doing what she was told.

'Erika. I don't need this right now. Surely you should be happy about this? Things aren't being brushed under the carpet. Neville Lomas's body will undergo another post-mortem.'

'I don't know how another post-mortem would change my investigation, sir,' said Erika. She looked to Melanie, who was listening but had one eye on her computer screen. Erika's hands felt tied that she couldn't discuss the meeting in the Palace of Westminster.

'You are an investigator, Erika? Yes?' Marsh snapped.

'Of course.'

'Then why would you want to stand in the way of further investigation?'

'I'm not, sir. I'm just asking questions.'

'Yes, yes, of course you are,' said Marsh impatiently. 'Now. What we're here for is an update from *you*. What are you able to tell us new about your investigations?'

Erika took them through everything that had happened over the past few days, finishing with the interviews the day before with Kirsty and Ella. Erika decided to omit her meeting with

Curly Sue, the revelation of the dossier, and that she was due to meet with a walker from Diamond Companions.

'So you're focusing in on the murder of Jamie Teague?' asked Marsh.

'Yes. That's the murder where we have the most available CCTV. We now have a timeline from the two girls, and hopefully, we can work backwards and try to plot the journey of Annabelle before she arrived at the Landmark hotel on the afternoon of Jamie Teague's murder.'

'Very good,' said Marsh. 'Are you aware that Jamie Teague's body will be released to the family for his funeral in a few days?'

'Yes. I saw it on the news. It would be helpful to be briefed on things like that beforehand, so I don't have to remember to tune in every evening,' said Erika.

'I didn't know about it, either. I think it was a decision made late yesterday,' said Melanie, looking up from her computer screen.

'But I assume that Cheri Shelton knew before I did, as the lead officer on the murder investigation?'

Marsh sat back and folded his arms. 'Erika, why do you assume everyone is against you?'

'And why do you seem to run police business like a reality TV show?' snapped Erika. 'It wasn't just on the news that Jamie Teague's body would be released. It announced his funeral would be held in three weeks! Based on the news that his body was being released, that decision would have to be made by the family.'

'You need to watch your tone, Erika,' said Melanie.

'Yes, *that's* the problem, isn't it? My tone.'

Erika hated meetings like this. They just seemed to get in the way of her doing her job. It even felt like Melanie was getting in the way, which was unusual. Melanie was always on her side.

There was an awkward silence. Erika stared at both of them.

Unapologetic. Melanie kept her eyes locked on to Erika's, and Marsh looked away.

Wimp, thought Erika.

'How have you been getting on with that contact we were given by Richard Gaynor at Westminster for Diamond Companions?' asked Marsh.

'It was an unlisted mobile phone number. Not helpful at all. If I don't hear back from them soon, I will have to consider getting a search warrant. I think our murderer could be a sex worker seeking revenge. There have been four victims; what about the fifth?'

Marsh shifted uncomfortably in his seat. 'The moment you have anything, any information, however small, from Diamond Companions, I want to know about it, and you're only to act upon the information after running it by me first. Do you understand?'

'Yes, sir.'

Erika pushed out of her chair and got up. She'd been in this position before, when she knew the evidence was being suppressed and her superiors were trying to keep her from investigating something. It was just depressing it was happening on Melanie's watch. A senior officer she had admired.

52

Erika went to the incident room and asked Moss and Peterson if she could speak to them privately.

'You look pissed off,' said Moss when they were inside her tiny office with the door closed.

'And it's only eight thirty am,' added Peterson.

Erika rubbed her tired eyes. 'Listen. I can't tell you exactly how I know this, but some kind of cover-up is happening with Neville Lomas. I've been warned off him.'

'Who warned you off? Someone in your meeting at Parliament?' asked Moss.

Erika nodded. 'And now Neville Lomas's body is being exhumed.'

'Exhumed? On what grounds?'

'Because the first post-mortem result, death by natural causes, was incorrect,' said Erika.

'Was it?' said Peterson. 'I read the report – Isaac's report, right? He said that due to Neville Lomas's history of asking sex workers to perform violent acts on him, and this mixed with his terrible health, he could have died of natural causes, but he recommended an open verdict?'

'Yes. But I believe the chief whip's office briefed the press with a statement before the report was even complete, saying he died of natural causes. And now that Neville Lomas's death has been linked to a serial murder, they're in danger of being exposed for that, so they want to exhume the body to cast doubts on Isaac's verdict,' said Erika.

'Is Isaac okay?'

'Not really. And I've got Marsh and Melanie looking very closely at our investigation, with the chief whip's office in the background . . .'

'And you need us to be discreet about some of the things we're going to investigate?' finished Moss.

'Yes. To the point where you only share what you find out with me.'

Peterson looked at Moss.

'I know I've never asked you to do this before, but I'm concerned about the team and leaks.'

'*Leaks?* Dahlia?' asked Peterson.

'I don't know. I don't know if she's even clever enough to be a mole. But Dan Fisk's name is featuring heavily in everything to do with Neville Lomas. And Dahlia was on his team, and now she's on ours. And I didn't have anything to do with it. I don't want to burden you with too much info. Let's just say the men in grey suits have been making appearances. Superintendent Dan Fisk has also suddenly taken a three-week holiday out of the country, which gets my alarm bells ringing.'

'What exactly do you want us to do?' asked Moss.

'I've got a meeting with a guy who worked as a walker for the Diamond Companions escort agency. When I get his details, can you run him through the system but find a way of doing it discreetly so it's not connected to me or this case?'

'Of course,' said Peterson. 'I've got a pal in Traffic.'

'Thank you. I also need something else which needs even

more *discretion*. I have the name of the young woman who was apparently blackmailing Neville Lomas. She's an illegal immigrant, and allegedly she was or still is pregnant with his child. All I know is that her name is Damsa Afridi, and she'd being held in an immigration centre here in the UK.'

'I've got a contact in immigration who could be discreet,' said Moss.

'No, I need you to search all of the immigration and detention centres in the UK, a broad search done by someone, or several officers, very junior where her name is buried amongst lots of other red herrings. I don't want the search to come back to you, me, or even this station.'

'What do you need to know?'

'Age, background, if she was a sex worker. Also if she's pregnant and if so how far gone. I need the team to carry on working on the Jamie Teague, Terry DeVille, and Jessica Goldman murders. I also want to find out the names of those women paid off by Cheri Shelton's agency, and I still want to see if we can talk to Rebecca Reid, the woman who accused Jamie Teague of rape. Cheri's already tried to bat me off with talk of NDAs. And we need to find some other information about Terry DeVille. He seemed to have no close friends. It was either his partner, Russel, or everyone else was a colleague.'

'I know that McGorry has been working on Terry DeVille,' said Peterson.

'And Crane and myself have been working on Jamie Teague,' said Moss. 'The sister and her OnlyFans profile are bothering me. I'm wondering if there's some link there with sex workers. I've asked to talk to her on the q.t. I don't know if she's going to bite.'

'Good. And thank you. I don't want to put you both in a bad position, but I need your help.'

'Are you sure you don't want to bring Crane and McGorry in on this?' asked Peterson. Erika shook her head.

'No. They're both working with Dahlia, and I don't want her to know about this, if she's been briefed to keep her eye on me and report back about our investigation. I don't like how she went over my head on that night in January at the Neville Lomas crime scene, and then she was parachuted into the Jamie Teague investigation.'

'That doesn't make sense, though, boss. It would mean that whoever parachuted her in had prior knowledge of these Annabelle murders and knew Jamie Teague's death was connected to Neville Lomas's death.'

The three of them were silent.

Erika put up her hands. 'No, we can't go down that road. If something is out of our control or pay grade, we won't know about it. Remember: we're here to catch a killer. I'm not interested in rich and influential people trying to save their bacon. So until we know more, I want to keep investigating discreetly until we have something really meaty that no one can ignore.'

Moss and Peterson nodded.

'There is one more thing. I also want to – and this could backfire – I also want to doorstep Neville Lomas's wife and find a way to talk to her.'

'I'll put some feelers out,' asked Moss.

Erika nodded. 'Somewhere public, where she can't run away or make a scene.'

53

Winter 2008

The night Casey died, Annabelle was very ill with the flu. It was snowing hard outside, and Annabelle lay in the dormitory, unable to sleep, sweating and shivering. A few hours after lights out, Sal opened the door and came striding into their dormitory, followed by Pipes. There had been no warning, footsteps, or sound of Pipes's key scraping on metal. They went to Casey's bed. Sal put her hand over Casey's mouth, and Pipes dragged her out. It happened quickly and quietly, and when they closed the door behind them, the room was plunged into darkness.

Annabelle got out of bed and stood up, unsteady on her feet. She tiptoed to the door and opened it quietly. They were at the end of the long, dimly lit corridor. Pipes and Sal were on either side of Casey, who was struggling against them. She bit down on Sal's hand and managed to break free.

'She bit me!' cried Sal in shock as Casey ran towards the main staircase. Pipes and Sal took off in pursuit, and Annabelle, not thinking about the consequences if she was caught, followed.

Casey started to run down the stairs. Annabelle would never

understand why she did this. Did Casey panic? Was she thinking she could hide? They were on the ground floor, and the stairs led into the basement.

The old manor house of Drexel Hill was a vast, long building, and the basement was open-plan, like a vast underground car park with no walls – just endless pillars, deep shadows, and spider-webs covering piles of old furniture and boxes. A long row of small windows close to the ceiling let in the light from the full moon, and the ground was solid, compacted earth. Annabelle followed Pipes and Sal as they pursued Casey without her footsteps being heard.

They stopped at the end of the long cellar next to an iron furnace, which had heated the house during the war. Annabelle ducked down between two stacks of wooden chairs close by, and watched them through the space between the chair legs.

'Have you got a torch? The little bitch could be anywhere,' said Sal. Pipes took his torch from his belt, and the beam moved over the piles of chairs, old tables, and bed-frames. Annabelle crouched, shivering. She felt spider-webs sticking to her hot, sweaty face, and her heart was thudding. Where was Casey? Had she doubled back and run upstairs?

There was a crash and a yell. Annabelle saw Pipes reach behind a pile of boxes and drag Casey out by her arm.

Sal hurried over. 'You bit me, you little bitch,' she cried, slapping Casey around the face.

To her credit, Casey fought back and landed a ringing slap on the side of Sal's head with her free hand, knocking her off her feet and out of sight behind a pillar.

'Stop it! Be quiet! Stay still,' Pipes growled, trying to keep hold of Casey, who was twisting and yelling.

'Get off me!' Casey screamed.

And just as she managed to break free, Sal reappeared from behind the pillar. Her glasses were gone, and she held a large spade. She swung it high and brought it down on Casey's head, hitting her twice.

'Little bitch!' cried Sal. She hit Casey a third time when she was already on the ground. She brought up the spade to hit her again, but Pipes stopped her. He pulled it from her grip, and they both stood over Casey's still form, out of breath. There was blood on her forehead and in her hair, and it shone black under the moonlight.

'What the fuck have you done?' said Pipes. It had all happened so fast. Annabelle stayed crouching in the shadows. She was so close to them, and she didn't dare move. She watched as Pipes dropped the shovel. He knelt down and shook Casey, trying to revive her.

'She's dead,' he said.

'Don't be ridiculous!' said Sal. 'She's pretending.' She knelt down and felt Casey's pulse.

'You killed her. Can't you control yourself?' growled Pipes.

It was the first time Annabelle had ever seen a dead body. She'd heard stories that dead people looked like they were sleeping, but there was something terrible about Casey in death. It was as if she had started to dry out. Her skin looked silky yellow, and even her hair, which was usually shiny, looked dull. Blood was above her eye and at the back of her head, soaking through her hair.

'Did you want her to escape? Did you?' said Sal, her voice trembling.

'What are we going to do?' Pipes also sounded scared. They stood for a moment, silent. Annabelle was pouring sweat, and she was terrified they would hear her heart thumping in her chest.

'They wanted us to light the furnace,' said Sal. 'Let's put her body inside. Burn her, and we can dump the ash.'

'What?'

'You heard me.'

Pipes vanished behind a pillar and returned with an old sheet. They unfolded it, draped it over Casey's body, and then rolled her into it. Practicality seemed to overtake them. Sal went to the furnace and opened the door. The opening was a metre square, and Sal shone the torch inside as Pipes picked up Casey's body like a carpet roll. Annabelle never forgot how Pipes placed her body inside the furnace, laying it down gently, and then the whine and clang of the metal door as it closed.

'Little cunt broke my glasses,' said Sal as she retrieved them from the floor. She kicked at the compacted soil floor to smooth over the bloodstains, and then they lit the pilot light. It gave a clicking sound, and with a whoomph, the basement was flooded with the golden glow of the flicking flames.

Annabelle shrank back into the shadows as she felt the heat spread through the freezing basement. She had to clamp her hand tight over her face to stop from crying out with the physical pain of loss. She sat for a long time, numb with horror and shock as the flames flickered and burned. Pipes and Sal stayed by the furnace, staring through the small glass window. And a terrible silence fell over the dark basement. When the sweet smell of burning flesh started to permeate the air, Annabelle could take it no longer. She tore herself away and stumbled back up to the dormitory, silent tears pouring down her hot cheeks and a thousand screams swallowed back and buried deep inside her chest. The girls were all sleeping, as if nothing were wrong. Annabelle went to the bathroom, stood on the sink, and retrieved the passport from its hiding place in the pipe. The heat from the furnace was rising, and the pipe felt warm. She went to bed and put it inside her pillow.

The following day, things carried on as usual and Drexel Hill basked in the warmth of the newly lit furnace. When one of the girls asked Sal about Casey, Sal said that she had moved away to another home.

And she was never spoken of again.

———————

15 years later
Friday, March 10, 2023

Annabelle watched through her binoculars as Pipes dug over the strip of soil. He'd been a tall, broad, imposing man when she lived at Drexel Hill, but now he seemed smaller; his shoulders sloped, his hair was thinning, and his face was fat and jowly. Pipes looked like he was digging under duress. He didn't want to be out in the cold, turning over the hard soil with an old spade. A moment later, he was joined by Sal, who somehow managed to look older but precisely the same as she had all those years ago. She carried two steaming mugs and wore her huge, thick glasses; although her hair was still shorn in a bowl cut, it was now steel-grey.

Since leaving Drexel Hill and gaining the independence of adulthood, Annabelle had kept tabs on Pipes and Sal. She'd hired a private detective to dig around. They'd lived together, platonically, for many years. Their house was small and tumble-down, surrounded by a large plot of land, and the closest neighbour was a good five-minute walk in either direction, and it was twenty-five miles away from Drexel Hill on the Kent borders.

Annabelle watched from the woods opposite, separated from Pipes and Sal's back garden by a freshly ploughed field. She was dressed in walking gear, with a waterproof jacket, a backpack, and binoculars. It was her birdwatching gear, and it had felt like a lucky break when she discovered a birdwatching hut across the field from where Pipes and Sal lived. Annabelle shifted on the wooden seat; her leg had gone dead, but she didn't want to move.

It was the perfect view, still and crystal-clear, like she was standing over them, staring into their eyes.

I see you, but you can't see me.

There were a couple of broken chairs to the side of the plot, and they both sat down heavily. Annabelle's binoculars were so powerful she could see that, as well as his tea, Pipes was drinking Carlsberg Special Brew extra-strong lager, and this was his second can of the morning. Sal unscrewed a hip flask and added what looked like whiskey to her mug of tea. Pipes held out his mug, and she poured him a measure. Annabelle trained the binoculars onto their faces and zoomed in. Sal was staring in her direction, which gave Annabelle the eerie feeling of locking eyes with her. She'd done this the last few times she'd visited, and she moved between Sal's face and Pipes's to try and see if there was any remorse in there.

She couldn't see any. There was only anger and dissatisfaction.

Annabelle watched through the binoculars as Pipes finished the last of his tea. Sal stood and straightened her back with difficulty. She went to the spade, pulled it from the earth, and began to dig. Her face creased with the effort. Annabelle thought of Casey. She lowered the binoculars, and the air blew through the wooden slats. Annabelle reached into her pocket and took out Casey's passport.

It wasn't the original one she'd taken from its hiding place the night Casey died. It had been renewed twice since then, most recently two years previously. Annabelle stared at her photo with Casey's name and details underneath, and then she saw Pipes and Sal as far-off figures through the hatch, him sitting hunched over his can of beer and Sal violently stabbing at the hard earth with her spade.

'Watch out. I'm coming for both of you,' she said.

54

Daniel, the walker from Diamond Companions, asked to meet Erika in a greasy spoon café on the corner of a residential street in Neasden in northwest London. She arrived at half eleven, and the café was almost empty. An elderly lady with Sellotape on her glasses, wearing a flowery housecoat and an old pair of slippers, was clearing dirty plates off the Formica tables. A lone man in high-visibility overalls sat at the counter, absorbed in his mobile phone, his hard hat and a steaming mug of tea beside him.

A radio played ABBA's 'Dancing Queen,' and there were posters on the wall for bingo nights, second-hand cars for sale, and some of those room-to-let ads with a phone number printed on tearable strips at the bottom of the paper. Erika noted how much a double room in a shared house now cost in outer London, and she wondered how anyone could afford to do anything after paying their rent.

Erika ordered a cup of tea and an egg bap and sat at a table by the window, steamed up at the edges, which she found comforting. She was biting into the roll when Daniel arrived, dressed in blue overalls covered in grease. He was a burly lad with buzz-cut red hair and a freckled complexion.

'Are you Erika?' he mumbled.

'Yes. Hi.'

They shook hands, and he went up to the counter and ordered.

'I was worried you'd be in uniform,' he said when he returned to the table.

'No. I'm plain clothes.' Erika opened her bag, took out two twenty-pound notes, and slid them across the table.

'I haven't told you nothing yet.'

'No, but we agreed on forty. Have you got anything to tell me?'

He stretched his arms and blew out his cheeks. 'All I know is that I made more money doing walking than I do now.'

'Are you doing an apprenticeship?'

He nodded. 'Mechanic. Four years. This is my last year.'

'I think that's the smart thing to do.'

'Really?'

'Yeah. You've got all these kids going off to university to study all kinds of stuff that bear no relation to the real world, and they come out with debt up to their eyes.'

He shrugged. 'Yeah, but it's a suspension of reality. A chance to grow. They say you only really go to university to meet people who can help you in the future.'

'I wouldn't know. I didn't go to university.'

He looked around and picked up a copy of one of the tabloid newspapers.

'I mean, look at this. The *Masked Singer* show. Everyone I work with keeps going on about it. And I can see it's fun, but should grown adults really be getting excited about who's dressed up as a singing prawn? Do you watch it?'

Erika looked at the article. 'No . . . I think twenty years ago, that would have been a kids' show on kids' TV, and now it's prime time. Scary. They want us all kept stupid.'

He nodded and laughed, and Erika felt they'd broken the ice a little. The old lady came back with his tea and egg roll.

'Thanks, love,' he said to her. And then to Erika: 'I don't know how I can help you?'

'How long did you work for Diamond Companions?'

'I've done nights and weekends, here and there, for the past four years.'

'What did the job entail?'

'You know. I'll walk a young woman into a hotel, restaurant, or apartment block and get her safely to the person she's booked to meet. Anything else she does is completely separate.'

Erika nodded. She pulled out a photo of Neville Lomas. 'Do you recognise him?'

'Yeah. Neville was North East Surrey's MP. Found dead in January. I never walked a client who visited him, but I follow politics.'

'Did you know any girls who visited him, hear any stories about him?' asked Erika.

'There was one woman. Candy, her name was; I don't think it was her real name. She said she used to do quite a few MPs. She said it was the right-wing ones always loved to get spanked and flogged. I can't remember if he was included in that.'

Erika showed him a photo of Jamie Teague.

'Teague? He paid for sex?' He shook his head. 'No. No. *He* wouldn't have to pay for sex.'

'What about top models who might have sex for a lot of money?'

'Diamond isn't a modelling agency. Well, they were classier than the poor girls who get trafficked. But the Diamond girls weren't the kind who got flown out of the country to some sultan's palace and paid fifty grand for their virginity. That could be the kind of model Jamie Teague hired . . . Probably from a modelling agency. Who might, you know, give him one for free for the publicity of being papped with him or for a nice chunk of ice.'

Erika was just putting away the photos when a picture of Terry DeVille fell out of her folder onto the table.

'What you got his photo for?' asked Daniel with an odd smile.

'He was our first victim. How do you know him?'

'I don't,' he said, putting up his hands. 'My guv'nor in the garage where I work has the UKTV Gold channel on all the bloody time. They've been showing repeats of that reality show he did years ago. *Find Me A Soap Star!*'

'I'd heard about it.'

'It was when they launched a new soap opera called *The Boulevard* on a cable channel a few years ago – the one set in that housing estate in Milton Keynes that got cancelled. The reality show, *Find Me A Soap Star!*, was Terry and another three judges auditioning a load of desperate actors for *The Boulevard*. Terry was the "nice" judge. You have to understand I don't watch it through choice. It's on in the background of the repair shop.'

'What do you think of him?' asked Erika, holding up the photo, which looked like it had been taken in the 1980s. Terry had long, wispy brown hair and a beard and wore big red-framed glasses.

'One girl I walked with said her friend had just overdosed at a casting director's house. She was distraught and had to have a drink in the bar before she went up to her punter.'

'Can you remember which bar?'

'It was at the Ritz Hotel.'

'When?'

Daniel blew his cheeks out and had to think about it. 'November, maybe later – there was Christmas decorations up.'

'And the casting director was Terry?' asked Erika, her hair prickling on the back of her neck.

'Yeah. Terry DeVille. It didn't mean anything at the time, but the name sticks in the mind, like Cruella de Vil.'

'What exactly did she say? Can you remember?'

'The friend was called . . . No. I've forgotten his name, but he went for casting, and somehow he overdosed. Terry called an ambulance, and the guy was taken to hospital, and then he died.'

'And this sex worker was friends with the guy who went to the casting at Terry DeVille's house?'

Erika thought back to the albums of Polaroids they'd found at Terry DeVille's house and the photos of all the young men.

'Yeah. I remember her saying that Terry got away with it because the police, you guys, couldn't prove anything. And Terry called the ambulance and spoke to the police. Didn't try and cover anything up.'

'Terry got away with what?'

'Well, killing her friend, or getting him into drugs that killed him.'

'What were the drugs?'

'I can't remember. I don't think it was anything really gnarly, like heroin, but it all rang a bell 'cos I've been watching the casting show.'

'Can you remember the name of the sex worker?'

'Yeah. She was a real stunner. Her name was Annabelle.'

55

Erika left Daniel inside the café with a fresh cup of tea and a bacon roll, and she came outside to call Moss.

'You're never going to believe it!' said Erika, struggling to hide her excitement and having to raise her voice above a red bus and a removal van going past.

'You're never going to believe *this*!' shouted Moss. She sounded angry.

'What? Are you okay?'

'Fine. I'm here with McGorry in Surrey. We heard Neville Lomas's wife, Isabella, was back in town, so we came to try and talk to her. When we arrived, we smelled smoke and called the emergency services.'

'Was there a fire?'

'Yes. The maid was in their back garden burning papers in a huge oil-drum . . . Hang on.' There was a click, and then Erika's phone rang again with a FaceTime video call from Moss. She was standing with McGorry in the large back garden of a mock Tudor manor house. Despite it being the second week of March, the lawn was cut neatly into stripes, but in the middle, an oil-drum was smoking atop a tarpaulin. Next to the drum was another plastic sheet, where scraps of paper with burnt edges sat in plastic containers, and a forensics officer in a white suit was picking more out of the oil-drum with a long pair of tongs.

'Can you see me?' asked Moss, turning the camera around to her face and McGorry beside her.

'Yes. Where's the maid?'

'Inside with a family liaison officer and a solicitor.'

'What paperwork was she burning?'

'Neville's diaries,' said Moss. She moved to the old drum with McGorry. Erika could see remnants of the cover of a plastic-bound diary with the year 2014 and another with the year 1999.

'Have you managed to salvage anything?'

'Not really. The maid was in the process of burning the last one. The plastic on the front caused such an acrid smell,' said Moss. She moved across the lawn to a set of white French doors. McGorry's arm reached to the handle and pushed the door open. Inside was an office with dark-green leather studded furniture and dark wooden shelves. Behind an empty polished desk, two of the shelves were empty.

'This is where his diaries were. I'm going to send you a screenshot of a magazine interview Neville Lomas did two years ago. He was pictured in front of this shelf with his diaries going back thirty years. And in the interview, he hints that one day he will write a tell-all exposé of the insider dealings of politics,' said Moss. 'They used this same picture in the tabloids this week.'

Erika stood on the side of the road and felt the warm, sooty fog on her face as another massive lorry rumbled past. She thought back to the tabloid newspaper article she'd seen at Folger Costume Hire, and the photo of Neville standing before a bookshelf in his office, beaming into the camera with tombstone-like teeth on display. Behind him on the shelf were a long row of desk diaries.

'Do you know who asked the maid to burn the diaries?' asked Erika.

'No, and she's not talking. She called in the family solicitor as soon as she knew we'd rumbled her.'

'Shit.'

'Are you okay?' asked Moss.

'Yeah. I think I have someone who's met Annabelle. Well, it could be someone else called Annabelle . . .' Erika explained her conversation with Daniel and the strange link to Terry DeVille and this Annabelle. 'I don't know if it's anything. It could be nothing, but if we can get Daniel to work with an E-fit artist, it's a start. We could have an actual picture of this Annabelle. We could then go back to the girls who were hired for the fake reality show.'

'Do you think he's a legit witness?'

'He was a walker for Diamond Companions, and he can link this Annabelle to Terry DeVille, which I never expected.'

Moss had stepped back out into the garden of Neville Lomas's house.

'What the hell do you think was in those diaries that warranted burning thirty years' worth of his life?' asked Erika.

'I don't know. The maid is seriously terrified. Someone put the fear of God up her to burn these diaries fast. She's covered in soot and burned her fingers on the fire. She was using petrol from the sit-down lawn-mower as an accelerant.'

'How fancy. Can we bring her in?' asked Erika.

'On what grounds? Her solicitor is pretty fearsome.'

'It wouldn't be unreasonable for her to talk to us informally when this is a murder investigation. Or for her to give us a written statement of why she did it? We have grounds to suspect that she's been burning evidence pertinent to a murder investigation.'

Moss peered at the screen. 'I've got another call coming in from Superintendent Hudson,' she said. 'Do you want me to see if I can patch you in on conference?'

'Yes,' said Erika, intrigued as to why Melanie would call Moss and not her.

Moss touched the screen, but the call ended. Another lorry rumbled past and honked its horn at Erika, who was standing too close to the edge of the pavement.

Daniel appeared at the door of the café. 'Erika. Are you going to be long? It's just I've got to get back to work.'

'Listen. I need you to come in and do an E-fit for us.'

'When?'

Erika checked her watch. It was coming up to midday. 'This afternoon. I want you to come with me to Lewisham station.'

He rolled his eyes and sighed. 'You said this would be an informal chat. I've got work. I've got a boss,' he said, his demeanour changing.

Erika lost patience. 'And I've got a quadruple-murder investigation. You can either come with me voluntarily, or I can arrest you here and now for obstructing the police.'

'Steady on, love,' he said, putting up his hands. 'No need to lose your rag.'

Erika returned her phone to her bag. 'I'll lose the tip of my boot up your arse if you're not careful.'

'You can't say that.'

'I just did.' Erika indicated where she'd parked her car. 'This way, please, and I can call your boss and straighten things out with him. His wife knows me.'

'How does his wife know you?'

'Wouldn't you like to know. Now, come on. Let's go.'

56

Traffic. Always bloody traffic, thought Erika as she weaved in and out of the cars parting in front of them, hurtling across London and back to Lewisham Row.

Daniel was beside her, his tall frame squashed into her front passenger seat, his knees against the dashboard.

'Why have you put on the blue lights and sirens?' he said, gripping the door as Erika slowed and sped through a tiny gap between two lorries and then over a red light.

'This is a murder investigation, and I think you are one of the only people I have alive who's seen the murderer,' said Erika. She picked up her radio and called into control, asking if they had the E-fit artist lined up.

'Yes. She's going to be at the station in forty minutes,' said the voice.

'What do you mean, the only person alive?' asked Daniel, looking at Erika nervously.

'She's killed everyone else who's seen her face.'

'No pressure, then.'

'No pressure,' said Erika with a smile.

'Jesus! Careful!' he said, gripping the inside of the door as Erika shot across another red light and took a sharp right.

'You don't get carsick, do you?'

'No.'

'It's okay. You're in safe hands with me,' Erika said, flooring it as a gap opened up in front of them.

Moss was just arriving in the car park at Lewisham Row as Erika parked with Daniel.

'What's happening with the maid?' asked Erika as they exited the car.

'The solicitor is going to provide us with a written statement from her,' said Moss. Daniel climbed out of the passenger side, and when he stood up, he towered above her.

'This is Daniel Blakeson,' said Erika.

'Blimey. You're tall.'

Daniel rolled his eyes, and said hello.

'Sorry. I don't have a filter,' added Moss. They walked to the station's entrance, where a woman was smoking. She wore cargo pants and a leather jacket and looked like someone who'd been brought in for questioning.

'Hiya,' she said.

'This is Kim Faulkner; she's our E-fit artist,' said Erika, introducing her to Daniel.

'You all right, mate?' said Kim.

Daniel looked surprised to see she was so informally dressed. 'Yeah. Nervous.'

'Ain't nothing to be nervous of. We have a cup of tea, a chat. They'll give us somewhere comfy, and then we'll start to talk about the features and body language of the person we're trying to recreate. I'll slowly build up the face based on your memory of her,' said Kim. She stubbed her half-smoked cigarette on the bottom of her Vans trainers and slipped it back into the packet.

'How long will it take?'

'Few hours, tops. We can charge some nice sandwiches and coffee on the Met Police tab.' She grinned.

Erika's phone rang, and she saw it was Marsh. She cancelled the call.

'Let's go in,' she said, opening the door. Moss and Erika left Daniel with Kim and went to the staff kitchen on the first floor. Erika's phone rang a second time. It was Marsh again. She cancelled the call and a moment later got a message:

> WHERE ARE YOU? IF YOU'RE AT THE
> STATION, COME UP TO MELANIE'S
> OFFICE NOW.

'Everything okay?' asked Moss as she filled the kettle.

'I think the shit's hitting the fan with us going to Neville Lomas's house. Marsh wants to talk to me.'

'If there is some kind of cover-up, it all seems to be getting rather inept,' said Moss.

'How far along are you and Peterson on the other things I asked you to do?'

'Working on it as fast as we can.'

There was a bing-bong sound, and a voice came over the public address system.

'Could DCI Foster please report to Superintendent Hudson's office immediately.' The kitchen door opened, and McGorry came in.

'Commander Marsh has just been down to the incident room looking for you,' he said to Erika.

The public address system chimed again; this time, it was

Marsh's voice, and she could hear from its shakiness that he was trying not to lose his cool.

'This is a message for DCI Erika Foster. Erika, if you are in the building, please come up to Superintendent Hudson's office immediately.' There was a rustle and crackle on the microphone. 'Find her. The desk sergeant saw her! The station isn't that fucking big!'

And then a voice said, 'Sir, you need to switch off the microphone.'

'Oh, fuck.'

There was more interference, and then the speaker fell silent. Moss looked at Erika, and they laughed.

'Boss . . . this isn't funny. This is the commander. Are you going to go up?' said McGorry.

'He can't be that good of a detective if he didn't think to look for me in the staff kitchen,' said Erika. She bit her lip. 'Sorry, that's not professional. What is it, John?'

McGorry had a piece of paper in his hand.

'I've just been talking to a casting director called Valerie Drummond. She worked with Terry DeVille and knew him quite well. She also said she knows about the young guy who overdosed at his house.'

'What's the address?'

'West London, again,' he said, showing her the paper.

Erika checked her watch. 'I'll get the train and go now. I only have to change at Waterloo to get to Barnes Bridge.' She was just at the door when the public address system chimed again with another message.

'Go through the custody suite and out the back entrance,' said Moss.

'Good idea. Please don't let anyone bother the E-fit artist,' said Erika. 'And when are we expecting this solicitor to get back to us with a statement from the maid who torched all of Neville Lomas's diaries?'

'Within twenty-four hours.'

'Can't we arrest her for destroying evidence?'

'We can, but we need to prove it was actually evidence she was burning. We should see what her statement says first.'

Erika nodded and hurried out of the kitchen as the message became more insistent, and her phone rang again. This time it was Melanie. Erika cancelled the call and put her phone on vibrate.

57

The light was fading when Erika arrived at Valerie Drummond's house in Richmond. It reminded Erika of her first home in the UK. The sun shone through the windows, catching the dust in its rays, and clocks ticked and chimed in the silence. It felt like the rest of the world was far away.

Valerie was a small, thin woman with a hunched back. Her hair was dyed a bright red and shorn in a bowl cut. She had a beaky nose, and her eyes were very bright, and she studied Erika very keenly when she invited her in and left her in the living room to make tea.

A fire crackled in the grate, and two cats were asleep on top of a raised platform with a scratching post next to the window.

'You know you can sit down, dear,' said Valerie. She appeared a moment later, giving the door a little kung fu kick with her tiny black shoe. There was something Mrs Overall–like in the way that she staggered inside with a tray laden with tea. Erika sat down in an armchair next to the cats.

'Not there, dear, that's my chair,' she said, tilting her head to the armchair opposite. Erika switched places as Valerie poured them each tea. With her hunched back and bright little eyes, she seemed to loom over Erika when she handed her a cup.

'Thank you. Do you still work as a casting director?' asked Erika.

'Yes, dear,' she said, sitting heavily into her chair and trying to get comfortable. Erika looked around at the room, shelves filled with books, from the classics to modern. And the walls were lined with framed posters from West End shows and films. Valerie took a sip of her tea and nodded in approval. 'There's more milk, but you shouldn't need it.'

Erika took a sip of her tea. It was excellent and strong.

'Your colleague said you wanted to know all about Terry?'

'Yes. We've had trouble finding people to talk to. It seems he didn't have many friends.'

'He had two very distinct sides to him. There was the lovable, almost cuddly side to him, and then there was the side of him that used to seek out dark encounters.'

'And by "dark encounters", you mean . . . ?'

'Sex with other men, dear. That's what I mean. When Terry was a young man, being homosexual was illegal. For him and presumably a whole generation of gay men, that's not easily forgotten. And I suppose he was never comfortable with being homosexual. He was very good at his job. And we cast several productions together. We worked on one of the longest-running musicals at the London Palladium and other long-running productions, and they not only need to be cast but recast every six or twelve months.'

'What is the main thing a casting director does?' asked Erika, realising that she didn't know much beyond auditions.

'Well, we have the job of asking actors to read for parts in plays or telly or films, but a big part of the job is going out there and seeing things, watching plays, talent showcases, keeping an eye on who's coming out of drama schools each year.'

'You must have seen thousands of actors.'

'But I've only been contacted and interviewed about one actor by the police,' said Valerie.

'When was this?'

'It was late in 2019. November time.'

'Can you tell me what happened?'

'Terry and myself were working on our latest round of castings for a musical. I forget which one. Zach Selby, that was his name, had just graduated from drama school. He was twenty-one, and as far as I know, he'd had a tough time growing up in a children's home. Zach left the home at sixteen and got a job in a theatre on the south coast, where he'd wowed whoever needed wowing. He was encouraged to apply for drama school, which he did, and he got into RADA, I think it was. Graduated with all the momentum and excitement required. I know that Terry went to Zach's graduation showcase and was wowed. He gave him his card and called him in for a general.'

'What's a general?'

'A general casting. I used to do a lot of general castings. It helps to see an actor and have them in your database, up top,' she said, tapping her forehead with a gnarled index finger.

'So, Terry did a general casting with Zach.'

Valerie raised an eyebrow. 'I think they did much more than casting, if you know what I mean. Terry became smitten quickly and told Zach he would help him become a famous actor. To cut a long story short, Zach's career stalled. And he blamed Terry, and at the same time, they were in a dysfunctional relationship. I quite liked Zach. Whenever you do castings, you often need another actor there to read in the other parts, and Zach did this for me for a time.'

'Why do you think it didn't work out for Zach with the acting?'

'I think Terry smothered him, was jealous and controlling.

Zach had a few chances that he blew, getting too drunk before an audition. Not showing up for one very big, influential casting director. And saying you fell asleep isn't an excuse that will redeem you. One day, I was doing some castings here. I have a lovely big music room next door, which I used back then. Zach and Terry arrived late, out of sorts, around halfway through the morning. They both kept vanishing to use the lavatory. Zach comes back looking worse for wear and collapses on the carpet. Blood gushing out of his nose, mouth, and eyes. Horrific, it was. Horrific. We called an ambulance, which arrived pretty fast, but he was pronounced dead by the time it arrived at the hospital.'

'I thought that Zach was at Terry's house when he was taken ill?'

'No. Zach was staying with Terry, and I think he was registered on some of the bills, but he collapsed here. Which was better for Terry – no disrespect to Zach.'

'His death was ruled accidental.'

'Yes, an accidental drug overdose.' Valerie put her hands on the armrests and went to get up. It took a couple of attempts before she could raise herself to her feet. She went to a small desk in the corner and picked up a book.

'This is the Spotlight Graduates directory.' She glanced at the cover. 'From 2018 to 2019. It has all the actors and actresses who graduated that year. Here are Zach's details.' Erika took the book and saw a picture of a good-looking young guy with a shock of dark, curly hair. He had beautiful brown eyes and a wide smile. 'Handsome, wasn't he?'

'Yes,' said Erika. She looked at the details under Zach's black-and-white head shot.

- Zach Selby
- Playing age: 16 to 21 years
- Height: 5 feet 11 inches (180cm)

- Memberships: Equity
- Appearance: White
- Eye colour: Brown
- Hair colour: Chestnut
- Hair length: Curly, mid-length
- Facial hair: No
- Voice quality: Strong
- Voice character: Natural
- Weight: 10 st 1 lb

'He was twenty-one when he died?'

'Yes.'

'And Zach Selby was his real legal name?'

'Yes.'

'Can you remember the name of the children's home or where it was?'

'No, dear. I'm not an encyclopaedia.'

'Can I keep this?'

Valerie nodded. Erika hesitated for a moment. She didn't want to tell her about the Polaroid photos they'd found in Terry's house. Maybe she should ask a different way.

It was now growing dark, and the light outside had almost gone. Valerie moved around the room, closing the long curtains and flicking on lamps. It was only five thirty pm. But it made Erika feel like the day had ended prematurely.

'Who do you think killed Terry?'

'I don't know, dear, but this Zach was the only person I'd ever seen Terry lose himself over. Call it him being in love. Terry knew how to compartmentalise his life, but Zach seemed to spill over into his work. He was devastated when Zach died.'

'Did he feel guilt?'

'I think so.'

'Why?'

'I think he never admitted it, but he destroyed the young lad.'

'Did you know any other people in Zach's life?'

Valerie was stroking one of her cats, and it turned its head sleepily to look at her. 'Not really.'

'Did you go to his funeral?'

'Yes. It was sparsely attended. Four of us in total, and the vicar. It was a cremation. Terry paid for it all.'

'Can you remember the other two guests?'

Valerie put her hand to her head, and for a moment Erika thought she was going to say no.

'There was a man from Brighton – an older man called Carl, I think. Homosexual. Terry told me Carl had also been in love with Zach. He'd given up his wife and children to be with him, and then Zach went off to drama school. And there was a young woman there who had been at the children's home with Zach. Her name was . . . Arabella.'

'Or was it Annabelle?'

'Yes. Beautiful girl with willowy features, long dark hair. Quite an intense person, from the brief words we exchanged. Yes, she said her name was Annabelle.'

58

Annabelle waited in the small, windy hut for the sun to go down. She watched Sal through the binoculars as she dug over the patch of earth behind their house. Around four pm, Pipes got up from his chair and began to cut logs from a woodpile next to the house with a log splitter. He'd cut only the first log when Sal turned, stabbed the spade back into the earth, and went to him.

Annabelle wished she could lip-read; Sal seemed to think he was splitting the logs incorrectly, and after some angry back-and-forth, Sal pointed to the woodpile stacked next to the house. Pipes stared at her for a long moment. His dead eyes and jowly face still. He removed his baseball cap, and the wind caught the wisps of hair clinging to his pale, balding head as he went inside. There was a carport beside the house with an ancient blue Volvo estate car. Sal carried on digging, and he emerged a few minutes later with another can of lager, put it down next to the woodpile, and picked up the axe. The crisp, wet thud of the firewood splitting carried across the field.

Annabelle watched them work as the light faded through shades of gold and dark blue, and then, when the night fell in a dark sheet, Sal dug over the rest of the plot, and Pipes carried a basket of wood inside. The light came on in the living room, and Pipes appeared with the wood basket to build a fire.

There were two other cottages on this deserted stretch of land. The one to the right was empty and up for sale, and the house to the left, which was farther away, had a light on in the window. It was too far away to make out anything inside.

It was only when it got dark that Annabelle dared to leave the hut to get some fresh air. There was a half moon, and it cast enough light over the forest for her to see. Annabelle returned to the hut and did an inventory; in her small rucksack, she had two lengths of climbing rope, a sharp hunting knife in a leather holster, wet wipes, latex gloves, her Polaroid camera loaded with new film, and a Taser. Annabelle checked that the small cartridge of compressed nitrogen was loaded into the Taser. This was used to fire the copper electrodes, which delivered the electric shock. Annabelle also had two additional nitrogen canisters in case she needed to reload.

She'd watched Pipes and Sal for several long days and evenings, and they rarely went out. They didn't have a dog. Sal usually went to bed early, and Pipes would often sit up until late watching TV or looking at porn on his laptop, and he would carry on drinking until he slept in a stupor.

Annabelle knew that this final one could be risky. That's why she'd left it until last. With all her other victims, she had found a way to meet and drug them, so when it came to tying them up, they were suitably incapacitated. She would deal with Sal first and then Pipes. He was weaker, out of shape, and had already drunk six cans of Special Brew, but he was still a powerfully built man.

Annabelle killed the next few hours by keeping busy. She walked the perimeter of the woods to keep her muscles from seizing up. She drank lots of water, ate a sandwich, and checked on the surrounding fields. There was no one else around on this cold March night.

The moment Erika left Valerie's house in Richmond and stepped into the dark street, she took out her phone. There were more missed calls from Marsh. She ignored them and phoned Moss.

'We need to organise another E-fit with Valerie Drummond. She's saying that a woman called Annabelle came to the funeral of Zach Selby,' she said.

'Kim's just finished working with Daniel on his E-fit. I'm going to scan it and send a copy over to you,' said Moss.

'Thanks. Is there anything from the solicitor for Neville Lomas's maid?'

'No. Tomorrow morning at the earliest, I've been told.'

'Who's still there at the station?'

'It's just me and McGorry.'

'Can you run a check on Zach Selby? Valerie Drummond says that Zach was listed on the utility bills at Terry DeVille's house a few years ago. See if you can work backwards and find out if there is anything else about him in the system – criminal records, past addresses, and so on.'

'Will do. It's another lead, boss; I feel we're working towards something.'

'Okay. I'll see you tomorrow,' said Erika. She walked back to the train station and ended up getting on a slow train back to Waterloo. Rush hour had now passed, and the carriage was half-empty going in the opposite direction of the commuter trains. She reflected on her conversation with Valerie and wondered why she wasn't feeling so positive. They seemed to be so far behind this Annabelle. It was crazy that they had hours of video of her, but because she was heavily disguised, they had to rely on E-fit drawings from Daniel, who last saw her a year or two ago.

Erika found an email from Isaac, with a link to an article in the *Daily Mail*.

Hi Erika – just arrived at my hotel in Iceland. I didn't expect to be here, I've always wanted to visit, but trying to enjoy myself. It seems very far away. Check out this newspaper article. Not as bad as I thought. Keep me posted. Isaac x

The body of Neville Lomas, the Conservative member of Parliament for North East Surrey, has been exhumed from his grave in Highgate Cemetery.

In January, forensic pathologist Dr Isaac Strong conducted a post-mortem and recorded an open verdict. In a dramatic U-turn, Dr Strong asked for the case to be reopened after casting doubts on his original ruling.

After new evidence has come to light, Neville Lomas is now believed to be the victim of the same serial murderer who killed Premiership footballer Jamie Teague.

A fresh verdict on the cause of death is expected to be recorded by Dr Maurice Calderwood, a Home Office forensic pathologist who has been brought in to replace Dr Strong.

Dr Calderwood was unable to comment on an ongoing murder investigation but was quoted as saying, 'The most important task I have right now is to respectfully conclude my investigation and return Mr Lomas's remains to his family so he can finally rest in peace.'

We contacted Dr Strong's office, but he was unavailable for comment. This paper understands he has taken a leave of absence from his role.

Would this news report be enough for the people in power to leave Isaac alone? She saw it wasn't only the *Daily Mail* who was covering the story. The BBC News website had put out a more neutral version, but they'd still named Isaac.

The train rumbled through the darkness towards Waterloo, and Erika saw her tired face reflected back at her in the glass. She thought back to the maid who had destroyed Neville Lomas's diaries, and how she'd burned her fingers and arm in her haste to get all of them destroyed.

59

Pipes and Sal didn't bother with curtains in their living room. At eleven pm, Annabelle saw Pipes through the binoculars, dozing in his armchair in the living room. Sal had retired to bed an hour earlier.

It was time.

She made sure her leather gloves were pulled on correctly, put her binoculars back into her rucksack, and left the small hut. The wind now screamed across the empty field. And Annabelle had to fight against it as she crossed. The lights from the house cast a glow over the grass outside. Pipes lay in his chair. His eyes closed, his baseball cap askew on his head.

Annabelle hurried around the side of the house, under the carport. The main entrance was locked and secure, made of UPVC plastic. Annabelle carried on around to the front of the house, facing the road. It was pitch black, and there was no traffic. The trees opposite shifted lazily in the breeze, like they were underwater.

On a previous visit, Annabelle had discovered they left the small utility room window unlocked, and she was relieved to see this was still the case. She slipped off her backpack and hitched herself up onto the high, narrow windowsill. She reached inside with her gloved hands, took the line of cleaning products off the sill inside, and dropped them onto the grass. She had to perch on the narrow windowsill, turn around, and climb backward. Her trousers caught on the window frame, and for a moment, she was hanging with her feet dangling above the floor, but after wiggling her hips, she slid inside, and her feet landed on the tiles inside with barely a sound.

Annabelle stood amongst the shelves of cleaning products, breathing to slow her thudding heart. The utility room led into the kitchen, where the lights were out, and beyond that she could see the hallway and a bright light shining from the living room, where the television was blaring.

Annabelle spotted a bathroom at the end of the hall and two bedrooms. She had her knife ready in its holster as she crept through the carpeted hall to Sal's bedroom, where the door was slightly ajar. Annabelle stopped on the threshold and listened. She could hear her snoring above the noise from the television in the living room.

Annabelle slipped the rucksack off one shoulder, took out the Taser, and held it out, ready to fire. She didn't know if she could face Sal again. The memory of her killing Casey with the shovel had haunted her dreams for so many years, and the smell of burning when they lit the furnace with Casey's body inside.

Annabelle had checked the Taser many times and practised firing it at her flat. She pushed the door open and entered. There was a thin net curtain on the window, and the light shining through the living room window next door suffused the room in a low light. Sal lay on her back, tucked under a thick blanket. Her glasses were on the nightstand, along with a set of dentures in a glass of water.

Ugh. Annabelle hadn't known Sal had dentures. Sal smelt the

same as she had all those years ago – stale sweat and garlic and, mixed in with it all, the ghostly scent of laundry detergent.

Annabelle stood over her but couldn't move. She'd fantasised about this moment for many years, and now she was here, she didn't know if she could do it. And then she heard Sal's words from the night she killed Casey: *'They wanted us to light the furnace . . . Let's put her body inside. Burn her, and we can dump the ash.'*

Annabelle leaned over and pulled back the blanket. Sal wore a thin, greying nightie, and her large breasts lay flat under each armpit. She opened her eyes, and a look of alarm crossed her face. Annabelle activated the Taser; the light on the front strobed, lighting up the faded crochet blanket, and the two copper wires shot out and hooked onto Sal's chest. She went rigid, her eyes rolled back in her head, and then she was still.

Annabelle placed the Taser on the bed and swung her rucksack around, opening the flap. Keeping her eyes on Sal, she took out a roll of masking tape and tore off a piece, sticking it over Sal's mouth. Then she took out a length of the rope. Sal's body was flabby and unwieldy. Annabelle had to climb onto the bed to turn her onto her front. She tied her hands tight behind her back. Sal woke up when Annabelle was tying the first knot, binding her feet together, and her strength was surprising. She twisted and fought. Annabelle got the second knot tied, and Sal slid off the bed, her head hitting the wall with a loud thud.

Annabelle grabbed Sal's legs and pulled her across the floor to where there was more space on the carpet. Her nightshirt rode up to show her white backside. When Annabelle flipped her over, the look in Sal's eyes terrified her. The anger and rage blazed. She made a loud moaning sound, and Annabelle gripped Sal's throat as she climbed on top of her, kneeling on her chest, extinguishing the loud moans. She clamped the heel of her hand under Sal's chin, pinched Sal's nose shut with her fingers, and squeezed. She put all her weight on Sal's chest, but still, Sal fought, trying to turn her head.

'I hate you,' Annabelle hissed through tears. 'Die, you fucking cunt. Die, die!' Sal fought some more, and as Annabelle pushed her full weight onto Sal's chest, she felt her ribcage sink with a crack and then another. Sal's body gave a final death rattle and spasm, and then she was still.

Annabelle remained on top of her with her hand over her mouth and counted three minutes. Only then did she dare climb off.

She was out of breath when she stood up. She unhooked the copper wires from the front of Sal's nightshirt and then returned to her bag, pulling out a pair of scissors, another length of rope, and the Polaroid camera.

Annabelle zoned out as she worked, and it was only when a loud advertisement for car insurance blaring out from the television in the next room ceased that she remembered Pipes.

Annabelle reloaded the Taser and slipped on the rucksack. She looked down at Sal's naked body and felt revulsion and a strange sense of anticlimax, of feeling cheated. Surely she should feel triumph and release? But she didn't. Sal's dead body didn't bring her any pleasure. She felt foolish. Embarrassed. Afraid, almost.

And Pipes was still in the next room.

Annabelle's mouth was dry, and she was sweating in her warm clothes and gloves. She swallowed and stepped back out into the hallway. The living room door was ajar, and the sound of the television grew louder. Through the gap, she could see Pipes lying back in the glare of a reading lamp with his eyes closed and mouth open. Keeping the Taser aimed in front, she pushed the living room door open and walked across the carpet. She stopped between the television and his chair. The bright colours from the TV adverts washed over the walls and Pipes's pale face.

Annabelle hadn't noticed that the automatic switch-off timer on the TV had been counting down, and the screen went blank, plunging the room into silence. Pipes opened his eyes and saw Annabelle standing in front of him. He froze and then started to pull himself up.

Annabelle heard herself shout 'No!' as she activated the Taser. The light on the front flashed, and the two copper wires hooked onto his chest. Pipes went rigid, his eyes rolled back in his head, and he slumped in his chair.

Annabelle stared at him for a moment. She'd stopped breathing. She took a deep inhale, and a voice in her head shouted, *GO! DO IT! TIE HIM UP!* She went to put the Taser down. *NO! RELOAD THE CARTRIDGE!* shouted the voice again. Her hands shook as she removed the empty nitrogen cartridge from the Taser unit. Pipes lay still in the chair as she fumbled. She dropped the new cartridge on the floor and bent down to retrieve it. When she looked up, Pipes was standing over her. He seemed even taller than when she was a little girl. The whites of his eyes blazed, and his pupils were tiny black pips of hate.

He grabbed her right hand, which held the Taser, and twisted. Annabelle yelped in pain and dropped it on the floor. Pipes brought his free hand up and punched her. Pain exploded in her face as her head snapped back, and she went down on the floor, seeing stars.

Pipes grunted and shuffled towards her. He looked down and saw the two copper wires were still hooked through the material of his pullover and into his chest. He yanked them out and dropped them on the carpet. Annabelle's head rolled, and she struggled to get up. Pipes leaned down, gripped the front of her coat, and heaved her onto her feet.

'Who are you? You fucking bitch!' His eyes were still dilated, and he spat drool over her face.

'I . . . I was at Drexel Hill,' she said, struggling to focus. He still looked confused.

Pipes looked her up and down and then grabbed a handful of her hair and dragged her along the carpet. The horror of the situation snapped Annabelle alert. He was going to kill her, just like Casey. There was no time to kill him. She only had time to run. Annabelle could feel the holster of the knife under her, and the backpack jabbing painfully into her spine. He had dragged her to the door when she managed to reach round and grab the hilt of the hunting knife. His legs were moving but she hit the bull's-eye and buried the knife up to its handle in his thigh muscle. He let go of her hair.

His scream was delayed, but when it came, it was chilling. He staggered back, and Annabelle scrambled to her feet and ran. She took a wrong turn out of the living room, and it was only when she hurtled into the tiny bathroom that she knew she had gone the wrong way.

Annabelle ran back down the hall to the front door. It was locked. She turned, picked up the door-keys from the hall table, and grabbed the keys for the Volvo parked outside.

Pipes appeared at the door, leaning on the door-frame. The knife sticking out of his leg. Annabelle tried two of the keys in the door as he tottered forward. He was wincing at the pain but wasn't pulling the knife out of his leg. He fired the Taser at her but missed. The third key unlocked the front door, and Annabelle ran into the cold air, slamming the door closed behind her.

The Volvo was parked farther back in the carport facing the road. It was ancient, and it took several attempts to get the doors to unlock. Annabelle got inside the driver's side and closed and locked the doors. Her legs and arms were shaking badly. She dropped the keys in the footwell, leaned down, and groped around on the floor to find them in the dim light. When she sat up, Pipes stood in front of the car. The knife was no longer sticking out of his leg, and she saw a growing bloodstain where he'd tied a piece of material around the wound. He was carrying the log-splitting axe in both hands. And his eyes were wild.

Annabelle pushed the key into the ignition, put the car in gear, and switched on the engine. It roared to life, and she floored the accelerator. Pipes's bad leg meant he didn't have the dexterity to move out of the way. The car hit him head-on, and Annabelle felt a violent jolt as she ran him over. She overshot the driveway and slammed on the brakes, skidding to a halt in the middle of the empty road.

Annabelle turned and saw Pipes's crumpled form lying in the driveway, in the shaft of light spilling through the open door. His right leg and arm were bent at funny angles, and his balding head was slick with blood, but he was still moving, struggling to get up.

A blind white rage overcame Annabelle. She gripped the back of the seat and turned to look out the rear windscreen. She put the car in reverse and drove more slowly this time; as she reversed back up the drive, she felt another crunch and jolt as she ran over his body. She braked, put the car in first, and drove back over him again, feeling the jolt of his skull under the front right wheel.

Annabelle drove backward and forward several times, crushing Pipes's body into a vast red smear. She must have blocked out the next few minutes because her next memory was of being back at her car, parked two miles away in a lay-by.

Only when she arrived at Heathrow Airport and turned her car back in to the car hire place did she realise she was missing a glove and her Polaroid camera.

60

Unusually for Erika, she fell asleep in all her clothes on the bed, and she didn't wake up until seven the next morning.

Her phone was dead, and as she groggily pulled herself to a standing position, she found her charger and plugged it in. After a hot shower, Erika emerged in a towel and saw her phone blinking with messages. The first was from Moss, with the E-fit image Kim had put together from Daniel's recollection of Annabelle.

E-fit images always had an eerie, dead-behind-the-eyes quality, but the photo chilled even Erika. The face was long and thin, with a small nose and piercing eyes. The woman's hair hung around her face, and her lips were drawn into a scowl.

'Who are you?' said Erika to the image as George padded over and rubbed himself against her legs. Erika also had more messages from Marsh, Melanie, and Igor – Igor! She'd forgotten all about Igor over the past day. The final message was from Moss, asking if she was okay and reminding her there was a briefing at eight am.

'Shit!' said Erika, seeing it was twenty to eight and she was still sitting in a towel.

The incident room was packed when Erika arrived, breathless and apologetic. The E-fit of Annabelle was up on the whiteboard, and Moss was waiting with a sheaf of papers.

'You okay, boss?' she asked.

'Fine. Long day yesterday. What do we have? I can update you all on my talk last night with Valerie Drummond.'

'Yes, and I have an interesting postscript to that,' said Moss. Erika told them about her conversation; Zach Selby's connection with Terry DeVille; and the girl, Annabelle, who was one of the only four guests who had attended his funeral.

'Using Terry DeVille's address, we ran a search on Zach Selby last night and this morning,' said Moss, taking over. 'He studied drama at the Royal Academy of Dramatic Art, a top London drama school. He studied for three years, until he was twenty-one. Before drama school, he'd lived in Brighton with a youth theatre director called Carl Trapp. Carl Trapp still lives in Brighton and is divorced from his wife . . .'

'Valerie mentioned something yesterday about Zach having a relationship with a man in Brighton,' said Erika. 'Although if he was sixteen years old and it was consensual, that's not going to factor into our investigation.'

Moss nodded.

'If we go back further, we've discovered that Zach Selby was in the state's custody. He was a resident at the Drexel Hill Children's Home close to Maidstone in Kent from age one until he left at age sixteen. He left Drexel Hill in 2013, and was rehoused a few months before it was closed down after systematic failures in safeguarding children . . .' Moss shook her head. 'I've accessed the Ofsted government inspection report for Drexel Hill. After their visit in 2013, two staff members were referred to the police and another six were fired. The place closed a month later, and all the children were rehoused.'

A phone rang, and Crane answered.

'The home was in an old manor house in the Kent countryside about thirty-five miles from London,' said Moss. 'After selling it to a private owner, it's been gutted and reopened as a health retreat.'

'Of course it has,' said Erika, her voice thick with irony.

Crane put his hand over the receiver. 'Sorry to interrupt. This is Grace Mahunda, one of our support workers who pulled the details of Drexel Hill for Moss. She's just seen a report on the duty log system. An incident has just been reported in a village ten miles outside Maidstone. A courier found a man and woman's bodies early this morning. They are believed to be Lewis Crowe and Sally Hunt. They both worked as orderlies at Drexel Hill Children's Home for ten years, until it closed in 2013.'

There was a silence in the incident room.

'Are there any more details of how they died?' asked Erika.

'The police are on the scene now, but there are quite a few oddities. Sally Hunt's body was found tied up in her bed. Lewis Crowe was shot with a Taser, stabbed, and then repeatedly run over by a car. The car was still sitting abandoned outside the house, and forensics are working there now.'

'Tied up? This is too much of a strange coincidence for my liking. Drexel Hill. Did either Lewis Crowe or Sally Hunt have criminal records?' asked Erika.

'Grace is already on it, and she's going to send it all through,' said Crane. Erika went over to the massive map of Greater London on the wall, which continued into the Kent borders. She saw Maidstone, just outside the M20 on the southeastern side of London. The room fell silent for a moment as Erika contemplated what was unfolding. Here she had two dead bodies connected to a failed children's home and a potential cover-up surrounding a politician. Her heart sank lower than it had felt when she'd arrived for work.

'Yes,' said Crane. 'Lewis Crowe was charged with possessing indecent images of children on his computer and was accused by two other staff members at Drexel Hill of violent, abusive behaviour towards children. He was on the sex offenders register for six years, and his licence expired four years ago,' said Crane.

'Did he go to jail?'

'No. Suspended sentence. It was his first offence.'

'First offence he got caught for, I bet,' said Erika. She saw the disgusted faces in the incident room and shared their horror. Erika looked at Annabelle's ghostly, thin face in the E-fit picture. How was she involved in all this? Was she the victim or the perpetrator?

'Have we got an E-fit artist lined up to go and visit Valerie Drummond in Richmond?'

'Yeah. Should be at her place in half an hour,' said Moss.

'I know you only have a first name, but see if you can pull a list of all the children who were residents at Drexel Hill in the last twenty or thirty years. It will be a lot of data, but see if we can narrow down all the residents and staff who had the name Annabelle.'

Everyone in the team nodded. Erika opened her purse and took out a sheaf of twenties. 'Okay, I need a volunteer for a coffee run. Please order your most extravagant coffee and cakes on me. I know it's a Saturday and we've had a long week, but I have a feeling we're inching closer to cracking this case. I appreciate all your hard work, but let's keep it going with sugar and caffeine.'

The incident room sprang to life. Erika went to Moss and Peterson.

'I'd like you two with me today. We need to follow up on all of this fast. I need a car to take us for a look at this crime scene.'

61

What struck Erika about Lewis Crowe and Sally Hunt's house was the deserted location: close to the motorway, but hidden within a deep crease of flat countryside and surrounded by forest.

They passed only two houses on the lonely stretch of road, and Moss questioned whether they had the correct address until they saw the cluster of police vehicles up ahead and realised the road was closed.

Moss parked in front of the police tape, and they all got out. The wind howled across the surrounding farmlands, making Erika's eyes water. Peterson and Moss pulled on their thick winter coats, and Erika was glad of her own warm coat and gloves. She heard a cawing sound, and when she shielded her eyes to look up, she spotted a group of crows circling high above.

They showed their ID to the officer at the cordon, and he followed their gaze to the birds circling.

'They're hungry,' he said. 'I was first on the scene. There was a group of them picking at the entrails.'

Moss closed her eyes for a second.

'Oh no,' she said. 'Do we need strong stomachs?'

The officer nodded. Peterson looked at Erika.

'Three of my colleagues barfed up their breakfasts . . . I didn't,' the officer finished proudly.

They ducked under the tape and were met by a plain clothes detective of a similar age to Erika.

'Hi. DI Becky Ashe,' she said, shaking hands with them all. As they rounded the corner of the house to a wooden carport, Erika saw a blue Volvo sitting at the edge of the drive with its bonnet pointing into the road. The front bumper and the car's number-plate were covered in dry blood, and there was blood spatter over the front windscreen. The door was open on the driver's side, and a forensics officer in a white overall worked inside.

'The body is behind the car,' said Becky. They gave the carport a wide berth, circling past and then stepping onto the grass. 'Do you believe this has something to do with your investigation?'

'Yes,' said Erika. She wanted to say more, but then they saw the driveway was a smear of red with the barely recognisable remains of a man. They were quiet for a moment.

'The deceased's head is almost detached from his body, but his face is remarkably intact. We were able to make a preliminary ID from the courier who found him. He's been taken to hospital. He went into shock shortly after we arrived. We believe the body we found inside belongs to Sally Hunt. The friend who lived with him.'

'Are there signs of a break-in?' asked Erika.

'No, but a window was open in the utility room.'

Erika, Moss, and Peterson suited up, and they went inside the house, passing Lewis Crowe's remains on the driveway.

They first went to the bedroom where forensics officers were working. The body of the woman had been left in a now-familiar tableau. She was naked and hog-tied, lying on her front. There was tape on her mouth, and her open eyes were magnified by a pair of substantial grimy-lensed glasses.

'What's that?' asked Moss, pointing down to the woman's vagina, from which something was protruding.

'Her false teeth,' said Becky. 'We also found the copper wires and a nitrogen canister from a Taser . . .'

'Whoever did this would have had to work hard to buy a Taser,' said Moss. 'Not easy to get hold of them here.'

'Unless they worked in law enforcement,' said Peterson.

'And we found these on the edge of the bed.' Becky held up three Polaroid photos of the victim, hog-tied on the bed. Erika noted that she appeared to be dead in all of them. They were all signed with the name:

ANNABELLE

'I can see this is all familiar to you?'

'Unfortunately, yes. Do you have a time of death?' asked Erika.

'Within the last twelve hours, between ten pm and midnight.'

They went into the living room, where a small table was overturned and magazines and cushions were strewn over the floor.

'We found this on the floor close to the door,' said Becky, holding up a clear plastic evidence bag with a Polaroid camera inside.

'Any fingerprints?' asked Erika, glancing at Moss and Peterson.

'No. But it looks like there is still film in the camera.' Erika looked around the room, trying to put it all together. She went to the picture window, looking over the surrounding fields and forest, and saw a small birdwatching hut nestled amongst the trees directly opposite. 'We still need to print the inside of the house,' said Becky. 'We have lifted three separate fingerprints from the inside of the car. And a leather glove was left in the driver's footwell.'

Erika quickly explained the nature of their investigation and how it could be linked to the murders of Neville Lomas, Jamie Teague, and two others.

'Can we get those prints fast-tracked through the system? I'd like them sent to my team working at Lewisham Row.'

'Of course. I've got my support van arriving any minute now.'

'Thank you.'

Erika gave Becky the contact details for Sergeant Crane and McGorry. And then Erika, Moss, and Peterson stood together at the window and looked over the bare field, the trees, and the hut.

'You thinking what I'm thinking?' asked Peterson. Erika nodded.

'If this was an intruder, then what a good place to watch their victims from,' said Moss.

'Let's go and take a look,' said Erika.

The distance across the ploughed field was deceiving, and it took five minutes to walk to the birdwatching hut. When they looked back, the house was tiny on the road, and the police cars and van were just small humps beside it.

The hut was sparse inside, just a long wooden bench underneath the two observation hatches, both closed. Erika went to the first hatch and was about to open it when she saw a pile of wood shavings on the wooden floor. ANNABELLE was scratched in stark, tall letters with a sharp knife.

'I wonder how long she watched them?' said Erika, pulling on a pair of latex gloves and opening the wooden hatch. A gust of cold air came inside, shifting the dust and wood shavings on the floor.

Moss and Peterson looked around.

'She could have been here for some time,' said Peterson. He

crouched down and peered at the bench. 'There's crumbs here from some kind of food.'

'She might have needed to pee, too,' said Moss.

'What do you think happened? She planned to do them both in her signature style, but something went wrong?' said Erika.

'She panicked,' said Peterson. 'Or the bloke was too strong for her. She dropped the Polaroid camera. And lost a glove.'

'God, I hope they manage to get a print. If we could just have a print off her, it would be something,' added Moss.

Erika looked around at the hut. 'If she did pee, we should get forensics in here and out back in the trees.'

62

I should have gone back, I should have gone back . . . The thought kept passing through Annabelle's head as she tried to sleep in the airport hotel room. The heating was blaring out full blast, and she couldn't find where to switch it off.

It had all been planned out perfectly. Annabelle would kill Pipes and Sal and leave them tied up and humiliated. She'd fantasised for so long about killing them both, binding them, and suffocating them. And that moment when the light went out of their eyes.

Killing Sal hadn't given her the comfort or revenge she'd hoped for. And what had happened to Pipes was a bloodbath . . . and she'd made some fatal errors. When Annabelle returned to the car hire drop-off at Heathrow Airport, she'd seen in the mirror how wild she looked. She'd changed her clothes before going inside the office. The arm had been torn on her sweater, and there was blood on her trousers. She had scrubbed her face and hands with wet wipes and did her best to cover a big bruise on her cheek with a bit of make-up.

She boarded the transfer bus to the hotel and tried to piece together how she'd returned to the hire car. She must have run down the dark lanes the two miles to where she'd parked. Pipes must have been dead; she remembered running over him in the car several times. But the glove. The fucking glove.

I should have gone back. I should have gone back and got the glove.

And the camera. No. The camera didn't matter. She had been careful to never touch it with her bare hands. Hadn't she? Yes. *Yes.*

Annabelle's alarm had gone off at five am, and in the cold light of her hotel room's bathroom mirror, the bruise looked worse. The whole side of her face was swollen and misshapen, and her skin had an angry purple hue. She showered and put on her expensive outfit: a Louis Vuitton print dress and black Chanel boots. She blow-dried her hair until it was sleek and poker-straight, and she spent almost an hour applying heavy make-up with smoky eyes and lots of shading. Finally, she added lots of jewellery. Her face was still an odd shape on the left-hand side, but the mauve hue on her skin was covered. And now she didn't look like a criminal on the run. She could pass for an attractive, mad, wealthy woman.

She checked her luggage. She had two heavy suitcases and her Louis Vuitton handbag, which contained make-up, a passport, her wallet, some painkillers, a paperback novel, and a small silver key, the only key on her person, which she slipped into the inside pocket.

She left the hotel at six thirty am and boarded the transfer bus to Heathrow Terminal Five, where she'd paid a small fortune for a first-class ticket to Los Angeles. With her passport in the name of Casey Silver, she was flying off to disappear and start a new life.

Annabelle arrived three hours before her flight was due to depart at eleven am. The first-class terminal was a beautiful glass-and-steel structure and almost empty.

She went to the check-in and presented herself with her two suitcases. The steward weighed her bags and then ran her passport through the magnetic stripe on the computer keyboard. There was a long moment whilst she stared at the screen.

'You have a visa or an ESTA?' she asked, turning the passport over and flicking through the pages. She arrived at the page with the B-1/B-2 visa, with Annabelle's photo and Casey's name. 'Ah yes, a visa.' She tapped at her screen, and after a slight frown and another long pause, the printer spat out Casey Silver's first-class air ticket and two labels for her luggage.

Annabelle gave a huge sigh of relief. She'd cleared the first big hurdle.

'You have a pleasant flight, Miss Silver,' said the steward, handing back her passport and tickets. Annabelle went through the security check with no problem and then headed to the first-class lounge, where she ordered a large vodka, took half a Xanax, and sat down to wait to board the plane.

Despite taking deep breaths, all she could think about was the glove. If she lost the glove, what did she touch?

Erika, Peterson, and Moss stopped at a petrol station on the M20 just outside London at 10.40 am. While Erika filled the car, Moss and Peterson went inside to buy coffee.

Erika had a strong stomach, but after seeing Lewis Crowe's remains strewn across the driveway outside his house, she could only contemplate drinking black coffee. Just as she joined Moss and Peterson at the small seating area outside, where they had coffee waiting, her phone rang. It was Crane. She put him on speakerphone.

'Boss. I got the fingerprints sent over by DI Ashe there. We've run all three through the system,' he said.

'And?'

'Lewis Crowe and Sally Hunt both have criminal records, for

assaulting a neighbour a few years ago during a boundary dispute on their land. Their fingerprints were in the car, as you'd expect. The third print didn't show up on the National Crime Database. However, we did a wide search through our other databases, and the prints belong to a twenty-five-year-old woman called Casey Silver. Her fingerprints were taken at the US embassy in London on February 9 for a visa application.'

'Where was her print found?' asked Erika.

'Three prints were found. One on the door handle of the Volvo, one on the leather glove left in the car footwell, and another on the dashboard. There's a level of urgency to this, boss. Casey Silver is booked on a flight to Los Angeles that departs from Heathrow in thirty minutes.'

'Shit . . .' Erika looked at Moss and Peterson and had a moment of panic. 'Do we have any prints from this Casey Silver from inside the house?'

'No. Another thing. Casey Silver was a resident at Drexel Hill Children's Home until 2008, but her records are incomplete.'

'What do you mean, "incomplete"?'

'There's nothing to say she ever left the children's home.'

Erika looked at the clock on the wall. The time changed from 10.50 to 10.51. 'What time is this flight taking off?'

'Eleven twenty, boss.'

'I'll call you back.'

Erika hung up the phone and dialled Melanie.

'I don't have time to explain. I need authorisation to stop a flight from Heathrow leaving . . .' Erika heard her phone beep and looked at the screen. It was a text from Crane with flight details. 'It's British Airways flight BA4591 departing Heathrow Terminal Five at eleven twenty am for LAX.'

'It's departing in twenty-eight minutes!' Melanie said.

'Try. Please try.'

Annabelle sat in first class with her belt tightly buckled, gripping the armrests of her seat as the huge airbus reached its slot on the runway. She saw out the window as the aeroplane's nose slowly turned, and then it came to a stop. Scorched and scarred with rubber wheel marks, the tarmac runway stretched out seemingly forever where the lights lining the sides blinked.

'Cabin crew, seats for take-off,' came the captain's voice through the intercom.

'First time flying?' asked an elegant woman sitting opposite. Annabelle nodded.

'Holiday or business?'

'A bit of both,' she said. She had a connecting flight booked from Los Angeles to Las Vegas. Annabelle had two weeks booked in the Bellagio hotel. Her plan was to meet a rich man, of which there were many in Vegas, and if that didn't work out, she was going to disappear. She had $10,000 in cash, and another $20,000 in a US checking account. Either way, it was easy to reinvent yourself in America.

The plane's engines ramped up to a higher pitch, and it felt like the plane was finally going to speed along the runway when a blue light appeared on Annabelle's side of the aircraft. The engines powered down, and two police cars with their lights flashing and sirens blaring pulled up to the side of the plane. A mobile set of stairs was also speeding up beside the police cars.

Annabelle looked to the two air stewards strapped into their seats at the front. The intercom rang, and one of the stewards got up and picked up the handset.

No. No, this can't be, thought Annabelle. *They can't have put things together so fast. I covered my tracks . . .* And then the voice in her head said, *The glove. You lost the glove – what did you touch?*

There was a thumping sound on the side of the aeroplane, and

Annabelle saw that two police officers had climbed the steps and were now at the plane door.

'Don't open it!' Annabelle heard herself cry. 'Those men aren't real police officers. They're terrorists!'

The woman next to her screamed, and suddenly, there was mayhem as the two air stewards were joined by a male steward from business class.

'They're terrorists, and if you let them in, they'll kill us all!' Annabelle shouted. She scrabbled around in her Louis Vuitton handbag and found the key in the small inside pocket.

The key. Her insurance policy. If they arrested her, they would search everything and find the key. Everything she owned was on this plane. In amongst the commotion and panic, as the air steward turned the handle to open the airplane door. Annabelle made a split-second decision – she put the key on the back of her tongue. It felt huge in her mouth, and wincing, she swallowed it.

63

It was early afternoon when the woman Erika believed was Annabelle was brought to Lewisham Row police station in a convoy of police cars.

Her arrest on British Airways flight BA4591 had been chaotic. The police finally gained entry to the aeroplane cabin, and amongst the mass panic inside, they had arrested Annabelle in connection with the murders of Lewis Crowe and Sally Hunt.

Erika and her team watched from the windows in the corridor, looking down at the custody entrance behind Lewisham Row as Annabelle was brought out of the police car, wearing handcuffs. She was a slight, well-dressed woman with long brown hair, an oversized designer handbag in the crook of her arm, and sunglasses on her head.

'Her passport says she's Casey Silver, and so do the fingerprints found at the crime scene,' said Erika. 'But Casey Silver disappeared in 2008.'

'She looks like the two E-fit images from Daniel and Valerie,' said Moss. They watched as she was escorted through the back doors leading into the custody suite, where Erika had asked that she be placed in a cell. Another car had pulled up behind the first, and a police officer removed two large suitcases encased in giant evidence bags.

———————

It wasn't until three hours later that Erika came face-to-face with the woman she believed was Annabelle.

A duty solicitor had been provided, and Erika sat opposite the two of them with Moss.

'It's seven pm on Saturday, March 11, 2023,' said Erika, looking up at the video camera recording in the corner of the room. She knew the whole team was watching from the video suite next door. 'I am Detective Chief Inspector Erika Foster. This is Detective Inspector Kate Moss, and we're joined by the suspect's legal representative, Maureen Clark. The suspect has a passport under the name Casey Silver, but we believe her real name is Annabelle Wallis.'

Erika stared at the young woman in front of her. She looked confident and sanguine.

'Can you confirm your full legal name?'

She glanced at her solicitor and folded her arms.

'What does it say in my passport?'

Her voice was smooth and a bit posh, thought Erika, like those condescending women who do the voice-overs for insurance commercials. Erika pulled out a photocopy of Casey Silver's passport photo page and a scanned image of a bank card. She slid them across the table.

'You have a passport with your photo in the name Casey Silver. But when you were arrested, you also had a bank card in your suitcase in the name of Annabelle Wallis. Which name is your legal name?'

Annabelle was silent and remained with her arms folded. She didn't look at the two pieces of paper.

'Do you have a photo ID in the name of Annabelle Wallis?' asked Moss.

'If we're asking about names, is your name really Kate Moss, like the supermodel?' she asked.

'Yes, I used to work as a lookalike, but I get paid better for being a detective inspector,' said Moss dryly. Erika saw the solicitor suppress a small smile. 'I'm interested to see how you talk your way out of all this,' Moss added, tapping the two pieces of paper on the desk between them. There was silence.

'An Annabelle Wallis has been renting an apartment in a complex in Canary Wharf for the past four years,' said Erika. 'Moreover, the property management company who rented the flat positively identified your photo, saying you are Annabelle Wallis.'

'What photo?'

'The photo we took in our custody suite,' said Erika.

'Your mugshot,' said Moss. Annabelle unfolded her arms and sat back. 'Why were you travelling on a passport with the name Casey Silver?'

'Is it illegal to go on holiday to America? I had the correct visa.'

'It's a criminal offence to have a forged passport,' said Erika.

'That's not forged. That's a genuine passport issued by the UK passport office.'

'Using an improperly obtained identity document is also a criminal offence.'

Annabelle sighed and leaned forward.

'Correct, Erika. Under Section 6 of the Identity Card Act 2010, it's an offence for a person without reasonable excuse to have in his or her possession or control a false identity document, an improperly obtained identity document, someone else's identity document, apparatus, or any article or material to his or her knowledge designed or adapted for making false identity documents . . . Any of these carry a maximum of two years' imprisonment or fine or both,' she said. 'If that's all you can charge me with, the maximum time I'll go down for is two years; I'll be out in one or less. Is that what you're going to charge me with?'

Maureen, the solicitor, could not suppress her surprise and raised an eyebrow.

'How did you come into the possession of a passport in the name of Casey Silver?' asked Erika. There was a long silence. Annabelle didn't reply or break eye contact. 'You've been arrested for the murders of Lewis Crowe and Sally Hunt. We are also interviewing you under caution in connection to the murders of Terry DeVille, Neville Lomas, Jamie Teague, and Jessica Goldman.'

'You think I murdered all of them and Jamie Teague, the Premiership footballer?' She rolled her eyes as if this was all ridiculous.

'Lewis Crowe and Sally Hunt were orderlies at Drexel Hill Children's Home. You were a Drexel Hill Children's Home resident from age eight until sixteen. Casey Silver was also a resident at Drexel Hill. This morning, the bodies of Lewis Crowe and Sally Hunt were found at their home near Maidstone in Kent.'

Erika placed photos of the crime scene in front of Annabelle. Pictures taken of Lewis Crowe's broken and bloodied body in the driveway and of Sally Hunt lying on her bedroom floor. Maureen, the solicitor, registered shock at the gore. Annabelle remained impassive. She glanced down at the photos and then up at Erika.

'I didn't kill them. I'll be honest, though. I'd like to shake the hand of the person who did. They were the worst kind of bullies, particularly Sal. Did you know, her name can also be used as Cockney rhyming slang – she was a real Sally Hunt.'

'We found three of your fingerprints inside the blue Volvo at the crime scene,' said Erika, indicating the blood-spattered bonnet of the car in the photo. 'One on the driver's door handle, one on a leather glove left in the car footwell, and another on the dashboard.'

Annabelle hesitated and seemed to lose her composure for only a split second. 'Whose fingerprints? Mine or Casey Silver's?'

'Both. When we arrested you today, we took your fingerprints. We also have on record, thanks to the American embassy, a matching set of fingerprints taken for a visa application on February 9 in the name of Casey Silver. You and Casey are the same person. Can you explain?'

Annabelle sighed and pressed her fingers to her forehead.

'I met Lewis Crowe a few weeks ago. He contacted me and wanted to make amends, part of some pathetic twelve-step Alcoholics Anonymous programme. I met him in his car. That would explain my prints being there. And I must have dropped a glove.'

'Why would your fingerprint be on the door of the driver's side?'

'He was still inside the car when I came around to the driver's side to say goodbye. I must have touched the door,' she said without missing a beat.

'Where did you meet him?'

'Outside his house.'

'And you didn't realise you'd dropped a glove inside? It must have been a cold day if you met him a few weeks ago.'

'It was a stressful meeting. Seeing him again after all these years.'

'Did you go into his house?'

'No. Did you find any prints or DNA evidence that I was inside the house?' Erika hesitated. They were still waiting to see whether there was any DNA evidence from inside the house or the hut across the fields. 'I thought not.'

'What happened to Casey Silver?' asked Erika. Annabelle looked to her solicitor.

'I can refuse to answer questions, yes?'

'That's correct.'

'I don't want to answer that.'

'Why don't you want to answer that? Are you afraid?'

Annabelle was silent. Erika took a deep breath and decided to change tack.

'Can you tell us where you were last year on Monday, November 7?'

'I'd have to check my diary,' she answered as if she were being asked if she was free to meet for coffee.

'What about Friday, January 13, this year?'

'Again, I'd have to check.'

'Friday, March 3?'

'Diary.'

'Where is this diary?' asked Moss. 'We didn't find one in your hand luggage or your checked-in bags from the hold.'

'It's all up here. I'll have to have a think,' she said, tapping her forehead.

'Did you work as a prostitute for Diamond Companions?'

'I worked as a companion. Which means attractive women like me are paid by fucking ugly rich men to go on dates. And before you ask. I never had sex with any of them, and I declared all of my earnings,' she replied confidently.

'Did you ever work with a walker called Daniel Blakeson?'

Annabelle thought about this for a moment. 'Maybe. What does he look like?'

'He identified you in this E-fit image,' said Moss, taking another printout from a folder and pushing it across the table.

'That's supposed to be me?' Annabelle laughed, holding up the image. Erika had to admit that the woman in the E-fit had a longer, harder face and smaller lips, but she didn't say anything.

'What about you? Do you think this looks like me?' she said, holding it up to her solicitor.

'I'm not here to comment,' said Maureen.

'Nuff said. When does this Daniel bloke remember seeing me?'

Erika had to consult her notes.

'He remembers talking to you at the Ritz Hotel in November 2019.'

'Then he probably did. I've worked there a lot as a companion.'

'Daniel linked you to Terry DeVille, the casting director. He said that when you spoke to him that night in November 2019, you were very upset because your friend Zach Selby had just died. Zach was an actor in a relationship with Terry DeVille,' said Erika, watching Annabelle carefully.

'Do you remember Terry DeVille?' asked Moss.

'I didn't. It didn't ring a bell. I only knew him through Zach mentioning it. Him.'

'Was Zach Selby a close friend?'

'Yes.'

'You were both residents at Drexel Hill Children's Home?'

'Yes,' she replied after a long pause. 'It wasn't a nice place.'

'What did Casey think of Drexel Hill?' asked Erika. She knew it was a clumsy question, but she was determined to circle back to what happened to Casey.

'No comment.'

'Did you know that Drexel Hill was shut down after an inspection in 2013? Sally Hunt and Lewis Crowe were both fired and referred to the police after reports of child abuse, and another six members of staff were suspended pending an inquiry. Did you witness or experience abuse at Drexel Hill?'

'Let me guess? The inquiry never happened? Lewis and Sal were never charged?'

'No. There wasn't enough evidence. And Drexel Hill was closed a month later, and all the children were rehomed. Do you have evidence of abuse you suffered or witnessed? Do you know what happened to Casey Silver?'

Erika thought she saw Annabelle react in a split second, but her face didn't move. She changed tack again, deciding to circle back on Casey later. Softly, softly.

'What about your other friend at Drexel Hill, Zach Selby? I spoke to Valerie Drummond, a casting director who was a close colleague with Terry DeVille. She told me that Terry was obsessed with Zach and got him into drugs.'

The following silence continued for almost a minute, and Erika kept eye contact with Annabelle, who, again, didn't look away.

'Terry took these photos of Zach,' said Erika. She opened the folder, took out a couple of Polaroid photos, and slid them across the table. They were pictures of Zach naked on the couch in Terry DeVille's house. 'We found these in a folder amongst pictures of other young men in Terry's house. Zach looks rather out of it. High, don't you think? Did he look like this before he met Terry?' Erika took out a headshot of Zach from the Spotlight Graduates directory, where he appeared happy and healthy, and lined it up with the Polaroids. 'This was taken just a few weeks before he met Terry.'

'If you say so.'

Erika tapped the pictures.

'These prove a link between you, Zach, and Terry DeVille, the first murder victim. We believe that Zach's death gave you a motive to kill Terry. You tied him up and suffocated him.'

Erika produced a series of computer printouts with the Polaroids from all the crime scenes.

'You signed these Polaroids,' said Erika, indicating the signature;

ANNABELLE

'Did I? Can you prove that? Have you got fingerprints?' said Annabelle. She winced, put a hand on her waist, and wiped her other hand across her brow. Erika could see the thick make-up was coming away.

'Where did you get those bruises?' asked Moss, indicating the side of Annabelle's head.

'The police threw me down on the floor when they arrested me on the plane. My head hit the bottom of one of the seats.' She winced again, groaned and rubbed at the side of her waist.

'Perhaps my client would like a break?' said Maureen. 'Officers?'

Erika thought she did look a little pale, but it was convenient timing to feign illness when she pulled out the Polaroid photos.

'Yes. I could do with a break,' said Annabelle, rubbing her stomach and wincing again.

'Okay, let's take ten minutes,' said Erika, wanting to scream with frustration. 'I'm pausing this interview at five thirteen pm.'

64

Erika and Moss came out of the interview room. The rest of her team, who had been watching in the viewing suite next door, filed out into the corridor to join them. They seemed frustrated, which mirrored how Erika felt.

'You okay?' asked Peterson in a low voice.

'Not really,' said Erika. 'You heard all of that?'

He nodded. 'You need to push more on the Drexel Hill stuff. Don't be afraid to go hard on her.'

'I know.'

The door to the interview room opened, and Annabelle was led out past them, wearing handcuffs, by two uniformed officers. They watched as she walked down the corridor. She was hunched over and moving oddly, as if she was in pain, as the uniformed officers led her into an open lift down to the cells.

'It must have been a real smackdown wrestling situation when they arrested her on the plane,' said McGorry when the lift doors had closed.

'No. I just think she's a bloody good actress,' said Moss.

Dahlia came over to Erika.

'Boss, can I have a word with you?' she asked.

'I need to go and talk to Superintendent Hudson,' said Erika.

'It's linked to all of this, I think,' said Dahlia, pulling an agonised face.

'Okay. Can we meet in my office in ten?' Erika said to Moss and Peterson.

Erika was dying for a cigarette, so they went outside to the car park. She lit up and exhaled, peering at Dahlia's anxious face.

'Well? What is it? It's cold out here,' she said.

'It's Superintendent Fisk. Dan.'

Erika knew the moment Dahlia called him 'Dan' what she would say.

'How long?'

'How long what?'

'How long were you having an affair with him?'

'Two years. But that's not what this is about. You know I told you he asked me to keep a special eye out when it came to Neville Lomas when I was on the beat around his flat?'

Erika nodded and took another deep inhale.

'There was something else I didn't tell you because Dan said it was very confidential.'

'Something is either confidential or not. There's no 'very'.'

'There are rumours amongst top brass that a sex worker in London has incriminating photos of several high-profile men.'

Erika's head snapped up when she heard this, but Dahlia was looking down at the ground.

'Incriminating how?' asked Erika, keeping her voice even.

'I don't know. Sex stuff. Drugs. Underage girls. They don't know for sure.'

'And Neville Lomas was one of the men in these incriminating photos?'

Dahlia shook her head.

'They weren't sure. It's just that Lomas often hosted parties there with other politicians, judges. . . people in finance.'

'Police officers?'

'Yeah. That's what Dan, Superintendent Fisk hinted at. . .'

Erika wondered if Dahlia could hear her heart thumping with excitement. The dossier had come up again. Curly Sue knew about it, and so did top brass, but Erika didn't want to let Dahlia off the hook. 'I really didn't know much at all. . .' Dahlia went on. 'He put me on as a beat officer for a whole year walking that bloody Thames Embankment path.'

'Did he arrange your promotion to my team? Were you his spy?'

Dahlia sighed, and tears rolled down her cheeks.

'I don't know.'

'You don't know? Come on.'

'I like to think I'm a good officer. I thought I'd been promoted for my performance.'

Erika almost added, *yeah for your performance in the sack,* but she stopped herself.

'A good officer would have come to me on the first day of this investigation and told me all of this. I would have seen that as you being loyal, and I would have protected you. It would have gone no further. Jesus, Dahlia! You've seen how this investigation has unfolded. You've seen how we've been blocked when we tried to investigate Neville Lomas's background.'

'But I didn't really know anything!'

'You knew that Neville Lomas and anyone around him was being protected by the police. And a dossier of photos? That would have been enough for me to have leverage over these arseholes.'

Erika thought it was safe to let Dahlia think she didn't know about the dossier, just in case Dan Fisk was still on speed dial.

'But, I'm telling you now,' Dahlia cried, her face screwing up with tears.

'Why are you telling me now?'

'I watched that interview with her. Annabelle. Casey. She's done awful things, but somehow, I felt sorry for her too, and then I realised how much damage I could cause not telling you. It could be evidence you need.'

'Oh, great. Thanks, Dahlia. Welcome to the case. You finally grew some balls.'

'He was right about you – Dan.'

'What was he right about? That I'm a bitch?'

'No. He told me to watch out for you. Nothing gets past you.'

'Does all of the top brass know about it? This dossier?'

'They have strong suspicions. They don't know if it's real. It's just rumours.'

Erika flicked her cigarette into the gutter. 'What are you going to do?' asked Dahlia in a small voice.

'I don't know. There's quite a lot going on. I certainly don't trust you to remain on my team.'

'No. Please. I know I've been stupid.'

'Go back inside and wait with the rest of the team. And don't say anything to anyone.'

Dahlia trudged back inside hanging her head, rather theatrically, in shame.

Where is this dossier? thought Erika.

65

'Would any of it stand up in court if we went to trial?' asked Erika. Annabelle's solicitor had requested another ten minutes' break before the interview resumed, and Erika's head was spinning. She was talking to Moss and Peterson in her office. There was a long pause.

'She's been meticulous about covering her tracks. No fingerprints or DNA at any crime scene,' said Peterson. 'Apart from Lewis Crowe's car.'

'I think that's where she slipped up, leaving her glove and those fingerprints in his car,' said Moss.

'And there's no CCTV or eyewitnesses from the Neville Lomas crime scene,' said Erika.

'And she was so bloody clever with the Jamie Teague murder. She could only pull it off if she went into a very public place with CCTV everywhere, so she wore a disguise the whole time and hired a group of women to be lookalikes . . . who all wore gloves. And we can't even prove she hired them,' said Moss.

'And then she killed the only person who saw her out of make-up, which we can't prove, either. And we haven't even questioned her about that yet,' finished Erika.

'Could we charge her for the Lewis Crowe murder? At least buy ourselves some time?' asked Moss.

'But with their personal history, and his history of sexual violence . . . and Annabelle's claims she met him in his car on his request. The CPS might throw it out, or even if we did manage to link his murder to her, the CPS could conclude that she was acting in self-defence.'

'And we're going to have to take a statement from Annabelle about her time at Drexel Hill Children's Home, and the alleged abuse by the staff which could include Lewis Crowe and Sally Hunt,' said Peterson.

'Jesus,' said Erika, putting her head in her hands. She rubbed her eyes and looked up at her two colleagues, who looked just as tired as she felt. 'Annabelle just admitted she was on the books of Diamond Companions. We have an E-fit from Daniel, who worked as a walker for the agency, where he positively identified her. That gives us the ability to secure a warrant first thing tomorrow morning to raid the premises of Diamond Companions. That could give us a link to Neville Lomas.'

'That he hired her as a "companion"?' said Moss. 'And what about Jamie Teague? We don't have any forensics or CCTV to link her to his death. We don't even have a motive. How did she know him? And if she did, why did she kill him?'

'She signed the Polaroids at every crime scene,' said Erika.

'*Almost* every crime scene,' said Peterson. 'What if we charged her for using an improperly obtained identity document?'

'And she gets bail, and a fine. She hasn't got a record, so it would be a first offence,' Erika snapped.

'I'm just thinking out loud,' he said. 'Do you really want to have to release her without charge?'

Six floors below Erika's office, Annabelle lay on the hard plastic bed in the prison cell in the custody suite of Lewisham Row station. She didn't know why it was called a suite; it was far from a hotel, but the room was strangely calming. Just a low bench, a stainless-steel toilet bowl, and walls scrubbed clean of graffiti, but not quite. The cramps in her stomach were intensifying. Sharp, stabbing pains increased if she tried to lie normally, so she had to scrunch herself up in a ball to bear the pain.

The police didn't have anything. She had to remember that. They might be able to charge her, but they would have to prove it in court, and she had several insurance policies. Annabelle groaned and rolled to her feet. The tiny cell was spinning, and she was burning up. She went to the hatch on the door and put her head against the cold metal. There was a small hole, and she could just see a circle of the dank concrete hall outside, lit with orange light. The ground seemed to lurch violently under her feet, and she felt she was lying against the door like it was underneath her. And then her knees gave way, and she hit the concrete floor.

'What happened with Rebecca Reid, the young woman who accused Jamie Teague of rape?' said Erika, pacing the tiny patch of floor available in her office. 'I asked McGorry if he could talk to her. There could be a link there to Annabelle.'

'She doesn't want to talk to us,' said Moss. 'Rebecca Reid made an official police statement when she reported the rape, and had to go through the hideous humiliation of a doctor's examination, and then she spent two days on the stand in court being questioned aggressively by Jamie Teague's defence team. She worked for Rush Models, and was hired to be photographed with him at a film premiere. The only reason Teague wasn't found guilty of rape is because she'd joked in a text message with another model about doing a kiss and tell on him. And he wore a condom when he raped her.'

'Then what's the link to Jamie Teague?' Erika said, raising her voice with frustration. Moss and Peterson were silent. 'Sorry. I wasn't shouting at you. What about his sister and this OnlyFans thing?'

'Cheri Shelton has squashed that like a bug. She's representing Karen now for modelling. It seems Karen Teague wanted to make a lot of money – she's always wanted to be famous and step out from behind her brother's shadow,' said Moss. Erika stopped pacing and sat back down behind her desk.

'We have more of a link with Terry DeVille to Annabelle. Valerie Drummond identified a woman called Annabelle who attended Zach Selby's funeral. She gave us an E-fit which matches the E-fit Daniel Blakeson, the walker from Diamond Companions, gave us. What if we talk to that guy Russel again? He was Terry's long-term companion. Spent the most time living with him. Could he give us a link to Annabelle, or at least we could show him the E-fit in case it triggers something, some kind of recollection?'

'He's been staying in a hostel in Neasden. McGorry's been keeping tabs on him,' said Peterson.

Erika got up again and walked around her desk, seeing the piles of paperwork, the case files which had been neglected during this labyrinthine case. She saw a look pass between Moss and Peterson.

'What is it?' she asked.

'It's about Damsa Afridi,' said Moss. 'The illegal immigrant you asked us to check out. There was nothing.'

'Nothing?'

Moss shook her head.

'Nothing in the system. We checked all eighteen immigration

detention centres in the UK. No one by the name of Damsa Afridi is being held pending deportation.'

'We also did a check on NHS records,' said Peterson. 'We figured that if she was pregnant or had just given birth, there would be records. There is no one in the system. We did find another Damsa Afridi, but she's seventy, and she's lived legally here her whole life.'

Erika smiled ruefully and shook her head.

'So it was all bullshit to throw me, us, off the scent.'

'What about this dossier Curly Sue mentioned?' asked Moss.

'Ah, yes. I was about to mention the dossier.' Erika told them about her earlier conversation with Dahlia. 'I was worried we only had the word of a retired sex worker with a drink problem. Curly Sue was two Negroni cocktails in when she told me, and slurring her words, but now we have confirmation, through Dan Fisk, that top brass think there's a dossier,' said Erika.

'What if it's just the same rumour that Curly Sue heard, only it's gone higher up?' asked Moss.

Suddenly, they heard a bell sounding from deep down in the station.

'Shit. That's the emergency alarm in the custody suite,' said Erika. They all hurried out of her office and took a lift down to the basement. When they emerged, they saw two paramedics with a stretcher wheeling Annabelle out of the custody suite. She was covered with a thick red blanket, and she was unconscious. One of the custody sergeants was accompanying the paramedics.

'What happened?' asked Erika, as they watched Annabelle being wheeled into the lift.

'I've been checking her every twenty minutes,' said the custody sergeant. 'She was lying on the floor, non-responsive. She'd been sick.'

'Do they know what it was? Drugs?' asked Erika as the lift doors closed.

'No. She'd been searched when we booked her. And we removed her shoes and her belt when she returned to the cells. The paramedics said it could be her appendix. They're taking her to Lewisham Hospital.'

Another lift opened, and Marsh walked into the reception area of the custody suite. His face was red, and he looked furious.

'And here she finally is!' he shouted.' Do you know how long I've been trying to reach you?'

Erika sighed.

'I'm sorry, sir. It's been a hectic and stressful few days, and I've got a lot of information to fill you in on.'

'Well, I hope so,' said Marsh, caught off guard.

'Come up to my office.'

Erika walked past Moss and Peterson as Marsh's mouth dropped open, and then he followed her into the lift.

66

At eleven pm, after a long meeting with Marsh, where she filled him in on everything, leaving out the rumours about the dossier, Erika arrived at Igor's flat. Someone was leaving, so she didn't have to ring the intercom. She took the lift up to his floor and knocked on his front door. He opened the door wearing his pyjamas. His eyes were bleary, and his hair was dishevelled.

'Hi. Did I wake you up?' Erika asked.

'No. I can't sleep,' said Igor.

'I'm sorry about everything. I love you.'

'I love you too, and I'm sorry,' he replied. Erika held up the bottle of whiskey she'd bought.

'Thirsty?'

'What are we celebrating?'

'Nothing. My key suspect has been hospitalised and is in intensive care. If she dies, then. . . I have no case.'

'Shit. Sorry. Tom has asked Denise if he can stay in London when she moves to Spain. He wants to finish his last year at school here.'

'That's great.'

'Denise has to agree to it.'

'Do you want me to threaten to arrest her?'

'For what?'

'I'm too tired to think right now,' said Erika with a smile.

Igor stood to one side.

'Come in, and open that bottle. I'll get the ice.'

Erika smiled and stepped into his flat, glad for once that she had the distraction of a life outside work.

There was no news on Annabelle's condition on Sunday morning. The hospital was still running tests on her, and the doctor described her condition as 'stable'. Erika was unsure how to proceed with the investigations. They weren't allowed access to Annabelle to continue questioning her, so she told her team to have Sunday morning free. Erika decided to visit the apartment Annabelle had been renting in Canary Wharf.

It was in one of the tower blocks next to West India Quay, looking out over the water and the cinema and restaurant complex. The doorman gave Erika the key and accompanied her as they travelled up to the sixteenth floor. It was a white, modern one-bedroom flat with echoing wood floors. There was no furniture, and the sun streamed in through the curtain-less windows.

'The previous tenant had the whole place scrubbed by a big cleaning crew,' said the doorman, a sprightly older man with a full head of salt-and-pepper hair.

'Was it a mess?' asked Erika.

'No. Far from it. Very tidy. A couple of times, I had to come up and let in the gasman or the meter reader.'

'Did the building management company pay for the cleaning?'

He blew out his cheeks and laughed. 'No. That lot wouldn't give you the steam off their piss. No, she did.'

'Annabelle Wallis?'

'Yes, Miss Wallis.'

'What can you tell me about her?' asked Erika, moving to the window and looking at the view of the London skyline. 'Did she ever have visitors?'

'Never. Not once that I saw. She always paid the rent on time. She was polite. Clean.'

'What about her post? Did you have to sort out letters for her?'

'Her rent included all bills, so they were in the landlord's name. I don't think she had a phone or internet put in. There was the occasional piece of junk mail.'

Erika moved around the small flat with the doorman trailing after her with a bemused look on his face. It was all so modern and beautiful. The bathroom was tiled in a pale white marble with thin threads of gold running through. The bedroom had a fitted wardrobe, and when Erika slid back the mirrored door, she saw a small safe inside. The door was ajar, and she opened it and peered inside. It was like the rest of the apartment: pristine and empty.

'Do all the apartments have a safe?'

'Yes. They're all rich folk.'

They came back into the small hallway. There was nothing to see.

'Do you have CCTV?'

''Course. Just downstairs in the lobby.'

'How long is it kept for?'

'Thirty days.'

They travelled back down to the lobby in silence, and as they came out of the lift, Erika's phone rang. It was Moss. The doorman went back behind his desk, and Erika answered the call.

'Boss. I'm at the hospital. They had to operate on Annabelle. She's fine, but you need to come and see this.'

Erika was just about to leave when the doorman shouted after her.

'There's one bit of junk mail for 'er. I didn't see it here in the box,' he said. Erika thanked him, took the envelope, and ran to get the tube.

'We found the cause of the obstruction in her small intestine,' said the surgeon, holding up a silver key in a clear plastic bag. Erika and Moss were outside the ward, where Annabelle was still unconscious, recovering from the small surgical procedure.

'That was an obstruction in her small intestine?' repeated Erika.

'Yes,' he said. He was a keen, curious-looking man. 'You see. It's only about five centimetres long, but the top of the key has this rounded end with the number stamped on it.'

Erika and Moss peered at the shiny silver key, which had thankfully been cleaned up. The number 456 was stamped into the rounded end.

'Do you think she swallowed it?' asked Moss.

'Yes. It's highly unlikely that a rectal insertion,' he said, rolling the *r* of 'rectal' 'would have travelled so far up through the bowel, through the large intestine, and into the small intestine.'

They all stared at the key.

'I bet it was difficult to swallow. I can't even take vitamin pills,' said Moss.

'Yes,' he agreed. 'I did see a patient last year. He was what they call a "professional regurgitator".' Moss pulled a face. 'Yes, he could swallow snooker balls, pocket watches, and even a mobile phone. He was rushed in one night with a Nokia 3310 stuck in his large intestine. It was a slightly more complicated operation, but he made a full recovery. And then, of course, we get what we call the "up the bottom crowd". But they're a different kettle of fish. You wouldn't believe the amount of people who get rushed into A&E claiming that they fell awkwardly on a fresh cucumber.'

'Can we take this with us?' asked Erika, holding up the key in the bag.

'Yes. Please do. I understand my patient is under police supervision?' he asked, with a bit of excitement in his eyes.

Erika nodded.

'What, er . . . what did Miss Wallis do?' he asked, looking around furtively and lowering his voice.

'We can't tell you.'

'Ah. It was worth a try.' He grinned.

'Can we talk to her when she wakes up?'

'We'll have to see how things are before we let you cross-examine her. She will make a full recovery, though. We used keyhole surgery, so she should be on her feet quickly.'

Erika and Moss came down to the canteen and ordered coffee. Here, Erika remembered the piece of mail the doorman at Annabelle's building had given her. She'd opened it on the train, and it hadn't made much sense. She showed the letter to Moss.

'It's a bill for a company called Vonnegüt and an address on Wardour Street,' said Moss, scanning the single sheet of paper. 'And the fee is four hundred pounds and listed as "April 2023 Sundries".'

Erika hadn't had time on the train, but now she pulled out her phone and googled it. 'It's a private bank.' They both looked at the key with 456 stamped on the top. 'Jesus. She swallowed the key for a safety deposit box.'

67

Erika had never noticed the small private bank tucked away on a corner of Wardour Street in London until she and Moss arrived at nine am the next morning. It was a tall, thin building pressed between a long-defunct embassy and a modern office for a film company. When Erika showed the silver key to the serene yet stern-looking woman at the marble desk in the foyer, she ushered them both down a sweeping set of steps into a vault that wouldn't be out of place in an old-fashioned heist movie.

'Do you need our ID?' Erika asked a tall man with a Germanic accent who was manning a desk.

'You have the key, which is enough ID. Follow me,' he said sternly, moving off down a corridor.

'And he's a poet and he don't know it,' muttered Moss as they followed.

He took them into a small area lined with gold-fronted safety deposit boxes.

'If I may,' he said, taking the key from Erika. He inserted it into box number 456 and turned it. The little door popped open, and he slid out the metal box inside. He showed Erika and Moss to a small cubicle with a curtain and left them alone. Erika could tell they were both nervous, because their hands were shaking and they couldn't work out how to get the wide lid open on the box. When they did, they found a cardboard folder with an elastic band around it.

Erika reached into her pocket and took out two pairs of latex gloves, a numbered evidence bag, and her police notebook. They pulled on the latex gloves in silence. A clock ticked somewhere out in the corridor.

'You do the honours,' said Moss, indicating the folder. Erika nodded and opened it.

Inside the folder was a smaller folder, like the ones they'd found at Terry DeVille's house. It was filled with explicit Polaroid photos. As Erika turned through them, she recognised some faces.

'Jesus Christ, isn't he . . . ?' said Moss.

'Yes, that's him,' said Erika, looking at the photo of the extremely high-profile politician. She carried on turning the pages.

'It's like the Who's Who of fetish and porn,' said Moss quietly. What disturbed Erika most was that the men looked like they had been drugged. No, that didn't disturb her. What disturbed her more was that this file even existed. She looked at Moss, who was very pale.

'The dossier exists,' said Erika.

'Why do you think she didn't want us to find it?'

'It could be her insurance policy.'

'I don't want to see any more,' said Moss. Erika nodded, took a deep breath, and went to close the folder. The pages in the album were made of see-through plastic, and just as she was closing the last one, Erika noticed the backs of the Polaroids. She stopped and stared.

'No . . . No,' said Erika, her heart starting to beat with excitement.

'What?' asked Moss.

'She thought she was so smart. She knew she didn't leave any forensic evidence. She thought she'd covered her tracks perfectly.' Erika quickly slid the cardboard folder into the numbered evidence bag and sealed it. She made a note in her police logbook and closed the safety deposit box. 'I think I know how we can link Annabelle to the murders,' said Erika. 'We need to find Russel Milligan.'

68

After five days of recuperating, Annabelle was transferred back into custody at Lewisham Row so Erika could continue the police interviews. The five-day delay had worked in Erika's favour, and she felt confident when she came face-to-face with Annabelle across the table again. Her solicitor was back, and this time, Erika was joined by Peterson as the rest of her team watched from the viewing suite next door.

Annabelle looked afraid. Erika expected her to be scared after the key was removed from her body in the emergency operation.

'How are you feeling?' asked Erika.

'Not great. I don't think I'm up to this.'

'The doctor has ruled you are fit to be questioned, but we're going to take it slow.'

Peterson had a box file on the table in front of him, and he opened it so Annabelle couldn't see what was inside and took out the silver key in a plastic evidence bag. He slid it across the table. 'Can you tell me how this ended up in your small intestine?'

'Someone here put it in my food. I ate a meal here last week. I was served a tray of spaghetti Bolognese in the custody suite. Which I ate.'

Annabelle's answer made Erika realise she was desperate.

'You acknowledge you swallowed the key?'

Annabelle hesitated and looked at her solicitor. Then she nodded.

'Can you tell me what this is?' asked Erika, sliding a copy of the Vonnegüt bank account letter across the table.

'I don't know.'

'It has your name on it. It confirms that you pay a monthly fee to rent safety deposit box number 456 in the vault of Vonegüt bank. The same number stamped on the key you swallowed, which opens the safety deposit box.'

'What if I told you I was being framed?'

'How so?'

'This has all been planted by someone.'

'Who?'

Annabelle sat back and folded her arms.

'We opened the safety deposit box. And found this folder, this dossier, inside,' said Peterson, taking out the cardboard file.

Annabelle's eyes grew wide. 'I know what's in it, but it's nothing to do with me.'

'We're not interested in these photos,' said Erika.

'You're not?' asked Annabelle. She looked surprised.

'Did you know that on the back of each Polaroid photo, there is a number unique to every Polaroid photo ever produced?' asked Erika. She flipped the dossier open. The solicitor couldn't hide her shock at what she saw. Erika took out one of the Polaroid photos wrapped in plastic and placed it on the table.

Annabelle stared blankly at her. When Erika recalled this moment in the years to come, she always remembered it was as if Annabelle's brain had crashed, like a screen freezing on a computer. Her eyes went blank, and she seemed to go into a trance.

'On the back of every Polaroid photo, if you can see, in very faint type, there is a ten- to eleven-digit code. Polaroid films produced before April 2018 will have a ten-digit code, while films produced after this date will have an eleven-digit code. Now, this is very important, particularly for this case. All of the photos in this dossier folder were manufactured after April 2018. So the digits on the back tell us so much information. The first two digits tell us which machine in which factory made the film, and the second digit tells which shift the film was produced on that day. All Polaroid factories now run two shifts – would you believe it? The next pairs of numbers tell us the day, month, and year of manufacture and, finally, the film type. All of the photos in this dossier, and those found at the murder scenes of Lewis Crowe and Sally Hunt, Jamie Teague, Neville Lomas, and Terry DeVille, were manufactured in the same factory, on the same date, and even during the same shift. That was the morning shift on February 10, 2019, in Enschede, in The Netherlands. Where all Polaroid film packs are manufactured.'

Erika looked over at Annabelle, who was still looking blankly at her.

'We've also talked to Terry DeVille's long-term companion, Russel Milligan. Using the E-fit images of you from casting director Valerie Drummond, he confirms that you worked casually a few times for Terry as his casting assistant in the summer of 2019. Around the time, Zach Selby entered into a relationship with Terry. He confirms you also asked to buy some Polaroid film boxes from them. You see, Terry bought Polaroid film in bulk. He had a wholesale business account and kept a huge amount of Polaroid film in the fridge at his house. We've traced the batch of film we found in his house using his business receipts. It all has the same time codes on the back: the morning shift, on February 10, 2019, in the Polaroid factory in Enschede, in The Netherlands. Your fingerprints in Lewis Crowe's car puts you at his house, along with three Polaroids with the same numbers.

You also left your Polaroid camera behind. You didn't leave fingerprints on it, but you did leave some of your DNA, an eyelash on the Polaroid camera viewfinder.

'So we have DNA evidence. We have the time codes on the manufacture of the Polaroid films, and we have Russel Milligan willing to go on record and testify in court that he sold you fifteen packs of Polaroid film back in February 2019.'

There was a long silence. And then Annabelle raised her arms and started to applaud with the dead look still in her eyes. As Erika, Peterson, and the solicitor stared at her, she carried on for a full minute.

'Well done, Detective. What happens now? You get a bonus?'

'No . . . I'd like to know why?'

There was a long silence. Annabelle looked beaten down.

'Why did I do it? Terry killed Zach with his obsession and mind games . . . Neville Lomas hired me and beat me so badly that I almost died, and no one wanted to know. No one cared.'

'Did you report him to the police?' asked Erika.

She nodded and stared at the table, a single tear falling from her eye. 'And nothing happened. Nothing. Jamie Teague did the same. Although he didn't beat me, he refused to hear the word "no".' Annabelle looked up at Erika. 'Did you know it was on the night he was acquitted of rape. The night he celebrated, that's when he raped me. He didn't care that he hurt another woman.' She wiped the tear away with the back of her hand.

'Annabelle. This doesn't have to be about you being guilty. You can tell us everything. Just because you're guilty doesn't mean other people can get away with what they did to you,' said Erika, feeling sudden compassion for her. 'And what they did to Casey?'

'Did you know that Sal and Lewis killed Casey Silver, in the basement of Drexel Hill? I saw them do it. Sal hit her over the head with a spade, and they burned her body in the furnace. It was November in 2008.'

Annabelle said this matter-of-factly, and as she stared at them, she looked dead behind the eyes.

'Why didn't you report it?' asked Erika. Annabelle shook her head. She seemed to be staring at something beyond the small interview room.

'I was *ten*. A minor. At the mercy of these bastards. Do you think it would have worked out well for me if I'd tried to report them? Who would I have told? They ran the place. You people. You think it's easy for a child in a place like that? They own you.'

Erika, Peterson, and the solicitor exchanged glances. Annabelle went on. 'I'm willing to make a statement all about my time there. The things I saw.' She seemed to come out of her trance-like state and she turned to Erika. 'Check the grounds at Drexel Hill. They planned to bury Casey's ashes from the furnace. You should check the grounds. Hopefully you'll find something and everyone will believe me.'

'We do believe you,' said Erika.

'Bullshit,' she said quietly. 'I killed Sal and Lewis for what they did to Casey, me, and all those children who didn't have anyone to love them. The only one I deeply regret is Jessica Goldman. She didn't deserve to die, and I'm sorry.'

There was a long silence. Erika pulled the dossier towards her and placed her hand on it, almost like she was trying to keep in all the awful images. 'Did you take these pictures?'

'Yes. It was, it is, my insurance policy. Those men always think they'll get away with it.'

'You were running away to America. It would have been a very complicated and time- consuming process to extradite you once you were there,' said Erika.

'If you'd even found me. I had money saved, and I have my looks, but I intend to live a long life, and it doesn't hurt to have an insurance policy like that,' she said, indicating the dossier. For once, Erika didn't know what to say.

'You seem disappointed, Detective. Like you wanted me to put up more of a fight?'

'No,' said Erika. The small and rather delicate-looking woman before her had just admitted to the murders, and Erika had proof.

'Do you believe I killed all those people?' asked Annabelle, turning to Maureen, her solicitor.

'I'm not here to have that kind of opinion,' said Maureen, visibly flustered.

'Yeah. I bet you think I should have green scales on my body. Or look like a monster. I was quite a monstrous-looking child, though – I think that saved me when I was at Drexel Hill. The men who came to the home in search of young boys and girls only wanted the pretty ones. I can show you some of them in that dossier.'

Erika kept her hand on the cardboard folder. 'Are you saying some of these men came to Drexel Hill when you lived there?'

'Yes . . .' Annabelle turned to her solicitor. 'I think I need to take a break. But everything I've said stands. I confess to everything.'

She got up to leave and was escorted by two police officers back to the custody suite.

When Erika entered the corridor outside the interview room, a whoop went up, and her colleagues flooded out of the observation suite.

'We got her!' shouted McGorry, hugging Crane, who was grinning from ear to ear. Moss and Peterson gave her a hug.

'Awesome, Erika. Awesome!' shouted Peterson above the noise.

'She's going down for a long time!' cried Moss. 'I'm buying the drinks when this is done and dusted!'

Erika congratulated her colleagues, but something troubled her and she couldn't work out why.

She'd caught Annabelle. She'd solved the case.

EPILOGUE

Six months later, September 15

By the time the Annabelle Wallis case went to trial, a lot had happened in Erika's life. She'd solved two more murder cases and added four to her caseload.

Igor's ex-wife, Denise, had moved to Spain in July, but she had agreed to let Tom stay with Igor and finish his last school year. Erika had taken some days off during the summer holidays with Tom and Igor, doing 'London things'. They'd visited Madame Tussauds, Buckingham Palace, and the Tower of London, where Erika wondered how a lot of her murder cases would have ended if she'd been a policewoman in the olden days, when criminals were hung, drawn, and quartered. Justice would have been quicker, with much less room for mistakes.

It was a bright Friday morning just after the kids had all gone back to school when Erika met Isaac, Moss, Peterson, and McGorry outside the huge anonymous brown-brick building of Southwark Crown Court for the opening day of the Annabelle Wallis murder trial. The court building sat with its back to the

River Thames, and the wind rushed off the water. The courtyard outside was crowded with people from the press, victims' relatives, and curious bystanders. It took so long to get through the security barriers that they almost missed the beginning of the case, and they had to make a mad dash through the busy corridors.

In courtroom one, the biggest, the public gallery was packed, and they just made it into their seats at the end. Erika saw Crane was already there, saving them seats, and she sat beside him. He looked very pale and shocked and was holding his mobile phone.

'Are you okay?' asked Erika.

'No,' he said. 'Did you see the news? Russel Milligan was found dead.'

'Dead?' Erika repeated. Isaac sat beside her, pulling his phone from his pocket. Moss and Peterson, who were beside him, leaned in to hear. 'I was talking to him just last night. He was fine . . .'

'Does it say how he died?' asked Moss.

'It says he was found in the bath in the hostel where he was staying. He'd drowned,' said Isaac. Erika went to ask more, but then the clerk said, 'All rise,' and everyone stood.

Annabelle looked thinner than she had six months prior, but she was dressed well and entered the dock, walking with confidence. The judge asked them to be seated and then read out the opening statement.

Erika cast her eyes around the courtroom. Melanie and Marsh hadn't chosen to attend the first day of the trial, which surprised her, and then, with a feeling of shock, she saw someone she recognised on the other side of the public gallery. It was only a glimpse, but she saw the man in the grey suit with the birthmark under his eye was just leaving the courtroom through the exit of the opposite side.

Erika felt someone's hand on her shoulder, and Isaac

indicated she should turn back to face front. Annabelle was now standing up and being addressed by the judge.

'And how do you plead?' he asked, his voice booming around the wood panelling.

Annabelle leaned towards the microphone and scanned the courtroom. When her eyes found Erika, she held her gaze for a long, defiant moment before answering,

'Not guilty.'

A NOTE FROM ROBERT

I love writing these Detective Erika Foster books and thank you for picking up *Lethal Vengeance*. This might be the first Erika Foster book you've read or the second, or you might have read the whole series. If you enjoyed *Lethal Vengeance*, please tell your friends and family. Word-of-mouth really is the best way for new readers to find my books.

I'm already planning to write the next book, and I want to keep writing more Detective Erika Foster novels for as long as you want to keep reading them. I'd like to ask you the question: what would you like to happen next? Erika Foster is certainly moving on with her life since the first book in the series. What kind of cases would you like to see her solve? And where do you think she'll be in five or ten years? I have a very clear idea of where I plan to take the story next, but it's always wonderful to hear feedback from you, dear reader.

I'd like to thank Henry Steadman for another terrific cover and thank you to Jan Cramer, for her fantastic performances narrating the Erika Foster audiobook editions. Thank you to my excellent editors, Haley Miller Swann, Kellie Osborne, and Tara Whitaker, and the skilled editors and translators from around the world who bring my work to life. And finally, a big hug and a thank you to my first reader, Janeken-Skywalker, and the rest of Team Bryndza/Raven Street Publishing: Maminko Vierka, Riky, and Lola. I love you all so much, and thank you for keeping me going with your love and support!

As I always say, there are many more books to come! My next book is *The Lost Victim*, which sees the return of Private Investigator Kate Marshall.

Rob

THE LOST VICTIM - NOW AVAILABLE TO PREORDER

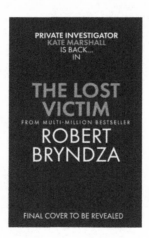

Private Investigators Kate Marshall and Tristan Harper return with a stunning new mystery crime thriller!

PUBLISHING JULY 11TH 2024
Paperback: 978-1-914547-26-3
Hardback: 978-1-914547-27-0

EMAIL SIGNUP

If you would like to be the first to know when my next book is out, sign up for my mailing list below using the QR code or the web address. Your email will never be shared, and you can unsubscribe at any time.

http://eepurl.com/duluLz

ABOUT THE AUTHOR

Robert Bryndza is best known for his page-turning crime and thriller novels, which have sold over five million copies. His crime debut, *The Girl in the Ice,* was released in February 2016, introducing Detective Chief Inspector Erika Foster. Within five months it sold one million copies, reaching number one in the Amazon UK, USA, and Australian charts. To date, *The Girl in the Ice* has sold over 2 million copies in the English language and has been sold into translation in 30 countries. It was nominated for the Goodreads Choice Award for Mystery & Thriller (2016); the Grand prix des lectrices de Elle in France (2018); and it won two reader voted awards, The Thrillzone Awards best debut thriller in The Netherlands (2018) and The Dead Good Papercut Award for best page turner at the Harrogate Crime Festival (2016).

Robert has released a further six novels in the Erika Foster series; *The Night Stalker*, *Dark Water*, *Last Breath*, *Cold Blood,* and *Deadly Secrets*, all of which have been global bestsellers, and in 2017 *Last Breath* was a Goodreads Choice Award nominee for Mystery and Thriller. *Fatal Witness* and *Lethal Vengeance* are the seventh and eighth Erika Foster novels.

Most recently, Robert created a new crime thriller series based around the central character Kate Marshall, a police officer turned private detective. The first book, *Nine Elms*, was an Amazon USA #1 bestseller and an Amazon UK top five bestseller, and the series has been sold into translation in 19 countries. The second book in the series is the global bestselling *Shadow Sands*, the third book is *Darkness Falls*, and the fourth is *Devil's Way*.

Robert was born in Lowestoft, on the east coast of England. He studied at Aberystwyth University, and the Guildford School of Acting, and was an actor for several years, but didn't find success until he took a play he'd written to the Edinburgh Festival. This led to the decision to change career and start writing. He self-published a bestselling series of romantic comedy novels before switching to writing crime. Robert lives with his husband in Slovakia, and is lucky enough to write full-time. You can find out more about the author at www.robertbryndza.com.

ALSO BY ROBERT BRYNDZA

STANDALONE CRIME THRILLER

Fear The Silence

KATE MARSHALL PRIVATE INVESTIGATOR SERIES

Nine Elms

Shadow Sands

Darkness Falls

Devil's Way

The Lost Victim

DETECTIVE ERIKA FOSTER CRIME THRILLER SERIES

The Girl in the Ice

The Night Stalker

Dark Water

Last Breath

Cold Blood

Deadly Secrets

Fatal Witness

Lethal Vengeance

COCO PINCHARD ROMANTIC COMEDY SERIES

The Not So Secret Emails Of Coco Pinchard

Coco Pinchard's Big Fat Tipsy Wedding

Coco Pinchard, The Consequences of Love and Sex

A Very Coco Christmas

Coco Pinchard's Must-Have Toy Story

STANDALONE ROMANTIC COMEDY

Miss Wrong and Mr Right

Raven Street Publishing

www.ravenstreetpublishing.com

Cover design by Henry Steadman

eBook ISBN: 978-1-914547-17-1

Paperback ISBN: 978-1-914547-19-5

Hardback ISBN: 978-1-914547-18-8

ALSO AVAILABLE AS AN AUDIOBOOK

Made in United States
North Haven, CT
08 February 2024